Cold Light

ALSO BY JENN ASHWORTH

A Kind of Intimacy

JENN ASHWORTH

Cold Light

WILLIAM MORROW

An Imprint of HarperCollins*Publishers*

COLD LIGHT. Copyright © 2011 by Jenn Ashworth. All rights reserved. Printed in the
United States of America. No part of this book may be used or reproduced in any
manner whatsoever without written permission except in the case of brief quotations
embodied in critical articles and reviews. For information address HarperCollins
Publishers, 10 East 53rd Street, New York, NY 10022.

HarperCollins books may be purchased for educational, business, or sales promo-
tional use. For information please write: Special Markets Department, HarperCollins
Publishers, 10 East 53rd Street, New York, NY 10022.

First published in Great Britain in 2011 by Sceptre, an imprint of Hodder & Stoughton,
an Hachette UK company.

FIRST U.S. EDITION

Library of Congress Cataloging-in-Publication Data has been applied for.

ISBN 978-0-06-207603-8

12 13 14 15 16 OV/RRD 10 9 8 7 6 5 4 3 2 1

Cold Light

Between interviews, they make us wait upstairs in a classroom. We're left alone but we're aware that in a nearby office we are being discussed. Teachers; her parents and mine; the nurse; social workers. And the pair of us with nothing to do but stare out of the windows at the bedlam occurring at the front of the school and wait.

We watch the cars arrive and unload. We lean on the sill, making palm prints in the dust. Emma rests her muscly thighs against the radiator. I pull leaves from a brown spider plant and we both look out of the window and say nothing. We listen. The glass muffles the crying and singing but we can still see the flowers and feel the atmosphere, which is shrieky and curious and raw.

These people who we don't know – who Chloe doesn't know – even turn up at the school in coaches. Every single one of them brings something. If it's not roses and baskets of silk flowers then it's stuffed bears and huge, handmade cards. So many ways of spelling her name.

They interview us alone, then together, then alone again. Because we're only fourteen, we're entitled to breaks. We don't discuss the questions we've been asked. We don't compare stories. I never know what Emma is going to say until she comes out and says it.

'They're putting candles out now,' she says blandly.

She nods towards a kneeling figure across the road from the school. He is pulling something out of a carrier bag, laying it out on the pavement. A bank of tea-lights blooms as quick as mushrooms to drip and sputter in the shelter where the school buses pick up. Emma leans forward, putting all her weight on her hands. Her breath makes clouds on the glass. Her school jumper smells like old towels.

I stare at the flickering candles and remember the time me and Chloe waited there in the rain on a day we were supposed to be at school.

'The wind'll blow them out,' I say. Emma nods and we wait, no one breaking the silence until Shanks comes back with another pair of police officers.

'What is it now?' I say, but not loud enough for Shanks to hear.

The police bring us cans of Coke and put their hands on our shoulders. Smile a lot, just to let us know that we aren't in trouble and we shouldn't be afraid of speaking out – of saying everything we knew about Chloe and her boyfriend. Sometimes they film us as we talk and make our parents sign pieces of paper afterwards to say it's all right, that they don't mind. I wonder if the cameras will be out this time, and what they'll do with the recording, and if we'll end up on the television again. Sometimes there are journalists waiting for us after school. They've promised to make special arrangements.

'Right then,' Shanks says, and I notice he's taken the pack of fags out of his breast pocket, and that today he's wearing a proper shirt and not a denim one.

'They just want another five minutes with each of you, one at a time, and then you can go back to classes.' He smiles, tries a joke, 'No getting out of Maths today, I'm afraid, girls. Who's first?'

Emma and I don't look at each other. She steps forward. I see her ponytail bob from side to side against her neck. I don't wonder what she is going to tell them. Shanks takes her away and I turn back to my window. Another coach has arrived.

1

They're showing it this afternoon. A ceremony to mark the first spadeful of earth, and when it's built, a ceremony to open the thing, I bet. I bring a bag of Doritos and a box of wine with me to the couch. Close the curtains, find the remote and settle in. The screen crackles with static as it warms up and I wonder, uneasily, what Emma is doing with herself tonight.

Beginning of this January, the council got together with the school and Chloe's parents and set up a memorial fund. There was a consultation and a vote at a meeting in the Empire Services Club. The crowd was so big it overflowed the bar and spilled onto the bowling green. Someone came round with a tray of tea in those beige plastic cups with the plastic frame holders you get to stop you squeezing too hard and covering yourself in boiling liquid. We voted, all together, for a memory. A memorial. A house. The upshot of it is the City has decided to build a summerhouse overlooking the banks of her pond.

It's not a pond and it's not hers. It's a concrete-bottomed pool, man-made and deeper than it looks. The yeast in the bread thrown to the ducks has polluted the water so there are no fish and no reeds – it's a dead, black disc surrounded by a tangle of grey and leafless trees and hawthorn: their branches are decorated with torn carrier bags and faded crisp packets.

It's not a place where anyone, least of all Chloe's parents, would want to *sit and rest a while*, as it will say on the bench. But the City has decided. The council is putting up the money. Terry did the publicity and the telethon appeal for donations, and because the wood was the place were Chloe and Carl used to go – for their *privacy* – the summerhouse, decorated with stone doves and plaster cupids, surrounded by trellis and its own decking tracing a walkway down to the dirty banks of the pond, was what they planned.

They've built a model which the camera in the studio zooms in on so that on the television it looks like the real thing. This summerhouse (a concrete folly) is half a monument to young love gone wrong and half a nice piece of publicity for the City's urban renewal programme: deprived areas, community cohesion – something for the teenagers to smoke their glue in. It's morbid and sentimental, it ticks all the right boxes for community enterprise funding, and now it's on *The City Today*.

This February has been wet and mild so the soil is easy to turn. The location camera shows the mayor attacking the cleared patch with a spade decked out like a maypole in pink and white ribbon. Chloe's parents, because of their guilt, wanted the memorial to be a celebration of love and life and St Valentine and as a concession to this the City has provided the ribbons for the spade and the pink and white balloons – *gratis*. The mayor isn't paying attention when he sinks the spade in but smiling at the pop of a few flashing cameras.

When the earth opens there's nothing to see but some plastic – thicker than ordinary bin-bags, but nothing like tarpaulin. The blade of the spade tears open the plastic and a corner of it catches underneath. Even then, it's nothing spectacular. Nothing, that is, we watching at home can *see*. No spectacle apart from a dirty fold of fabric that comes up with the soil as the mayor leans back and jiggles the spade so that the blade turns up the first clod. It could be anything – the cover from a pram, an old shower curtain, the material from an umbrella.

In fact, it's a blue North Face jacket – waterproof and indestructible.

Terry peers into the hole, smiles, and then leans into the

camera. The black bulb of the microphone is at his mouth. He says something, but I'm watching the weather girl who is standing next to him. She's holding a white candle in one hand and a pink balloon in the other. They must have used helium – the string is straight up like a plumb line and the balloon floats over her head like an idea. Her smile freezes, then fades. Terry is still talking but the people behind him are screwing up their faces and coughing.

It's the smell.

When the mayor heaves the spade backwards again, straining the row of buttons that bisects his belly, there's an audible groan of disgust from the crowd and the weather girl lets go of her balloon, leans to the side and vomits a clear string of bile onto the ground. I watch the balloon float upwards, out of camera shot.

There's chaos. The doves are flapping at the wire of the boxes they are stacked in. I don't know if it's because they can smell something too, or because the people around them are suddenly moving, jostling each other away from the little hole, talking too loudly. The camera doesn't wobble, but pans away from the crowd, focuses on the still black water of the pond.

That's what you get if you want to do these things live. Unforeseen events. Things are falling apart. Things have been falling apart long before the mayor cracked open the ground and unleashed a smell that had Terry's weather girl vomiting into the bushes.

Terry apologises for the interruption and promises they're getting a van out to the scene post haste but for the time being he's going to have to hand back to the studio.

'We will be back and when we are, we'll tell you exactly what's going on here,' he says. He rakes a hand through his dishevelled hair, twitches his tie and hands back to Fiona, who is waiting on her couch, legs neatly crossed at the ankle and pressed together at the knee. She's wearing an expensive camel-coloured two-piece suit with patent leather black shoes. Fiona wants Terry's job. Beautiful.

'That's our Terry. Calm in a crisis, a consummate professional,' she says, and the man practically bows. Fiona simpers. 'First at the scene again. I think we'll be in for a long one tonight, won't we, Terry?' The link is cut before he can reply and Fiona is left nodding at thin air and the programme's logo on the screen behind her sofa.

'We'll be back,' she says, 'after this,' and the adverts are as harried, jangling and garish as they usually are.

I let my eyes move to the window and sniff the air, which smells of crisps and fags, and the damp washing on the cold radiator. I don't need to examine the screen. I can watch it again, whenever I like. It'll be on YouTube before morning. I make a coffee, walk back to my couch slowly. There'll be time to decide how I feel about this later.

Terry was totally cool – though that's no surprise. He was in his element, because if Terry had an element it would be unexplained deaths, or euphemistically reported rapes. Fiona was right: he's always first on the scene or the screen, bursting with bad news. She's been hovering around, waiting for his job for years, but he's the award winner. He's the one we remember telling us about the pest that stalked the parks here ten years ago – the publicity and his campaign, even his tacit endorsement of the vigilante groups that sprang up, are supposed to have had more to do with the attacks ending than the efforts of the police, who could never give us a name. Not officially.

Terry Best. Famous for a cool head and a pink shirt. Various ties, often seasonal. But always, always the pink shirt. Sometimes his fans send him in different coloured shirts for Christmas and urge him to ring the changes, but he is never seen wearing anything but pink. He might only have one shirt, or five hundred that are all the same. Woolworths sell pink shirts and they did a special promotion for them in the window with a big poster of Terry. It didn't say it in so many words but it strongly suggested that Terry Best bought his shirts from Woolworths. The management of *The City Today* complained and told them to take it down.

There's a postcard you can buy in the bus station kiosk – him, with his thumbs up to the camera. The caption along the bottom, which is done in the same kind of glowing green writing as the *Twin Peaks* opening credits (although I don't think many people will have noticed that) says: REAL MEN WEAR PINK. That's never been banned, mainly because it isn't advertising anything except for Terry himself.

Terry's more of a fixture in some people's lives than their families are because whatever happens, good or bad – he's there. If you were expecting bad news, Terry would be the one you'd want to tell you. Most of the people who live in the City have a story about seeing him getting on a bus; complaining about the wait at the post office; carrying a rolled-up towel into the swimming baths. I've seen him once before myself, or at least I think it was him – suit jacket, pink shirt – hauling a heavy-looking bin-bag from the back of his car, and dumping it on a verge by the side of the road. I mentioned it to my boss and she got breathless and asked me what was inside the bag. When I said I'd never checked, she refused to give me any overtime for a month.

He isn't a regular at the shopping centre, but apparently he's been in. Bobbed into Primark for two packets of navy blue socks. There's a rumour that the manager wanted to give him the staff discount, messed up putting her card number into the till, and ended up just giving him the lot for free. She didn't even ask for a signed picture to put near the revolving doors.

It is hard to explain to people who don't live round here how important Terry is. Without ageing or changing his shirt, he has presented the local news bulletin every evening for twenty years which means he has been a part of most of the important things that have ever happened in this area. Every time the Ribble flooded. The time they tried to do a music festival in the park. That pub riot they had, and the ongoing debate about the multi-storey car park on top of the bus station. He opens the new markets, welcomes in the Whitsun fair and turns on the Christmas lights every year. He presents the children's book club certificates at the library, and he guest speaks at the AGM of the Real Ale Society.

I don't expect the programme to return to its coverage of the memorial, but it does. Terry and his crew have shifted them-selves, and sharpish. What started as jolly coverage of a foundation-laying ceremony quickly turns into breaking news and is piped into my room. The suddenly obscene decorated spade is hidden away; the mayor swaps his wellingtons for dress shoes, and Terry changes his tie. They reassemble in time for the police to arrive and erect their white tent over the place where the summerhouse was going to be.

This coverage will play all night. Chloe, upstaged at last. They haven't named the body yet, but I know it is Wilson. I know.

2

Chloe had fine blonde hair that lay flat against her head and fell, limp and transparent, across her shoulders. The wallpaper in her mother's front room was old-fashioned: green and brown and pink and livid with birds that looked like bright pressed flowers. The birds looked crushed and angry, their beaks squashed open.

Our plans went like this: Chloe would get a job at the perfume counter in Debenhams; I'd get a job in the cafe on the top floor, or failing that, Woolworths – who Chloe said would take anyone. We'd save up our money, and then we'd rent a flat. She'd progress to the make-up counter, or the VIP personal shopper's lounge.

The flat would have a balcony because Chloe didn't think it was hygienic to smoke inside, and I wanted to get a rabbit. We'd be good about paying the rent and the bills, but we'd spend the rest of our money on skirts and beads and blue bottles of alcohol in nightclubs. We'd have wallpaper like her mother's but we were going to draw it ourselves so it'd be limited edition and worth a bundle. We'd have ashtrays made out of blue glass, and dream-catchers in the windows. We were going to eat Arctic Roll whenever we felt like it, and watch Leonardo DiCaprio in *Titanic* and *Romeo and Juliet* every night.

I never got a job at a cafe, and I never tried Woolworths. I clean the shopping centre. It's my job to put out the yellow triangles before I mop: little slipping stick men to warn you of what you'll get if you walk on wet floors. I use the motorised floor polisher with protectors jammed over my ears while the television screens mounted overhead show the shopping channel, the talk-shows, the consumer revenge panels. I don't get paid much, but after all the shops in town went 24-hours there's as much work as I want. There's nothing else to do but work. It's not Woolworths or a perfume counter, but I have my own trolley and I know my way round the service corridors even in the dark. I do all right.

Chloe, who did not grow up to clean a shopping centre, or anything else, sits in my head while I stand on the escalator in the centre of the arcade, pressing a duster against the handrail on either side and walking slowly against the flow. Light bounces through the pointy glass atrium ceiling and I change escalators and she slides out a poster from the centre of her new *Smash Hits*. She is squeezing the staples closed with the flat edge of a scissor blade. All the posters: the walls of her bedroom jangling with eyes. Everything she owns has a face stuck to it. You can't get away with coveting any of her things because most of the time her possessions stare back.

We had a perfect summer together – the last summer before Emma involved herself in our lives. And then summer turned into autumn and we went back to school and things started to change. I think of the times we went to Avenham Park and we are there and she is taking my arm. I feel the inside of her wrist against the crook of my elbow. We're laughing, following the footpath around the edges of the rose-beds and kicking at empty conker cases. Someone has been here before us and collected everything and we find the conkers bobbing in the turned-off fountain, swelled with water. Their shiny skins are split. Lichen spreads over stone faces and we walk around and around until it gets dark. She slips a hand into my pocket. Later, I find a packet of cigarettes. I hide it under my mattress and learn how to smoke in the shed.

Or she is sitting next to me in class. We're at the back, the eyes of the teacher on us. Something has been said. Maybe we've been passing notes again. There are always new boys to talk about. What we like changes, mysteriously, from one week to the next. A matter for constant discussion. There are lists. We compare ratings. We invent love lives for our teachers, as intricate as soap operas.

The eyes of the other girls are slick and curious and hostile. Emma is there, but ghostly. We aren't paying attention to her yet. When someone bitches, Chloe sticks up her fingers and hurls pieces of broken pencil eraser. We write our names on the desks in Tipp-Ex, our initials intertwined like a monogram.

She is leaning into the mirror. The basin, toilet and bath aren't white, they're blue plastic in a shade called 'aqua' and it seems exotic. She is plucking hairs out of her eyebrows with a pair of tweezers. It hurts. She flinches away and her eyes water, but she is grinning.

'Fuck me,' she says. It's still a new word for her. 'The natural look is very hard work,' she quotes into the glass, and laughs.

Because I am standing behind her I can see myself over her shoulder: a pale face surrounded by a frizzing halo of woolly brown hair. An expression that looks stupid but is just myopic. I am watching my own eyebrows. My face is chubby and whiter than hers. The brows are like someone has drawn a loaded paintbrush across my forehead. Chloe says I'm not delicate enough; there's no arch. This is going to be a painstaking operation and I am waiting my turn. Chloe always tests the water for both of us. If she deems this desirable, I will follow on after.

'We need to do something with that,' she says, and spins around. I am caught in her stare, but it isn't my eyebrows she's looking at, it is my hair. The tweezers clatter into the sink and she twirls away. Eggs are broken into a bowl, beaten, poured onto my head. She wraps my head in clingfilm. Her fingernails dig into my scalp as she pats and rubs. She layers on more clingfilm, then hot, wet towels, then dry towels.

Slime that feels like snot and smells like nothing drips into my ears. My neck aches. We watch the clock. Twenty minutes, the magazine says, then I will have hair like Chloe's. She starts to rinse me and the water she runs is too hot and the eggs scramble. When I have picked the last piece of egg out of my hair and poked it down the plughole she is still snorting and rolling and wiping her eyes on the bathmat.

I smile. She is my best friend.

She was special, even when she was alive – but not in the picture-perfect, pure and polished way people think of her now. Being dead has turned her into a final draft. She did things I'd have felt false and ridiculous even trying. She dried her hair upside down with the diffuser, tried scented panty liners, smeared Vaseline on her eyelids and said things like 'T-zone' and 'accent colour' and 'handbag-must-have'. Once Carl arrived in our lives, she'd talk raucously about fingering and cumming and blow-jobs, and I would listen – hot and horrified and compelled. She smelled like sweat and hairspray and cigarettes and I smelled like lavender ironing water and Vosene. I'm not sure why it mattered, but it did.

The process of making Chloe into a saint began in 1998.

A funeral wasn't enough. First, they named a rose for her. For her, not after her, because there was already a Chloe rose: some other dead girl. They called it the Juliet, after an especially moving broadcast by Terry which we all remember, and which some of us taped to watch again later. So she wasn't herself – she stood for something. And stood for it using someone else's name and a four-hundred-year-old story that wasn't even true. No one minded.

The teachers planted the Juliet roses in the brand-new school flower-beds and huddled in the corridors to talk about Chloe fading. No one did any real work for weeks. Lesson plans and homework, Bunsen burners and hockey sticks, protractors and rough-books – they are ordinary objects but in school, one down, us leftovers stared at them as if they were strange things and their continuing existence became an insult to her memory. We cleared them away and slunk between classrooms, whispering. Even some of the boys cried. The teachers turned up late, blue shadows under their eyes. They let us see them smoking in the car park, and pretended they'd noticed her getting thinner, the cracks in her lips and the fineness of her hair.

Second, there was an investigation. Ofsted, or the National Health. Back then that was the kind of thing they were supposed to be doing: even in a city like ours where we had Terry, and our own ways of dealing with things. Should someone have stepped in? Could they have made her speak to Patsy? Where was her doctor in all of this? Her form tutor? The head? That helped. Kept the interest going for months, with interim reports and preliminary findings and conclusive recommendations about food and teen mental health and drop-in advice centres (*Chloe House*) until she was famous.

And the thing is, I was famous too, because I'd been her best friend. And Emma. People wanted to talk to us. They were kind. There were that many pictures of us in the paper and on Terry's show – and that's why I don't mind wearing my glasses now when before I used to leave them in the house and put up with things being blurred. I let my hair grow out and tuck it into big hats, like a Rasta, if I'm planning to go out anywhere busy during daylight hours. No one looks these days. I don't have friends at work. When people talk to me, I tap the ear-protectors and shrug, and after a while they stop trying.

Third, there were the interviews. They asked all sorts. How we spent our time, what we did together, what Chloe thought about her future, her boyfriend, her weight, her parents, her GCSE options.

'Did she have other friends that you might not have known about? Did she go out to pubs?'

I told them about her New Year's Eve party. I told them about the wallpaper, and the perfume counter, and the flat, and

Woolworths. I told them about the glass ashtrays, and her poster collection. Emma told them about her gentle nature, her shyness covered up by extroversion, her determination to come top of the class. She talked about how kind Chloe was to animals, and a collection of glass owls I didn't know she owned. All of those things got into the newspapers. Every single time Emma came up with a fact, I provided one more and she ran out of things to say first, and at the end I was still holding Chloe's secret in my mouth, like the time we put buttons under our tongues to make us sound posh when we made prank phone calls.

They asked us if we had any photographs of her doing ordinary teenage stuff. Singing into a hairbrush, for example – or dressed up to go to a disco. Carrying a loaded tray through McDonald's. That sort of thing.

'We need something to give to the media,' the policewoman explained. They already had her school photograph, but they wanted something more personal – showing a side to her that only girls her own age would have known. Showing Chloe larking about with us, her friends.

Emma shrugged, and I couldn't give them a photograph either.

One of the things that we did together, I could have said, was lock ourselves in her bedroom for hours and hours and hours. Whole afternoons – rows of them. Chloe insisted. She'd put on her special underwear and her silky dressing gown, pull out the Polaroid camera that Carl had given her and get me to take her picture.

'Did you know,' I could have said, 'that Polaroid film costs ten pounds a box, and you only get ten pictures from each film? That's a pound a picture, and she had drawers of the stuff because Carl gave it to her, and the clothes, and the camera, and she got me to do it because she could never work out the timer on her own.'

So yes, there are pictures. Pictures that never found their way back to Carl or to the police. Even I wasn't supposed to have them. I'd pretend the film had overexposed and pocket a few each time. These pictures were too private for anyone to see. Chloe, kneeling on her bed with the dressing gown falling off her shoulders. Chloe, shaking her hair and staring into the camera, not smiling. Chloe, her lipstick smudged across her cheek, posing with an unlit cigarette. Chloe on all fours, her hair falling around her face and her mouth slightly open. She is out of focus in this one. Her expression is a blur, her hair must have been moving.

There's more. Chloe from behind, her hands on her hips, pretending to unlace the thing she was wearing. I remember the red marks on her skin from the cheap, too-tight corset – the way she'd run her thumb under the edge of it and squirm between every photograph. Her eyes are dark and dull and unreadable. There's something about her look I should have noticed at the time. She doesn't seem unhappy, she looks bored. Her face shows she wasn't fully committed to what she was doing. It felt ridiculous. We didn't know what we were doing.

Polaroid film doesn't keep well. I don't want to use up these pictures, so I look at them only rarely. The colours are disintegrating: her face is the same shade as her hair; her limbs are smudged; the decoration on the corset – I remember a film of lace and some ribbons I'd have to arrange at the back – has dissolved. She's fading. I keep them in the dark, in a drawer, but they're on their way out. By the time they get that summerhouse finished, she'll be gone.

I never showed anyone these pictures. Never said a word. I was her best friend. I kept all the secrets she trusted me with. Could she have taken pictures like this with Emma? After ten years, it is still difficult for me to accept that I will probably never know.

I also have in my possession a picture of Emma and me, taken around this time. I leave the television flickering its news onto the blank walls of my flat, and get it from the drawer where I hide it. It is old but not faded. We are pretending to dig a hole in the school beds. The Juliet rose bushes are lined up beside us, their roots wrapped in wet gauze. Emma has her hand resting on the spade and is staring at the camera. My fingers rest on her arm. We were told to pause like that. Not smiling, touching each other. The picture was in a newspaper – our pale faces, blank as masks and frozen in a spotlight of attention.

People wanted to know if Chloe had confided, if we'd noticed the signs. I said nothing. Emma and I glanced at each other, and the photographer took another photograph. That's the one I have.

3

Chloe wanted to go into Debenhams to look at earrings. We were supposed to be Christmas shopping but I think she had her eye out for something special to wear to her New Year's Eve party. She'd lingered at the perfume and make-up counters, tried things on, used all the eye-shadow testers and had been shooed away. Her shoplifting habit was a secret but I knew about it because I was the one she told her secrets to. It goes without saying. Sometimes I got the blame, but that was okay – it was what close friends did for each other. She moved quickly between the aisles and displays and slid between and around people without touching them. Like a slinky. I followed her. People blocked my way after letting her pass only a second before. I always followed her.

'Look at this!'

She went to a basket filled with Christmas decorations. She was like a much younger child in that way – always gravitated to anything shiny or wrapped up. I think she liked Christmas a lot more than she would admit. She only ever described anything as 'all right' or 'boring' but that year, I think she was excited.

When I caught up with her she was already opening boxes and taking small glass reindeer out of their tissue paper beds. She laughed at them, and held them up against her ears. The broken boxes and tissue paper lay around her feet.

'What about these for my mum?' she said, and jiggled the ornaments until the little bells on their harnesses rattled.

'What are you doing?' I laughed. I couldn't help it.

We had a lot of running jokes going on between us about people that we knew – mainly people at our school or members

17

of our families. Her mother's habit of always wearing large, bright earrings was something that we laughed about a lot. I thought these people didn't know that we were laughing at them. Or I made myself forget what being laughed at felt like. We underestimated ourselves. Who cared? We were just girls – a nuisance, harmless, too loud in shops.

'What about this?' I said. I picked up one of the pieces of discarded tissue paper and held it against my top lip. 'Hello, Chloe,' I said, in a pretend deep voice. 'Have you seen my new car? It's a real pussy wagon!'

Chloe looked, blinked her metallic eyes once, twice, and turned half away. 'Who's that?' she said. She made her face go very still and serious.

I waggled the paper. 'I've got a box of chocolates for you, Chloe, come here and give us a kiss!'

'That's not really funny, actually,' she informed me.

The last time we saw Carl he'd been growing a moustache. He obviously wasn't used to the feel of it on his face because while Chloe had been talking to him I'd noticed him stroking it repeatedly. I was going to point it out to her – a fault or at least a potential embarrassment it was my duty to bring to her attention – but they'd left me alone and I'd had to sit on the bandstand and hold her bag while she disappeared into his car. I'd looked inside her purse at the picture on her bus pass, the pretend student ID card she'd got hold of from someone's older brother, who fancied her. A bracelet made with tiny beads that looked like glass but were only blue plastic. I'd smoked her cigarettes while I waited and the impression of Carl, the joke about the pussy wagon, was my attempt at revenge. Chloe was the one who was in charge of deciding what exactly was funny and what wasn't. She was right. It was a feeble joke. I let the scrap of tissue paper drop into the basket.

'Come over here,' Chloe said and stepped behind a tall revolving rack. It was hung with strings of beads, velvet chokers with butterfly clasps and earrings pinned onto pieces of card. She began to turn the display.

'Stand there,' she said, her fingers slowly grazing the coloured things, 'and just chat to me.'

'What about?'

'It doesn't matter. Whatever you like. No one's listening to you.'

This was confusing. Chloe continued to twirl the stand and examine the beads. She weighed them in her hands and pretended to be deciding. There was a mirror built into the top of the rack. She adjusted it downwards like it was in a car, and smiled at herself.

A fat woman edged by us and poked me with the point on her closed umbrella. It snagged my ankle and I made a little noise, an involuntary gasp. The woman turned and frowned at me. I stared back at her until she tutted and walked away then I bent and pulled up the leg of my jeans. There was a graze on the sticking-out bone of my ankle, weeping clear fluid and not blood. I could see Chloe's feet too, and the little squares of black cardboard that were dropping between them.

'Talk then,' Chloe said.

'That woman just hit me with her umbrella!' I looked for her grey head in the crowd. 'She never even said sorry!'

'Did she?' Chloe said. 'Did it hurt?'

'It wrecked!' I said, freshly outraged. 'And then she looked at me as if I was the one who'd done something wrong. Fat bitch.'

The Christmas music and the bubble of people talking was loud, but Chloe was still nodding at me.

'I don't know why people think they can just walk about and do what they like,' I went on. 'Shall we go and find her? Tell her what's what? I reckon we should. Chloe?'

'Right,' she said, 'that's enough now.'

I thought she was telling me to stop whining but she glanced upwards at a red light blinking in the swivelling black eye-socket of a camera, and then behind my shoulder. I saw a flick of movement in the corner of my eye, but didn't turn to see what it was – I was more interested in what Chloe was doing.

'Got to go,' she said, and slipped away giggling. I could hear her laughing long after she'd gone.

The security guard put his hand on my shoulder and not hers. It had happened before, but still, I never saw it coming. She told me once that I got caught and not her because I stood there looking ashamed of myself. I had a guilty-looking face, apparently: a magnet for suspicious shop assistants and men with brown shirts and walkie-talkies.

I turned limply. You always had to go to an office or a staff room somewhere. He walked behind me and tried to hold onto my elbow.

'I'm not going to run,' I said, 'but take your hands off me or I will go home and tell my dad you touched me.'

He recoiled because I said it like Chloe had told me to – the emphasis is on the word 'touched'.

And then you leg it, she'd said, but I didn't. I walked slightly in front of him, as if I was leading him. I only let him stand beside me when I was not sure which way I needed to go next. He tapped my shoulder but didn't hold onto it.

This was the same winter the City was plagued by an anonymous pervert who was cornering young girls in parks and bus stations and exposing himself to them. The news coverage about it was feverish. There were more police in the public places, and talk about a curfew. No man wanted to hear the word *touched* said about him by a fourteen-year-old. Chloe knew this.

In the back room, I let him have my real name.

'Where do you live?'

I shrugged. 'You can't ask me anything without my dad here,' I said and emptied out my pockets. A cigarette lighter and a packet of Polos.

'That it? What about your coat?'

'I've nothing,' I said. 'You can't keep me.'

I flicked open my jacket to show him there was nothing inside.

'What about your friend? What's her name?' He had a note-book in front of him, but the pencil was on the desk, not in his hand. He looked hot and bored.

Even in the back room the sound of 'White Christmas' on pan pipes floated in. There was a cold cup of coffee and an out-of-date copy of the *Mirror* on the desk in front of him. He looked at the newspaper longingly.

I smiled. 'I don't know what you're talking about.'

'The blonde. The pretty one. You know who I mean. What's her name?'

'You really shouldn't be conducting an interview with me without my parents here. Can I have your name? And what's that number on your sleeve? That'd come in handy too, thanks.'

I wrote the number down on the notepad using his pencil, then tore off a strip of paper and tucked it into my back pocket. He sighed.

'Laura Webb. I'll remember you. You at the Valley School?'

I nodded. He must have seen the badge on my rucksack.

'That means you must live round here. Walking distance. I'll find out your address. Talk to your parents. They'll tell me who your good-looking mate was.'

'She never took anything,' I said, 'and I've got nothing either.'

I scooped up the mints and the lighter, and walked out. I sauntered home, waiting for Chloe to pop out from somewhere, her pockets rattling with jewellery. By the time I got there the security guard had gone through the phone book and called Barbara to tell her that I was banned from our Debenhams and all other Debenhams in the entire chain – for life.

I didn't catch up with Chloe that afternoon. She'd seen me getting caught, I suppose, and bombed it home. It might seem heartless, but there was no point in both of us getting caught, and, as she'd probably say, it served me right for not being as observant as she was.

When I got back home Barbara was waiting for me. She opened the door before I'd even gone up the path. Sometimes she hovered in the hallway and yanked the door inwards when my key was in the lock, but that day she pulled it back and stared at me while I was still fumbling with the gate. Her fringe was stuck to her forehead and she was wearing an apron with a recipe for Scotch Broth written down the front of it. We had a matching tea-towel and set of soup dishes.

'Get inside, you,' she said, and looked past me into the street as if there was going to be a van full of policemen parked outside and a man in a white overall unrolling crime-scene tape between the cherry tree and the gatepost. I wasn't quick enough: she grabbed my shoulder and pulled me into the house.

That was twice I'd been manhandled. Three times if you count the woman with the umbrella, which I did count, because she hadn't apologised. I was made to turn out my pockets again. I'd expected this, and I'd tucked the cigarette lighter into the waist of my jeans, so I was all right.

'I didn't do anything,' I said.

'They telephoned me just for fun then, did they?' Barbara said quickly. 'Was it that Chloe?'

'Chloe went home.'

Barbara sighed and leaned forward, her hands flat on the table.

'What did you take? What is it that you need so much you'd steal it?'

'Nothing. I didn't take anything.'

'I know we don't have money, but—'

'I didn't take anything.'

She sighed. Picked her hands up from the table and put them into the front of her apron. Waited a while before speaking.

'If I didn't seriously think you'd spoil yet another Christmas for your father,' she said, 'I'd tell him about this.'

I didn't say anything. By 'yet another Christmas' I think she meant the year before when I got the chickenpox. Because Donald and Barbara had never had it, I gave it to them too, and because Donald didn't do much, his immune system was rubbish and he had to spend a week in bed and miss everything.

She confiscated the Polo mints.

Except for the sudden, unexpected freeze on Christmas Eve and a hailstorm during the night that settled and pretended to be snow, Christmas Day went as usual that year.

I'd bought Donald a compendium of magic tricks. I'd got it months before from a remainder bookshop. I'd bought it too early. By Christmas he'd gone off magic and moved on to fish. Still, he pretended he liked it and sat with the box on his knees while we watched the Queen and waited for the turkey to be ready. I'd also saved up and bought Barbara a bottle of the perfume that Chloe's mum always wore. She wouldn't open the box and try it on and when Donald went to sleep she put it on top of the television.

'That can stay up there until the shops open,' she said.

I stared at it and listened to Donald snoring from his chair. The box stared back. The lights on the Christmas tree were reflected in the silver foil writing on the box and the twinkling dragged my eye back to it no matter where in the room I looked. Barbara got tipsy.

'You want me to swap it?' I said. Hurt. Barbara shushed me. Pointed at Donald. 'Charity shop,' she said, slurring slightly. 'I am,' she poured another glass, 'not comfortable receiving stolen goods.'

'You can't nick perfume,' I whispered back. 'They keep it locked up behind the counter. The boxes on the shelves are just for show.'

'So you've been "scoping it out" then,' Barbara said.

'Everyone knows that,' I said. 'It's like fags and razor blades. The dear, small things.'

'Fags?' she said, and changed the channel on the telly without asking. I couldn't wait for it to be Boxing Day so I could go out on the park with Chloe and compare what we'd got.

4

There are Debenhams department stores all over the world. They've got them in Israel, in Russia, in Australia. Years later I told Emma the story about me being banned from them and she laughed, but when I told her that I'd never actually been in a Debenhams since, *ever*, she insisted we leave the park where we'd been sitting sharing a bottle of cider on a bench in the Japanese water garden, and go into town. The very same Debenhams, and although I don't think it occurred to her, I kept expecting to see Chloe hovering somewhere, one eye on the security cameras. Blonde girls caught my eye and I stared at them sniffing their wrists at the perfume counters and holding dresses against themselves in front of long smudgeless mirrors. They were nothing like ghosts.

Emma and I had a cup of coffee in the cafe at the top. It's on a mezzanine, except everyone calls it the rotunda, and the chairs and tables are against glass panels so that you can look through and down at everyone inspecting the racks, picking things up and putting them down and queueing for changing rooms.

Emma took the paper packets of sugar, tipped them into her saucer and slowly ate them, licking her finger and dabbing it at the grains until they were all gone.

'Now it's your turn,' I said.

'My turn for what?'

'Tell me something about her that I don't know. I told you about the shoplifting, didn't I? You and her went out together. Without me. Tell me what you got up to.'

Emma shook her head and told me I should take something. 'Go down there and put something in your pocket. Some earrings. Sunglasses. Something little.'

'No!' I said. Louder than I'd meant to. 'Tell me about Chloe. Do you really think she . . .' I couldn't look her in the eye. '. . . did what they said she did?'

No one says suicide. It makes us all look bad. We say *tragedy*.

'Go on,' Emma said, and smiled into her cup. 'Or are you too scared?'

We're grown up now and Chloe is still sitting with us, waiting to be impressed.

'We're too conspicuous to shoplift,' I said.

People were already staring. Two grown women acting like guilty schoolgirls. Laughing too loudly. Our coats were faded, stained, past their best. We might have smelled like cheap vodka and onions, or unwashed knickers and yesterday's Stella Artois.

'You already got blamed,' she said. 'You should get something out of it.'

That's the way her mind works. Emma likes to go on walks and let down people's tyres or break off their wing mirrors as a kind of revenge because she thinks cars are killing the planet. She's got a WWF badge and an embroidered rainbow on the lapel of her jacket. She's got a car, but she makes up for it by only driving when she's a bit pissed, covering the rust with Greenpeace stickers, and volunteering for things. She's shy of people but she cares about plants and animals. She hates men and she's angry at everything.

'If I get pulled in for shoplifting, I'll get the sack,' I said.

When I think about work, I hear the piped music, the squeak of squeegee against the glass lift doors. See green plastic plants sunk in a pot of what looks like brown baked beans, but is really just polystyrene painted to look like pebbles. It's not much. It's home.

'I need my job.'

Emma shrugged. She doesn't have a job other than the kinds of volunteering that you can't get sacked from, so it doesn't matter to her.

'Let's go then,' she said, and made a clucking noise under her breath as I squeezed past her to get out of my seat. She moved and her saucer tipped, sending grains of sugar pattering to the marble-effect floor. 'We'll find a pub.'

It wasn't as easy as that. We stopped again for another look in Women's Accessories. That was where it had happened. She insisted it was time to face up to my past.

'Look,' she said, and plucked a red and white chiffon scarf from a basket on the counter, swished it through the air like a streamer, and then wound it around her hand. She was laughing, and someone passed between us and frowned. Emma's got brown teeth because she smokes hundreds of roll-ups a day. She stinks. My hair, when it's not folded into a knot and covered up with the crocheted hat, is a matted dark swirl of damp and sweat-smelling curls. We don't do make-up. I've got acne scars and Emma's always running with cold sores.

We're not the kind of girls we used to be.

I watched Emma twirling but I never caught the moment when she made the streamer disappear, or how it got from her pocket to mine. Some sleight of hand. A knack, a magic trick. Chloe will have shown her it. A familiar spark of jealousy. How come Emma got to know that, and not me?

5

A morning sometime in the winter before she died. The three of us went into town; it must have been before Christmas because the daft music was playing in all the shops and the tinsel in every window made my eyes ache. Town was so busy that I kept losing them – chasing them between racks of clothes and shoes that seemed to grow and divide and close in on me like a dream while my eyes itched with tears because I couldn't help but feel the two of them were doing it on purpose, and really wanted me to go away.

'Come on, Lola!'

I followed them around the shopping centre – it was as if they had a list. Jessops, Superdrug, Wilkinson. Emma was wearing a cardigan that belonged to Chloe – a pale blue thing that crossed over at the front and tied at the waist with a ribbon. It was too delicate for her square, broad shoulders. She was taller than me and Chloe. I thought about how unfeminine that was and wondered if she'd stayed over at Chloe's last night.

'Are you coming, or not?'

Carl was going to meet us in the multi-storey car park over the bus station. He was right at the top, and we went up to him in the lift. It smelled weird in there, like bleach and piss and the thin chicken soup you could buy in plastic cups from the vending machines in the bus station. The doors were painted orange and slid shut with a rickety clank that was not reassuring.

'Are you sure he's going to be there, Chloe?' Emma said. 'If I'm not home by three my dad'll murder me.'

Chloe smiled. 'He'll be there,' she said. 'He's never let us down before, has he?'

'He better not.'

'Who cares about your dad anyway? *I'm* going to stay out all night.'

'Your mum'll have kittens if you do,' I said. 'You'll never get let out at the weekend again.'

'She sent me to stay with my grandma,' Chloe said, 'told me to telephone and make the arrangements myself.'

'Why? Are they going away?' Emma asked, and at the same time I thought about the empty house, the lockable drinks cabinet Chloe could get into with a Kirby grip, her father's computer and her mother's expensive, strictly-not-allowed-to-be-taken-out-of-the-box, massaging foot spa.

'Nah,' Chloe said, and the lift moved upwards slowly, leaving my stomach behind it, 'they're having *marital problems*.'

Emma frowned. 'Are they going to split up?'

'I doubt it. She's found out about him and his fancy piece. She chucked the wedding teapot at him.' She looked at us slyly, as if checking how we were going to react. I looked at Emma, who had drawn her face into a picture of mature concern. Panhead.

'Are you all right?' she asked.

Chloe laughed. 'I think it's disgusting, him shagging a primary school teacher. He should be past it, at his age. He's got hair in his ears and he cuts his toenails in the bath and pokes the bits down the plughole. I'm going to go to her school and tell her that,' she started pointing at the air in front of her, the tip of her finger stabbing in time with her words, 'right in front of her class. Say he's a dirty old man with sweat marks on his work shirts and he said "goodness gracious" when some prick ran into the back of us at the traffic lights. Then she won't want to shag him,' she clicked her tongue against her teeth and winked, 'problem solved!'

I giggled. Chloe was amazing. The thing was, something crazy like that was always a possibility with her.

'How did your mum find out?' Emma said.

'Yeah, did she catch them at it? In your parents' bed?'

'Nothing like that.' Chloe shook her head. 'I heard him talking to her on the phone on the upstairs extension. Smooch-smoochy talk. He sounded like a right penis. He pissed me off so I told her myself.'

Emma looked uncertain and as if she was about to tell Chloe what a bad idea that had been when the lift doors juddered open and Chloe darted through the doors first.

'Come on, lardy-guts!' she called.

The car park was dim and windy and Carl had parked his car at the front. He was sitting on the curved concrete ledge looking out over the main road and the shops. He had dark hair three months away from its last cut and it fell shaggily over his ears and the collar of his jacket. When he turned, I noticed he'd got rid of the moustache and I smiled but I didn't say anything.

'All right, my girls!' he said, grinned, and jumped down jauntily as we approached. Chloe and Emma, and then me, started to run, and the sound of our shoes bounced around the metal and concrete. A car came around the corner and had to brake hard to avoid Emma and Chloe. The driver beeped her horn and Chloe stuck out her tongue. Emma held onto the edge of her coat and pulled her back when she tried to run out in front of it again. She was always like that when Carl was around.

'You been busy?'

'It was packed, Carl, just like you said.' Chloe was using the special, older voice she always put on to talk to him. Carl put his arm around her shoulders, brought her in to him and kissed the top of her head. Then he moved around his car and popped open the boot.

'Stick it all in there then, will you?'

Emma leaned over the boot, untied the blue cardigan and let

several yellow and black boxes of camera film fall out. Chloe giggled, and held Emma's coat while she took the cardigan off and gave it back to her.

'There's a knack to it,' Emma explained. 'You need to choose what you're wearing better. That jumper's no good. Too baggy. Everything'll drop out the bottom.'

'Right,' I said, realising too late that this was some sort of competition.

'Or you could do it like Chloe does,' Emma went on.

Chloe winked and took an elastic band off her wrist. Carl laughed as she pulled at the cuff of her jacket that had been tucked into it, and shook little boxes of screws and nails out of her sleeve.

'You're a genius,' he said. 'I'd never have thought of that. A real Bobby Dazzler!'

Bobby Dazzler! That was the sort of thing dinner ladies, or your granny would say to you. Sometimes Carl spoke English like he didn't understand it.

'What do you want with those screws?' I asked.

'Carl's doing a darkroom in his house,' Chloe said. Carl nudged her shoulder. 'It's all right. She won't say anything.'

I frowned. Who cares about his darkroom?

'He needs to black out the windows,' she explained. 'You can't develop pictures in daylight. It won't work.'

Emma had walked away from the car and was staring over the edge of the concrete lip, looking down at the buses going in and out of the station below. People jumped off here, and the gap was supposed to be netted off to stop them, but no one could agree on whose job it was to pay for it. The inside of the lip was covered in graffiti – not the good, interesting kind you got on the trains in big cities, but hearts and pairs of breasts and erect penises spraying cum into the air.

'Emma, get back over here. I thought you were in a rush to go?'

Emma didn't react for a few seconds – as if she didn't hear

him – and he blinked slowly and opened his mouth to call her again when she turned and looked at him as if she was waking up from a long sleep.

'All right,' she said, and headed towards the car – but in her own time, not walking, not sauntering, but shuffling. Chloe didn't hurry her.

I didn't understand why Carl would want them to get such small, insignificant things for him. He had a job – surely he could afford stuff like this? And I didn't know Emma was in on the secret of Chloe's boyfriend – someone too old for school, too old for Chloe. I was under strict instructions to say nothing to anyone about him. When had she confided in Emma?

'What did you get, Lola?' Chloe said.

I shrugged, and showed her a handful of chocolate eclairs I'd snagged from the pick 'n' mix bins in Woolworths.

'You want one?' My teeth and fingers were already sticky with chocolate. It was a comforting, disgusting feeling – my molars tacky and clamping together when I spoke.

'Nah.' She shook her head. 'Stuff like that's really bad for your skin, you know? I'm avoiding it. Detoxifying so I can have what I want over Christmas and New Year without breaking out.'

I didn't bother asking if Carl wanted me to put my things in the boot too. He was giving us all a lift home, apparently, because the sky had turned white and snow was expected any minute. He wasn't going to have his girls trudge through town in the sleet getting their feet wet and giving themselves pneumonia.

'You coming in the car as well, Lola?' Carl said. He usually ignored me, and because I wasn't expecting to be spoken to I flustered over my answer, and Chloe and Emma laughed as I tripped over a dangling loop of seatbelt and stumbled into the back.

'Can Emma sit in the front this time?' Chloe said, and Carl shrugged and said why not, and Emma looked pleased with herself and I was pleased too because that meant I got to sit in the back with Chloe – but she leaned forward and talked to Carl all the way back.

I have the scarf Emma lifted from Debenhams that day. I keep it in my sock drawer, under the bad socks I only keep to punish myself with if I've been too lazy to keep up with the laundry. It still has the tags on.

I wonder if she did it on purpose? She wouldn't answer my question about Chloe. Wouldn't tell me what she remembered. But she'd steal in front of me: show me the knack of it just to remind me that there was plenty I didn't know about the things she and Chloe did together.

Emma will ask me about this scarf one of these days. Will laugh at me still never going back into Debenhams, laugh if she knew I wear my hair the way it is and choose the glasses I do because, after our months of being secondhand celebrities, I don't want anyone else to look at me.

6

Christmas might have been dull, but I hadn't expected anything better. I'd grown out of it. I'd grown out of everything. Everything was boring except for the endless trips around the park with Chloe. Wandering aimlessly, waiting for the boys to turn up, and lately, waiting for Chloe and Carl to be finished in the back of his car.

When I was out with Chloe I felt on the brink of things. She was going to get Carl to drive us to Manchester and get us into a real nightclub, where famous people went. Footballers. People out of *Kerrang!* She said he was going to take us to buy dresses and let us wear them in a place where we could have cocktails and sushi and no one would bother asking us for ID because they all knew Carl and if we were with him, we'd be all right. It was going to happen; any day now. She hadn't asked him when yet; she was waiting for the right time. But when the right time happened we'd be going, the three of us.

I'd been looking forward to Boxing Day, when I'd be allowed out again. Chloe and I had arranged to meet in Avenham Park, the place with the rose garden and the fountain and the Victorian promenade along the river. That was the place we went. It was good – near to town and the shops and the Spar that didn't want ID, and friends from our year were always there. That was where we were going. That's what the plan was. Chloe was going to sneak out a bottle. But Carl had arrived, picked us up in his car and driven us to Cuerden Valley Park. Not really a park, but a nature reserve – a large woodland with a man-made lake and paths and red bins for the dog crap and hides for the bird-watchers. We couldn't have walked there.

'Why've we got to come all this way?' I said.

'Every man and his dog are out walking off their Christmas dinner,' Carl said irritably. 'I wanted a bit of peace.'

It was always parks. Parks, or the industrial land around the docks, or nature reserves, or the train station at night, or the back of the bus station, parked on the dark bit of the empty aprons while the buses were all safe and away at the depot. Never the cinema or the fairground or ten-pin bowling.

'Peace and goodwill to all men,' I said. I don't know why. It was the sort of meaningless playing with words and phrases that Chloe and I did when we were alone together – chattering into each other's ears across linked arms as we walked. It wasn't supposed to mean anything; it was just a way of touching each other when we were out and about. Automatic. Chloe laughed. Carl stopped, turned off the engine, and looked between the front seats at me.

'Go on then, get out of it, will you?'

He was more abrupt than usual. He didn't tell us jokes, hadn't brought any sweets or magazines or fags for me. He rushed me out of the car: he must have missed Chloe.

'Go and stand guard.'

He actually said that, and pointed out of the car window with his thumb. If he was chocolate he'd go on and eat himself, and I was about to tell him that, looking towards Chloe for moral support. She had a charm bracelet tinkling on her tiny wrist, and big gold hoops in her ears. He'd passed them to her, still in their Elizabeth Duke bag, and she'd ripped into them that eagerly she didn't notice he hadn't bothered wrapping them and hadn't brought anything for me.

'Chloe?'

But Chloe was looking at him, her lips pursed.

I nearly said: she practises that in the mirror, she read about it in *Just Seventeen*.

She pushed her tongue up behind her front teeth and pointed

her wet lips at him because she'd read an article that said it looked sexy. Her hair was scraped back into a scrunchie, apart from two long strands at the front. She'd wet those with spit and curled them around her finger while she was waiting for him to come and get us. You got near her, and those curled ribbons of hair smelled like her morning breath. I wanted to tell him that, too.

'Chop chop, then,' Carl said, and reached back to pull the catch on the door. Chloe didn't say anything so I had to get out.

I walked away quickly, before I had the chance to go off on one. I didn't trust myself, but I didn't much feel like walking home either. Carl would have been a prick about it, would have driven off laughing and left me to make my own way home. I knew that and I knew Chloe wouldn't stick up for me while he was there so I did as I was told. I stood guard, waiting a little way away from the car by the edge of the car park. It was cold and I pulled the sleeves of my cardigan down over my hands. I stamped my feet on the earth, shifted my weight from one foot to the other.

It was just a car park; there wasn't anywhere to walk but I walked anyway, a tiny circle in front of the sign with the map of the reserve on it, the drawings of cowslips and stoats and other rare things to look out for. Someone had put a lighter to the plastic over the map and burned it in places. The plastic had dripped down and blackened. The drips obscured some of the writing.

This is shit, I thought, and glanced at the shapes in the car, hunched and indistinct except for the alarming flash of Chloe's new white jumper. I put my hands inside the sleeves of my coat and held them in front of me like a muff. I should have brought gloves. I should have stayed at home. Carl was saying something to Chloe. I couldn't see him clearly, but I could see Chloe tugging at the fluff around the hood of her coat, laughing carefully, nodding her head.

I don't know why everything Chloe wore or owned had to be white or pastel pink or baby blue. Why it all had to be cashmere or feathers, fluffy or baby-soft. It was like a trademark she had. A kind of 'thing' that she was known for. People could go into shops and see white cross-over cardigans with fluff around the cuffs and nod and say, 'That's so Chloe.' It meant she had personality. She was easy to buy presents for.

I knew I didn't have a thing. I'm nondescript. I'd never even tried to have a thing. Harder to get presents for. The gifts under the tree were a total washout. Donald and Barbara had bought me book tokens and a new black coat. It was plain, perfect for school. It wasn't really a present. It just proved it: I had no personality. Even Barbara could tell, otherwise she'd have bought me something decent. I stood there in the cold and tried to think about presents; really good presents I could ask for in the summer when it was my birthday. I couldn't even think of anything. It was something I needed to talk to Chloe about. She had the best ideas.

Chloe and Carl were still talking in the car. I carried on pacing. I didn't even know what I was supposed to be looking out for anyway. Keeping guard. What a prick. We were in the visitors' car park on the edge of a nature reserve – a pretend wilderness with regimented trees, a man-made lake and a bit of conserved woodland that backed onto a fucking Asda. You could see the letters from the big green sign through the trees, some angles.

Stand guard. No one was going to be there: it was Boxing Day. People were at home, watching films. I hadn't even seen a dog walker. Guard – and I was the one stood on the edge of the woods, on my own, with that flasher roaming about in the bushes. If Barbara knew, she'd have a fit. She'd bought me a rape alarm and I'd stuffed it into the back of the kitchen junk drawer, but now I was thinking it would be a useful thing to have. I imagined creeping towards the car and setting it off, making the pair of them jump out of their skins. I sighed and turned around. I was going to signal to Chloe and get her to get Carl to take us home, or take me home at least.

Chloe was up on her knees. She was turning and climbing between the front seats. She tipped forward and fell into the back face-first. A few seconds later the driver's side door opened. Carl got out, rubbing his mouth.

I turned my head away quickly in case he thought I was being a perv and spying, but he didn't look at me. He slammed the door with such force that the car rocked. He got into the back with Chloe.

This is shit, I thought again, and turned my back on both of them. On the car, on Chloe's new cashmere jumper. On Christmas, on the whole fucking year just gone. Fucking Carl, I thought, and walked slowly away from them around the edge of the car park where the earth turned into grass and under-growth and hedge. I counted my steps, balanced as long as I could on one foot in the middle of a step and leaned so far forward I was falling and had to stamp my other foot down hard to keep my balance. I knew I looked stupid, like a baby, playing like that.

It didn't matter. The car park, probably the whole reserve, was deserted anyway, and Carl wouldn't have been looking at me. He never looked at me.

The man had come out from between the bushes. He'd edged sideways and cringed his face away from the dead brown brambles. The branches had sprung back after him and snagged at the sleeves of his jacket.

'Oi,' he said, but friendly. He was carrying a football, a brand new one, and there was a scratch on the back of his hand. It wasn't deep but blood was beading in the groove and he hadn't noticed. He came towards me, smiling, and made no move to open his coat or unzip his fly.

'Oi, nothing.' I wasn't in the mood to be nice. 'Oi, yourself.'

'What you doing here?' he said, as if he knew me.

I just looked at him. His voice sounded strange. Like he was deaf, or making fun of someone who was. Like he was a child. He didn't look like a child though. Too big. Too old to be carrying a football. The kids had been out all morning; I'd seen them on the street. Carrying kites and trying new bikes, testing the ice-rink pavements with new rollerblades. But this boy, this man, must have been older than me. Carl's age, even – which I'd guessed was twenty-three. He'd told us he was twenty-one.

I looked at his his hands again.

'What are you doing here? Excuse me?'

He was loud. Irritated, but extremely polite. It was strange.

I was about to tell him to mind his own business, tell him to bugger off, when I realised what he was. One of those – I forgot the word, but I knew there was one.

Barbara called them angels and said they weren't like real people. More like children, or animals. According to her, they can't do right or wrong because they don't have souls of their own, not in the same way normal people do. They aren't account-able for their actions, like tiny children aren't.

Mongs. That was it.

That's what they were called at school. I'd spoken to one before – its parents brought it to church one Christmas. They kept it at home the rest of the time, but it wanted to see the nativity. It was all right. I thought it was all right.

'I'm just waiting,' I said, and shrugged. I decided to speak to him like he was a real person, and nodded at his football. 'Did you get that for Christmas?'

'Yah, got it for Christmas. Brand new. Best one available in the shops. To buy,' he said, and smiled.

His teeth were funny. They weren't disgusting or anything like that, there were just gaps between every single one. Made them look like baby teeth, even though they couldn't have been, because he was taller than me and I didn't have any baby teeth at all by then. Can't even remember losing the last one.

He was wearing a good waterproof jacket – an expensive one – and a purple scarf knotted under his chin and tucked in underneath it. Someone had wrapped him up before letting him out to play with his new ball. There was someone looking after him. I imagined his mum, maybe the same age as Barbara, which is older than usual. Embarrassing.

That's what happens when you let yourself get old before you have babies. I remembered it then, from Biology. I imagined wrinkled hands tying that scarf around his neck and tucking it in. Someone white-haired kissing him on the head before sending him out to play with his new ball. He probably got teased about how old his mum was, like I used to before I started knocking about with Chloe.

Actually, that would probably be the last thing he'd get teased about. Would be if his school was anything like mine was, anyway. Mongs go to school all together though, don't they? So maybe he would. Except he couldn't have been at school anymore, by then. I couldn't work out how old he was, but I felt protective towards him.

'Santa bring you anything good?' he said, and looked at me out of the corner of his eye. His eyes were funny too. I should have known right away. All their eyes are like that. I couldn't tell if he was joking or not, about Santa. He might have been smiling, but his face didn't have the creases in the right place so I couldn't tell. Even dogs sometimes look like they're smiling.

'Yeah,' I said, 'Topshop vouchers. A few albums. You like listening to music?'

He didn't answer me and I shook my head and turned away. I can't believe, I thought, I can't fucking believe I am standing out here in the freezing cold talking to a Mong about what Santa brought me. For fuck's sake.

'Ginger Spice!' he said, and I realised he'd been struggling to remember. 'I like her. I like her. I like her.' He looked around, checking, I could tell, to see if anyone was listening.

'Big titties.'

I laughed, but in a friendly way.

'Yes, she has,' I said. 'You shouldn't talk like that.'

'That girl in the car your friend?' he asked.

'Yeah,' I said. There was no point asking him if he had any fags with him. He probably only got three quid a week pocket money or something. And spent it all on sherbet fountains and *Monster In My Pocket*.

'I saw that girl's titties.'

'What girl?'

'That girl in the car. White jumper. Saw her take it off. That her boyfriend?'

'Carl's not her boyfriend. Just a bloke.'

'He was kissing her.'

'Knobhead,' I said, though I wasn't surprised. I walked away from him, still talking, muttering under my breath.

'I've got to hang about here in the cold until he's finished with his jailbait. Don't know what they expect me to do.'

I'd finished talking before I realised he'd come with me, trotting along just beside. I stopped and turned.

'Look,' I said, trying to sound adult and reasonable. 'You shouldn't be hanging around watching them. Sneaking about in the bushes. It's pervy. Carl – that man in the car – he wouldn't like it. He'd shout at you. You should go home. Aren't you cold?'

He stopped just behind me. He held out his ball for me to take.

'I'm not playing with you,' I said loudly, hoping to scare him away, even though it was a bit tight. 'Get on home, will you?'

'Hold it for me a minute. I want to get into my pocket. Share with you. One to yourself, swear to God.'

I sighed, almost groaned, and took the ball off him. He went through all the pockets in his expensive jacket until he found what he was looking for. A pack of ten Embassy. He opened it, only two gone, gave it to me, and took the ball back. I looked at the packet and laughed.

'You smoke?'

'Every day. All the time. Whenever I like,' he said. 'My dad told the man in the Paki shop not to give me them anymore, but he still does. I'm old enough. I had Christmas money. I can buy whatever I like with it.'

'You shouldn't say that,' I said. 'What's your name?'

'Wilson.'

'Wilson, you shouldn't say "Paki" – it isn't nice.'

'Sorry. Sorry. Why isn't it nice?'

'They just don't like it.' I didn't think there was any point explaining it to him. He wouldn't get it anyway. 'If they heard you, they might not sell you the fags anymore.'

'None of them?' Wilson looked stricken, and I had to take a deep breath to stop myself laughing. It was so cold the air hurt my nose on the way in and reminded me that, actually, I could do with a fag.

'Where's your lighter?' I said. 'Shall we have one now?'

'I've dropped it,' Wilson said. He looked crestfallen and I felt bad for reminding him.

'It doesn't matter,' I said quickly.

'It was ace. It was my best thing. Had a woman in a costume on it.'

'What kind of costume?' I said, thinking about fancy dress and Halloween.

'For swimming in. When you pressed the button to get the fire to go on, it disappeared and you could see her titties. It was great.'

He looked miserable again. I was ready to believe the lighter really was his best thing.

'Where did you drop it?'

'In there. In those trees.'

'We could go and have a look?'

He shook his head. 'Pine needles. Old leaves, spiders and things. I've already been looking. I'll get another one though. I will. Whenever I like.'

'All right then. We'll use mine,' I said, getting it out of my pocket.

When we'd finished the fags and Wilson had gone behind a tree to be sick, I handed the packet back to him. I could have taken it. He'd probably forgotten, or would be too scared to ask me for it. But I didn't.

'What's your name?' he asked.

He'd got the ball under his arm, his other hand jammed into his pocket. I could see his fingers fumbling through the material, turning the fag packet around and around.

'It's Lola,' I said. Because I'd decided to speak to him like a normal person, I explained it to him, like I always had to when I met someone new.

'It's not my real name. I'm called Laura. That's what it says on my birth certificate. School register. Laura Madeline Webb. With two "b"s – not like the spider. But when I was little I couldn't say it.' I rolled my eyes. 'Laura. Lola. My parents thought it was cute. And Lola's the name of a girl in a song they liked when they were younger. So that's what everyone calls me. Even teachers, sometimes.'

He was waiting patiently for me to finish, he wasn't interested at all. I laughed.

'What? What do you want?'

'Lola, what's jailbait mean?'

'Oh. You shouldn't say it. I was just in a bad mood. Because of the cold.'

'What does it mean though? What does it mean?'

'Nothing.'

'Lola Webb, what does jailbait mean?'

I didn't want to be talking to him about sex. There was no way of telling what he already knew and what his parents had left him hazy on. There were some things, I supposed, he'd never need a practical knowledge of and what Chloe and Carl were doing in the car right now was probably one of them.

'I gave you a fag. I was your best friend! Now you're ignoring me?'

'For God's sake. It means a girl who's too young to have sex with. Someone younger than sixteen. But pretty, I suppose. Like bait, for fish. She's too young to have sex with a man without the man getting into trouble, in case he forced her to do it. Or tried to get her drunk or something. But because she's pretty it makes the man want to have sex with her a lot. Even though he's too old and he isn't supposed to. And if anyone found out that he did it he could go to jail. Because he took the bait. So it's not a nice word, really. You shouldn't say it.'

Wilson didn't say anything for a while. We stood next to each other under the trees looking at the white sky and watching our breath on the air. The sun was going down already. It must have been about three.

'My dad takes me fishing sometimes,' Wilson said. 'He gave me a baccy tin and I've got to go digging and fill it up with worms. Best worms are black. That means they've eaten a lot. Fish like them ones best, eat them up quick.'

'Yeah?' I said, looking towards the car. I was too far away to see anything, but they must have been done by then. My feet were so cold they hurt. It was freezing.

'I've been fishing here before,' Wilson said, and nodded back towards the woods. 'There's a pond through there.'

'I know. You wouldn't be able to get anything now though,' I said. 'It's all frozen over.'

Wilson nodded. 'I've been from there. Been to see. Do you think the fish are all right under there?'

I shrugged. 'Probably. They have fish in colder countries than ours. Polar bears eat fish.'

'I can't wait until it thaws out,' Wilson said. 'Cold water is all right, but when it's all iced up there's no fishing, and it's shit,' he giggled, 'it's well shit.'

'You could skate on it though,' I said.

'Not interested in skating,' Wilson said, and shook his head. 'I'm interested in digging up worms and going fishing.'

'I've been out skating on that pond before,' I said. 'It's ace. Sliding along like nobody's business. Faster than anything. Even if you fall, it doesn't hurt that much because you carry on sliding. Just so long as you wear your gloves, and the right sort of shoes.'

'Boring,' Wilson said, 'plus, my dad would batter me if he saw me out on the ice. I've had serious warnings about it.'

'Yes,' I said, 'me as well. Everyone's parents do. There's a video they show in school. Have you seen it?'

Wilson shook his head. I wondered if he'd even been to school. Missed out on the icy ponds, fireworks and giant hogweed safety videos. Big loss.

'I've been out all the same though,' I said, 'because it's fucking brilliant.'

'What did your dad say? Did he batter you?'

I shook my head. 'Nah, course not. If they don't know, then you can't catch it, can you?'

'He'd know,' Wilson said, and shook his head, 'my dad always knows. And he'd stop me going fishing. Fishing's the main thing. And the worms.'

'Right.'

'I got a massive one once. A worm about as big as a skate-board.'

'Right.'

'Yeah.' He held out his hands to show me. 'I dug it out of our garden, this big. Bigger than the fish we got, my dad said.'

But his ball had dropped and was rolling away between his feet, down the gentle incline towards the tatty hedge, and he turned away to get it. I followed him, bending under the branches, and got it before he did.

Wilson was laughing and I was pulling a dead leaf out of my hair when we came out from between the bushes. The first thing I saw was Carl, standing under the burned sign with Chloe. I thought they were looking at the picture of the stoat before I realised they were looking for me. Wilson came up behind me as Carl turned, looking pleased with himself. His hands in his pockets and his elbows were jutting out like handles.

'This your boyfriend?' he called. He was sneering at me, lazily, but only for effect. He put his fingers on Chloe's shoulder, squeezing her there and guiding her over the gravel towards me and Wilson, but his eyes were hazy and kept darting back to the car.

Chloe was twitching. She looked a state – her hair was a mess and she kept patting at it. She was biting at the skin on her lips and rearranging the collar on her jumper to cover the tiny purple marks on her neck.

'Yeah, he's my boyfriend, Carl. We've been meeting in secret all this time because we knew you couldn't handle the competition,' I said, before I could stop myself. And bang goes the lift home, I thought.

Carl looked surprised, and then laughed right at me. A real laugh, open and genuine.

'Cheeky bitch,' he said, and laughed again, shaking his head like he didn't know I could be funny. Thought I was scared of him. Chloe looked at Carl, didn't like it.

'You cow!' she mouthed poisonously. I looked away.

Wilson started to laugh too, and Carl laughed with him for a while, exaggerating and slapping his thigh. It went on until Carl reached over and pushed the ball through Wilson's arms.

It rolled between his feet and through the grass. Wilson chased it but it went into the hedge again before he could grab it. When he bent over to pull it out Carl put his foot in the middle of Wilson's backside and gently pushed until he toppled over. When he got up his face was red, his hair stuck up in tufts. His nose was running and he was outraged. It did look funny.

I stepped away from Wilson and went to stand nearer to Carl and Chloe. Wilson scowled and rubbed the back of his trousers with his free hand.

'You and your jailbait, yeah!' he said. 'I'll tell my dad you and your jailbait did this to my hand,' he said, and held up the hand with the scratch that I thought he hadn't noticed.

'Wilson.' I said it quietly, because Carl wasn't laughing now, wasn't doing anything except looking at him with slack, dull eyes.

'Tell him you and your jailbait made my face bleed. Ripped my new coat. Took my ball. He'll have you.'

'Shut up, Wilson,' I said, not looking at him. I tried to take a step sideways, to get between Carl and him, but Wilson was already coming forward, getting as close to Carl as he could, standing up straight as if he was preparing to fight. Wilson was bigger than Carl – taller, wider – Donald would have called his trainers canoes. But he was soft and slow and he didn't know what Carl was like.

'What did you say?' Carl asked quietly, as if he was genuinely interested. He cupped a hand behind his ear. 'Didn't hear you, mate. Speak up a bit. Go on. Don't be shy.'

'Tell my dad. Not scared of you. Bullies only pick on people they're scared of. You're just jealous. You and the jailbait!'

'Say that again for me, will you?'

Carl didn't look angry, he was glittering with calm. He was hard – but relaxed – teeth not even clenched, arms loose at his sides, fingers curled against his palms. He snapped his arm like a whip and clipped Wilson around the side of the head before he could duck. It was the sort of thing his dad probably did to him when he caught him smoking.

He'll be all right, I thought. It was a hard slap though, and made a noise like Carl had hit wood.

Wilson put his free hand on his head like it was starting to rain. He cried with his mouth open. Spit bubbled between his gappy teeth and snot came out of his nose. It was noisy. He was wailing in his sing-song hooty voice, still going on about his dad and jailbait. It was like it was a foreign word, one he didn't understand. I don't think he'd ever heard it before and it was the novelty of it that was making it stick in his mind. That, and because it had something to do with sex. But I could tell Carl couldn't stand it.

Chloe laughed.

'You stupid monger,' she said, hawked, and spat at his shoes. There was blood in the spit from where she'd bitten her lip.

Wilson cried louder and dropped his ball again. He bent over and tried to wipe the thick froth off the toe of his shoe. Carl raised his foot and I thought he was going to kick Wilson in the head. I opened my mouth but I was frozen, and then Carl let it fly and kicked the ball, really belted it. It went right over the hawthorn hedge and disappeared into the bushes and woods behind.

'Aw, what did you do that for?' Wilson said. He rubbed his hand clean on his coat then rubbed his face with his hand. He was still ready to smile and forgive us. He was still ready for it to be a joke.

'Go on then, go and get it,' Carl said. 'I'll give you a head-start.'

Wilson disappeared through the hedge. 'Are you going to count me?' he called, as if it was hide and seek. I could hear him crunching through dry twigs and leaves, blundering through the edges of the woods. He was counting himself, 'Seven crocodile . . . eight crocodile . . . nine croco—'

Carl cupped his hands around his mouth.

'I'm going to come and fucking belt you!' he bellowed, the pitch of his voice sliding upwards. 'Ready or noooo-ot!'

Chloe laughed, and from deep in the woods came the faint sound of wailing.

'I bet he just shat himself,' Carl said.

'Let's go, shall we?' I said.

Carl shook his head. He was grinning and counting down from five silently, holding up his fingers to Chloe who was smiling and tugging at her collar. When he got to zero all his fingers were tucked into his palm and he clenched them into a fist and set off running, forcing his way through the hedge with a shout.

'Better get moving!' he called, and I could hear Wilson shrieking. It was so high-pitched, so obviously terrified, that I think I might have laughed if I'd heard it before I met him.

I might have laughed.

I think I laughed.

We waited. Chloe took a pot of lip balm from her pocket and pulled one of her gloves off with her teeth so she could apply it. I moved away from her and tried to look through the hedge.

'Where is he? Shall we go after him?'

'What's your problem?' she said.

'Forget it.'

'You've had a face on you all afternoon. We didn't need to bring you out, you know. If you wanted to stay in and watch *It's a Wonderful Life* with your grand— I mean, your parents, you should have just said.'

'Fuck off, will you?' I said, and stepped away, even though there was nowhere to go.

'Be glad to. Been trying to get ten minutes with Carl without you cracking on for the last hour.'

'You've been in the car for the last hour,' I said. 'If all he wants to do is get off with you, why don't you go back to his

49

house? Why have I got to come all the time? Is he into being watched or something?'

Chloe smirked. 'His mum would be as keen on me as my parents would be on him,' she said. 'It's complicated.'

I scowled. 'You could always go and hide out in his *dark-room*,' I said and Chloe laughed again.

'You're so jealous,' she said, 'and anyway, Carl's been busy. We've got to snatch our time when we can take it. It isn't easy for us, you know.'

I hated it when she pulled that 'us' stuff on me – rubbing it in, always, that she had a boyfriend and I didn't. It wasn't fair. I didn't even want a boyfriend, not really. But now Chloe had one it was the next big thing I needed to do, and suitable candidates had been slow in appearing.

'It'd be nice if we could do something, for once, without him or Emma turning up,' I said. 'It didn't used to be like this.'

'Never mind,' she giggled, 'you found a friend, didn't you?'

'I want to go home.'

I started to pace away, remembered there were no buses, and stepped back. It must have looked like I was jumping, or running on the spot. Chloe was smoothing her eyebrows with her finger and didn't notice me.

'I should have brought Emma,' she said lightly. Pretending to talk to herself – pretending she'd forgotten I was there. 'Emma never moans like this. Emma's glad when me and Carl decide to bring her out in the car for a bit.'

I stepped away and didn't answer.

Bring you out! As if I was a dog, a big stupid kid like Wilson. It was me and her that were supposed to be going out. Out to the park, walk about and see if anyone else from school was there. It had been empty, but someone was bound to have turned up sooner or later. Once the parents had crashed out in front of the telly someone would have come along with some booze. It was almost guaranteed.

But no. After about ten minutes Chloe had got cold, decided it wasn't safe – *what with the flasher* – and phoned Carl to come and get her. Which was, I realised belatedly, exactly what she had planned to do all along. I was just the audience.

'You've turned into a right bitch since you've started seeing him, do you know that?' I said.

'You *are* jealous,' she said mildly.

'Of what?'

There was a moment or two of silence. Rows like this were becoming normal. It was nothing that wouldn't blow over but it irritated me that it was always me who made the first move to reconcile and not Chloe. Like she knew she could do without me fine, for as long as it took. It was all down to Carl. The summer just gone; we'd spent more or less every day together. I'd sleep at her house, she'd sleep at mine – sometimes even in the same bed.

We watched the stage version of *Bottom* and videos of *Carry on Emmannuelle* and *Barbarella*. We ate with her parents, who I actually think really liked me, and thought because I was quiet I was possibly a good influence on Chloe, who they worried had a tendency to run wild and get out of hand. Then, late October or early November she'd started seeing him – and overnight she'd changed, and even started encouraging Emma, who'd been nothing but a hanger-on up until Carl had come on the scene. It was all getting away from me.

'You're a slag,' I said.

Chloe didn't look at me, didn't look hurt. She rubbed a hand over the mark on her neck.

'Give it a rest, will you?' she said wearily. 'You're being really, really immature, you know that? Do you want to come to my party, or not?'

I opened my mouth and I was about to say more, to really go off on one, when I heard the crackle of someone running towards us through the woods. Chloe tucked her lip balm into her coat pocket and put her gloves on fastidiously. I remember the sticky, sickly smell of the grease she put on her mouth. Peach melba, or peach crush. Something thick and orange. We both turned to the hedge and waited.

When Carl came out he was panting slightly and his eyes were bright. I'd never seen anyone look like that before, not even in films. It was an 'ideas' expression. Something new, something shining, deep in his mind. He was wiping his boots on the grass as if he'd stepped in dog-dirt.

'What did you do with him?' Chloe asked. She went over and tried to put her arm through his. He shook his head and shrugged her away.

'Get off pawing at me, will you?'

Carl wiped his mouth and hawked up snot, spat on the grass, wiped his mouth again. 'He ran off. Quick little bastard. Can they all move like that?'

I shrugged, and Chloe tittered and tried to hold his hand.

'You want to go back in the car?' she said, and moved her face so those loops of hair fell over her eyes. Carl was taller than her – a lot taller. She looked up at him through her eyelashes.

'Get in the car,' he said, and pushed her so hard she had to run a few steps for her feet to catch up with her body. She nearly fell and I was about to say something. I took another look at Carl and thought better of it. Chloe didn't say anything either, just carried on moving. She didn't look back at him. Trotted over to the car and didn't wait, like she usually did, for him to open the door for her.

'In the back,' he gestured with his thumb, 'both of you. I'm taking you home.'

'What's the rush?' Chloe said, once we were strapped in and on the move. 'I thought we had plans?'

She drew out 'plans', just so that I wouldn't miss the refer- ence – wouldn't be able to take my mind away from what she and Carl would be doing as soon as I was out of the way. We were on the road that circled the outside edge of the park – spooning the trees and the Asda superstore.

'That's the rush,' Carl said, and slowed the car to a crawl. He tapped his knuckle against the window and we looked into the Asda car park.

The shutters were down and the lights were off in the super-market, but there was a van in the car park – a beige- and oatmeal-coloured Bambi camper with a sheet draped over the side of it. On the sheet someone had painted something in red paint or thick marker, and there were several men with scarves wrapped around their faces standing around admiring it. One of them looked in our direction. Carl put his foot down and we were on our way back towards the City.

'Who were they?' I asked. I felt sick.

'Group of lads getting together to go through the woods, bus station, places like that. Looking for this pest.' Carl laughed, and looked at me in the rear-view mirror. 'Think they can do a better job than the police – slipping about on the ice all tooled up with potato peelers and bike chains.'

'They're a vigilante group,' Chloe said knowledgeably. 'Someone asked my dad if he wanted to be in it. Fathers only. He said he wasn't sure if it was mob mentality or grassroots action. My mum went to one of their meetings and said they were a load of council-dossers and doleys.'

'Your dad not going in on it?' Carl said, and I looked away from the mirror and shook my head.

'There's some tea in the fridge for you, Lo.'

The house was overwhelmingly hot after outside, and it smelled of turkey and pine needles and Donald's feet. That special Sunday dinner and Christmas smell. I used to really like it.

'I'm not hungry. I'm going to bed,' I shouted from the doorway,

53

trying to get up the stairs before they could come out of the living room and grill me.

'Bed? Bed?' Barbara managed to get to the bottom of the stairs before I could cross the upstairs landing and get into the bathroom. 'You can't go to bed. It's barely four o'clock. Come and have some cheese and crackers and watch the film with your father.'

'I'm really tired.'

Barbara stared up into the dim hollow of the upstairs landing. I couldn't hear much from the living room, but I bet it was *It's a Wonderful Life* they were watching. You could practically guarantee it.

'Have you been drinking?'

'No. No, I haven't.' She carried on staring. 'I haven't. Smell my breath if you want.'

'And you've not had another falling out with that Chloe, have you?' Barbara took a step and put her hand on the immaculate cream receiver of the hall telephone. 'I was hoping you were going to start seeing a bit less of her. Shall I call her mother?'

'I'm just tired. I'm going to have a sleep. I'll be back down in a bit, right? I'll watch the end of the film with you later.'

Even I could hear it: my voice, thin and pleading. It wasn't a lie. I really was very tired – although there was something else to it too, the way that those men in the car park might have been wearing their scarves over their faces because it was cold, but there was another reason. I thought of them crashing through the undergrowth, shouting into the stillness of the woods, and shivered.

'Leave her alone, Barbara. She says she's wanting her bed.'

Donald's voice rumbled around the open living room door. I could imagine him sitting there with the remote control and a jar of pickled onions. A bottle of Newkie Brown and a glass between his feet.

'He's waiting for you,' I said. 'You'd better go in to him.'

*

When I opened my eyes someone had turned my bedroom light off and pulled the duvet up to my chin. I was roasting and I think that's what woke me up. I looked around me. If I'd gone back to sleep that second I wouldn't have remembered anything about waking up at all. It's a fact, that – people wake up ten times in the night, on average, but as long as you surface for less than three minutes you never remember it.

That night I woke up worrying. It was dark. I could hear the telly downstairs and Barbara laughing every now and again.

I used to get sent to bed after my tea as a punishment when I was little. I would get out of bed and lie on the floor with my ear against the carpet, listening to the echo of Terry doing the six o'clock news between the floorboards. I could always imagine Donald and Barbara very clearly. Having a great time and completely forgetting about me.

It was still Boxing Day and I imagined them again. Barbara was going to stand up at the end of the film and brush imaginary crumbs from the front of her skirt.

'Well, that's that for another year,' she'd say, and turn the lights on the Christmas tree off. Donald would nod absently.

'You did us proud, love.'

And they'd laugh as if that was the remains of a hilarious joke the pair of them started years and years ago, before I was born and when they were still young.

I lay there, something fluttering in my stomach, and wondered about how long they were married before I was born. Fourteen years, which is ages. And I thought about how old they were when they had me. Old. They didn't go to work anymore. They didn't look too much like old people, they could still walk and everything, but when it came to getting picked up and parents' evenings and things like that, it was humiliating.

Didn't they really want to have children? Didn't they worry about me turning out funny, like Wilson? Didn't they realise I'd get hammered for it at school? In my bed I tried to muster up the energy to hate them again but Wilson was in my head, those hands tucking the ends of the scarf into his jacket, and my throat got so tight I felt like I was going to suffocate.

7

It was New Year's Eve and I should have been at Chloe's house, not at home with too many boxes of Ritz crackers. Barbara had bought them cheap because the boxes had fallen off the display and had to be patched up with brown tape.

Chloe had said there was going to be a party, with cousins and friends of the family. There would be a room set aside just for us, with films up to certificate fifteen, and a limited amount of booze. Her mother had said she could invite one friend, and it was a toss-up between me and Emma right up until the last minute. But on the last day of school, Chloe had hugged me and said she was going to lend me her pointy shoes. I'd bought some white tights to match. The tights were still in the packet and Chloe hadn't called me since Boxing Day.

I could have telephoned her. We both had our mobile phones – heavy, brickish objects we flashed about at school. We had no one to send messages to but each other because hardly anyone else had them. They were secrets from our parents. Donald would have been suspicious about radio waves that near to your head, and Barbara liked to listen on the upstairs extension. People at school knew, of course. We'd let them beep and then refuse to let anyone else have a go. Other girls were jealous, or hated us. Not even Emma had one. I loved that phone. It was what made me special.

I never forgot, because Chloe never wanted me to forget, that we only had them because Carl worked in Currys. He liked to keep tabs on her, and it wasn't as if he could ring her at home. She gave her first one to me and told Carl she'd lost it so he'd get her another. Now and again, she'd promise to get Emma one. Emma would shrug and pretend she didn't care, but when she thought I wasn't looking she stared at Chloe's phone like it was a lump of chocolate.

I didn't ring Chloe. I remembered her saying 'bring you out' and I was angry. It was her turn to phone me, and she hadn't. By tea-time on New Year's Eve I was in a full-blown sulk, loitering sullenly around the kitchen and thinking about Emma's lumpy feet in Chloe's pointy shoes, wearing her glitter eye-shadow and drinking my share of the limited amount of alcohol. I wasn't going to ring and invite myself. Wasn't going to act desperate. Barbara had her own plans for the three of us, and was standing at the draining board hacking tomatoes into garnishes.

'Will you take that look off your face and put a dress on?' she said, without turning. 'We're going to have a nice evening,' she insisted, 'the three of us together. It's going to be quiet, and civilised, and *nice*.'

Donald sat at the kitchen table and flattened empty corn-flake packets. He was making Secchi disks by cutting circles out of the cardboard and using a black marker pen and a bottle of Tipp-Ex for the design. He used my school ruler to divide the circles into half, and then four, and then started to colour in the quarters. The kitchen stank of solvents instead of cocktails. The point of these disks was to measure the transparency of sea water. The depth to which light from the surface could penetrate. Donald had a theory. He always had a theory.

'I think twelve should be enough, for the first outing,' he said.

I was almost at the bottom of the stairs, escaping to the silence of my room with a bag of clementines and a magazine, but Barbara turned and looked at me pointedly, pursed her lips, and nodded at the kitchen chair next to Donald's. She wasn't fond of his projects and the effect they had on his moods but we had a deal: when she was cooking or otherwise occupied it was my job to babysit him, and how I did that was up to me.

'What are you going to do to make them waterproof?' I asked.

I'd asked the same question the last time, and the time before that.

'I could cover them with sticky tape, I suppose,' he said thoughtfully, as if he'd never considered it.

'How long do they need to last in the water for? Sticky tape might not be enough.'

'I really don't know.' Donald smiled and shrugged and started colouring in with his black marker. I watched him, and I wondered if all families were like this: sitting in kitchens, speaking their lines and acting in a soap they already knew the ending to. For a minute, the peaceful, vacant expression Donald had on while he was colouring, the way the rims of his eyelids were pink – it reminded me of Wilson.

I picked up a pen, started to help, and asked another question – something not in the script – just to take the thought away.

'Are you going to get the boat soon?'

Donald nodded. He looked excited.

'I need to collect all the evidence for the article before the spring sets in. The tides, the organisms in the water – they'll all change once it starts getting light.'

Donald looked up as he spoke but carried on moving his marker. The nib of the pen slipped from the edge of the cardboard and made a mark on the table, but he didn't notice.

'As soon as I've got my statistics,' he went on, back onto his script, 'I can write up the article and send it off whenever I like. I've got months before they'll be deciding on the trip.'

I wasn't really listening. It was the kind of thing he said a lot when he was planning his application to the *National Geographic* Field Trip *Sea Eye* Programme. It was an annual programme and this year they were accepting proposals from parties interested in coming along on the first manned trip of a deep-sea submersible in years. Last year, it had been the jungle somewhere, and the year before, one of the Poles.

Donald hadn't been interested then – he was still on magic or hot air balloons. But this year, it had caught his eye and he was determined to impress them with his investigations and win a place as a research assistant. Barbara told him it was for PhD students and university professors and they didn't mean people like him. She said there was more to being an assistant on a trip like that than typing up, making tea, and cleaning lenses.

'You've not got the qualifications,' she'd say.

If he was in a good mood Donald would just shrug at this. 'So?' he'd say, grinning. 'So? Anyone that can read can find out what they need to do to conduct an investigation. I've trained myself,' he tapped his head, 'all up here. Whole world of it. Information's free, isn't it?'

Barbara would put the yellow magazines in the bin when he was sleeping. It didn't work because I'd bring them back into the house for him.

I made a lot of effort to keep him off the subject when Chloe was around. I knew how it would sound and what him and his junk room and his felt-tip pens would look like to someone outside the family who didn't know his phases.

'*Blockbusters*'s on now,' I'd say, or something like it. It was like rolling a ball for a dog – he'd chase it into the living room and Barbara would feed the video cassette into its slot and close the door on the theme tune and Chloe and I would have the kitchen, my bedroom – the house – to ourselves. When that didn't work, there were the magazines – brought back in from the bin in the shed, pushed under his door. That's what I did.

'You're getting it on the table, Dad,' I said, under my breath.

I was aware of Barbara at my back, still slicing at the tomatoes, and the tension in the room – Donald was a soap bubble and we all needed to keep him away from the walls and the floor, just by blowing.

'I reckon if I write it all out you could type it up for me, couldn't you, love?' He stopped colouring, and I moved the cardboard closer to his pen and rubbed at the marks with the cuff of my jumper.

'I can use the computer at school, I suppose,' I said. 'As long as it isn't too long.'

'I'm not sure yet. It depends what I find. I have some theories about the water-flows that are going to need a lot of backing up so they make sense to someone else. There are organisms there that should not be there. I'm not sure if it's light, or temperature, or mineral deposits, or what. Need to get out there and do a spot of investigation.' He twirled the disk. 'That's what the measuring is for. Science is precise measurement, and nothing more. Remember that one, for when you do your exams,' he said, then pointed at me, smiled, and carried on, lost in the whirl of his own words.

I didn't need to listen. Donald's talking was disposable. I'd heard the speech about precise measurement many, many times before. The *Sea Eye* application had come out of nowhere, one of Donald's fussy little projects, and there had been a lot of them. Most of the time they hadn't amounted to much more than the hoarding of books and papers and magazine pictures pasted up on the walls of his room. But this one, this latest 'spell' had gone a bit further than the other ones I could remember. Sometimes I thought he really would find something out about the water at Morecambe – something new – and then I would help him write an article about it and then he would send the article to the scientist who was in charge of the *Sea Eye* and then he would be allowed to go too.

People discover new things all the time, so why not someone who is actually trying to? That would make Donald happy and everything would be normal. Not 'back to normal', because as long as I could remember I'd seen Donald being a bit weird, but it would get normal, and once it was, Barbara would loosen up a bit and I'd magically get on a bit better at school and everything would be easier than it was.

Barbara had her back to us; the knife nestled between her fingers like a pen.

'Why your father thinks taking a friend's wreck of a boat out through the quicksand into the rip-tides and whirlpools of Morecambe Bay, very possibly illegally, when he can barely swim, is totally beyond me,' she said, without turning. She'd been holding it in for long enough, and couldn't wait any longer.

'You could come, Barbie, if you wanted to. I could do with a hand for the note-taking,' he said. 'Your mother's got lovely handwriting.'

I snorted and Barbara's shoulder blades moved together, although she didn't make a sound. She could have been laughing or just coughing silently.

'Think of it,' Donald said, standing up and scraping his chair back. He waved his hands in the air. I thought he looked like Michael Aspel. 'Think of the romance. The sand, the sea. Floating in the moonlight . . .'

'. . . through a tide of untreated sewage,' Barbara said, rolling her 'r's.

Donald shrugged.

'Your mother's no imagination, you know that? She knows it, of course – otherwise why pick a man of vision, like myself?' He winked. There was a moment of silence. 'And you know what I found out at the library today?' He started paddling through the papers on the table, sticking his pale, sausagey fingers between the flaps of scuffed paper folders.

'I'm wanting to set the table now, Donald.'

'And I can do that for you in a while,' he said. 'Go back to your tomato-carving and hold your horses one minute, will you?'

She sighed, but didn't say anything else.

He turned back to me.

'Now, Lola, have a look at this. Two years' more education on you than your father ever had, so here's a little test for you. Tell me what you think's going on here. We'll have a battle. Your qualifications against my self-training. A pound for you, if you guess it right.'

He slapped the coin onto the table and I pulled the paper towards me. It was boring, having to stand in for Barbara like this.

The sheet of paper was a grainy photocopy of a picture in a magazine but at first I thought it was a copy of a painting. A dragon. The creature had teeth; milky, almost transparent teeth. They looked like they were made of cartilage, or ice. It was all mouth, with eyes like shrunken walnuts pressed into the sides of its head.

'Another fish, Dad? You going to go and catch one of these?'

'Not likely,' he replied. 'These live so far under the sea that they'd probably implode and turn into fish paste if we brought them up to the top.'

'Really?' I was interested, in spite of myself. He'd told me stories before. Fish that crawl along the bottom of the sea like worms, fish that make their own light, transparent, poisonous jellyfish the size of cars that fly about in groups as big as football stadiums.

I examined the picture, even though Barbara was crashing cutlery about. Partly it was because Donald had not been as enthusiastic as this about anything, not for months. Partly it was to make up for the bad Christmas present. I was scared that the shine on him would go out and he'd go back to staying in bed again if someone didn't play along with him.

'Oh I don't know,' Donald said, but he was still smiling, 'I might have filled in the facts a little. Embellished, here and there. Why shouldn't I? She's a mythical-looking creature though, isn't she?'

'It's a female one?' I asked doubtfully. I leaned over and put my face closer to the picture, staring into its shadows. 'How can you tell?'

Donald slapped his hands on the table. I jumped back. This

was the other side of the coin: sudden outbursts and enthusiasm over nothing.

'By God, she's getting close! You're costing me a fortune. Have a look. Make your guess.'

Barbara muttered from the sink, 'For God's sake,' but she didn't turn, didn't tell us to stop and clear the table. I kept one eye on her back.

'Is it pregnant?' I asked, looking at the picture again. It was round, but fish don't get pregnant with babies like animals do, do they? They can't, because there is such a thing as fish-eggs, and people eat them. 'What's that, stuck to it?'

'That's your guess?' Donald said, pushing the pound coin towards me with his finger and then sliding it away, teasing. He hadn't teased me like that for ages. It was only a pound, but I snatched for it and he hid it under his palm and laughed. I was worried he was beginning to think I was too old for it. Or by the time he came out of himself, I really would be too old for it.

I stared again, but the dots of ink that made up the picture were too big and the more I looked, the less I could see. The best thing, I thought, would be to put it to one side and then quickly glance at it. Let it think you'd forgotten all about it and then take it by surprise, so that the blots and shadows would stay making sense and not scramble themselves into a puzzle under the bright light of being looked at.

'Is it a baby fish, hanging on the side? It's a very blurry picture, Dad.'

'I'll give you fifty pee for that,' Donald said, standing up and rattling the change in his pockets, 'because it is another fish, but it's not her baby.'

'What then?' I said, and took the pound off the table while Donald was occupied sifting through his pockets for a fifty-pence piece.

'It's the male of the species, who has bitten her on the side and is pumping his generative fluids into her through a tube between his mouth and her egg-chamber. The process takes such a long time that over the days, or weeks, or months – even years – we don't really know – he shrinks, his own organs die away and he relies on her totally for his food supply.'

'So it is like a baby, then?'

'In some ways, yes,' Donald said, and risked a look at Barbara. I couldn't tell if she was listening, or ignoring.

'More accurately, he is a parasite, because he contributes nothing to the female but those generative fluids I mentioned earlier. In fact, you could even say –' he flipped fifty pence onto the table. For a minute I was disappointed: I wanted him to pretend to pull it out of my ear.

'Yes?'

'You could even say that he's more of a testicle than a parasite, Lola.'

Then Barbara did turn around. She put the knife down first, very gently on the side of the sink. She put the tomato she'd been working on next to it. Very slowly, so it wouldn't roll away. She even pushed it with her first finger to make sure it was sitting on its flat, cut end, and the half-done petals were facing the ceiling. She wiped her hands on the front of her apron. Then she turned around.

I wasn't looking at Donald anymore. I wasn't looking at anything. I was keeping my eyes very still on the table, noticing the white specks on the wood where the Tipp-Ex had smudged over the sides of the card and dried.

'What a disgusting thing to say,' Barbara said.

I won't forget the way she said 'disgusting' – the word split down the middle with a 'g' as hard as her teeth. There was a tick of silence. I waited for Donald to fold the paper up and tuck it all back inside the folder. I waited for him to put his hands together and close his eyes. His shoulders were always a good indicator. If they sloped away from his neck it meant it was a bad day. A bad month. It meant he might not reply if you talked to him, or he might start saying something then leave it in the middle, as if he'd tired himself out with the effort of talking. But if his shoulders were up straight, making a corner at his neck, then he was all right. He kept them up, but his face looked as if it was making him tired to do it.

'I'll set this table for you,' I said to Barbara, and started slotting the paper back into the folders. I was careful not to crease the edges, but I did it quickly, and stacked them on top of the washing machine. Then I took one of the green scrubby cloths to the table and got rid of all the white marks.

I did get away to my room with my magazine in the end. I lay on my bed in the dim winter light until Barbara shouted for me. I turned pages without seeing them and rested my feet on the creaking radiator. I only bought the magazines for the free things and the problem pages. Flip-flops with blue flowers on the t-bar where it crossed over the big toe. Eye-shadow triples in little cakes that would fall out of the case and crumble if you weren't careful and didn't hold them like they were trays of water that could spill.

The pages were shiny and they smelled like fish. The problem pages. Questions about odour down there and boyfriends who wouldn't take no for an answer. You would if you loved me. And there was always a helpline. Numbers to ring to find out the answers to your problems. Brook Advisory for the babies. A clinic for periods, and the diseases. Vox-pops about the best place for that first kiss, and a picture of some long-faced woman with a red bow in her hair and dark-framed glasses – chewing on a pen with a telephone at her ear. She was the person to ring if you had problems with your friends.

Problems with friends. You had to have friends to have problems with them in the first place. I imagined what it would be like to be married, to sleep next to the same person for thirty or forty years, and then have them leave you. Not, I decided, as bad as this. I knew, without knowing how I knew it, that adults didn't feel humiliation the same way.

I flicked through the magazine backwards. Past the adverts for psychics, tarot readings, boob jobs, nose jobs, special tights that would hoik your gut in and make your belly disappear, before and after pictures of chins, of eyes, of spotty foreheads and all-over tans. Pictures of shoes and bags and coats and scarves, past the feature about how you can tell if a man puts a powder in your glass when you're away at the toilet, and onto the quizzes. They had a special section of their own and the pages were trimmed with a blue border like a Victorian condolence letter.

We always did the quizzes together, and compared our answers. *What kind of girlfriend are you?* Multiple choice. Chloe read the questions and filled in her answers with a cross, mine with a tick. We added the scores up at the end. I remembered Chloe adding up on her fingers. She wore tiny gold rings sometimes, with pear-shaped cubic zirconia or hearts etched with her initials.

Did Emma have a boyfriend? I couldn't see it. She was oily and her hands were square and grey and constantly tugging at the elastic of her socks. Had Chloe got her a boyfriend? Some friend of Carl's? I imagined them out together. Pointy shoes, Christmas perfume – two couples in the car. Carl did handbrake turns in supermarket car parks at night because he liked to hear Chloe squeal. I'd hang on to her in the back, bracing myself against the passenger door as Chloe hurtled into me – her hair flying, her jaw clacking together. I never squealed, but I bet Emma screamed her heart out. Once she knew what was expected, she was compliant. She liked to know the steps. She practised gymnastics until the size of her calves made her socks uncomfortable and her bleeding stopped.

The next quiz was about skin type and I poked my forehead and tried to think about T-zones with dry, tight patches, and stared out of the window. The frost on the grass was thickening. Each blade was coated in its own grey-blue skin of icing sugar. There were darker oblongs on the path where the ice had melted under the strong yellow light from the glass panes in the front door. I didn't think about anything else. It was just ice. The clouds were heavy and the temperature had stayed in the minus figures since Christmas Day – but no snow yet. I let the magazine slide down the side of the bed. When I dozed I dreamed about Carl pushing an old-fashioned sledge down a big hill. In the dream I watched him, and felt scared, but I was too small and too far away to do anything to stop him.

Ten to midnight, and there was a man on the telly with blond crimped hair like a woman singing a song called 'The Final Countdown'. Not a good song, in fact I thought it was a really bad song, but I knew, because Donald was humming and tapping his feet on the rug in front of the gas-fire, that the tune was going to stick in my head for days.

Barbara had called me down when the buffet had been prepared and primped and spread over the coffee table. You didn't know if you were supposed to eat it or take a picture of it. The tomatoes had shrunk, and sat on tea plates in their puddles of leaked rosy fluid.

'Well, this is nice, isn't it?' Barbara said, and patted her knees. There was a stack of green napkins with golden bells on them. A pile of them – as if this was a proper party – and she'd folded the one on the top into a fan. So much effort.

I looked at the Christmas tree, stripped of all the crackers and foil-wrapped chocolate bells. About now, I thought, looking at the clock and imagining spray cans full of silly string, and pearl-coloured balloons filled with white and silver confetti. Everyone would be kissing everyone else on the stroke of midnight – Chloe and the friends of the family and the limited amount of alcohol. All the adults would be so wrecked she'd have no problem sneaking out to meet Carl either. I imagined their mouths going like fish – the moist chomping I heard whenever they forgot I was there. At least there'd have been the cousins to talk to. Donald rubbed my head, grinned at me and turned back to the television.

'Na, na na na,' he was singing now, under his breath. 'I've never danced to this one.'

Barbara yawned and got up.

'I'd better empty the bins. Give the cooker top a once-over. Shan't be two ticks.'

She was tipsy. Her lips were soft and her words were frayed at the edges and blurring into each other. It was a kind of tradition with Barbara, a family custom she was trying to pass on to me. Not getting tipsy, because even though it was New Year's Eve, I hadn't even been allowed a sip. No. Getting clean.

The house had to be totally clean on the strike of midnight, something to do with throwing away all the muck of the past year and making sure you go into the new one clean and new. When I was little I always used to have a bath and my fingernails cut before the bells, always had to be inspected and passed: new Christmas pyjamas that had to be fresh on, fresh from the packet that evening. But the cleaning was a laugh, because Donald was sitting there in a crumpled shirt stained with tomato soup and with smudges of black marker pen on his fingers.

Barbara was emptying the pedal bin in the kitchen and calling through to us. The man on the television leaned over his microphone and shook his hair over his face.

'I'm just taking this out to the wheelie,' she said. 'I won't be a minute.'

I moved from my cushion on the floor in front of the television and sat on the sofa next to Donald. I had to squeeze myself through the small gap between his knees and the coffee table, which was groaning with saucers of crackers and cheese on sticks and little dishes of pickled onions. Curly strips of cucumber and the special tomatoes. They looked like wet, fleshy roses. Vol-au-vents had prawns sticking out of the top like they were trying to somersault their way out onto the carpet, and I didn't blame them.

Hardly anything had been eaten, and I looked at it for a second, looked at the little bottle of sherry and the two tiny gold-rimmed glasses that were only used once a year. *What that is, is pathetic*, I thought. Not even sparkling wine. I took a handful of the things on the table and shoved them into my mouth one by one, pushing something more in every time I swallowed. It took a few minutes, but it made the table look more respectable.

'Can I have a beer, Dad? Seeing as it's New Year?'

Donald looked blankly at the television. The song had changed and I knew that one. It was Prince, or the Artist Formerly Known As, or whatever, singing something about 'partying like it's 1999'. I didn't think it was funny, or entertaining, or even ironic.

'Best not, love,' he said after a while, when I'd already thought he was going to ignore me. 'Your mother wouldn't like it.'

'It's New Year, though,' I said. 'Chloe's parents let her drink on special occasions. They say it stops you being an alcoholic when you're older.'

'Do they,' he said blandly. He looked away from the television and let his eyes rest on the coffee table.

'Do you want something to eat, Dad? Shall I get you a plate? You never had much tea, did you?'

Donald looked at the things on the table as if he wasn't sure if they were food or Christmas tree ornaments. I started talking, not realising how much I sounded like Barbara until I'd stopped.

'I'll just go in and get you a plate, and you can sit with it on your knee and pick at it here and there if you fancy it. It looks a lot, laid out like that, doesn't it?' I got up. I carried on from the kitchen, 'You should think of it like your supper.'

I was getting a plate from the drainer when I saw the green glass bottle on the side near the cooker.

It isn't fair that I'm not even allowed a little bit to drink on New Year's Eve, I thought. It's taking away my human rights. It could be argued that taking away someone's basic human rights is a form of mental or emotional abuse.

The striplight was on in the kitchen and the curtains were open: the back garden was nothing behind the kitchen window because it was dark outside, pitch black and hailing in tapping gusts that came and went, and Barbara was still out there messing about with the wheelie bin. And probably getting an ideal view of me in here with a plate in my hand, eyeing up the booze and leaving my father to his own devices. I went back into the sitting room, loaded up the plate, sat down.

'Cheese gives me nightmares,' Donald said, and I was about to tell him that I knew the book where that came from because we had to read it in English in the last week of school, and all write essays about it. And it was all right, because it was a kind of Christmassy book and got everyone in the mood, and I did well on that essay too, so it would be a safe thing to bring up. And sometimes Donald liked to hear about interesting facts like that.

The picture on the television changed quickly, from the music programme to the adverts. The first picture was bright yellow because it was an advert for summer-smelling washing powder, and the shock of it in his eyes must have startled Donald because he moved slightly and the plate tipped and the cheese cubes fell onto his lap and some of them bounced onto the rug. I was going to have to clean all that up and where was Barbara, who had been out with that bin in the hailstones for about a million years?

I didn't move to collect the food from the carpet, and Donald didn't acknowledge it even though some of it still rested in the creases of his shirt and trousers.

'Some weather we're having, eh?'

I nodded. 'Hail every day for a week, apart from Christmas Day. Did you put a bet on this year?'

'Yes, same as usual. And it's not a white Christmas, no matter how white it is, unless there's a flake falling in London on Christmas Day itself.'

'What's so good about London?'

'It's where the weather's measured. It only counts as weather if it snows down south.'

When neither of us was speaking, you could hear the hail battering against the windows.

'It even snows under the sea, you know,' Donald said.

That was the thing with my dad – half of the things he said sounded as if they couldn't possibly be true, and you'd be an idiot for believing them.

Barbara came in then, round lumps of hail in her hair, which was clipped up in some kind of roll on the back of her head. I got up quick, and gestured towards Donald and the lumps of cheese.

'I just remembered, I forgot to empty the bin in my bedroom. There's some paper in it. Some orange peel and stuff. I'd better go and take it out?'

Barbara looked at Donald and made her mouth go thin, like a letter box. She nodded at me quickly.

'Put your coat on when you go outside, it's evil out there. And hang it up in the hall over the radiator when you get back in. And make sure you latch the gate properly after you. I don't want it banging to and fro half the night.'

I ran out of the living room like there was nothing in the world I wanted to do more than empty my bin. It wasn't really a lie. I did go upstairs and empty the paper and orange peel into a carrier bag. And I knotted the bag at the top and stood on one leg on the kitchen lino to pull my trainers on through the laces that I never, never untied unless Barbara was watching. Barbara, who probably wished I had never been born.

And then I took the green bottle from the side and poured half of what was in there into a mug and took the mug and the bag out of the back door, through the hail and the wind and the black, and into the garden shed.

The shed was going to be pitch black too, and freezing, maybe a bit scary, but I had the cigarette lighter and I waved it about a bit until I had the courage to close the door behind me. It wasn't so bad. There was a set of folding chairs in there for the summer, and one was already unfolded. It must be another one of Donald's secret hiding places. And the chair was sitting in front of the little, book-sized pane of dusty glass in the side of the shed. I could sit in it and see the lit window of the kitchen and the green bottle on the worktop and my latest school report stuck to the fridge with a magnet in the shape of a Coca-Cola bottle. And the kitchen door was open so I could see the flicker of the television and the very edge of the couch, with Barbara's hand and wrist lying on the arm of it, her nails painted a funny kind of brown.

This is as crap as Christmas, I thought, as I flicked the lighter. I imagined the whole world blowing up: a mushroom cloud the size of a planet, and everything dead in the time it took for me to tap the tiny wheel against the flint with my thumb. The light from the wobbling flame turned the window into a mirror and the house, the bottle, the couch and Barbara's arm disappeared. The noise of the hail on the corrugated roof of the shed was amazingly loud and comforting.

I laughed then, because Crap As Christmas sounded funny, and I said it out loud and laughed again because it was even funnier the second time around. The next time anyone asked me my opinion of anything at all, I decided I was going to say, 'What, that's as crap as Christmas.'

My cigarette was lit and I let the lighter go out, then I was in the dark with the hail sounding like someone throwing stones at the window, and I thought about Emma, out in the thick of it and having to cadge a lift home, or even pay for a taxi and wait for it in the freezing cold because Chloe had buggered off with Carl somewhere. And Carl and Chloe, parked under a bridge in the dark, his hands inside her clothes and the pair of them panting and pawing at each other, filling the car with their hot breath until bang! the battery on the car goes dead, or the heater packs in – and it being too dark for her to get her jeans back on properly before the AA man comes to rescue them. Ha.

These were nice thoughts. I took a sip of the clear stuff in my mug. Because it was so, so cold and because I didn't really like the taste I drank it quick. Then I flicked the lighter again, holding it downwards so I could see what was lying about. I was looking for something to put the dog-end in. I was hoping for a glass jar with a hard circle of paint in the bottom, a tin lid, or even the lip of a rusting trowel. I swept the lighter through the air in slow arcs.

'Typical.' I hardly ever talk to myself. I swore. 'So hypocritical.'

There were about twenty cigarette ends on the floor, a big flattened heap of them, and they'd been under my feet the whole time. One was stuck to the side of my trainer and I had to stamp my foot to get it off me. I dropped my own cig on the floor along with the rest of them, some faded, some fresh, all kissed on the orange edge of the filter with a ring of brown lipstick.

8

The world was getting whiter and whiter. It was the kind of white you can feel even before you get out of bed and look out of the window because of the cold, bright quality of the light coming in between the curtains. It was the Saturday before the start of school and I'd still not heard anything from Chloe.

Barbara turned off her vacuum cleaner to listen to another news broadcast about the unusually cold weather. Apart from the aftermath of a New Year's Eve street brawl which had started when one of the patrolling vigilante groups had noticed an old man pissing against the window of Tammy Girl and taken it the wrong way, there had been nothing new to report. It was January. It was freezing. Frosty. A bit of the river had frozen over. Big deal.

Donald had been in a strange, restless mood that morning. Barbara had given him a toilet roll and sent him wandering about the house mopping the condensation from the inside of the windows. He dabbed with wads of toilet paper that left fibres sticking to the glass and the mess agitated him even more so now he was busy rubbing at the glass with the cuffs of his shirt. Yet even he was caught by the afternoon broadcast and had drifted towards the front room to watch it with us.

Terry, wearing what looked like a ladies' mink coat and matching hat, stood on the old tram bridge over the Ribble and talked about climate change and global warming as the camera zoomed in on the lacy frill of ice working its way across the river from either bank. Baffled ducks skated along the rim and plopped into freezing, fast-flowing water that was brown and opaque. Things protruded from the water: trolleys, old bikes and prams, dented traffic cones wearing wreaths of twigs and slime. On the far bank, a mattress had been wedged against the bare earth by a broken wheelie bin, half filled with mud. The top part of the mattress bent forward, as if bowing to its invisible audience. In the morning broadcast Terry had said this was the coldest winter on record for eighty years, but now his researchers had revised the figure to eighty-four, and there were pictures of yellow trucks moving slowly along the emptied ring road, spewing salt and grit behind them.

'But it's not all doom and gloom,' Terry said, and grinned.

Barbara leaned on the vacuum cleaner and wound the lead around her hand, catching it expertly on her elbow in a series of swift, jerky movements that never caused her to take her eyes off the screen.

'He's had his teeth fixed again, hasn't he, Lola? A polish, at the very least. What do you think?'

I was draped over an armchair pretending not to be interested although secretly I was hoping for the school pipes to go, for the holidays to be extended and for school to be cancelled – indefinitely.

'Indeed, the young ladies of our city will be most pleased with an unexpected side effect of this cold snap,' Terry said.

Barbara leaned forward.

'The spate of unpleasant incidents that has been plaguing our city's parks, gardens, train stations and other remote places,' he went on cheerfully, 'seems to have dried up. As we reported, there was an attack on Christmas Eve when a man accosted a fifteen-year-old girl outside the city train station on her way to visit her grandmother, exposing himself to her before attempting to assault her. The man has still not been identified,' Terry twitched camply at his hat and grimaced, 'and the girl's name has not been released to us at this time.'

'It's still getting to him, isn't it?' Barbara said.

Fiona, by virtue of being a woman, had managed to get an exclusive interview with one of the earliest victims – a thirteen-year-old who'd been felt up behind a pub in Chorley. It was persistently rumoured that Terry wasn't going to rest until he got one of the victims to recount her experience live on his evening broadcast, or even better, unveiled the identity of the flasher himself. That's why he didn't condemn the vigilante patrols – even though the police did. Barbara said they were Terry's eyes and ears on the ground. He was determined to get to the next girl first.

'But thankfully it has now been over ten days since that attack, and while our community action patrols continue to search the City's dark places, it seems the rest of us can sigh with relief. Our Friends in the South may make jokes about the Lancastrian Man's famed tolerance for the cold but it seems for the time being our girls are safe. The weather is a touch too nippy even for the most prolific pest our city has ever seen.'

'That's ridiculous,' said Barbara – suddenly grumpy. She turned the television over. A Christmas Special *Cluedo* was playing on the other side, and I settled in to watch it.

'I've no problem with that flasher staying at home in front of his Calor Gas,' Donald said. His hand reached through the air, bumped my shoulder, and squeezed. 'No one with a daughter would.'

'He'll be at it again, come the spring. You can guarantee it. Him having a Christmas holiday isn't the same as him being caught and having his –' Barbara stopped, looked at me, coughed, 'people like that – they've not got a choice about it. There's something wrong with them upstairs.'

She clattered the vacuum away into its cupboard and emerged without her apron, tying her hair back with an elastic band.

'Come on. Let's go out. We've been stuck in the house for days. I've sucked the flowers off the carpet, and we'll be down to boards if I can't get out for some fresh air soon.'

'It's freezing out there,' I said. 'Were you watching something different to us just then?' I turned my face back to the television: Leslie Grantham as Colonel Mustard accusing Mrs White of something unspeakable, but it popped and the screen went blank. Barbara was holding the remote control, and she tucked it away in its holder by the side of Donald's chair.

'If it's not frost, it's flashers,' she said. 'We're entitled to get out of the house. We're going stir crazy. Look at your father.' Donald was twitching the antimacassar on the back of my chair. 'And anyway,' she raised her eyebrows, looked at me meaningfully, although whatever it was she did mean was lost on me, 'you've got a little errand to do, haven't you, *Laura*? Come on. Shoes and coats. Lola, you can wear your new one. Just don't let me see you dragging your cuffs along the railings.'

She stood Donald in front of the hall mirror to go over him with the lint roller before she would open the front door and let us out.

Even though I should have been prepared for it, the cold outside shocked my lungs, bit the insides of my nose and made my teeth ache. We were two weeks past the longest night of the year, but winter was working backwards and spring felt like it was getting further and further away. The paths and the walls of the house were scratched with frost and without saying a word to each other Barbara and I stood on either side of Donald – not touching, but hovering as he navigated the slippery, glittering pavement. We walked all the way into town like that, up Fishergate Hill and past the train station where the girl had been flashed at, three abreast under the white, freezing sky. Barbara tutted and shook her head at people who didn't want to let us by.

It was a bright, bright day. All the smooth surfaces – car bonnets, illuminated advertisements in bus shelters, the green and gold plastic litter bins – were coated with their own thickening layer of white, and Donald's coat was a light beige sports jacket that was dated and gleaming and wasn't right for the weather, but it was all he would wear.

This walk to the shops felt like a special occasion. I knew that we weren't quite like other families: I had few memories of my parents outside our house. I knew they went out walking some afternoons when I was at school, and Barbara drove them both to the supermarket twice a month, but it was always during the day so I didn't see it. There were never any seaside holidays or weeks in Spain. I didn't even get day trips to Windermere or Grizedale or Blackpool. Nothing like that.

The only trip away I could remember was to a Pontin's in North Wales. I must have been five or six years old. A dim memory of a dark pub with seats upholstered with a blue plaid fabric like the seats on the City buses. It was a variety night with Orville the Duck. I was sitting between Donald's legs under the table pouring a can of cheap supermarket bitter into an empty pint glass. Barbara had bought a pint of lemonade, made me drink it, and then kept the glass in her lap. My mouth and hair were sticky. The brown fluid turned white as it hit the glass, and it fizzed over her patent leather court shoes.

'Tip the glass! Tip the glass!' I remember her hissing, and kicking her feet out of the puddle.

It was because of the money. Neither of them worked. Barbara had been a cleaner, a dinner lady and an office help, but now she was nothing and Donald got money from the City to stay at home and she had an allowance of some kind for looking after him. It was also because of Donald. The more interesting and colourful Donald's spare room became, the less he needed to leave it to go into the outside world. The things going on in his head were much more real to him, more real, even, than the documentaries and nature programmes he liked to watch on the television. Gradually I learned that if we wanted to talk to Donald, we had to go into that place with him.

Even so, we weren't that unusual. We might have been bigger home-bodies than most, but no one we knew left the City very often. It just wasn't done.

When we got to the shopping centre, Barbara took Donald's arm and pulled us through the revolving doors together. The three of us were wedged into a single segment of the turning mechanism. The blast of the hot air heater was directed down at us, and Donald started to sweat heavily.

'Don't worry,' I said, and pointed through the glass, 'they've still got the Christmas trees up.'

'Your father isn't a child,' Barbara said, and I let the sigh out, very slowly between my teeth so she couldn't hear it, and the door completed its revolution and we were spat into the warmth and twinkling lights of the shopping centre. It was still prickling with silver tinsel and the air was clogged with the dry, solvent smell of spray-on frost.

'Where are we going?' I said, and peered across Donald to Barbara, who was heading towards Boots and brandishing a handbag so brown and shiny it looked like it was made of wood. Brandish is right – she carried it over her wrist, held in front of her like a weapon. I wanted to walk away. I wanted to turn and melt into the crowd like a curl of steam. I knew, then, what she was going to do, but Donald was smiling and tugging me gently along, a fold of my new coat gripped between his finger and thumb.

The decorations in Boots were more subdued. When we got to the perfume counter the woman who was supposed to be serving was kneeling on the top of a short stepladder. There was another ladder on the back of her tights, disappearing up her skirt. She was winding a red ribbon around the display cases on the shelf behind her. Red, heart-shaped stickers dotted the boxes and bottles because there was a special offer for Valentine's Day and they were putting the displays up for it already. She didn't notice us until Barbara dropped her handbag heavily on the glass counter.

Barbara coughed. 'Excuse me, miss?'

The woman turned then hopped, heavily, down from the ladder, staring at Donald and tweaking the hem of her skirt downwards. I wanted to say, 'He's not like *that*,' loud, and in a tone like Barbara's – but Barbara spoke first.

'My daughter,' she said, with such clear dignity I could tell she had rehearsed it, and imagined her standing barefoot on the linoleum in her bedroom, straightening the rosebud cover on her single bed and muttering it like a prayer, 'wants to return an item she removed from this counter without paying.'

I watched the shop assistant's face change. I tried to imagine what we looked like to her. The three of us: Barbara in her shabby, aggressively clean houndstooth coat and cracked leather gloves; Donald, rocking slightly and smiling as if he was about to be given a present; and me – jeans at high-water mark, school shoes and the Christmas-Present-School-Coat, shoulders speckled with fine grains of snow that to an unsympathetic eye could have looked like dandruff. And all of us lined up in order of size, staring back at her and her abandoned packet of paper hearts.

Barbara retrieved the white and blue and silver perfume box from her bag. She closed the clasp with a snap (the noise it made was as satisfied as she was) and placed the perfume carefully on the counter.

'Here it is,' she said, and gestured towards it. She didn't look at me – her neck was rigid with fright. 'She'd like to make up for her actions in some way. What do you suggest?'

The shop assistant glanced at me. I looked at the red hearts and said nothing.

'Wouldn't you, Lola?' Barbara prompted. As if she was getting ready for a fight, she pulled off her gloves and laid them over the pursed mouth of her handbag.

'Are you sure?' the shop assistant said. She gestured behind her without looking, like a weathergirl. 'These are display boxes. We aren't missing anything.'

'It's Valentine's Day soon!' Donald announced, and put his hand on the counter. 'Have you got a boyfriend, young lady?' The assistant moved her eyes from Barbara to Donald, who had opened his wallet and was proffering an expired credit card, and then back to Barbara again. The credit card was green and white and orange – clearly an antique and the sort of object that would turn up as a curiosity in a jumble sale, and get snapped up by someone collecting props for a retro television programme.

'Whatever's number one,' Donald said, 'whatever you'd want your man to buy you. That's what I'll have, for my Barbie. And something light and flowery for my little girl. Cost no object.' He raised his arm, dropped it around Barbara's shoulders, clutched her, shook her a little. 'She's young at heart, isn't she?' He actually winked – 'Isn't she just!' and waved the card at the assistant. She didn't take it. Barbara said nothing and the assistant looked at us as if we were all mental.

'My mother thinks—' I began, trying for that tone of injured dignity Barbara had managed so well.

'Maybe,' Barbara interrupted me, 'we can come to an arrangement. Will you take the perfume back into stock? Can you do that for us, at least?'

The assistant glanced at the box and shook her head.

'There are health and safety—'

'I see. Of course. I should have – Donald,' she turned, 'put your wallet away.'

There was a moment when nobody spoke. The tinkling music in the shop seemed louder, but I could still hear Donald's polyester trousers rustling as he tucked his wallet away.

'Maybe,' Barbara said, and I knew in that instant that she wouldn't be defeated, 'Lola could work here for a few Saturdays. To earn the money back.'

I opened my mouth – this was Chloe's ideal job – we already knew you had to be sixteen to work on the perfume counter and if I got this job some underhand way, she'd kill me – but Barbara held up her hand, her fingers poised delicately. Her nails were painted neatly but the skin on the back of her hand was slack.

'Miss,' she said, as if it was the assistant who had started to protest, and not me, 'my daughter did something wrong. Of which she is ashamed. Deeply. As a family, we are ashamed. Deeply. We are not destitute. Not enough to steal something. So she can work for you, to pay off the debt and make it right.'

'There are all sorts of considerations to take into account,' the assistant said. 'There's an induction. A training programme. We have to interview her properly. Equality and Diversity. I'm afraid it doesn't really work like . . .'

Barbara was sagging. The handles on her handbag flopped forward.

'How much was it then?' she asked, her mouth tight.

The assistant scanned the barcode and looked at the numbers on the till.

'Nineteen pounds and ninety-nine pence,' she said brightly. Barbara flinched and opened her purse, and the assistant asked if we wanted it gift-wrapped, and I said, 'I only paid twelve for it. Eleven ninety-nine. Was there a sale?' and Barbara told me to shut up, and the shop assistant said, 'You paid already?'

I wanted to laugh. I wanted to walk away, to shout at someone – Barbara, if I had the nerve, but Barbara was fumbling out a worn, carefully folded tenner and counting the coins onto the counter. She didn't say anything, but her posture was loud enough: *this is our food money*, and watching her labouriously count was painful.

'We'll settle this with your company now,' Barbara said, 'and deal with the matter at home. Lola will apologise,' she finished counting and pushed the heap of money across the glass with a flourish, 'in writing.'

There was some further talk about the address of head office, the correct title of the CEO, and a scrap of paper was scrawled on and passed over the counter. Barbara asked for assurances that the matter was closed now, that the police wouldn't be involved in the light of my confession. The assistant muttered something in return but by this point I wasn't listening.

At some point during Barbara's counting – between the click of the coins on the glass counter and Barbara's snuffly, starting-a-cold breathing – I had become aware of a difference in the quality of the air beside me. Nothing more than that. I looked, and Donald was gone. Barbara noticed just after I did and she left the coins scattered on the counter, looped the handbag over her elbow, and we ran.

It wasn't the first time Donald had disappeared. He used to vanish from the house once every few months – like a cat. Sometimes he came back after a few hours, bright and cheerful with a new magazine tucked under his arm – just like anyone else's father. One time, he strolled through the front gate after a nine-hour absence with a Homer Simpson cap and a tin of Cherry Coke. Another time a neighbour called us at five in the morning to ask us if we knew that Donald had climbed over the bolted gates of the Gas Board car park and was now unable to get out. That was the thing. His vanishings were probably nothing, but they could have been anything – Donald brought with him the constant reminder that bad things could happen.

Barbara and I left Boots and hurried through the shopping centre, looking through windows, checking behind displays of cut-price advent calendars and Christmas cards.

Usually I enjoyed the symmetry and regularity of the way the building is designed: the smooth shine of the fake marble floors, the smoky glass of the lifts and doors, and the faintly chlorinated smell of the warm, recycled air. The architects, I think, wanted people to drift from floor to floor with no conception of the light or the weather outside, no worry about moving too far away from a public convenience, litter bin or water fountain. It made searching the place a slow, frustrating business though – full of false starts and back-tracking. The centre is built like a wheel on two floors – with a round central area that encircles an indoor fountain, artificial plants and a cafe. The shops are ranked along the spokes of the wheel and we tried to work through them methodically: John Lewis, Sweeten's, Menzies, Bon Marché.

The shops were busy with families out returning unwanted presents, spending their gift vouchers or examining the sales racks. We moved slowly, always peering around heads or jostling for space between bags and buggies and elbows. Whenever we reached the centre, I huddled into Barbara's wake, hiding from the boys sitting around the edge of the fountain. They were leaning over in brand-new sports tops and trainers, close to the water – fishing out coins or blowing the paper skins off straws in a private competition.

We rode the escalators upwards and waited outside the men's on either side of the door like two stone lions. Barbara asked a man to go in and check the cubicles. We waited.

'He was all right this morning, wasn't he?' I said.

'Fine. Fine,' said Barbara.

The man we asked to help took ages. I thought about urinals, rows and rows of them lined up like seats in a white porcelain auditorium. And rows of men, too – standing with their hands in front of them, moving the weight from one foot to another, the way I sometimes saw them in the bus station alley, or down the back end of the park. The idea was dirty and exciting and my cheeks tingled and, without meaning to, I thought about Chloe and Carl.

'We should check the library,' I said. 'He'll have gone to the library; his research.'

Barbara didn't say anything, but rapped on the door with her knuckles and used a voice like Margaret Thatcher – pretend posh

– to call through the crack. The sound echoed inside, rattling along the tiles with the smell of piss and yellow disinfectant. I peered over her shoulder but there was nothing to see except torn scraps of toilet paper sticking to puddles on the floor.

'He's been pestering me to take his books back,' I said, 'and I haven't done it yet. I bet he's worried about the fines. He'll have gone in to see about it.'

'You shouldn't encourage him,' Barbara said quickly, 'it isn't fair. His projects. All those books. The papers!'

'What do you mean?'

Encourage. It was a new idea. I had thought Barbara and I had a kind of agreement about this. She took charge of the practical things. Changed his bed in the middle of the night, checked on him during the day when things went too quiet. Took care of the bills and his razors, complaints from the neighbours about things he tried to build in the garden. His meals and prescriptions.

I typed. I did research with him. I listened to his stories and sorted out library fines. Stuck pictures into scrapbooks. Taped things off the telly. I took it all very seriously, accepted token and sometimes not-so-token payments for my services, and it wasn't my fault I liked my part of the deal better than Barbara liked hers. We were supposed to keep each other's secrets, Barbara and I. I'd say nothing about the occasions when I'd come home from school and Donald would still be in his pyjamas, distressed and ravenous. Barbara would put on a video and close the door on him when Chloe came round. It was a deal.

'I don't encourage him,' I said.

'This report he's writing. Three typewriter ribbons in a month. He tried to oil the thing with a lump of lard and I've had to send it to be repaired.'

'I said I'd type it up for him at school. When we go back. I'll do it for him at lunchtime, on the computers.'

'That isn't the point,' Barbara said. She leaned back against the wall and closed her eyes. A strand of hair fell over her face and she did nothing to tidy it away. 'You've got to stop condoning him. Joining in. I know you think you're helping, but you're not. Do you understand?'

She stood upright and looked at me. 'Lola? You know it's all in his mind, don't you? This trip he thinks he's going on. Making money out of his idea? Glow-in-the-dark shrubbery? You know it isn't right, don't you?' She looked frightened.

'Yes,' I said, 'all right. He's just making it up.'

She sighed. 'Not making it up. Your father isn't a liar, Lola. He thinks it's all perfectly reasonable. That's why he's taking so much time over it. It needs to be just right. But it isn't—' she cut herself off. 'Let me put it this way. It would hurt him, very badly, not to be accepted onto this mission – not to get to talk to the scientists about his big idea, wouldn't it?'

'Yes,' I said, 'sure. He'd be gutted. That's why I've been—'

'No,' Barbara said firmly. 'That's encouragement. If you care about him, you won't be helping him to make it better – you'll be distracting him from it. Getting him to think about other, more ordinary things. Saving him from the disappointment.'

A man came out of the toilets then – the man who we'd asked to help us. He was drying his hands on the front of his jeans and looked surprised we were still there.

'My husband?' Barbara asked. The man shrugged and walked away without even looking at her properly.

'Come on,' she said, and tugged at the sleeve of my coat. 'We can't stop looking. He could be anywhere. We'll talk more about this later.'

We found Donald in WHSmith. Barbara saw him through the window and pulled me inside. He was crouching over a pool of spilled newspapers, the rack at an angle behind him. Donald murmured calmly as people stepped over the mess. He was struggling to put the pages in the right order and every page looked the same: pictures of the half-frozen river, the leafless, whitened trees, the bundled kids sliding down hills on metal tea-trays, reams and reams of closely printed columns about global warming.

I saw his neat fingers shuffling over the pages and heard the whisper of the paper. His head was bent forward and the bald patch on his scalp was shiny and humiliating. Barbara pushed past me and knelt beside him to fold the papers, working slowly, saying nothing, bumping her shoulder against his.

I hesitated on the mat in front of the automatic doors, feeling them slide close and bounce open behind me, the electronic sensor under my feet not sure what to do with a weight that hesitated so long.

Are you staying or going?

The draught at the back of my neck was icy.

I was thinking about Chloe again – of course. I'd stopped imagining her and Emma at the New Year's party now – the booze, the streamers, the late-night trip out in Carl's car. Now I was thinking about when I'd see her next – how I was going to approach her. I'd almost decided to pretend I'd forgotten about her because I'd been whisked away to a last-minute party of my own. It would have been transparent and ridiculous. Chloe would have smirked and then let me tell my story as if she was doing me a favour. Emma would have openly laughed and passed me the packet of photographs – her and Chloe in party dresses, hair up, doing 'Auld Lang Syne'. Even worse if they walked past WHSmith and saw me kneeling on the carpet with my whole family, fumbling with newspapers while the shop assistants stared.

The doors bumped closed, and then opened again behind my back. Barbara looked up.

'Go home,' she said quietly. 'Go and peel the potatoes and we'll be with you shortly.'

I went.

9

The buzzer sounds.

It is a thrumming, crackling noise that I cannot stand. The casing on the intercom unit isn't screwed down tight and the plastic rattles against the wall and the noise rattles around the flat and right into my teeth and skull. It's horrible but I've never done anything to fix it because I don't get people coming round that often.

I turn away from the television and scramble towards the hallway. I pull my hair straight and brush Dorito crumbs off my jumper. My teeth will be grey and blue with wine, but tough.

'Hello?'

Emma's voice crackles out of the box. 'It's me. Are you going to let me in?'

I am reluctant to open the door but the buzzer sounds again, right next to my ear. I feel the noise before I hear it, throbbing along my jaw.

'Emma?'

'Come on. It's cold out here. Open the door.'

I imagine her, hunched in the lobby, whispering urgently into the box. Angry, no doubt, at me dithering.

'Have you seen what happened?' Her voice is nasal and echoing. 'I've been watching for –' I think I can hear her sigh, 'for two hours. Caught it by accident, just as he started digging. I didn't realise there was an anniversary coming up.'

That is a lie, and we both know it.

'I saw it,' I say. 'They've cancelled the nine o'clock film.'

'Lola?'

'I was going to watch it,' I explain. I think of my evening routine. The film, the crisps, the wine. I can't remember the last time I had someone in my flat.

'Lola? I'm still standing here.'

'Okay,' I say at last. 'I'm going to buzz you in now. Don't come up in the lift – someone's pissed in it.'

The warning about the lift may or may not be true. It usually stinks, but I'm more concerned about giving myself a few extra minutes to tidy my flat than I am about Emma stepping in something unpleasant.

I pause in front of the television with an armful of wet towels from the bathroom. It's dark outside – darker still down by the pond where there are no streetlamps. Terry is pointing at the tent, saying something about dogs and evidence. He says 'painstaking process'. I mute the sound, dump the towels in front of the washer and start grabbing dishes and taking them into the kitchenette. I run out of space in the sink and start to stack sticky bowls and mugs in the cupboard under it, next to the ranks of green glass bottles, saved for recycling. There's a knock – hesitant and unfriendly. I lift the snib and stand back. Emma shuffles in smelling of alcohol and musty flannels.

'Did you catch the bus?' I say, stupidly.

Emma shakes her head. 'I waited, but it didn't come.'

'Is it that bad?'

She moves past me and looks around at the sagging couch, the wine box, the stained carpet and bare walls. She paces, too wound up to sit down. There's a browning umbrella plant and a row of videos on the windowsill. They're covered in a fur of dust so thick it looks like mould. I watch her looking at my things.

'I drove. Probably shouldn't have,' she lifts an imaginary glass, 'but I got sick of waiting and the roads are empty anyway. Everyone glued to the box tonight, eh?'

'Yes,' I say. 'Terry's going to do an appeal. Witnesses, a phone-in. The works.'

'Oh, God,' she says and then she sits down with one elbow on her knee and her forehead resting on her palm. 'This is never going to stop, is it?'

I shrug. 'Not if he can help it.'

'All this time, and he's still—' She breaks off, yanks her hand through her hair and looks up at me. 'I didn't want to stay at home in case his researchers started ringing for an interview again. I couldn't stand it.'

I look at her, and remember. The two years Terry tried to get us on the air and wouldn't take no for an answer. As if the police weren't enough, people wanted us to answer questions on Terry's programme as well. Emma wasn't like Chloe – she never wanted to be famous.

'No one knows about me here. I'm Laura now, not Lola. They won't ring.'

She sighs, but it isn't quite relief. 'I hoped you'd say that.'

We look at the television again: Terry's mouth moving sound-lessly, the dark shapes of the trees against the sky and the phone-in number scrolling along the bottom of the screen. You don't need to hear what he's saying to catch his mood – the excitement in the way he holds his head to one side and draws shapes with his hands in the air.

'Don't they know who it is yet? Haven't they said anything about that?' She curls her fingers against her palms and rests her knuckles against her mouth as if she's trying to cram her words back down her throat.

I shake my head. 'Not yet.'

'Fucking hell.' Her voice is muffled by the sleeve of her coat. 'Have you got anything in to drink?'

'Coffee,' I say, and she shakes her head. I nudge the box of wine on the floor in front of the sofa with my foot. 'There's that, but it's shit. I'll get you a glass.'

'In other cities, people go out for romantic meals on Valentine's Day. You've just got me,' she says, and although there is humour in it, neither of us laughs.

No one's celebrated Valentine's Day round here properly for years. For us, it's the day we remember the couple who drowned themselves because they were forbidden from seeing each other. Women who didn't know Chloe wear her picture in lockets around their necks and sigh, hoping they'll be loved like that one day too.

'Well, we can make do,' I say. She raises her head as I hand her a glass and looks around her again.

'Nice place,' she says, mildly and without sarcasm.

'It's council,' I say. 'There's a legal limit on how bad they can let it get.'

'Not the lift, though,' she says and looks at the television. 'Do they know who it is yet?' She glugs at the wine and doesn't realise she's repeating herself.

10

Emma had always been at the Valley School with me, but I'd not paid much attention to her. I'd kept my head down generally, until Chloe had arrived at the end of Year Eight and made the girls who'd been picking on me find someone else to torture. But one day when I hadn't been looking, she started to get closer and closer to Chloe and because Chloe was my best friend, I started to see more of her. It started in the October half term when Chloe turned up with Emma at my house. It was the first time I'd really spoken to Emma, and the first time I realised that Chloe did things without me being there, things that I didn't know about.

'Let me in,' she'd said, and thrown herself through the front door as if she was being chased. I held the door open and looked over the hedge and along the street, but nothing moved except the bits of *Evening Post* and flyers about personal safety and self-defence classes blowing about on the pavement along with the drifts of leaves in the gutter.

'We ran all the way,' she said, panting. 'I'm knackered.'

Emma nodded at me seriously and hurried in after her. She'd never been in my house before. I shut the door. Chloe was leaning against the hall radiator with one hand resting on her chest. The ends of her fingernails were perfect crescents because she had a soft white pencil she used to colour in the undersides with. Emma went and stood next to her, then, after a minute's thought, put her arm around Chloe's shoulders.

'What's up with you two?' I said.

Emma knew better than to tell Chloe's story for her and Chloe didn't answer – couldn't speak, at first. She waved a hand at me to wait while she caught her breath. Her eye-liner was smudged and there was a streak of dirt on the sleeve of her pale jacket.

'Shh,' she said, and pointed at the living room door. Barbara was in there with Donald watching *Antiques Roadshow*. It was an old one. Barbara had a stack of them she'd taped off the telly because they kept Donald calm when they were on, and sent him off on harmless missions to the attic once the programmes had finished.

'Can we go in your room?' Chloe said eventually.

'All right.'

The three of us traipsed up the stairs – Chloe first, leading the way, then Emma, then me, closing all the doors behind us. In my room, Chloe took the seat in front of my desk. Emma sat on the bed. She didn't take her coat off. I hovered between them, and eventually leaned against the wall. It was an awkward place to be, having nowhere to sit in my own room. There were things lying around – open books and magazines, tapes without their cases, dirty clothes. Chloe was used to it, but with Emma there I realised the place looked shabby and uncared for. I was embarrassed about the peeling gloss on the windowsill, the broken chair fixed with brown tape and the tired anaglypta on the walls. Emma gathered the pages of a tattered copy of *Sugar* and laid it on my desk.

'What is it?' I said. I looked at Emma, who shook her head.

'Let her tell you herself.'

'Give me a minute,' Chloe said, and I saw that she was pleased with herself: almost smiling and showing all the other signs that she was carrying a secret she couldn't wait to be rid of. Something 'confidential' that she was desperate for me to ask her about.

'I knew I was coming round to yours,' she said, 'so I decided to set off early and walk. I couldn't remember if I was still grounded or not, and if I'd asked for a lift, or some money, it'd have reminded them. So I just came out the back way.'

'What happened?' I said.

This was Chloe's soap opera and I knew the part I was supposed to play. She fed me my lines and I cooperated, half-amused at the state of her, and more curious than I wanted to be.

'Did they catch you?'

'You won't believe it,' she said and laughed helplessly. Emma smiled mechanically. Her mouth was dark and tacky with lipstick.

'Let me get a grip of myself.'

It was a short walk between Chloe's house and mine. I lived in a poky row of terraces in a warren of streets tucked into the north bank of the Ribble and quietly subsiding. Chloe lived on the south side of the river, at the top of the hill and around the corner from our school. Her house had a conservatory and a greenhouse. The road bridged the river and carried on in both directions – past Chloe's house and out of the the City towards Southport, and past my house where it turned into Fishergate Hill and led you towards the train station, into town and the shopping centres. The walk might have taken her half an hour, but that day, Chloe said, she'd taken a detour that involved walking along the Ribble, over the tram bridge and through Avenham Park. She'd have come out of the park at the end of a long street about fifteen minutes' walk from my house, and added an hour onto her journey.

'Why did you take the long way round?' I said. It was something we did sometimes – for fun, or to kill time – but not unless we really couldn't think of anything else to do and hardly ever since the summer.

'I wanted to smoke,' Chloe replied. 'I was hardly going to march down the hill with a fag hanging out of my mouth, was I?'

'Long way to go for a fag,' I said, and Chloe shrugged.

'Walking's good for you. You should try it next time you feel like a plate of chips, you porker.'

'Fuck off.'

Chloe gave me the finger.

Emma giggled and I realised she'd been drinking. I couldn't smell booze on Chloe so they hadn't been out together, which was something. I never had Emma down as the type to hang about the park with a bottle though. 'It's not that far,' she chipped in, 'not if you're fit. I've walked that way loads of times.'

I tried to stare at Emma coolly, keeping my eyes steady and without moving my mouth at all. She was wearing make-up — a lot of it — and I'd never seen her that way before. The thick mascara and brown eye-shadow made her look ill and bruised.

'Not to my house, you haven't,' I said.

Chloe broke in. 'Pack it in, you two. I was walking along that big line of trees to the side of the river, you know the path that goes behind the bandstand, yeah? I was going along there, and I heard something crackle. I thought it was a bird or a squirrel or something. I took my headphones off,' she was still wearing them around her neck, the wire snaking down under her cardigan to the black box at the waistband of her jeans, 'and I carry on walking. I'm not scared or anything, it isn't like it's the middle of the night, right?'

'Okay,' I said. Her eyes were bright and wet with amusement.

'This guy steps out from the bushes,' she laughed again, a strange, sobbing sound. 'He didn't jump out or shout or anything — just stepped out. If I hadn't have heard the crackle first, and I only heard that because my tape was between tracks, I probably wouldn't have noticed him. But I did notice him just step out. And you know what the first thing I noticed was?'

'What?' I said.

'He was wearing a mask —' she paused, and leaned forward, 'and that's not even the worst thing.'

I imagined the man in the cape from *The Phantom of the Opera*.

'What sort of mask?'

'Halloween,' she waved her hands around her face, 'bright green, flat head. Bolts. What did you say it was, Emma?'

'Frankenstein,' Emma said quietly.

'Frankenstein's Monster, actually. Frankenstein was the—'

'Whatever he had a mask on. Every Spar in the City is selling them. Brown hair poking out the top. Jeans. Boots. Nothing special.'

I was getting impatient.

'You tell her this bit, Em,' Chloe said. I looked at Emma, who cringed. Chloe tapped her knee gently, and I've been there – I know it's her way of dishing out her commands.

'Well,' Emma started eventually. Maybe she was feeling shy because Chloe and I were staring at her so hard. 'He came out from the bushes, wearing his mask, and Chloe stopped and stared at him – like you would, you know? And then he gets a bit closer to her and says, *Trick or Treat?* And Chloe, she says, are you not a bit old for that, still walking over to him because she's convinced it's someone that she knows.'

'One of the Year Elevens,' Chloe interrupted, 'pissing about.'

'Yes, but it wasn't,' Emma said. She didn't look at me, and spoke too quickly, the words running into each other as the blush spread up the sides of her neck. 'Because when she got right close to him, he opened the front of his jeans and showed her his cock.'

Chloe leaned over her knees and sobbed with laughter. 'Right out there,' she said, 'right in the park! It was just hanging out!'

Emma nodded urgently, as if I was about to accuse the pair of them of making it up.

'Just lying there, like he expected me to do something with it. Why do they do that? Do you know why they get cheap thrills from that? I mean, it wasn't a big deal to me.'

'What did it look like?' I said.

'Just like you'd expect,' she said, 'only bigger.' She stood up. 'It was *massive*!'

'What did you do?'

'I told him,' she said lightly, 'it looked just like a cock, only smaller. Then I kicked a pile of leaves at him, and walked round the other way.'

She winked, stagily.

'Did you see this?'

Emma was sitting on the bed, her hands pressed together and held between her knees. She jumped, as if she wasn't expecting to be spoken to. When she looked at me she opened her eyes wide and I noticed her pupils – huge and glassy.

'No,' Chloe said quickly. 'I ran into Emma afterwards.'

'And was it – you know?'

Chloe grinned. 'Was it what?'

'Erect?' I was whispering.

Chloe fell back over her knees and howled with laughter. 'You perv!' she squealed. Emma swayed slightly, and smiled a little too late.

I moved towards the desk, hurt.

'You should tell the police,' I said. 'It's that pest, isn't it?'

'He didn't try anything,' Emma said. She had her hair up – something complicated with Kirby grips and half a tin of Elnett. When she moved her head, her fringe stayed flat and stiff over her forehead. What was she doing dressed up like that and wandering around the park on her own?

'No, I'm not going to bother.'

Chloe went and sat next to Emma. The divan rocked on its wheels. 'He probably expected me to scream or something, but I didn't. It was hilarious.'

'What did he do? How did you get rid of him?'

Chloe glanced at Emma. 'He just went away, back into the bushes. I didn't follow him. I put my earphones back in, and carried on walking. Prick.'

'She was hardly going to chase after him, was she?' Emma said.

'Ask him for a second helping!'

I looked at Chloe. 'It *was* that pest.'

'Probably.'

'They're appealing for any information. They said the smallest detail could be the key that unlocks the whole case.'

Chloe laughed. 'It was a pretty big detail.'

'She didn't really get a good look at him, not even what he was wearing,' Emma said.

'She could give a description anyway,' I said to Emma.

'What of? A mask? There's been nothing about a mask in the newspapers. Terry hasn't said anything about a mask,' Chloe said.

'Well that proves it,' I said, 'they do that all the time. Keep one detail back so that they can tell if someone calls in with a hoax. I've seen it on *Crimestoppers*. That's how they'll know you're telling the truth. It's too weird to make up.'

'She doesn't want to go to the police,' Emma said, 'she's already told you that.'

'This is my room, thanks, Emma,' I said, 'and I'm not forcing her to do anything, am I? Just saying that they're trying to catch this weirdo. If you know something, and don't say it, you can get yourself into trouble. Barbara says they progress from one thing to another. He'll be dragging girls into cars if he's not caught.'

'No one's saying anything,' Chloe said. 'If I tell my mother about this she'll never let me out of the house again. None of us will get out this side of Christmas. Is that what you want?'

'If they catch him, she'll let you out. And if you did go to the police,' I paused, just for effect, 'Terry and Fiona would interview you. Fiona talked to that other girl, didn't she? They had an actress do her voice but it was still her in the studio. You're fifteen in March – you could go on the telly and get interviewed for real.'

Chloe hesitated. I knew she was imagining herself 'in make-up', sitting in front of a mirror framed with lightbulbs. I think she might have changed her mind, except Emma said, 'Then you'd have to tell your mum why you took the long way round –' she smoked an imaginary cigarette, 'where you got your fags from. How you find the money.'

'She wouldn't care about that,' I said, but Chloe pursed her lips and shook her head. She'd made up her mind.

'It's not going to happen, *Laura*,' Chloe said, 'and we wouldn't have come round here to tell you about it if we'd known you'd be such a granny.'

'What did you tell me for then?' I sat on the desk chair Chloe had vacated, and looked at the two of them together. Emma wasn't pretty, not like Chloe, but they suited each other. Like negatives of each other, one brown, one blonde, in jeans, slouch socks and smudged make-up.

'We thought you'd think it was a laugh,' Chloe said.

'It *was* funny,' Emma said weakly.

'See?'

I looked away, felt humble and stupid and young.

Chloe and Emma got their way, and instead of telling anyone else, we carried on telling the story to each other. I think it made Chloe feel special, and almost famous, and because she'd found Emma first and had told her while the whole incident was still fresh in her mind, that was the thing that had brought them together. She'd often rely on Emma to fill in the details, or elaborate on the shape of the mask or the exact intonation of the words the man had spoken.

The story was theirs, really – I was just the person who they told it to. Just audience. Whenever there was another sighting of the pest, or something new about the case appeared in the local news, she'd look meaningfully at Emma and I would try to join in with their laughter but it never worked. Sometimes I thought if Emma would just mind her own business,

Chloe would do the right thing and report the flasher to the police. That was ridiculous though. I'd yet to meet the person who could coax Chloe into doing anything she didn't feel like doing.

The next time the three of us went to the park she showed us the exact place where it had happened, as if she knew I didn't quite believe her. Just where she said, on a track through an unkempt, almost wooded area of the park, and behind the bandstand where lots of hawthorn and holly had been planted to discourage people from sleeping or injecting there. She didn't seem scared or upset, not on any of the occasions that we spoke about it, but she did once claim that she'd had a dream about the man – still in his mask and his light brown boots, crunching through the leaves and staring at her through the eyeholes.

'Right here,' she said, 'that's where he came out.'

'Okay,' I'd said, and she moved around me quickly, standing on the path with her hands on her hips.

'And here's where I was, just walking along like this.'

'Right,' I said.

Emma was nodding furiously.

'And what were you doing in the park?' I said to Emma. 'Wandering around on your own. That's not a good idea.'

Emma looked away and Chloe rolled her eyes.

'She was in a bush, stoned off her tits and fucking her boyfriend – what do you think she was doing?' she said, and she laughed, and Emma laughed too, and the two of them were laughing so hard I thought it was a joke – that even the *idea* of Emma having a boyfriend when Chloe didn't was hilarious – so I joined in with the laughing and didn't ask her again.

Apart from the dream, which she had mentioned more in the spirit of entertaining me than confiding a worry, Chloe didn't seem interested in talking about it anymore. After her initial excitement and hysteria the whole incident seemed to be boring to her. The evening when she showed me where it had happened was the time that she took me to meet Carl, and soon after that whenever we were in the park he managed to turn up too, so at least she didn't need to worry about strange men in the bushes creeping up and surprising her anymore.

11

I stand and look at Emma sitting on my couch and I wait for a second, as if she is going to say something else. Nothing. So I sit next to her. We watch the pictures change on the soundless television. Nothing new. The replay of the replay of the discovery: the mayor leaning back on his spade, the balloon floating upwards into the damp air.

'Were you watching it when it happened?' Emma says.

'Yes.'

'Are you sure I didn't miss anything? On my way over here? Do they know if it was a man or a woman? How old they were, even? Those things must be quick to find out.'

I shake my head. 'Nothing like that,' I say.

'Did you think about going down there for the ground-breaking?'

The police have set up a cordon with yellow tape and uniformed officers. Terry is standing in front of it, gesticulating behind him at the comings and goings of the forensics people. They really do wear all-in-one suits made out of white carrier bags. I thought that only happened in films. Now and again, someone just out of the camera shot catches Terry's eye and he nods, or frowns slightly. It's busy there. There's a crowd. The first lot turned up early, for Chloe's memorial. Now it is dark and the body is being dug out of the clasp of soil, the ghouls have come out.

'No,' I say carefully, 'did you?'

She shakes her head. 'I was scared someone would recognise me.'

I remember something. 'You know what I was thinking of tonight?' I say. 'That time you and me and Chloe went into town, nicking stuff, and Carl came to pick us up. Do you remember? It was freezing – the cars were slipping all over the roads but he insisted on driving us back.'

Emma nods. 'I remember,' she says. 'Chloe walked out with half a make-up counter up her jumper and all you managed to swipe was a handful of toffees out of the pick 'n' mix.'

'No,' I say, 'that's not right. You got a load of camera film and Chloe got some weird stuff – screws and bolts and nails and things. Carl had sent you out with a shopping list. He wanted the stuff for his darkroom. I wonder if he ever finished it?'

Emma frowns. 'It wasn't a proper darkroom. He nailed a load of scrap wood over the window in the back bedroom and put a red lightbulb in. Took the wallpaper off the walls and moved all the furniture out apart from the bed. I don't think he knew what he was doing with that, not really. His mum would have gone mad if she'd seen it.'

'How do you know?'

She shrugs. 'He told me. Showed me up there one time. His mum never went upstairs. She was half deaf, in a wheelchair. No idea what was going on half the time, or pretended not to know.'

'I never knew you went to his house,' I say, and Emma shrugs again and asks me if there's any more wine. We settle into the couch, watching each other as much as the television.

It's funny, how me and Emma have stayed in touch. Or not, when you think about it. I haven't kept up with anyone else from school, but Emma was the only other one who really knew Chloe. That's not to say that she was as close to Chloe as I was, just that it makes sense that the two of us would stick together.

It happened without either of us planning it. I ran away from Barbara when I was sixteen. Wanted to get away – partly from her and partly from Terry's researchers, who were still desperate to get us on the show for the inside scoop on Chloe. I didn't get far. Felt like, in the end, I needed to stay put and keep an eye on things. Everyone was still so cut up over the loss of Chloe. It had been two years and nothing was normal. So I ran away but only got four miles across the City, talked to a youth worker, came to live in this flat, found a job at the shopping centre across the road, and settled.

I started going by 'Laura' again, changed my last name and didn't speak to anyone.

Then one day, I saw Emma. I was twitching the hood of my duffel coat over my face, trying to get out of the wind and light a cigarette. I was half in and half out of the entrance to the flats when Emma walked right past me in a gale of perfume and chinking metal bangles and the clatter of knee-high boots. I could have touched her, easily. She was with two other girls and laughing her way through a story about a bouncer on the door of a nightclub who'd lifted her off her feet and twirled her around in the street with such force her skirt blew up, her knickers were on show and the taxi drivers on the rank had flashed their lights and beeped their horns.

She says now she never saw me, but I know that's rot. Her eyes flicked over me. Her make-up was blurred. Dangling earrings in her ears and the three of them carrying around their own pocket of noise and the friendly fug of alcohol. I waited in the doorway until they passed by and turned a corner. I felt trembly and insubstantial: a bit of dry grass. I was shaking. I wanted to shake her. Why should she have all this – the friends, and the nightclub nights out, and the earrings and the perfume and the drunken laughing in the night – when it was not possible, would not ever be possible, for me to have those things? Friends. She had friends. For a while there, I saw how far the scales had tipped in her direction and I wanted to kill her. Put my hands on her skin and pull out her earrings and scream my secret into the whorl of her ear and kill her.

That night I started dreaming about Chloe. I hadn't forgotten about her. In my dreams she skated and slid. They were always silent dreams – as if someone had muted the sound on a film – but I could see her laughing and watch her blue lips move, trace the shapes she made while she was shouting. They weren't good dreams.

A year or two after I saw Emma outside the flats, she sent me a postcard. It was addressed to me by name – my old name and the block of flats. No number, but the postie knew me so it got to me safe. Of course he knew me – I've been here years, staying put in this damp box in the sky while everyone else moves on. He's a good lad. He's never let on, never asked me a question, never stared, never tipped off Terry's researchers. I don't know if it's pity or professionalism, but either way I am grateful for it. The picture on the postcard was of the train station. Miniature daffodils and ivy in wooden planters on the platforms. No dirty pigeons. No drunks. No tramps. A sunny day.

After I'd read it, I'd stared at the picture until my clammy hands warped the card. The train waiting at the platform. Her handwriting. Postmark. Stamp – not the Queen's head, but a robin perched on the handle of a spade, the spade driven into a hillock of earth. Wondering if it was significant. If she was trying to tell me something. And she was a liar too. A sly one, like Chloe. She hadn't been so drunk she didn't recognise me, not so drunk she didn't notice the name of the block of flats where I lived.

Emma is much less stupid than she looks.

We drink together a fair bit these days. It isn't exactly what you'd call social. We make trips to the park, to Debenhams. Take each other on guided tours over the topography of our memories.

'Look,' she'll say, 'here's where me and Chloe first went and got our ears pierced.'

I'll have to take her to HMV just to keep up and show her where I distracted the security by flashing my new bra at the cameras while Chloe ran out of the door with the second series of *Dawson's Creek* up her jumper. Emma will watch patiently, and then take me to Boots and show me the exact brand of icy-white glitter that Chloe liked to stroke over her brow-bone on special occasions. Like New Year's Eve.

She doesn't come to the flat, but I meet her once or twice a month in a Thirties-themed cafe called Brucciani's that we choose because it's almost exactly half way between her place and mine. I have to get there first and order for us – if she looks through the windows and sees that I'm not there she'll turn around and go home. We don't talk much. I tend to sit opposite her, look at her dirty hair and dull eyes and try to guess what she is thinking. She looks different now.

I wonder about those other girls – her friends. The make-up and the boots and going-out clothes. Making friends with the bouncers. These days, she can't hold down a real job and doesn't even raise her eyes to the waitress when she is paying for her tea. I don't know where her friends are now. I don't know if she still likes a drink, a dance, a kebab on the way home. I don't think there's a boyfriend. Is she into girls? I think about the photographs I took of Chloe, wonder if she ever handed the camera to Emma. I try to picture them kissing, their mouths working wetly together. It doesn't work. Emma hates to be touched – it's like she's bruised all over.

On our visits to Brucciani's, we make attempts at small-talk like normal people do. Emma will ask about my job. I will ask after her family, who I don't think she is in touch with anymore. It's always a relief when the waitress comes with the tray of tea. There are a few minutes of distraction bestowed by the individual metal teapots, the condensation on the flick-up lid, the scald to the ball of the thumb as I pour and the tea slopping onto my saucer. I take those minutes gratefully and I mop the table with napkins more carefully than is necessary.

Most of the time we sit in silence. Often, we'll give up and escape outdoors, past Winkley Square and back into the park. The fountain is still there, the rockery and the Japanese water garden and the folly at the top of the hill. We sit on one of the benches and more often than not, Emma will slip me a tenner and send me away to the off licence. She always pays because she won't talk to strangers: it's one of her phobias. It's the reason she can't get a job anyone would actually pay her for. Even I'm not that bad. I take the money and come back with a half bottle of vodka or a few cans inside my coat and we will sit there like that for most of the afternoon. Even in the rain: the damp won't kill us. Sometimes we see other girls there doing the same as us, and we'll shout over at them and offer them cigarettes and see if they'll come and join us. Emma's more confident when she's pissed, more likely to nudge my shoulder with hers, tell me a joke, offer a secret. She'll wipe the neck of the bottle on her sleeve and offer it to whoever is sitting on the next bench.

The other girls never want to come and sit with us. To them, we're too old.

The last time we were due to meet – about a week ago – Emma never turned up. I waited until nearly closing time and the cafe was almost empty. In there the waitresses wear black dresses and white aprons – a caricature of a maid's outfit that might sound erotic, but isn't. The dresses are Teflon and spotted with margarine and dropped coffee. They glide between the tables, wiping and lifting chairs. I was far away, thinking about worms as long as freshwater trout, as long as skateboards, even, and the girl behind the counter shouted over to me – told me to order now if I wanted anything else because she was going to cash up the till. I shook my head. There were wet rings under her arms.

I was sweating too. Wondering what Emma was up to, why she hadn't come. It was the anniversary coming up, I thought. The memory of it. The way flowers were starting to appear on the verges outside the school again, in the windows of the bank and post office. You couldn't open a paper without Chloe's face smiling out at you. Happy Valentine's Day. The patron saint of lovers and dead schoolgirls. It was bound to make her twitchy. Erratic. Maybe she'd want to talk to someone. I ignored the waitress, who was tutting and slamming the till closed, and waited.

'You never came, the last time,' I say. 'I sat there for ages.'

If you say you're going to be somewhere, you should show up. No questions asked. Take me and Chloe – for all her faults, she never once let me down like that. What Chloe and I had was rare and special and it isn't really fair to compare Emma to her in that way, but all the same, I am pissed off.

Emma's eyes are glued to the screen and she has that look people get when they're immersed in television – slack, absent, stupid.

'I sat there like a lemon, waiting. I looked like a dick.'

'There was an emergency at work,' she said. 'I needed to stay and help out.'

'Emergency?'

I don't believe her. Emma doesn't 'work'. She claims incapacity benefit for depression, anxiety attacks and phobias. She volunteers at a dogs' home sixteen hours a week and because they can't pay her they let her take her pick of the clothes people donate to sell in their charity shop.

Emma nods. 'There was a holdall of puppies dumped around the back of the office. I only noticed it because one of them squeaked as I walked past. Would have walked right past otherwise. I got them out – newborn ones – and I had to wait until the on-call vet turned up.' She turns to me, and suddenly smiles. 'We only lost four of them.'

'That's good,' I say. I want to ask her what they did with the dead ones, but I don't.

Emma nods, turns back to the television and makes herself another roll-up.

'I thought you were giving up?'

She pulls a face. 'Too late for that. I started at school. Chloe used to give them to me. I'll probably smoke forever. The earlier you start,' she sucked at the tube hungrily, 'the harder it is to stop. More than half my life now.'

'Me too,' I say. 'I wonder how many other people she passed that habit on to?'

Emma turns her head and stares at me as if I've said something shocking and blasphemous. The branch of Nationwide on the high street kept a framed photograph of Chloe and an ever-fresh bunch of Juliet roses in the window for three years. No one is allowed to say anything bad about Chloe. Chloe was born beautiful, had no ugly duckling phase, and stayed beautiful. The world didn't dirty her: Chloe would have got to thirty and still had her unmarked skin and fine, pale hair.

The thing is, Emma and I both know that if either of us had drowned ourselves the news wouldn't have made page six. At fourteen, Emma was sullen and sallow and buck-toothed, but when she was with Chloe and me she laughed a lot and it wasn't so noticeable. I wonder if she still likes children. I know she likes her job in the dogs' home, feeding and cleaning the kennels. She told me in a rare moment of confiding that she stays longer than she needs to in order to wash the dogs and brush their coats because she thinks it increases their chances of being adopted. This, and what I remember about her from school, are the only things that I know about her.

Sometimes I am consumed with curiosity and I imagine myself

following her home and looking through her bathroom window while she unwraps soap and pulls a comb through her hair. I picture her alone, in a bare and empty flat – but maybe that's just because that's how I live. The walls are white, the sink and toilet are white, she uses white soap and a rough white towel to take the dog smell off her angular, yellow body. I imagine her nipples: as small and dark as melanomas.

When I am feeling kinder, I imagine Emma with the dogs. I've been to the dogs' home once before, with Donald. There's a narrow walkway between rows of wire cages, concrete floors with channels, and glinting metal plugholes. The noise of the dogs barking and throwing themselves against the rattling wire panels and the stink of piss and fur and meat and Jeyes Fluid is nearly overwhelming. I try not to hate Emma, and I imagine the dogs falling quiet as she passes by them with a brush and a tartan blanket that smells of Persil. In this dream life I have made for her they lick her hands and she smiles and talks to them in the high-pitched, expressionless voice she was saving for her children.

Yes. I try not to hate her, and I give her cleanliness and solitude in her white flat, and I give her her dogs, but I don't call on her and I don't ask exactly where she lives. I don't know what she thinks she knows about me and Chloe and I don't want to know.

'Well don't stand me up next time,' I say weakly, and Emma ignores me. She finishes her wine, holds her glass out to me and smiles, and I push the tap on the box and top it up for her. We stare at the television. The remote control lies between us, untouched.

'This is just the regional news,' Emma says. 'I bet for the rest of the country things are going on as usual.'

I nod, and I can't tell by the tone of her voice if she thinks this is a bad idea or not. The rest of the country is a vague, fuzzy place. It might not even exist.

Terry is talking about how they date long-buried bodies. There are tests they can do on the organisms of the bacteria on the remains. Any insects or larvae remaining. They know how fast certain materials are supposed to decay. There's carbon-dating. It is not going to take all that long for people to start putting two and two together.

'You think all this is going to outshine Chloe?' Emma says scornfully and gestures towards the screen with her wine glass. 'After all this time?'

'Maybe,' I say. 'We'll have to wait and see, I suppose.'

My words hang in the air. Emma turns her attention back to the screen. I feel the wine churning in my stomach. I do not want to wait and see. I want to press stop, but real life, as I am constantly reminded, does not work like that.

Something that often surprised people about Chloe: she loved her cars. She bought *Top Gear* as well as *Just Seventeen*, and she knew all the makes and models and engine sizes. Could have had a conversation with anyone about it and held her own, but most of her conversations were with me and Emma, who knew nothing and could only nod. But if she liked her cars, she liked the boys that drove them even more and what she liked best of all was the combination.

When we walked – from one of our houses to the shop for cigarettes and an attempt to buy booze, or from school to one of our houses, or aimlessly around the streets, in circles with arms linked like lovers or old ladies – sooner or later we would hear that sound. A car slowing to draw up beside us on the pavement, the passengers whooping and gesturing and the driver revving the engine as if the mechanical mess under the bonnet that worked the car was part of his body and the growling and pinking of the engine was a language.

She loved it. Even better if the windows were down and the music was booming into the street. Bare forearms hanging out, with palms slapping the outside of the door in a lazy rhythm. The boy driving – although he would have seemed like a man to us – jerked his head. Not an invitation, exactly. An appraisal. She'd been passed. All her parts in working order, and fit for a closer inspection some other time.

I can see her posture change – her head lifts and her chin juts, and her eyes dart about: looking, and not looking at the same time. Not wanting to appear too interested, although she jabs me with her elbow and giggles as we turn the corner, and sometimes, turns right around, puts one hand on a cocked hip, and, smiling that brilliant smile of hers, gives them the finger. It is a complicated dance I don't know the steps for.

What about me? I probably just turned away from the road and walked a bit quicker. I wasn't shy; I was scared. Donald and Barbara liked to draw my attention to all those stories in the news: young girls dragged into vans, into bushes, ambushed in quiet places, given something nasty to drink and then undressed. They made a nasty incident with a boy, an attack, an assault, a too-rough groping at a disco, sound like a rite of passage I should try to avoid, even though the avoidance of it would be futile: they'd all get me in the end. They would all get all of us in the end. It was a certainty.

Chloe wasn't scared – whatever was going to happen was going to happen – and she was standing on the pavement grinning at cars and welcoming it with open arms. When I was on my own the cars didn't come. When I was with Emma and not Chloe, the cars didn't come. It was her. Her blonde head, which caught the sun, shone and drew the eye. Some smell she had on her. She was willing. There were rumours about her that she took no pains to dispel although I don't think, despite her raised eyebrows and veiled references, she'd had much experience at all until a man in a mask approached her in the park.

Soon after that she started going with Carl, who had his own car, had a job, topped up the credit on our mobile phones, gave us cigarettes and bottles of orange-flavoured alcohol. Carried mints to freshen Chloe's breath when she threw up from too many of the bottles. Was generous, sometimes sullen, tolerated me, sometimes Emma, and didn't like us knowing that he'd quite like to be able to grow a proper moustache.

This is my secret: I still have Chloe's mobile phone. For a long time I would dial the number to hear her voice on the answering service. I bet her mother did too. I used to think her answer machine message, and any messages people recorded for her, were trapped inside the phone itself, like letters inside a post box. That's why I stole it from her. It wasn't the phone I wanted, it was the messages.

But now I know that the recording service exists somewhere else, probably powered by a computer that lasts forever. I know you don't, if you're the police, even need the phone to listen to the messages people left for the person who owned it. So I am regularly amazed that no one checked it after she died. She flashed the phone about at school; everyone knew about it, but I suppose us girls were used to keeping things to ourselves and no one who was questioned about Chloe mentioned it.

Carl and I were the only people who rang her because we were the only people in the world who knew her number. Her message is more personal than most and directed at the two of us, in a fake American accent that I cringed to listen to, even at the time.

'Lo, Carl – you know what to do. Keep it clean on the answer machine! Wait for the beep. Hit it!'

My voice is in there too, hoarse and panicked. I used to listen to my own frantic voice telling her to frigging ring me back – blurting out on record what I'd been trying to tell her in person for nearly a month.

I'd sit in my room and listen to it, and feel cold and blank inside, and listen to it again, again and again until the battery ran out – and I would wonder what she was playing at.

12

I went to sleep on New Year's Eve that year with my mobile in my hand, in case she called to wish me happy New Year. Nothing. I didn't hear from her until we were back at school. But just as I thought things had been ruined between us for good, she decided to confide in me again.

She strode up to me as we were filing out of morning registration.

'All right?'

She always did have a fantastic smile. It worked on almost everyone.

'All right, nothing,' I said, and turned away. Started walking – as if the Geography block was the place I most wanted to be in the world.

'What you ignoring me for?' she said, and jogged along beside me. She pulled at my arm and I stopped. She turned on that smile again – full beam. She had her hair up in a high ponytail, and she shook her head, twitching it as she spoke. 'Come on, don't be like that.'

'Where did you disappear to? What's your problem?' I didn't want to mention the party. It sounded petty and needy.

'You know what it's like sometimes. My parents invited all the cousins round. We had family staying.'

'Yeah,' I said, 'for your party. I thought I was coming?' I didn't want to cry. 'I waited up.'

I felt the tears coming anyway, and turned my head away so she wouldn't see. She stepped to the side so she could maintain eye contact with me, and I started walking again.

'What did I do? I didn't do anything to you. Is it to do with Carl? Did you ask Emma instead?'

Chloe threw her arm around my shoulders and squeezed me.

'Don't be like that,' she said, and laughed, 'there'll be loads of parties. You're my best friend, I wasn't blanking you.'

I sniffed.

'Then what was it?'

I stared at her, waiting for an excuse that would make everything all right. If she'd been ill, or grounded, or her parents had found out about Carl and banned her from using the phone. Or if there'd been a death in the family, or if the marital problems had got worse and Nathan had left them both. Any of those things. I really badly needed it to be one of those things. Chloe stared back. She looked tired. Her make-up was lighter than usual and I could see little red patches on her cheeks under her eyes, like the start of eczema.

'Well?'

She sighed. Squeezed me again. Put her head on my shoulder. I felt her hair prickle the side of my neck.

'I need to talk to you.' Her voice was muffled. 'There's something wrong with me.'

'You're telling me.'

I said it quickly, without thinking about it. Chloe opened her mouth, huffed, flicked her hair. She expected people to make allowances for her, and they did. Her father was terrified of her – put it all down to hormones and monthly cycles. Her mother thought she should have had a sibling and tolerated a lot because of that. School knew her history – the fact that this was the fourth high school she'd been to and the City would either have to keep her in it, or pay for another Education Welfare Officer and a Home Tutor.

'I can't believe you just said that to me. I cannot believe it.' She was as incredulous as ever, and I was scared. Yes, she was being selfish and unreasonable and she probably had spent half of the Christmas holidays in the back of Carl's car and the other half telling Emma about it, but she was talking to me now – and what if she never spoke to me again?

'What's up with you then? Tell me.'

'I'm *trying* to tell you. I actually thought you were my friend?' Chloe said.

She did look worried. Genuinely. It didn't look like she was trying to be excused from cross-country and she didn't look hungover, or pretending to be. She looked like she'd been crying. But I'd seen Chloe cry on command. She cried sometimes if Carl didn't text her to check if she'd got home all right after she had been out with him. She cried when Amanda shouted at her. Still, it looked like she had been crying that morning and then had gone and got a piece of toilet roll and tried to fix her make-up. There were tiny pieces of damp tissue sticking to her eyelashes.

'Don't stare at me. Come in the toilet. I mean it, I'll talk to you but you've got to promise not to tell anyone. On your own life.'

I followed Chloe into the girls' toilets. Whatever was wrong with her would be my fault – I could predict it, guarantee it and would bet my life on it. But it was a relief all the same. The alternative – that her silence would be carried on publicly in the great staring arena of our lives at the high school – wasn't something I'd dared to think about.

'Are you coming, or not?' Chloe hissed at me over her shoulder. She knew I didn't like to spend time in there.

My toilet at home smelled like the little yellow block Barbara put in the cistern and the bowl of dried-up flowers and pine cones and things that was always on the window ledge. But the bogs at school smelled like what they were used for, and cigs, and blood. They smelled like everyone was on their period and had just done PE. It was horrible. I always tried to time myself so I went at home just before I left and then again as soon as I got back.

We went inside past the prefects who were waiting near the door. It was their job to make sure that no one was using the toilets for smoking or writing on the walls. Inside there were a group of Year Elevens standing by the mirrors in a huddle. They were smoking and writing on the walls and taking turns listening to something on someone's personal stereo. Even though they were not the girls who'd bugged me when I was in Year Seven and Eight, I didn't look at them. I looked at Chloe's bag which was just in front of my face. It was light pink and she had written 'Carl' on it in biro and drawn a heart around it. Chloe walked quickly right into the cubicle that was furthest away from the door. I paused by the cracked sink and Chloe frowned at me again.

'Get in here, will you?'

I followed her into the cubicle. There was a poster on the inside of the door about chlamydia, and lots of writing with Tipp-Ex pen or scratched into the paint with a compass: lists of names of people accused of having chlamydia, and who they'd got it from. The door caught on my rucksack as I tried to close it behind me. I turned to take it off and elbowed Chloe in the stomach.

Chloe said, 'For fuck's sake,' under her breath and I was about to tell her to get lost but the girls waiting under the mirror had noticed us, struggling with our bags in the doorway of the cubicle.

'Look at them two,' someone said.

'Look at the lezzies.'

There was a little chorus of whooping and two of the girls said 'Woooo' at the same time, which made the rest of them laugh.

'Let's be friends,' said someone else.

That is something that they all said, even the boys. Sometimes I said it too, but it was ages before I knew what it meant. It was the sort of thing people said to you quietly in the dinner queue.

You had to say it in a certain tone of voice or it didn't work. Lessbefrens. Like that. I didn't think it was a great joke, actually, but I was wrong – Chloe told me it was hilarious.

'Shut up, you slags,' Chloe shouted over the top of the cubicle. I was facing the door and I slid the bolt across and looked at the letters and pictures on the inside of the door until the banging outside stopped.

'What's the matter with you?' I said.

A disaster to do with Carl, no doubt. Nothing too bad, but bad enough to get Chloe worked up. Although I'd heard about rows with Carl before and listened to them and agreed to go and stay at her house and drink Bacardi Breezers and watch *Titanic* to make her feel better, I did not feel like doing that today.

'I can't tell you unless you promise you're going to keep it to yourself. It's confidential.'

'Right,' I said. Confidential was a word that Chloe used quite a lot.

'I'm sorry about the party. I had other things on my mind.'

'What?'

'I'm trying to tell you.'

'Did you cancel it then?'

'No, it wasn't cancelled. Just forget about the fucking party, will you? You know I would have called you, would have let you know what was going on if I could have done,' she said.

'Right.'

'Don't be like that. It's serious.' She paused, and I wondered if she was about to start lying to me. 'Me and Carl had sex,' she said, not smiling, but with a pale, blank look about her face. She wouldn't meet my eye. 'Like, properly, all the way in.'

'For God's sake. You've been going on about this party for weeks and then you flake out on me just because you fancied screwing your boyfriend instead?'

I kept my voice down but I could hear the chatting outside,

the taps running. Those girls weren't paying any attention to us anymore. I put my hand on the door.

'Lola!' There was something about her voice, something high-pitched and fragile, that made me stay.

'I know about all this already,' I said, 'so you fucked me off for Carl. Surprise surprise. We're going to be late for Food Tech.'

'You don't know . . .' She bowed her head and scratched the back of her neck. 'We weren't even doing it before.'

'I thought you said . . .'

'We did other things,' she said quickly, 'just as good as. We might as well have been. I mean, I had my clothes off and stuff, didn't I?'

'Right,' I said.

'It was his idea!' Chloe said shrilly, 'to hang on a bit. Until I was fully ready. That's what he said. There was no rush. He was happy with the other stuff. The pictures and that.'

I didn't say anything. I knew for a fact that Chloe had been hinting, if not actually saying, that she and Carl had been having sex for ages. Since about two days after they met. She had been going on about how big his cock was and how much better it was to be going out with someone who was more mature and experienced than the little boys in our school. She'd been carrying on like this, holding it over me, for weeks and weeks.

'Anyway. We've done it now, but something went wrong.'

'What do you mean?'

'It hurts, like, loads.'

'It's meant to hurt, isn't it?' I pulled a face, and thought about ruptures. We didn't get sex education until we were in Year Ten but I reckoned I knew the basics.

'I know that. I'm not thick.' Chloe shook her head, but still wouldn't look at me. 'I mean, I knew it was going to hurt the first time. Like when it was going in. You'd expect it to, wouldn't you? Emma said I might get a bit of bleeding. I know about that.'

121

How come Emma was suddenly a world expert? Who'd shag her?

'Did it bleed?' This was like the eyebrow-plucking, the leg-waxing, the pierced ears. There was a reason I always let Chloe go first.

'I don't know. It was dark. And then I was wearing my black going-out knickers, so if I did, it didn't show. Anyway. That's not the point. Stop being a perv.'

'Then what's the problem?'

'That was like a full eleven days ago and it's still really hurting. Like every time I go to the toilet it really stings. It burns. It's horrible.'

Chloe looked upwards and ran her index finger along her lower eyelid. First one, then the other.

'Eleven days?' I counted. 'That was Boxing Day. You had sex with him for the first time when I was hanging around outside the car?'

I couldn't believe it. I could not, seriously, believe what I was hearing.

'I'm supposed to be your best mate,' I said. 'It was fucking cold, waiting for you outside that car. We were supposed to be hanging out that day.'

'No,' she said, impatient – as if I was missing the point. 'Later on. At night.'

'You went back out?'

'This really isn't the issue here.'

Chloe sounded like my mother. She sounded like a teacher. She was deliberately trying to make me feel like a dick, for no reason. Just because she'd been taken out in the dark to have sex with some weird guy in the back seat of a car she thought she could take me into the toilet and get everyone to call me a lezzer and then talk down to me.

'Well, I'm pleased for you,' I said.

When I first thought Chloe was having sex I was sort of interested in it, not in a lezzer-type way, but just curious about knowing the facts and how much on a scale of one to ten it hurt, and whether it was embarrassing having to have no clothes on or whether you just kind of got carried away in the moment and didn't mind. But then you'd still probably mind afterwards, when you'd settled down a bit, and then you'd have to put your clothes back on in front of someone else and not make a mess out of it and I was sort of curious about that too.

And I'd asked, and Chloe had made out like it was some big private secret and wouldn't tell me, and it was all because the silly bitch didn't even know because she hadn't even done it yet.

'Don't be like that. I'm trying to tell you,' Chloe said. 'Something's wrong. I went to the doctor's and they had this leaflet in the waiting room. I only read the first page, then I was too scared to go in.'

Chloe sat down on the closed lid of the toilet and opened her bag and showed me it. It had been folded and unfolded and folded again and the paper was fraying in places. It was a leaflet about being pregnant.

'It's this bit, here.'

I read the part that Chloe pointed to. It said that for some women one of the very first signs of being pregnant is the need to pass urine very frequently. It said this is because the womb is growing downwards and pressing on the bladder. That might also cause backache.

'Do you think that's what it is? Are you peeing all the time?' I turned the leaflet over. There was a picture of a woman standing sideways, cut in half with the bubble of her stomach turned into a diagram. Just like the picture of the woman with one foot up on the toilet on the instructions inside a Tampax box. A line-drawing of something half-evolved inside her womb. A hagfish, or a deep sea shrimp.

'What else could it be? I've had to go, like, ten times a day. And it hurts all up my back as well.'

'Maybe it's something else.'

I tried to think of something else to suggest, but I couldn't.

Chloe shook her head and held her hand out for the leaflet. She pulled a length of tissue paper from the roll and blew her nose on it noisily.

'What has Carl said?'

'I haven't said anything to him.'

'Well you should. If you are – it's his fault, isn't it? He can help you get it sorted out. Go to the doctor's with you or something.'

'I can't go to the doctor.'

We had been whispering but Chloe said this out loud, forcefully. She shook her head a lot and her eyes filled up with tears.

'I wasn't even that into it,' she said, 'but he spent loads on me for Christmas.' She put her arm out and at first I thought she wanted a hug, and I leaned back a bit, but something on her wrist rattled and I saw the gold bracelet with little charms on it, tinkling under the cuff of her school shirt. 'See?' she said, and the charms rattled until I nodded and she moved her arm down again.

I do not want to be hearing this, I thought. I do not want to have to go home and think about this and be responsible for not telling anyone. Still, who else was Chloe going to tell? I was just glad it wasn't Emma. I imagined Chloe getting fatter and fatter, and having to give up school and probably getting killed, literally, by her parents when they found out. I thought about Donald and Barbara finding out. I thought about them banning me from going outside or watching television or listening to music or reading magazines until I was eighteen years old. I thought about them probably taking me to the doctor to make sure I was still sealed up down below and not infected or pregnant. Then I thought about going to the doctor and having to take my clothes off in front of someone and having someone shine a torch in my privates.

'No,' I said, 'I see what you mean. And they'd probably tell your mum, wouldn't they?'

Chloe put her elbows on her knees and her head in her hands. I could see the top of her head where her French plait started and the dark patches on her grey skirt where her tears were sliding off the bottom of her face and falling onto her clothes.

'You'll have to tell Carl, then,' I said quickly, being practical instead of touching her. 'Get him to find out. There's a tablet you can take. He might be able to get it for you. Maybe he's got a friend who's got a girlfriend who's older than us. She can go to the doctor and say that she needs it. Then she can get it and give it to Carl. And he can give it to you. I've got some Christmas money left over if there's a prescription charge. You can have it for that if you like.'

'What if it's loads?'

'Carl can give it to you, can't he? He should at least go halves with you?'

Saying that made me think of one of the chat-up lines that the boys had been going round with. Not that someone had said it to me, but I had overheard boys saying it to Chloe.

What happened was this: one of the boys would sit next to a girl and chat to her for a bit about other things. Like home-work or music or someone else who they both knew. That was usually how it worked. Then when the other boys had edged closer so that they could hear, he would look at the girl quite seriously and say, 'Feel like going halves on a bastard?'

This was the boys' version of 'let's be friends' and they thought that it was the funniest thing anyone had ever said. It got to a point where people were saying it to each other about five or six times in every lesson and even the teachers had heard about it.

'I can't tell Carl. He'll go mad.'

I forgot to whisper.

'Well it's his fault, isn't it? How can he go mad? Did he not make sure it was – you know – covered, or anything?'

Chloe looked horrified.

'You are such a perv!' she said.

'Well you have to do something about it,' I said, 'other than sit crying.'

Chloe stood up. She reached behind me and opened the door.

'Thanks for all your support,' she said, emphatically biting down on the 't'. 'Just leave me alone and I'll deal with it myself. You tell anyone and I swear to God you'll regret it.'

I was speechless for a second or two. Couldn't think of what to say, and didn't know what I had said that was so wrong. Chloe's hair-trigger temper shocked me even though I should have been used to it, and underneath it all I had the nagging feeling that there was something else going on that she wasn't telling me about.

Chloe was right out of the toilets and along the corridor before I could pick up my bag and get out of the cubicle. The girls under the mirror had gone. I washed my hands even though I hadn't been, because I had touched the handle on the outside of the door and the bolt on the inside and the holder for the toilet roll and all of those places are crawling with germs.

I didn't see Chloe for the rest of the day. When afternoon registration was over we usually went to the neck of the corridor where the school turned into the leisure centre, and bought Skips and Kit-Kats and Coke from the vending machines in the atrium before taking our separate ways home. I waited there for her but not for very long. Our school wasn't the sort of place where it was all right to hang around on your own for any length of time, especially for me. I knew Chloe had things on her mind, important things, but they weren't any reason to fly off the handle when all I was doing was trying to help. It was all down to Carl, anyway. Obviously. That day was the first time I'd seen or heard from her since Boxing Day, and she hadn't even asked me how I was, which, considering how she had been acting since she'd been letting Carl knock her off, was just rich.

And he hadn't even been knocking her off!

I couldn't even tell what was so good about Carl anyway. I felt the plastic lump of the mobile phone in my pocket and wanted to throw it away. That was him as well. Some plastic piece of shit from Chloe, as if I was meant to be grateful. And other things too, like lifts in the car, and CDs or videos or packets of fags sometimes. Just to get Chloe to let him poke her, and make sure I didn't say anything to anyone because he was clearly too old for her.

And he wasn't even good-looking, either. He had horrible greasy hair and the white shirts he had to wear for work were all grey at the collar, and he had spots on his neck, and even if he did have a car, it was a shit car. I tried to imagine him shagging Chloe in it. I couldn't believe they'd gone back out on Boxing Day after they'd dropped me off. That made me feel something. I remembered the scary atmosphere in the car all the way home, which I'd thought was down to Wilson getting on Carl's nerves but it wasn't to do with Wilson, it was to do with me, who was in the way.

So what happened then? I was half way to the bus stop, walking fast because it was freezing and I'd lost my gloves. Probably the two of them went and parked round the back of some garage and did it with the engine in the car still running. I tried to think what Carl would have looked like with no clothes on.

I'd seen his chest before. Just once, when he was taking his work shirt off in the car and putting on a tee-shirt instead because he was going to take the two of us out for a burger. It was all white and thin, you could see the moles on his ribs and the fat brown lumps of his nipples. He probably didn't take his clothes off completely when he did it with Chloe, it was too cold for that. I thought about the jutting-out bones of his hips, and the black semi-circles of dirt under his fingernails. I had a feeling. I can't describe it. Like a trickle of warm water down my back and over the skin of my arms. I tried out the thought again: Carl, lifting his bum off the seat so he could flick his belt open. The feeling came again, but weaker this time.

I put my hood up, licked my cracked lips, and decided to think about how to get Chloe away from Carl, and make everything go back to normal, as good as it had been in the summer. There was still hope: after all, it was me who she'd confided in. She'd asked for my help – mine – not Carl's, not even Emma's. Even if there was more to the story than she was telling me, half a secret is better than no secret at all and this was her way of letting me know I was special to her, and that she needed me. And that was true even if her worry made her phrase it badly, made her moodier and more abrupt than she might have been otherwise.

13

When I got in to school for morning reg the first thing I noticed was how much more noise there was than usual. But I was in a good mood and didn't catch any of the excited conversations taking place around me until later. I was feeling sparky and determined to sort Chloe out. I had an advert for the Brook Advisory Centre which I had torn out of my magazine and kept safe between the pages of my homework diary to show Chloe when we were on our own. The free phone number on the advert was printed in a friendly, loopy font that looked like handwriting, and when I'd rung it I'd found out the nearest clinic was in Manchester. *Confidentiality Guaranteed.* Chloe was going to be so pleased I'd worked out a way to solve her problem without involving anyone she didn't want to know. It would really show her that I was her true friend and not Emma. And once we'd sorted out her problem, I could get to work on getting rid of Carl, just by pointing out that he was the one who had caused the trouble and she hadn't trusted him to help her. She'd had to rely completely on me.

The room was an art room during the day when the classes were on but in the morning it was just a classroom with the paint and clay packed away in lockable cupboards. Rightly, they didn't trust us and kept everything interesting locked up so that no one could mess about with it when we were supposed to be sitting still and answering our names on the register, listening to daily devotion and collecting passes for free school dinners (me) and detentions (Chloe). But that day everyone was out of their seats and I couldn't see Chloe anywhere. They were all talking at once and I couldn't hear what they were saying. I just caught the mood of it, which was excited and pleased and a bit nasty. It was the same kind of feeling there had been in the air when someone looked out of the wide windows in the side of the Geography block and saw two dogs mating on the football pitch – right there in the middle of the astro-turf. That had been bedlam although when I glanced through the paint- and spit-speckled window I didn't see anything except seagulls in the yard swooping and pecking at crisp packets.

I walked very slowly towards the moving crowd of black blazers and blue pullovers. I walked and looked at the drawings of apples and lightbulbs and screwed-up pieces of newspaper stuck to the walls. I was hoping Shanks would come in and order us all into our seats before I reached the middle of the room.

'Is it that pest?' I asked no one in particular. 'Has he started up again?'

No one answered, the knot of bodies was thick. School was all right as long as there were teachers around to keep every-thing reasonable. I stepped slowly, wondering if the pest had got one of us. It was possible. Two of the earliest victims had been pupils at the girls' school round the corner. I imagined the man in the Halloween mask loitering in the woods where we ran for cross-country and felt a secret, shivery thrill. Then I heard someone say something about Chloe.

There was only one person sitting down and everyone else was gathered around her like they were waiting for her to sign an autograph. Emma. Emma was fast turning into the sort of girl who wears a black lacy bra under her white school shirt just so that when she takes off her jumper everyone can see it She was opening and closing her school bag as if there was some-thing inside that was much more interesting than anything else.

'I was going to go in the ambulance,' she said, looking at her bag instead of anyone in particular, 'but they didn't know what was wrong with her. Could have been contagious.'

She turned her head and smiled beatifically in answer to a question that I didn't hear.

'My mum will probably drive me in to visit her after school, if she's well enough to take visitors. I'll tell her you said that, shall I? *I'm* going to organise a collection.'

I knew they were talking about Chloe – who else would have caused such interest? She could have had a hundred friends if she'd wanted them, but for some reason she preferred to have one at a time, and no one, not even me, could figure out why she'd picked me. Emma looked at me, and I expected some kind of special word, a privileged piece of information.

'I'm here now,' I wanted to say. 'I can take charge.'

Emma smiled comfortably, flicked her coat over her knee, and said nothing.

She was a fucking liar – her mum wouldn't be giving her a lift anywhere. Chloe had already let me in on the facts about that. Emma lived in Ashton with her dad and three older brothers – all crammed into a house with not enough bedrooms. She actually shared a bedroom with her seventeen-year-old brother, which was disgusting. Her mum got depressed and left them all when Emma was two. Now, according to Chloe, her dad had got religion and was all right with the boys, but didn't know what to do with Emma – especially since she 'started growing up and getting tits, you know?' I'd seen Emma with her father once, walking between stalls at the school Spring Fayre. He never dared look at her – it was as if she was naked.

When Shanks came in to read the register he clapped his hands loudly. It made a good sound, a loud, hollow sound. Yesterday, the first day back, we'd had morning assembly so this was the first proper registration of the year and I'd not seen him in ages. He carried on clapping as he walked between the tables and to the front of the classroom, and by the time he was standing in front of his desk, leaning back on it and crossing his legs in front of him, everyone in the class was shuffling quietly to their seats and shoving their bags under the tables.

He was all right, like that, Mr Shanks. If we'd known his first name we could probably have called him by it when none of the other teachers were around, and he wouldn't have minded, but wouldn't have made a big deal out of it either, like he was trying to be our 'mate'. He was just natural. And also, he always made jokes, but the sort of jokes that it didn't really matter if you laughed or not. You could just smile at those jokes, or nod a bit, and that was enough, it wasn't awkward.

'I suppose I can assume from the noise that you've all had quiet, God-fearing, homework-filled Christmas holidays and come in fresh as daisies, free from hangovers, and anxious to start work,' he started.

A few people who sat on the table along the back of the room groaned and said, 'Whatever, sir,' but he only smiled and clicked his fingers at them, making his hands into two little guns at the end of the click which he pointed at the back row, shot, and then blew the imaginary smoke away.

'Chaps and Chapesses, let's get coats in bags and the registration done before I let you loose on my unfortunate colleagues,' he said, and reached for his book. There were more groans and shuffling as people reached for their coats, and then hush as he read out the names.

The school had a ridiculous rule. No one was allowed to carry their coat around with them. There weren't any cloakrooms so you had to get a locker which cost money for the year, or put it in your bag. And there weren't enough lockers. My coat was damp because it had snowed that morning: needles of frost flying about in the thickened air and collecting where they fell on my face and my hands and all over the new coat. So the wet coat was going to smudge the writing in the books in my bag and that would be one thing. It was also going to smell like old curtains by the time I got home, and Barbara would be checking it because it was new, and she would notice, and that would be another thing.

I struggled furiously with the coat and thought about Chloe being off school with a baby and her parents probably knowing everything by now and probably ringing up Barbara and Donald in the middle of the day – or even coming round to see them. They'd have long conversations about bad influences and Debenhams and things getting out of hand, and tell them that Chloe would be moving school again and it was probably best not to keep in touch.

Barbara would nod and look sympathetic and thank them for taking the trouble, then she would go up the stairs and take all the magazines and posters and hairspray out of my bedroom. I could see it. At the very least I was going to be on my own at school *all day*, and then back home to get a bollocking about the coat and the books and Chloe. Fucking Emma. I sighed and turned the coat inside out so the wet bit wouldn't touch my books, then rolled it up as tightly as I could. When I looked up, registration was over, everyone had gone, and Shanks was staring at me.

'You're working that coat into shreds,' he observed. 'Leave it in my office, if you're so determined to follow the letter of the law.'

'Thanks, sir.'

We went to his office.

'You've heard about Chloe, have you?' Shanks said, and shook his head.

I nodded. 'Emma was—'

'Emma's her best friend, yes?'

I didn't dignify that with a response.

'She's gone to the hospital,' Shanks said. 'Not to worry though. It isn't serious. I expect she'll be back at school within the week.'

'Sir, it's nothing to do with a baby, is it?' I asked, and bit my lip as soon as I'd spoken, hoping that he hadn't heard me.

Shanks didn't say anything. He sat down, leaned back on the stool and busied himself rearranging the things on his desk. There were mugs and mugs of pens and pencils and paint-brushes, an ashtray, empty bottles of water and jointed wooden models for drawing and half-eaten apples and jars of elastic bands and all sorts. He pulled them backwards and forwards and didn't look at me. Shanks was the only grown man I'd met since the attacks started who showed no fear at being alone with one of us girls. I remembered the security guard taking his hand off my shoulder like I was a bomb about to explode. Maybe that means Shanks is the pest. The thought of it sent a stream of bubbles rolling down my spine.

'That's a question, isn't it?' he said, and then stopped. I cringed, bit the inside of my cheeks, and waited.

'No,' he said finally, 'it isn't anything to do with a baby. Not hers or anyone else's. No babies involved. Which, from the look of you, I can see is something of a relief.'

'Yes,' I said, and looked at his hands, not moving the things about in his office anymore, but resting on his knees. There was paint right under his nails, and he hadn't even started the lessons for the day yet. That must mean he never used a nailbrush, or he painted at home, even before breakfast.

I imagined him dipping a paintbrush into the soft yolk of an egg and painting something on a slice of toast. I wondered if he had a wife, or a woman who he lived with. Even the friendly teachers were still a bit mysterious. They ended up knowing loads more about us then we did about them, which wasn't really fair.

'Perhaps, when you do go and see our Chloe,' Shanks said carefully, 'you could let her know, in your own inimitable way, with all the compassion and subtlety of your sex –'

I blushed. I could not believe he had taken me into his back room and just said 'sex' to me like that. Chloe was going to have an absolute fit when I told her.

'— that she can pop her head around the door when she comes back if she fancies a chat, about anything. Or perhaps one of the female teachers, if she'd prefer.'

'Can I go?' I stuttered, not waiting for him to nod before I left the room and hurried, still clutching the damp coat, with my open bag shedding paper and books onto the corridor, to my first class.

There was supposed to be a bus after school at twenty past three which everyone crammed onto. For three years I had been walking slowly and catching the bus at three forty because it wasn't as busy. The day Chloe collapsed outside the school gates and was taken away to hospital the first bus must have been delayed or cancelled because even at a quarter to four, the queue meandered out of the shelter and along the pavement. They were other people from school mainly, not friends, but familiar faces – elbowing each other into the path of oncoming traffic or kicking at crisp packets and dented pop cans.

I'd noticed before that all the same kind of people caught the later bus. It probably wouldn't be obvious to anyone else, but to us, it was clear what that meant. People who don't want to be around other people, either waiting for the bus, or actually in the bus. Because we were together but we didn't want to be together we respected each other's silence and personal space and that was good. There was no pushing and cramming and spitting on other people's coats. No girls with pelmet skirts, thigh-high socks, personal stereos and cigarette-smelling hair, crispy with hairspray. The later bus had a different atmosphere. Once everyone was on we sat quietly and had our seats all to ourselves. No one actually read but there was the feeling that we could if we wanted to.

That day there were at least thirty people hanging around and more sitting on the low wall in front of the Spar shop. I was lost in my own thoughts – puzzling over what my next move should be when it came to Emma and Chloe and wondering what was wrong with her. When I saw the queue I walked right past – didn't even think about it, didn't pause for a second. I pulled the sleeves of my coat over my hands and no one paid any attention to me. It was just as easy to walk into town and get the bus from there. Could walk all the way home, if it came down to it – and the burning up of calories would probably do me good.

I stopped in front of the Spar and felt the coins inside my pocket, just to make sure I had enough for a can of Coke before I walked in. There was a sign stuck to the inside of the glass of the front door and it said, in black capital letters, that only one child was allowed inside at any one time.

I was looking through the window to see if there was anyone else – anyone in school uniform that is – still in there when I noticed another poster, with Wilson's face right bang in the middle of it, and some writing underneath.

I think my body knew what that poster was about before my brain did. Even before I was conscious of what the writing said I felt the blood going out of my face and my hands jump up to my stomach on their own as if I was expecting to be hit. I had to go and sit on the bench over the road from the bus stop and look at the toes of my shoes for a while. Deep breaths, and ducking my head so the cold zip of my coat rested under my chin. And once I was calm, I was unsure, and convinced that I was getting carried away with myself and making it all up.

I walked back slowly in front of all those people who were still not paying any attention to me. The bus hadn't come yet, and I stood there for longer, pretending that I was waiting for it, but drifting back towards the shop just so I could have another look, read it properly and make sure. The second time I was there outside the door the man behind the counter waved his hand at me angrily as if I was looking for something to steal. I walked away quickly in case he remembered my face.

It was no good though. Running away from the shop wasn't going to get rid of what I had just seen, and I wouldn't be able to forget it either. From the shop and the bus stop the road dropped downwards and as I walked along the pavement my perspective changed and I got a clear view, right the way down the hill to the bridge over the river at the bottom, then along the flat bit past the allotments and into town. It was almost twilight and the street lights were slowly coming on pink: they looked like lollies all along the road, and I saw, very clearly, that there were more posters taped to every single lamppost the whole way along – on both sides. I was going to have to pass at least ten or fifteen of them. More if they went on into town and in the bus station.

And they will do, I thought, because it was Wilson's mum and dad that had made the posters. They won't have stopped at just a few up on lampposts in the suburbs. The town centre is going to be plastered with them and wherever I go I'm going to have to look at his face, or at least, the most recent picture of him blown up and taking up almost all of the space on the paper. I can't believe I hadn't noticed them before. I'd been so obsessed with Chloe and her New Year's Eve party that I'd hardly left the house between Boxing Day and the start of school. My last trip into town had been to return the perfume with Barbara and Donald, and Donald had been such a handful and the whole trip so humiliating I'd hardly raised my head to look at anything. Barbara was right: I really did walk around with my head stuck up my jumper sometimes.

The most recent picture must have been taken on Christmas Day, because Wilson was wearing a red paper party hat out of a cracker, slightly askew on his head. He looked surprised, caught in a laugh or a shout, with watery eyes and an open mouth, curved in an expression that was extraordinarily happy and oblivious to the fact that his gappy teeth were on display and his face was shiny with sweat. There were other things that I hadn't noticed before, mainly how fine his hair was, how it fell limply over his forehead and receded at the temples, that there were lines around the corners of his eyes.

Wilson was much older than I'd thought when I met him. But what should that matter? His mum and dad weren't entering him for a beautiful baby contest – they'd chosen a picture they had on hand, showing not only his face, but the reason for their worry and his vulnerability, which were the same thing. And they'd put the picture on a poster and printed out hundreds of copies and spent hours and hours sticking them up all over the place like he was a priceless, irreplaceable pedigree dog that they'd lost and promised a reward to get back.

I tore one of the posters from a lamppost, screwed it into my pocket, and ran. It was still icy outside: each day seemed to be a little colder than the last and the ground was treacherous. I turned my ankle on a frozen puddle, fell, and when I did get home I came through the back door limping. It was dark outside.

14

Barbara was standing at the cooker with her lips pursed at a spoon. The kitchen was roasting: the windows running with condensation and the net curtain sticking to them. The television was on in the front room and turned up loud with the doors open so she could listen to it while she was cooking. Terry, of course, running a phone-in about the proposed curfew – should the City still go ahead with its plans to keep us in after eight o'clock, seeing as it looked like the pest had stopped for the winter?

'Mum?'

She laid the spoon down on a saucer and looked at me, eyebrows raised. Before she could speak to me and tell me to do anything, I told her Chloe was in hospital.

'I need to go and see her. I want to talk to her and see if she's all right. Can I have some money for a bus?'

'Can I have some money for a bus, what?'

'Please. Please can I have some money for the bus to go and see Chloe. She's in the hospital.'

'What's wrong with her? Where have you been?'

'I don't know exactly,' I said.

Barbara turned the radio down.

'You don't know what's wrong with Chloe, or you don't know where you've been?' she said, and went back to the pot.

'I missed the bus,' I said.

Barbara paused. 'So, if you didn't get the bus, you still have your bus fare. If you still have your bus fare, you don't need more money to go to the hospital.'

'It's miles!'

'Enough, and take your coat off. Hang it up – *properly*. There's a nasty bug going about. She won't want company if she's got that.'

Despite the commands, the stirring, the checking of the new coat and homework diary and the tutting about the scuffed shoes from my fall, Barbara seemed to be in an unusually good mood. She had on her best apron, which was dark in patches from the washing-up water, and her face was flushed. I didn't need to ask why she was so happy, because she was itching to tell me herself.

'I saw that Terry Best today,' Barbara said when I came back into the kitchen after getting changed. She was smiling and stirring so vigorously her shoulders shook. Her cheeks were red, her hair crinkled with the steam.

'Great,' I said.

'I popped into the garage on the way back from town for your father's papers and a bottle of milk,' she went on, 'and there he was – larger than life. Pink shirt –' she stirred the air over her head with her fingers, 'that hair. Do you think it's all his?'

'I just need a bit of money for the bus,' I said, 'so I can go and see her.'

'Hmm,' Barbara said. I bit my lip. It looked like she was weighing it up.

'Do you know what he was doing?' she said.

'Who?'

'Terry.' She dropped the spoon into the sink and started to open and close cupboards, bringing out plates and setting the table. 'That's your problem, Lola. You've no natural curiosity. You don't care about anything unless it's spelled out to you, letters six foot high and two inches away from your nose. Have you put your shoes away?'

'Yes, I've put them away.'

'I'll check. He was asking the man behind the counter if he

140

could buy fifty pee's worth of petrol,' she said triumphantly. 'There, isn't that funny?'

'Hilarious.'

'I didn't even know you could do that,' she said, and put the plates in the oven to warm up. 'Still, your father likes to put the petrol in the car. He says if I get to drive, he gets to do the fuelling.'

I interrupted her. 'Can I go? I need two pounds, that's it.'

'What happened to your Christmas money?'

I shrugged, and didn't want to tell her I was saving it for Chloe's prescription charge. 'That's my *own* money,' I said, and Barbara tutted, tucked a tea-towel into the oven handle to dry, and looked at me.

'I'm not sure I want you going out that far on your own at night,' she said. 'It's dark. And anyway, you'd think –' She went to the bottom of the stairs, shouted my father's name at the top of her voice, and then used the broom she kept there to bang on the ceiling a couple of times.

'What? You'd think what?' I said.

'You'd think on his wages, he'd be able to afford more than fifty pee's worth.' She shook her head, and pointed through to the front room with a pot-scourer. 'It isn't safe for you to be out wandering the streets.'

'He's stopped, hasn't he?'

'For the time being, perhaps. But no one's been caught.'

'If you give me the money,' I said, 'I can get a taxi back.'

Barbara shook her head. She'd already decided. 'Hanging about near the taxi rank after dark is even worse,' she said. 'I can't let you do that, I'm afraid. Much too dangerous. You know, when I was your age some man offered my brother a bag of Everton mints to drop his trousers for half a minute. Didn't lay a hand on him, just wanted to have a look. He came back with the paper bag, pleased as punch, and my father took his belt to him.'

'Was it a taxi driver?' I muttered.

'That isn't the point, and you'll get nowhere being clever about it. I've said no, and that's that.'

She went to the stairs and shouted again, but there was no sign that Donald had heard, or was planning to come down for his tea.

'I really need to see her,' I said. That was a mistake. If you sounded like you really, really wanted something, it let her know it was something worth withholding – something to discipline you with.

'We'll see how things go tonight,' Barbara said, turning back to her pans, 'and maybe you can go tomorrow. Why don't you make her a nice card?'

I had excuses prepared – something about important home-work that she needed to have, or the coursework handing-in dates. I was going to tell her that Chloe's mother would prob-ably give me a lift home but I gave up then and when I went upstairs I let the door slam. If I wasn't going to be allowed to go anyway, there wasn't any point in me tiptoeing around.

Donald was sitting in his blue chair with a stack of papers on his knee. I could see him through the crack in the door, and because it was ajar, it was all right to go in. He acted surprised when he looked up and saw me, as if he'd been asleep. I wondered what the pair of them did all day when I was out at school – if they even spoke to each other at all without me being there to carry messages up the stairs.

'Mum says tea's nearly ready,' I said.

'What was all that about down there? Banging?'

'Nothing.'

I huffed and perched on the edge of his table. It wasn't really a desk, though he used it as one. It was the old folding table we used to eat off in the kitchen while he and Barbara were saving up for a proper one. There were scuff marks on the white Formica top and a brown ring from a hot pan left carelessly. Now it was filled with jam jars stuffed with buttons and paper clips and the pebbles Donald picked up on his walks. An old toast rack stuffed with newspapers and magazines. Stacks of hardback books with strips of torn paper hanging out of them to mark important passages he wanted to copy out later. Strange graphs and diagrams that he'd drawn with such force the paper was torn in places and the impression scored onto the surface of the table so deep that if you wanted, you could close your eyes and get the drift of Donald's thinking through your fingertips.

'Chloe's not well and she's gone to hospital and Barbara won't give me the money to get the bus and go and see her.'

Donald didn't shake his head or look concerned and get me to tell him what was wrong with Chloe. He acted like he hadn't heard me at all.

'Do you know what I found out today?' he said softly. He reached down the side of his chair, picked up a small green drinking glass and took a sip.

'Terry Best buys petrol in tiny amounts,' I said. 'My Uncle Ron dropped his pants for a few toffees. I don't know.'

Donald laughed, as if what I'd said was the height of wit.

'I never knew that about Ronald,' he said, 'but I'm not shocked about it, no I'm not. He looks like he lives at the mercy of his sweet tooth.'

I sighed. Donald had got round me. Making fun of him was like making fun of Wilson. It was easy enough to do, but you only ended up making yourself feel bad. Uncle Ron was a fairer target – bloated, angrier and more opinionated than Barbara, and apt to go missing for months at a time, turning up once or twice a year for a meal and a loan of some money. Barbara always gave him whatever she had on her, and it made me glad I didn't have any siblings.

'What did you find out?' I said, and went to sit on the arm of the chair.

'I was doing some more preparation for the *Sea Eye* application,' Donald said. 'I'm close to finishing, so you'd better root out a suitcase for me, but I've had a brainwave. I thought I'd better add a few lines – maybe even a whole page, on why I'd be a suitable passenger.'

I opened my mouth to say something, but I couldn't think of any response, so I kept quiet.

'They do it with astronauts. Psychological evaluations. No point sending someone up there who's claustrophobic, is there?'

'I suppose not.'

'Well, I thought I might as well put something in about not being afraid of the water. Not being scared of drowning. Just to reassure them that if they did pick me, that wouldn't be a limiting factor. Save them wasting their time on the head-doctors.'

'You can't swim,' I said, and then bit my lip, hating that I sounded like Barbara.

'I won't be swimming down there,' Donald said, settling back into his chair and resting the glass on top of the papers on his knee. 'If all goes according to plan, I won't even be getting wet. And if anything did go wrong with the submersible, and there was, say, a hull breach,' he was watching me carefully, checking to see if I looked worried or not, 'then I wouldn't drown, either.'

'How do you work that out?' I say, imagining a zeppelin-shaped metal box under the water, a tear in the side, and water pouring in.

'The pressure,' he said simply, 'the water would rush in at such high pressure it would be more like a blade than a spray. Cut you into slices before you knew anything about it.'

'That's disgusting.'

'I find it quite a comforting thought, actually, don't you?' He didn't wait for me to reply. 'Much rather go like that, doing something interesting, than with some nurse banging on my chest and struggling to get my false teeth out.'

'Dad!'

'You're worried,' he said abruptly, and I knew we weren't talking about the *Sea Eye*.

'She's not that ill,' I said, 'but there was something I wanted to talk to her about. I wanted to do it today.'

'So it can't wait then?'

'No, not really.'

'I see. And nothing you'd trust me to help you out with? Or should I not ask? Between girls only?'

'Something like that.'

Donald hmmed. He tidied his papers up slowly and put them on the floor next to his chair. He heaved himself up. I was almost as tall as him, and with the two of us standing, the box room became tiny and I could smell glue and old books and the tea on his breath. His slippers were trodden flat on the heel.

'It's nothing bad. I'm not in trouble. Neither of us are.'

Donald didn't say anything. He was pulling out drawers and turning over the contents carefully. Hairbrushes, a Care Bears video I thought had been thrown away long ago. Some of my baby clothes, stained headscarves and threadbare gloves that Barbara had tried to give to charity, boxes of Lemsips, shoelaces, train tickets, chalk. I saw him bring out an old Stork tub, the writing on it faded and the lid held on by an elastic band. He held it in front of him.

'You know they've not caught that man,' he said.

'Mum said.'

'The last one was only fifteen. Christmas Eve! Her family won't have had much fun this year,' he said.

'I'll be careful.'

'I bet she was being careful, too,' he said quietly. He was still holding the tub and rubbing his fingers over the top of it absently. 'Someone needs to do something about it. A plan. A strategy.'

'The school are saying they're going to put on extra buses, so no one needs to walk home. They were going to do it just for the girls, but Danny Towers's mum said that was sexist, and if they were doing it for one, they'd have to do it for all.'

'It's the girls he's after though, isn't it?'

'The pretty ones,' I said. 'I'm in no danger.'

Donald smiled, put down the tub and came towards me. I thought he was going to touch my hair, pat my arm, but at the last minute he let his hand drop to the side.

'I've got an idea. Something to sort all this out. I need to get my application finished, collect a final piece of evidence, get it typed up and sent off. Once I'm on that vessel—'

I remembered then what Barbara had told me in the shopping centre the time that he'd gone missing.

'You know, Dad, you might not win. They'll get loads of applications.'

'It isn't a lottery, sweetheart. They're looking for quality. And once I'm on that vessel, working alongside the scientists, the biologists, the oceanographers – I'll be able to tell them my idea. That's why I need your help. Think of yourself as a kind of research assistant.'

I liked the sound of that. And I thought again about what Barbara had said about encouragement, and then shrugged it off. Barbara was paranoid and she took the fun out of everything. Donald's interests weren't doing him or anyone else any harm. And if I could get a little something out of it myself, who was that hurting?

'Assistants get paid,' I said, and Donald went back, picked up his tub.

'The good ones do,' he said, slipped the rubber band aside and opened it. 'If I knew,' he said, pulling out a folded ten-pound note, 'all the ins and outs of it, the full situation, would I,' he put the money on the table next to where I was sitting, 'help you out?'

'I don't know,' I said, and I put my hand over it.

'It's for a taxi,' he said, 'I don't want you messing about waiting for a bus.'

'All right,' I said. Ten pounds was a fortune. There was no way I was going to waste it on a taxi.

'I mean it,' he said – trying to sound like Barbara.

'Yes.' I smiled. 'And I promise I'll take your library books back tomorrow.'

'And I have the draft application. It needs typing.'

'I can do that at school. Put it under my door and I'll take it in with me. Okay?'

We shook hands on it, Donald and I. He looked solemn and Barbara banged on the kitchen ceiling with the broom, making the boards under our feet vibrate.

15

After Donald had given me the money I ate tea with him and Barbara: grey mashed potatoes and tinned peas with a Fray Bentos steak and kidney pie. The brown salty gravy had spilled down the sides of the tin to burn on the bottom of the oven and it made the kitchen stink. I ate quickly, the ten-pound note tucked into my sleeve. While Barbara was washing up, I lifted my coat from the hooks in the hall and snuck out the back.

The streets were empty – partly because of the ice which was thickening on the streets day by day and causing hundreds of minor bumps and slips across the City. And partly because of the flasher, of course. I don't think anyone really believed that he'd stopped for good. We were holding our breaths, especially us girls.

The bus dropped me outside the hospital and no one spoke to me as I hurried through the corridors looking for Chloe's ward. I was going in prepared with the advert for the Brook Advisory Centre and the poster with Wilson's face on it. I had my action plan sorted out in my head. I was going to find out if she still needed an appointment at the clinic – and offer to arrange it all for her if she did. And I was going to show her the poster.

Carl had chased Wilson into the woods and then he'd gone missing. It looked fishy and it was down to us to tell the police, even if that meant she couldn't see him anymore. And once Carl was out of the picture, things would go back to normal between us. Although I wasn't going to come right out and say it like that, I reminded myself.

When I'd found the right bay, Chloe's bed was obvious. There were four pink heart-shaped helium balloons tied to the end of it. There were three other beds in the bay, each one stuffed with a crunched-up, colourless geriatric and surrounded by a batch of visitors. I knew without having to ask that Chloe had refused to go into the children's ward.

Nathan was sitting on the edge of her bed and scrutinising marks on a chart. He was wearing a green V-neck jumper over a blue shirt. Amanda sat in a plastic chair slowly turning the pages of a magazine. I couldn't see Chloe because Amanda's chair was in the way, but I could see her feet – two lumps under the waffle blanket.

'Oh, it's Laura come to see you. Look, it's Laura!'

Amanda always said everything as if she was announcing the Second Coming. It must have been exhausting to be so constantly enthusiastic. Nathan looked up from the chart, and then back to it. Chloe was wearing light pink pyjamas and had her hair tied up neatly. She was leaning back on five overstuffed white pillows – so white they made her skin look sallow. But really, she looked fine. Tired, but fine.

'Hey,' I said, but she only rolled her eyes at me, and out of habit, I rolled mine back. There was a pink and silver *Point Romance* book face down on her lap. She picked it up, closed it and shoved it into her bedside locker.

'Sit down, why don't you?' she said, but there wasn't a chair.

Amanda jumped up. 'You go, go on,' she said, and made Nathan go and get another chair. She directed him with one hand, and with the other she opened the second layer of a box of chocolates so I could have the other strawberry creme. The bags under her eyes were purple: being Chloe's mother must have been exhausting too.

'You help yourself, sweetheart. I know you like the pink ones, don't you?'

I saw straight away there was no way I was going to be able

to talk to Chloe on her own, and I folded the poster, which I'd been carrying in my hands the whole time, over and over into a triangle. When I couldn't get it any smaller, I put it in my back pocket. I crushed the chocolate against the roof of my mouth with my tongue. It shattered and the greasy strawberry filling covered my teeth. It tasted like Calpol.

If it had been me in the bed, Chloe coming to visit and Donald and Barbara cluttering the place up, Chloe would have found a way out of it. She'd have shaken her head and pursed her lips – behaved like an adult – and shooed them off to the cafeteria for a cup of coffee and (winking at Barbara), 'Maybe a smoke?' They'd have both gone, too, swept along by the force of what-ever it was Chloe wanted. I imagined them blinking over coffee they didn't like or want, wondering how they'd got there and what had made them buy it. I glanced at Amanda, arranging white flowers busily in a plastic water jug, and I didn't even try.

'You are funny,' Chloe said, in her grown-up voice. 'Come all the way here and don't say anything?'

'Don't be ungrateful,' Amanda said quickly. 'Laura's come on the bus on her own to come and see you.'

On my own. As if I was six years old and couldn't be trusted with the change for my fare. During all my careful planning and the times I'd rehearsed what I was going to say while I waited for the bus to bring me here *(it's not your fault Carl did some-thing daft – but you can't let him drag you down with him)* I hadn't considered how I was going to approach things with Chloe's mother looking over my shoulder. It was irritating.

'So, are you all right?' I said.

She looked all right. Her parents weren't pissed off with her so she couldn't be pregnant – or if she was, they didn't know about it. The fact she was surrounded by doctors who'd prob-ably take one look at her blonde hair and kohl-rimmed eyes and check for that kind of thing first of all meant that more likely than not, the whole thing had been a false alarm. Or she'd been lying. One or the other. But here she was in hospital all the same. What was wrong with her? I started to think she'd been pretending. Her hair was done nicely. She had pink lip balm on and her pyjamas looked brand new.

'I'm fine,' she said, and smiled at me broadly, 'fine. A bit tired, but all right.'

There was a television on a cabinet at the end of the ward. Another repeat of *The Crystal Maze* was on and Nathan put the chart down and drifted over to watch it.

'She collapsed right in front of the school, did you know?' Amanda said, and put her hand on her chest. 'I've been worrying myself sick. Her father nearly had a heart attack. A *literal* heart attack.'

I nodded. Of course I knew, or I wouldn't be here, I wanted to say.

'Emma helped her. Little angel. Went and got a coat to put under her head, ran to find a teacher. She would have come with you in the ambulance too, if she'd been allowed, wouldn't she, Chloe?'

Chloe smirked. Amanda patted her leg absently.

'She's always had people around, wanting to help her,' she said, 'since she was a baby. It's because you're such a pretty little thing. People think you can't shift for yourself.'

No one was listening to Amanda. I was trying to stare into Chloe's head and invent telepathy using willpower alone. I raised my eyebrows at her and she smiled again, and shrugged slightly.

'Thank God for Emma,' Amanda murmured again, still patting Chloe's feet. 'Who knows what would have happened to you otherwise? Young girl, lying unconscious and vulnerable on the pavement. Doesn't bear thinking about, does it?'

I turned away in frustration and saw the blue light from the television bouncing off the shining dome of Nathan's head.

'I'm sure someone would have come along sooner or later,' I said.

Even if it had been a perv – he wouldn't have done to Chloe anything that she didn't already do with Carl, so it didn't matter, did it? Fucking Emma. Chloe was all right. She was having the time of her life.

'What did the doctor say?' I asked.

Chloe leaned back against her pillows, took her time choosing another chocolate, put her head on one side and sighed.

'An infection,' she said, 'that got out of hand. I'm going home tomorrow.'

She waved her arm at me and I saw the thin white bandage on her wrist and the tube leading to a drip on a stand by the side of her bed.

'It's antibiotics,' she said proudly, 'double strength.'

Someone had hung a small stuffed penguin holding a heart from the top of the drip stand. The heart had blue and white swirly writing on it. *Get Well Soon*. Chloe followed my eye.

'Emma brought that,' she said. 'Cute, isn't it?'

'She's been already?'

She nodded. 'Got a taxi over here straight from school. They weren't going to let her in because she was too early for visiting hours, but she said she was my sister.' Chloe laughed. 'Cheeky cow.'

'You don't faint with infections,' I said.

'I had a fever,' Chloe insisted, but without much energy. 'God, look at my chart, why don't you?'

'It was in the waterworks, right up to the kidneys,' Amanda whispered with impossible enthusiasm, 'you know.'

I thought she meant Chloe had picked something up from drinking the water at school, which wouldn't have surprised me. If you asked for water in the dining room you got it in a little polystyrene cup – we all encouraged each other to break the cups into fragments after we'd used them because it was a certainty that if they were thrown out whole, the dinner ladies would fish them out of the bin and reuse them.

Amanda nodded meaningfully towards Chloe's thighs.

'She means my bladder,' Chloe said loudly, pointing her thumbs at her stomach, 'kidneys, pee-hole – the lot. It was horrendous.' She said 'horrendous' even louder than she'd said 'pee-hole', never taking her eyes off Amanda, and smiling when her mother flinched.

'I just can't understand why you didn't get me to take you to the doctor when it first started,' Amanda said, shook her head at Chloe, and stood up to fiddle with the cards again.

I felt the triangle of the poster poke me through my jeans pocket.

'Don't start,' Chloe said. Amanda opened her mouth – was about, I think, to try some discipline, when Nathan stood up and, with his back still to us, motioned towards the television. *The Crystal Maze* had finished and the news had started.

'Turn it up! See if they've caught that pest!'

Nathan obeyed the warbly voice from across the room, and turned the dial.

Terry appeared on time, waving to cameramen and production assistants as he strutted through the studio before sliding onto the couch and drumming the coffee table in time with the final chime of the theme music, as he always did. Fiona didn't get a walk through – she was always sitting there on the couch waiting for him to arrive. He smiled. His face was pleasingly asymmetrical: one raised eyebrow, one dimple in his cheek. His hair parted on the side and black and matt and luxuriant – dense as an old fur coat.

'That's some tie,' Amanda said breathily.

And it was. Not Santa or reindeer now Twelfth Night was over, but a snowman with black twigs for arms and lumps of coal for eyes and mouth. Terry was the sort of man that appealed to everyone's mother.

'Good evening,' Terry said, 'and welcome to *The City Today* at six o'clock.' His tone was cordial enough, but his smile had faded, which always meant bad news.

'Police reports have been coming through to us all afternoon concerning the recent disappearance of a local man: Daniel Wilson, from the Longton area of the City.'

They put his picture on the screen. Wilson, in his red paper party hat, grinning open-mouthed and missing. Missing since the afternoon of the 26th when he went out for a walk after a late breakfast. Vulnerable adult. No sign. And in this weather.

It was all I could do not to nudge Chloe but her eyes were glued to the screen anyway. *That's what I've been trying to tell you*, I wanted to say.

'While his parents have been postering the City with their son's likeness for the past few days, the police have only now taken up the case. The missing man, after all, is an adult,' Terry said. He leaned back into the couch. This was run of the mill news, hardly connected to his story of the moment, and so of little interest to him. Fiona, as if a switch had been flicked, sparked into life, smiled and picked up the autocue where he'd left off.

'We're running a phone number along the bottom of the screen right now,' she gestured lop-sidedly with her fingers pointing downwards, 'and if you've got any information – anything at all, give us a call and we'll make sure to pass it on to the police. *The City Today* has a long history of harnessing the goodwill of the community to resolve cases like this, don't we, team?'

The camera swung around suddenly to reveal the backside of the studio, where the laminate flooring and cream partitions gave way to chalk-marked black felt and a gaggle of camera men and production staff, in jeans, nodding furiously.

'The police are working on retracing Wilson's steps as he left home that morning and walked across town – and anything you can give us will be helpful. According to his parents, Wilson was a bit of a local legend, wasn't he, Terry?'

'He was a well-known member of his local community,' Terry

said mechanically. 'Despite his obvious challenges he was a keen fisherman and rambler and would often be seen out and about walking through the area. He was especially interested in football, following no particular team but enjoying a kick about in the park most weekends.'

'We're told he was particularly fond of striking up conversations and meeting new people,' Fiona said, 'which means lots of you out there will be familiar with his face. Can we show that photo again?'

The telly was a rubbish one – just a mini-sized colour portable. The picture jumped and fizzed.

'Move the aerial,' Chloe said. Nathan obeyed her. 'It's all your fillings, interfering with the reception.'

I ignored her because with Chloe, the sooner she had the last word, the sooner she'd stop. Nathan pushed the thin hoop of wire backwards and forwards until the picture resolved itself and the crackling stopped.

We settled on her bed. I imagined Wilson, wandering around town and introducing himself, asking questions, trying to be friendly and getting on people's nerves.

And then dropping out of the world as if he'd never existed.

Terry outlined Wilson's last known movements – tracing his appearance on the CCTV cameras that had tracked him on his long walk through the City. They broadcast grainy black and white footage of Wilson standing in front of a petrol station watching a man fill his tyres with air. The camera seemed to loom up on Wilson, its eye catching him in a private moment as he tenderly pulled something out of his pocket, unwrapped it, and started to eat it.

'That,' Terry informed us, 'was a sausage roll left over from the Christmas Night buffet – wrapped in a piece of kitchen roll by Wilson's mother, and very possibly his final meal.'

Chloe snorted with laughter. I started at her. She was engrossed with the pictures on the screen – staring intently. Even though she'd only seen him for a minute it just wasn't possible that she didn't recognise him – didn't she realise that the three of us were probably the last people to see him?

'While the police aren't expressing grave concern just yet, they'd still like to speak with the individuals connected with a,' he used his fingers to scrape a pair of speech marks in the air, '*vigilante gang* seen gathering in the grounds of a nature reserve across town later that afternoon. This group, made up largely of the fathers, uncles and elder brothers of the young girls who've been attacked recently, has vowed to scour the City's dark and out of the way places until this man is found.'

Terry paused meaningfully. Fiona, next to him on the couch, shuffled papers reverently. 'Our phone lines are open,' he added, in a subdued tone.

I was sitting right next to Chloe. Could feel the lump of her knee against the small of my back. I turned my head, tried to catch her eye, but she was pulling a lock of her hair straight and examining it for split ends. When I nudged her, she hissed at me.

'Shut up!'

Chloe laughed. I think it was nerves. When I looked at her, she looked away. Nathan stood up, and there was a chorus of chatter and complaints from the other beds and their visitors. He hunched, like he was making an exit in the cinema before the closing credits had stopped rolling.

'Sorry, sorry,' he said, 'just need to phone work. Tell them when I'm next in.'

'Buy me some pop while you're out there,' Chloe demanded. Amanda looked over her shoulder at Nathan as he left, counting the coins in his palm.

'He won't know what to get,' she said weakly. 'I'd better do it. Won't be two ticks, girls,' she said, her heels clacking on the hard floor as she hurried after him. 'You'll look after her, won't you, sweet?'

I didn't get time to answer before she was gone.

'No fucking way he's ringing work,' Chloe said bitterly. 'Bet you any money he's on the phone to that primary school teacher.' Something occurred to her and she smiled. 'I bet I've ruined his plans. He was supposed to be at a,' she drew a heavy pair of quotation marks in the air, copying Terry, 'health and safety presentation tonight.'

'Chloe, that's that man we saw on Boxing Day,' I said.

'Oh, be quiet,' she said, shaking her head.

'It is,' I said. 'I talked to him. He had a football. It was definitely him.'

'So?' She shrugged.

'What if he's dead? What if we were the last people to see him? Carl chased him off, didn't he? You can't let him—'

'You heard what they said,' she interrupted me. 'He probably ran into those vigilante guys and got duffed up a bit. He'll be too embarrassed to go home.'

'Chloe . . .'

'Not. My. Problem.'

Was it possible? Could it be that Wilson really had run away from Carl straight into that group of men and got himself into trouble that way?

I thought about them, standing around near the camper van in the Asda car park. They were cold, and lazy, and there to get their pictures taken and rant a bit to the journos, and then go home and get a pat on the back from their wives and girlfriends. I bet they'd spent more time on the sign on the side of the van than they had on the actual search. It wasn't likely they'd actually find the flasher, not like Terry was saying.

And if they did find someone, what would they do to him? Rough him up a bit, certainly, but kill him? These were adults Terry was talking about. A community action group he'd endorsed himself. It wasn't possible. But I knew, one way or the other, Wilson had never made it out of those woods. And I knew, and the knowledge was sneaking into my gut like cold water, that it wasn't the group of lazy vigilantes we'd seen in the Asda car park that day who were going to be held responsible – but that it was me, Chloe and Carl.

'We shouldn't have to take the blame for something Carl did,' I said.

Chloe turned her head and looked at me. '*I* never spoke to him. *You* were the one getting cosy with him. *You* were the one that went off into the woods with him.'

'We were looking for his ball.'

Chloe snorted.

'It wasn't like that.'

'He was talking about tits, and jailbait. Course it was like that.'

'Don't be stupid. We've got to say. We saw him last. Carl scared the shit out of him. Look, I've got this poster.' I pulled the hard triangle out of my pocket and started to unfold it but Chloe knocked it out of my hand.

'Take that away,' she said suddenly, 'it's nothing to do with us.'

'If we went to the police now,' I said, 'you'd get to go on the television. We could say, if you like, that you talked to him last instead of me. Then they'd definitely want to interview you. You'd probably get to go on Terry's show.'

I remembered I'd tried this with her once before when I was trying to convince her to report the flasher. She hadn't listened to me then, but it was worth a try. Everyone knew Chloe would love to go on the telly.

'No,' she said.

Chloe continued to inspect the frayed ends of her hair.

'Carl did something to him,' I said. 'I know he's your boyfriend and it's not your fault he's done something daft, but you can't let yourself be dragged down with him.'

'Never mind about Carl,' she said. She started playing with the charm bracelet on her wrist, twisting it around and around, as if she was giving herself a Chinese burn. Charm bracelet. A charmed life.

'You just don't want Nathan and Amanda to know about him,' I said, and huffed, 'that's so selfish.'

'Fuck off,' Chloe said. She helped herself to another soft centre. Her eyelashes were sticky and she was chewing rapidly. 'I told you he was a perv,' she said, and started picking at the raw skin around her fingernails.

'He wasn't,' I insisted.

Chloe laughed and looked away from me. 'They all are,' she said, and shook her head as if the thoughts were cobwebs clinging to her hair.

'He just liked chatting to people.'

She shook her head again. 'He should talk to people his own age,' she said, and rubbed the back of her neck. 'It's weird. Chatting girls up.'

There was something I wanted to say – a thought or a feeling that I couldn't grab onto quick enough. For Wilson, Chloe and me and girls like us were just the right age – the same age that he felt he was. He'd have no more wanted anything to do with girls his own age than we would have wanted to socialise with our fathers' friends. But the idea was foggy so I said nothing, and Chloe took it for agreement.

'I bet he was watching me and Carl in the car,' Chloe said, 'probably having a wank behind a hedge the whole time. He took you off into the bushes, talked about your tits.' She lifted her thumb to her lips and bit. I've seen her tear strips of skin away from the flesh with her teeth, and lick away the blood without flinching. She would never dream of biting her finger-nails and spoiling her nail polish, but she chewed at her skin until her school books were covered with bloody fingerprints.

'No,' I said, 'no. I think we should say something. You're just trying to keep Carl out of trouble. It wasn't like that. He wasn't like that.'

Chloe turned in the bed quickly, and tucked her knees under her. I heard her joints cracking.

'Shut up about Carl!' she said, too loudly. The woman in the bed opposite her stared, put a finger over her mouth and shushed. Chloe smiled back until she had her full attention and then slowly mouthed the the f-word at her.

'I don't know why you're so interested in defending him all of a sudden,' she said. 'Why would you even care? He's nothing to us. Not unless something did go on in the woods . . . eh?' She giggled, and carried on in a low, regular voice that it was impossible to interrupt or ignore. When Chloe gets onto something, she won't let it go.

'Are you *that* desperate for a boyfriend? I knew you were jealous, but I didn't know it was that bad. Shanks not giving you the cheap thrills anymore? I saw you, peeping through the car window to see what me and Carl were up to. Did you tell him to take you into the woods and give you a fingering? Did you like it? Did you get a Mong to pop your cherry and now you're feeling bad about it?'

'All right, girls?' We heard Amanda before we saw her, clicking along the corridor and complimenting the nurses on the Christmas decorations in the ward – 'Very festive!' Before she took her seat beside Chloe, she leaned over the television and changed the channel. Terry had gone out in a crescendo of theme tune and left Fiona listing the schools that were closed due to the bad weather. No one complained.

'Where's Dad?' Chloe said.

'He had to go back to the office. Something there that needed dealing with.' Amanda's eyes were red and it embarrassed me to look at her. 'He said he'd call by tomorrow morning, and he sent his love.'

Chloe looked at me knowingly and laughed.

'He said he'd leave me some money for some more magazines.'

'Did he? Oh, I don't think—'

'Did you get my pop?'

Chloe held her hand out, a little white paw. Amanda put a bottle of fizzy water into it.

'That'll have to do. You know the doctor says you've to lay off it – stick to water until everything's clear.'

Chloe took a deep breath, was about to start – I could see it coming. And something came over me.

'Oh,' I said slowly, 'a urinary tract infection.' Amanda nodded.

'Well, I bet that's a weight off your mind,' I said. 'You were really scared, weren't you?' I turned my back on Chloe. 'She thought she was going to get in all kinds of trouble.'

My hands, still in my lap, were trembling. Too late to stop now though. Amanda was staring at me.

'What do you mean, trouble? She wouldn't get in trouble for getting *ill*,' Amanda said.

'She thought Carl might have given her something,' I said brightly. I remembered the word on the inside of the toilet door, and heard Chloe's teeth grinding.

'Chlamydia. Unwanted pregnancy. Something like that. But an infection, well, that's nothing, is it? Did she get it from Carl, or could she not narrow it down that much?'

I stood up, pulled the collar of my jacket up against my neck and put my chair neatly at the end of the bed.

'Who's Carl?' Amanda said, with a little less enthusiasm, and not looking at me. Chloe went red, and squirmed in the bed, but attached to that drip, she couldn't go anywhere.

'Some lad,' I said, and edged away. 'He's all right. He's got a really nice car.'

'Car?' Amanda said faintly. She reached up and pulled at one of her earrings. I'd forgotten to check, but I noticed them then, twirling under her fingers: black enamelled cats wearing red and white Santa hats and clutching mistletoe above their heads in the end of their tails. The berries on the mistletoe glittered. Glass, or cubic zirconia.

What made me do that? I knew better than anyone else that the game was there to be played – there was no half-time, the rules were set in stone and no one ever, ever got a second chance.

There were two full years of school before I met Chloe. Years when I was bumped and jostled. My bag thrown down the stairwells. The boys did that, and it wasn't too bad. The girls would come up to me, concerned. Touch my arm gently, and smile. Tell me, in a hushed voice, that there was a spot of blood on the back of my skirt and did I know about it. Every day. Sometimes twice a day. You couldn't ignore something like that. It was impossible not to put your hand up, ask to go to the toilet. Slide the bolt closed in the cubicle, pull everything down with trembling hands and check. Then the long slow trip back to the classroom – teachers asking me if I had a gastric condition amid girls' laughter smothered only by the shining curtains of their hair. *Always Maxi* scrawled on in red felt-tip pen, and stuck to the back of my jumper by their adhesive wings.

Two and a half years, then Chloe arrived in my form, transferred from another school.

'It wasn't meeting my needs,' she'd said.

She'd been kicked out. Was on her last chance. There was a spare chair next to me that no one else wanted to sit in. Because it was her first day she didn't know she was supposed to sit somewhere else too. We became friends. Other girls liked her or were scared of her. They started to leave me alone.

Chloe saved me. We had a special bond and she was ruining it, and it was all because of Carl. I thought about him and as I sat on the edge of Chloe's hospital bed with that poster and the stupid Brook leaflet jabbing me through my pocket, Emma's penguin dangling over my head, I snapped.

*

'Where does this Carl live?' Amanda was saying. I might as well have not been there, except Chloe wasn't looking at her mother but leaning forward in the bed and shooting me a boiling look that made me want to leg it.

'Forget it,' Chloe said. 'Just shut up.'

'Chloe,' Amanda wailed, 'your father'll have to hear about this. Just wait until he gets back from his meeting . . .'

Chloe scrabbled at the sheets and it was only the tube attaching her to the drip that stopped her getting out of bed completely and coming for me. I ignored the feeling in my stomach, turned, and ran.

16

When I got out of the hospital it was properly dark. I checked how much money I had left and decided to get to Cuerden on my own and retrace Wilson's path through the woods myself. I knew it was far too dark to be out at night and I was going to have to switch buses at the station and it would take me ages and ages to get there and get home again. I knew that I was going to get a roasting when I got home, but compared to what I knew I had coming from Chloe, a grounding from Barbara was nothing. I was mad enough to feel invincible and I was determined that I was going to find something to implicate Carl in Wilson's disappearance. It shouldn't be too difficult, after all – we were there, weren't we? That was the truth. And Carl chased him off into those woods. All I needed to find (I skipped through hazily remembered plots of *Columbo* in my mind as I paced in the bus shelter) was a dropped cigarette packet. A set of tyre tracks. Something, anything, to prove that he was there even if Chloe was stupid enough to stick up for him and say he wasn't.

When the 125 left the station it was empty. I sat at the back, lit a cigarette and tried to blow smoke rings at my reflection in the window. I thought about Wilson. It would not be nice if he was still there in the woods, if he fell down and hurt himself running away from Carl. I started to feel sick because I was thinking about Wilson lying in the wet plants and leaf-skeletons, lying from Boxing Day afternoon until now, even through New Year's Eve: the night when there are parties everywhere, and fireworks in the sky, and drinking and party poppers and no one was supposed to be on their own. I imagined the creatures that would scuttle out from under the leaves and about his hurt hand hanging onto his new ball and the wrinkly, looking-after hands, waiting for him at home for all this time. I think I might have been enjoying myself, in some horrible way, but I stopped myself as soon as I started trying to imagine his mother.

Most people who run away and go missing are young girls. They were like me. No, they were like Chloe – they have older boyfriends and they go out at night too much. And then someone grabs them and takes them away in a van. Or they are young girls whose parents are too busy drinking and injecting themselves to notice that they haven't been to school but have got on a train and gone to London. Don't notice until their girl has been swallowed up into the grey of the pavements and the big buildings and the all-night clubs of the capital city, hundreds of miles away. I could do it, I thought. That idea, or the smoke, made me dizzy. That is what happens. They hardly put it on the news anymore. What does not happen, I decided, blowing smoke at the corner of the little window, is grown-up men vanishing. Even if they are a bit funny, like a Mong, like Wilson is, going out with their football and then never coming home. Especially at this time of year.

I ran across the car park with my hood up in case anyone else was there. Didn't stop to look at the stoat and the cowslip on the sign. To me, it felt safer in the woods than it was in the car park.

When we were driving here on Boxing Day, Carl told Chloe that people go to this car park in their cars at night to have sex. And sometimes, he said, they leave the lights inside the car on and one of the back windows open so that people can stand about and watch and even put their hands through the window if they feel like it.

'It's called dogging,' he said, and looked over his shoulder at me – he wanted to see if I'd heard and was blushing.

Chloe laughed. 'That's so weird!'

I nearly told Chloe he was just making it up and trying to put ideas in her head. He was obviously trying to acclimatise her for something he was planning on doing to her himself, but as usual, they were in the front so speaking to the backs of their heads would have been pointless. Before I could say anything he had turned the music up loud and revved the engine.

That night there was a car in the car park but it was dark inside and I couldn't see if anyone was in it. I ran past it anyway, leapt over a ridge in the soil, and was in the woods. The moonlight coming through the trees was bluish and faint. I couldn't see my legs because I was wearing jeans, but my white trainers flashed in and out in front of me as I stepped. When I stood still it was absolutely silent until my ears got used to the space and then I could hear cars somewhere far away. And when I moved, the crack of sticks and the rustle of frozen leaves was almost deafening. I tried to tiptoe, but that made it worse.

It was stupid, being there. Stupid being in a dark place on my own at night, even though I had my house keys with me. The keys had a little metal ornament on them that was shaped like an upside-down tear-drop. When the attacks had first started, me and Chloe had scraped the edge of the tear-drop into a point against a wall. I held it in my hand inside my pocket and tested the point against my thumb. It didn't hurt, but I thought if I needed to, I could take someone's eye out with it.

I saw nothing, and as I went on it got darker. The things in the undergrowth that caught my eye, that I thought might be something to do with Carl, turned out to be plastic carrier bags caught against twigs, a curved piece of green and yellow plastic, and hundreds and hundreds of crisp packets. An old chest freezer was there, along with a bike frame and an old buggy and a mattress that someone had tried to set fire to. It all smelled rank and catty, and as I knew these things weren't evidence of anything

I walked right past them to find the path and follow the steps downwards out of the trees and onto the cleared and gravelled walkway that goes around the pond.

In the summer there are ducks and plants and things, and it is a nice place to come and walk about. There used to be loads of ducklings too, but someone got sick of their pet terrapins, released them into the water and, the story goes, every spring the terrapins swim about under the surface and snap the legs off the little birds swimming on the top. I don't know if that's true. I've never seen them.

That night it was frozen solid, just like I'd told Wilson. Like everyone else, I'd made promises to Barbara and Donald that I would never, ever walk on the pond when it was frozen. All our parents made us swear down that we wouldn't do it. Out of the trees it was a bit lighter and I could see stones and cans and big sticks lying on top of the ice. People do it all the time. Throw heavy things onto it as hard as they can. If it doesn't break – if it doesn't crack at all – then it is all right to walk on. Someone had even chucked a hub-cap out there. I could see the grooves where it had skidded across the top. I went around the outside carefully, not looking for anything anymore, but shivering and stamping my feet against the sparkle of frost growing on the path. The metal poles with the signs on had scales of ice on them and I remembered the boy who licked one of them to see if his tongue would stick, for a dare.

It was freezing. More freezing there than it was even in the woods, because the wind was skating across the frozen lid of the water and making my hair fly about and slap my ears. I tucked it all into the back of my hood and walked on. There was a lump in the ice – a disturbance in the flat surface. I walked fast to get to it, squinting to see, and not wanting to look at the same time. My teeth were chattering. It was too cold to hang about here and it was too cold a fortnight ago, and he might have been a bit soft, but if he could have, he would have gone home, or got on a bus, or tried to find a cafe or something when he got cold, and before it got dark, even if Carl had really, really scared him.

There used to be a wooden jetty thing poking out from the path and onto the water. There was a railing around it, to show it wasn't for boats. It wasn't for anything, except walking out over the water right into the middle of the pond. But people were using it for the banned things: feeding the ducks and fishing. And in the summer people used to jump off the end to go swimming. The water at the edge of the pond was too full of reeds and bread and floating carrier bags and pop bottles to wade through, but if you jumped off the edge of the wooden platform you got in where the water was clear. And they took it away – because of the fish and the bread and the jumping – the thinking being that it was only a matter of time before someone took a stupid dive and cracked their head open on the concrete bottom.

Some of the posts were still there though, and they were sticking out of the top of the ice like trees that had been lopped off before the branches started. The lump in the ice was between the two poles furthest away from the edge. I got as close to where the ice started as I could without stepping on it, and looked. If I'd have been braver, I would have walked out on the ice, or stood on the flat tops of the old wooden poles and used them like stepping stones to get to the middle of the water. I wasn't that brave. I just leaned forward, and squinted against the wind, and stared at it a bit until the shape resolved itself into an object.

It was a football. Half a football, really. The other half was under the water, and the skin of the ice had frozen around it and locked it into place. My heart started to rattle. I remembered Wilson's new Christmas football and I made myself think about the park-keeper or the nature warden or whatever he was called – the man who hauls the bike frames and shopping trolleys out of the pond with a rope, the man who takes the primary school kids around on the stoat and cowslip walks. He'll have put it in there so he can pull it out later and leave an air hole for the fish. It would make sense to use a football rather than a ping-pong ball or a tennis ball, because this pond is much bigger than most people's garden ponds – it's a lake really – and would have more fish in it, and the fish would need more air, and so there would need to be a bigger hole.

All true facts.

And I heard my own voice, telling Wilson about ice skating on the lake. Recommending it, saying that what his parents didn't know wouldn't hurt him. I could call up the picture as easy as anything – Wilson blundering through the woods while Carl called through the trees behind him. Crashing through the undergrowth, branches snapping and sounding like gunshot. He'd have been scared – wanting to get away fast. And when he came out between the trees and saw the pond in front of him, its surface as flat as a pavement, it would have made sense for him to dash right across it rather than wasting time following the path around it. The shortest distance between two parallel points.

Carl was only chasing him, after all. It was me who'd told him it was safe to walk on the ice. My fault.

I turned away from the lake and ran off in the opposite direction to the one I'd come in. I slipped on the frosty path, and lurched into the woods again, running through the dark with sticks hitting me in the face and leaves sparkling and sliding under the heels of my trainers.

When I got onto the main road the cold air was burning my lungs and I pulled my phone out of my pocket and tried to call Chloe. The call went right through to the answer machine. She probably wasn't allowed to have it with her in the hospital, or she'd turned it off and put it under her mattress because she didn't want her parents to find it. I guessed at the time, checked a bus timetable and finally gave up and telephoned Carl.

He answered right away. I could hear loud music, someone laughing.

'Carl,' I said, and I was still panting. Probably sounded to him like one of those dirty hoax callers.

'What's up?' he said, in his funny, bored voice. 'What are you calling me for, little girl?'

I felt humiliated and angry. This whole adventure had been to get him into trouble and show Chloe how much better off she'd be without him. Instead, all I'd done was find out that I was probably responsible for something terrible happening myself. And Carl was the only one I could rely on to pick me up and tell me what to do.

'Where are you? I need you to come and get me.'

'I can't hear what you're saying. What is it?'

His friends were with him. I could hear the sound of the car engine revving too, and imagined him doing handbrake turns in a supermarket car park, taking his hand off the wheel to make an opening and closing beak in the air. I swallowed, tried to think clearly.

'Hurry up, I've got another call waiting.' I heard him chewing on something, the sound of his mouth working against the handset. 'Lola? What are you after?'

'Chloe's ill,' I said at last, 'she's in hospital. You've got to come and meet me right now.'

'What is it?' he said, more seriously. The music faded.

'I'm at Cuerden,' I said. 'Come right now. I need a lift.'

'*Cuerden*? What are you doing *there*?'

Carl sounded scared. The music in the background stopped abruptly.

'Just come quick, will you? I'm fucking freezing.'

I hung up, went and sat on the bench, and crossed my fingers.

Chloe normally managed to get Carl to do what she wanted, so he must be quite stupid.

He arrived fifteen minutes later and shoved the passenger side door open while he was still pulling into the kerb.

'What's up with Chloe?' Carl said. 'Has she done something to herself?'

'No,' I said.

'I was supposed to be meeting her tonight,' he looked at his watch, 'after her mum and dad go to sleep. Is Emma with you?'

'No!' I said. 'Chloe's in the hospital, she can't meet you.'

'What's she done?'

'She thought she might be pregnant, but it's all right, she isn't,' I said.

Carl shook his head, and laughed quietly. 'Silly cow. She turned up at the hospital for that?'

He pulled out and started to drive back towards the city centre.

'It wasn't that, nothing to do with that. It was something else,' I said quickly. 'I don't know what exactly. An infection.'

Carl didn't say anything – as if Chloe being ill was my fault.

'She's going home tomorrow morning. It wasn't anything serious.'

I tried laughing but in the car it sounded really fake and it made me cringe. 'You know what she's like,' I said, and swallowed hard.

'Did she tell anyone about it? Did she tell anyone about me?'

'I don't know what you mean,' I said.

Chloe was probably explaining all about Carl to Amanda and Nathan right now. Still, there was no need to tell him that. The lights on the dashboard were blinking green and red and I wanted to find out which ones belonged to the heater, but I didn't dare. I pushed my feet against the bottom of the car. A crisp packet crackled loudly and I lifted my bum off the seat to get the poster out of my pocket to show to him.

'Does anyone know you called me?' Carl said, and jerked

his hand out to adjust the heating. He talked too loudly –
almost shouting. That, and his elbow jabbing me as he twisted
the dial made me jump and drop the folded paper. It dropped
between my knees, down into the dark and I bent over to get
it.

'I want to show you,' I said, and I was struggling and unfas-
tening my seatbelt. 'I want you to look at this. It's that boy who
we saw on Boxing Day.'

I straightened up and offered him the paper, still folded and
warm from my back pocket, but he knocked my arm away as
he turned the steering wheel to navigate a roundabout.

I didn't think much of Carl but he was a grown-up, and yet
somehow one of us too. He was moody and unpredictable and
he said really horrible things to me sometimes, but when we'd
all had a drink he'd put his arms around mine and Chloe's shoulders and say we were 'his girls'. Of all the people I knew, Carl
was someone who knew what to do with a secret – especially
one that might get you into trouble.

'Who else did she tell?' We stopped jerkily at a set of traffic
lights. 'Stop waving that paper about and answer me.'

He did shout then, and lift home or not, I put my hand on
the door handle.

'How would I know? You don't have to be such an arsehole,
Carl. You're not *my* boyfriend.'

There were a few moments of silence, during which I cried
a little. Carl didn't reach out a hand and touch me, or pat my
back or anything like that. He smiled. I could smell fags and
something spicy on his breath or in his clothes. His face was
pale and it looked blue in the dark.

It's never properly dark, not in cities. The streetlamps and
shop windows throw their light up into the air in a hundred
thousand pinpricks that stain the night green and yellow.

The lights changed and we started moving again. He turned
off the main road before he should have, and in a few minutes

he'd parked under the arches of the bridge that goes over the Ribble.

'I'll take you home in a bit.'

He waited for me to stop crying and after a few minutes lit a cigarette, lit a second one from the glowing tip of the first, tapped my shoulder and made me take it.

'Talk,' he said, 'slowly.'

I gulped at the smoke, burning my throat and swallowing back a cough so he wouldn't laugh at me.

'I've done something,' I said, 'I've done something terrible. I've got to go to the police. I'm going to get locked up.'

I was still finding it hard to get myself under control. I carried on sucking at the cigarette and the car slowly filled with smoke. Carl used his thumb and his first finger to rub his eyebrows.

'For God's sake. Show me your bit of paper, then,' he said.

I wanted to go home. Even if it did mean getting a taxi and hoping it was Donald and not Barbara up to pay for it when I got back. But this was important. It was about Wilson, not me. I was going to do the right thing even if Carl did shout at me and behave like a prick – which was nothing unusual or surprising because he was always like that to me, and even worse to Chloe.

Carl had his hand out. The ends of his fingers were as wide as his knuckles and his nails were chewed short. I gave him the paper and didn't talk, let him have some peace to look at it. Carl's lips moved as he read and when he'd finished with it, he folded it up along its creases like it was a map.

'I heard about that,' he said. He put his hands on the steering wheel as if the car was moving and we were driving somewhere, flexing and unflexing his elbows. 'It's been on the telly.'

'It's that boy we met on Boxing Day,' I said, 'the one you chased away.'

I tried not to sound accusing, but it came out like that anyway.

'No, it isn't,' Carl said, 'it's just some Mong. They all look like that.'

'It's him,' I said, 'he told me his name.'

'I forgot you talked to him,' Carl said. He didn't say anything else for a long time.

'Yes,' I said, 'I talked to him and we were chatting about the pond, and the ice – the frozen top. You know how at our school we all go out there, and skid across it and that?'

Carl didn't reply. I caught myself chewing my hair, and I tucked it behind my ears and felt the soggy end of it stick to my cheek.

'I told him to go out on the ice – just for a laugh. I thought he might like it. And then you chased him off – and he was probably scared – you said you were going to batter him, and so he ran right out onto the pond and,' I gulped again, and Carl motioned for me to put the cigarette out in an empty Coke tin he was holding between his thighs, 'he went through. His ball is there, right in the top of the ice. Frozen in. I saw it.'

For a long while, Carl didn't say anything. I wondered what he was thinking. He might have been coming up with a plan.

'What were you doing poking about in the bushes anyway? This time of night?'

I shrugged and Carl seemed to accept it.

'I think we should go and explain,' I said. 'I think we should ring the number on the poster.'

'We? Nah,' he said, and laughed. He moved his face nearer to mine and I could see the wet of his eyeballs and the gleam of the gold chain he wore around his neck. I followed it with my eyes down to where it disappeared into his tee-shirt. Chloe told me that he never took it off, even when he was in the bath. Like she'd know.

'But this is important,' I said, and I heard myself in the dim hollow of the car, whining over the hum of the heater, even though when I formed the words in my mind I wanted them to sound reasonable.

'Oh, I know it is,' Carl said, and instead of moving back away

174

from me he came in even closer until his arm was pressed against mine. He was holding onto the edge of my seat. The car was getting hotter and the warm air was hitting me in the face, blowing my fringe about, and I wanted to rub my eyes, which felt sticky, but I kept my hands still.

'You've done a daft thing,' he said, and I nodded, 'but it isn't like you meant it. Isn't like you pushed him out there with your bare hands, is it? You never touched him.'

I started to tell him again about the football and what it meant, but Carl brushed my lips with fingers that smelled like fags and curry, and I stopped talking.

'I know you're not like Chloe,' Carl said, and touched my hand. 'She can be a bit . . . overdramatic. It's her age. You're much more sensible though.'

'Sensible. Thanks. Great.'

'I didn't mean it like that. I mean,' he paused, 'you think things through before you dive in. You're careful not to get yourself into a mess you won't be able to talk your way out of.' He smiled at me.

'We need to tell them,' I said, 'because if they find out from someone else it'll look like we were trying to hide something.'

'No one saw us with him, so who's going to tell?' said Carl. 'The way I see it, there's no point involving ourselves if we don't have to.'

'But—'

'It was dead. Everyone was tucked up in the house sleeping off their Chrimbo dinners.'

'There were those guys near Asda. The vigilantes?'

Carl sighed with exaggerated patience. 'So say someone did see us? Goes to the police, gives them our description? It's a no-goer. You were at Chloe's house. She was at your house. I was nowhere near. It's all worked out, isn't it?'

I nodded slowly.

'But I've no way of proving it,' Carl said easily, 'and when I come to think of it – Chloe doesn't either. And neither do you, if we're going to split hairs,' he smiled at me, 'but even that doesn't have to be a problem. Look. Say the police came around to your house tonight. Say you turned the corner and there they were, outside the house. You go in and there's two of them sitting on your mother's suite, and they've come that sudden she hasn't even been able to clear your father away.'

He stopped to let me picture it, and I did.

'So you go in there, and they ask what you were up to on such and such a day. Where did you go? Who were you with? Who did you talk to? Normally, you might get away with saying that you can't remember. But this is Boxing Day that they're asking about. Everyone knows what they were up to on Boxing Day. You see what I mean?'

'Yeah, but—'

He interrupted me. 'You can get your mum to swear you were in the house with her all day and all night. She's got to say it straight out, without even looking at you. They'll dig into it. She'll have to be ready to name the television programmes you watched, tell them what you had for tea, what time you went to bed, whether you got up for a piss in the night. Do you think your mum would do that for you?' He didn't wait for me to answer. 'Mine would,' he said, 'which is why I'm not worried.'

The idea of Barbara lying to anyone at all (*the truth hurts, does it?*) was unimaginable: the police, even less. Barbara took cups of tea out to the traffic wardens checking the residents' permits on our street. She wasn't like Carl's mum. She was respectable. What would Amanda say? Chloe always managed to get her own way. She'd think of something.

'No one's going to find out,' Carl said, waving his hand lazily in an arc. 'You don't need to worry about that Mong. He's not going to be telling anyone your name, is he? Not if you're right about what's happened.' His hand flopped down onto my knee and perched there for a second before squeezing then moving on through the air. 'About what *you* made happen.'

'I thought you said it wasn't my fault. That I never touched him?'

'Don't get worked up. Figure of speech,' he paused, 'but it wasn't me telling him to go skating, was it?'

I wound down the window, threw out the cigarette. Carl offered me another and I shook my head.

'Who else have you told? How long have you been worrying about this?'

'All day,' I admitted. I didn't tell him that less than three hours before I was trying to convince Chloe to call the police and have him taken away. Of course I didn't. But the guilt was drifting off me like a smell.

'Chloe's been – under the weather, out of action – this isn't the sort of thing you'd tell your parents about, so,' his hand bumped my knee again, 'it probably seems more important than it actually is, because you've been thinking about it so much with no one to talk to. Did you know twenty people go missing every day?'

I shook my head and tried to imagine them – twenty people out of assembly disappearing – just popping out of existence and leaving nothing behind but gaps in the crowd. Soon, I thought, there weren't going to be any people left.

'Most of them come back,' Carl said. 'They don't bother putting it on the news. If they did, they wouldn't have time for anything else. If you're wrong about what happened, and this Wilson does turn up after a few days, then you've not got nothing to worry about. We didn't do anything. Just a bit of banter. Nothing nasty in it, was there?'

I wasn't listening then. I was looking at his hand on the edge of his seat, creeping towards my knee. I was noticing the way he had loosened his seatbelt and edged so far towards me that the handbrake was jabbing into the side of his thigh.

I didn't even know he liked me like that.

'I'm not going to try and get one over on you,' Carl said. 'I think we both know you're cleverer than Chloe gives you credit for. I don't need to "handle" you like I have to with her. No hysterics.'

I felt pleased. My heart was beating in my throat and I didn't think about what Carl had done to Chloe to make her hysterical. Carl drew a circle in the air in front of his ear, and I thought he was trying to say that I was mad.

'You've let it build itself up in your mind. Talking to me was the right thing to do.'

'Yes,' I said, 'but—'

'If you ring this number,' the page appeared and he tapped on it before making it vanish again. His hands were big and clumsy but I could imagine him being able to work good magic tricks and make things disappear, 'they're going to ask you who you were with. Want to know how you got there. And then they're going to want to know why I was taking you and Chloe out. And if they asked me, I might need to stick to what we started with, and say I've never heard of you, and I was never there.'

I finally realised what his problem was, and I blurted it out without thinking, 'you'd get in trouble, about Chloe. Because she's only—'

'Don't tell me,' Carl said quickly and he shook his head at my not understanding. He laughed. 'I'm not worried about that,' he said loudly.

There was a chip in one of Carl's teeth and he tapped his fingernail against it. It made a hollow sound and he blew the air out of his cheeks and changed the shape of his mouth to adjust the sound like his whole head was a drum he wanted to tune up and play. That's why he'd be good at the magic tricks. I put my finger on it then, even though the feeling about him was one that I'd had all along. He fidgeted all the time. He was constantly tapping or drumming or folding up train tickets or picking at the plastic trim on the inside of his car. When people like that are given a coin or a pack of cards or even a pencil and paper, they start to work out ways to do magic – even if they do have clumsy hands, like Carl did.

I was thinking all this when Carl leaned over and kissed the side of my neck. It gave me a shock, and my arms flew out as if I was falling, or defending myself. I was embarrassed about that. He laughed softly and I felt his teeth against my skin. I hunched my shoulders and moved my head back and the triangle shapes of the whites of his eyes were grinning at me and then he did it again.

I wasn't prepared for the feel of his tongue to come out and start poking at my teeth, up along my gum line and swirling around like I was a room he was trying to break into – my mouth the lock. While all this was going on, he'd started pressing his hands under my coat and against my jumper. He was tugging the material upwards and I felt how rough his hands were when the jumper gave way suddenly and he put his hands against my stomach and started to slide them upwards.

This is not something I like doing, I thought, and was pushed back into the seat. He was still kissing me. I could smell his saliva on the side of my neck and feel it drying on my face. I thought of the tiny bruises on Chloe's neck and shot out my arm behind me for the car door handle.

When it clunked open the river-smelling wind forced it closed again right away but the noise was enough to get Carl to stop. He took his hands out of the front of my jumper and leaned back.

I was worried he might have been offended or embarrassed.

'I'm – I should . . .' I said, sounding even to myself like a ten-year-old.

'Not into it then,' he said, and laughed. His mouth was shiny. 'You're more interested in Chloe?'

I could feel how hot my face was and I was glad it was dark.

'I'm going,' I said, but didn't sound as outraged as I felt. Carl didn't try to stop me and he didn't start the car engine and follow as I ran away under the bridge and through the park towards home.

17

The next day, I turned up at Chloe's house after school. Nathan let me in and I was glad it was him answering the door and not her mother. Amanda would have made me hot chocolate and asked me to tell her more about Carl. She'd have hung around with me and Chloe, reading our magazines and sniffing our perfume samples and trying to join in with what we were talking about. Nathan only nodded and pointed with his thumb to the conservatory.

'Heartbreak Hotel's that way,' he said. 'Tell her to turn it down, will you?'

I could hear the tinny noise of *TOTP* on the colour portable and I walked towards it. The mantelpiece in the front room was decked with get well soon cards from the other girls and before I had the chance to wonder who had brought them round, I heard Emma's voice.

'Shanks'll get you out of PE for a bit when you come back, you lucky bitch,' she said, and they were laughing as I went through.

'Who let *you* in?' Chloe said venomously.

She and Emma were sitting on the small wicker love-seat, with their feet in matching pink slipper socks up on the wicker coffee table. She'd opened up her Christmas selection boxes and the floor around them was scattered with screwed-up funsize Crunchie wrappers.

I smiled and sat down on the leather pouffe.

'You're in the way of the telly.'

'Don't be like that,' I said meekly. 'I just wanted to see if you were all right. They let you out of hospital?'

'Obviously.'

Emma was keeping quiet. To show willing, I caught her eye and smiled at her, feeling vile and small and creeping. So the plan to get Chloe and Carl apart had backfired. Fine. But I needed friends now more than ever, and if that meant learning to like Emma, well then, so be it.

'What are you watching?'

'Oh for God's sake,' Chloe said lightly, and leaned back into the love-seat. 'Pass me that jug, will you?'

I handed her the jug of juice from the coffee table and Emma held up her beaker while she poured herself a glass of it.

'I can't believe what you did to me. I can't believe it. You shouldn't even be here.'

Her teeth were brown with chocolate.

'I didn't mean to,' I said. 'I was upset. I was stressed.' I glanced at Emma. Did she know about Wilson and what had happened on Boxing Day? Did she know the whole thing was my fault? It was so hard to know what to say, what not to say.

'Shut up,' Chloe said. 'We're in here trying to work out how I can get in touch with Carl when I can't leave the house and they've put a block on the house phone and you're fucking me off whining about how stressed you are. What have you got to be stressed about?' I opened my mouth but she went on, 'Nothing, that's what. It's my life that's been ruined, not yours.'

'The house phone is blocked off. You need a pin number to make outgoing calls. Her dad set it up,' Emma explained. 'And they've not told her what else – how long she's grounded for. They're waiting until she feels better and they've discussed it,' she added darkly.

It was obvious she had been helping Chloe with her plan of action when it came to evading whatever punishment Chloe's parents decided on. And that wasn't fair. It had always been me who'd had to cover for her, stand guard and take messages to Carl when she couldn't get out. It was me and not Emma who understood the intricacies of the way they were with each other – the games, the ignored phone calls, the crocodile tears and the romantic moments they shared in the back of his car. As someone outside the situation looking in, I probably understood more about what was going on between them than they did themselves. Emma didn't know anything.

'There's always your mobile,' I said.

Chloe screwed up her face and mimicked me. *'There's always your mobile!* As if I didn't think of that. No credit on it, and I can't get credit if I can't get out of the house, can't get any money, can't get hold of Carl to tell him to get some for me. Genius.'

'I said I'd get some for you,' Emma said, 'or I'll ring him from my house, tell him what's happened.' Chloe put her head on Emma's shoulder and squeezed her arm.

'I want to talk to him myself,' she said and she didn't sound angry anymore. It was the same tone of voice she used with Shanks when he was going to mark her up for being late or not turning up for registration at all. (*It's private women's problems, sir – not my fault I was late.*)

'You shouldn't be spending your money on me. *You* didn't do anything wrong,' Chloe said, and tucked a strand of Emma's dark hair behind her ear affectionately. I gritted my teeth – the two of them pawing at each other like that. It was disgusting. Chloe looked at me, her plucked bald eyebrows raised, and finally I caught on.

'I've got a bit of money on me,' I said. The change from the tenner Donald had given me the night before. 'It isn't much, but it'd go towards. I can give you that, if you want?'

Chloe blinked slowly, her mouth screwed up. She was marking a tally in her head. How much would I need to do to make it up to her?

'How much?'

I counted out the coins from my pocket onto the table in front of them. Six pounds.

'Is that all?' Chloe scowled at me. 'You know they're probably going to ground me for months?'

'Listen,' I said, 'my Christmas money is at home. I can go and get it for you. Or give you my phone, if you want.'

'Never mind,' she said, and slid the money off the table into her cupped palm. She tucked it away into the pocket of her jeans. 'Have you got any fags?'

I shook my head.

Emma unwrapped a small square bar of Turkish Delight and let the shiny pink wrapper fall onto the tiles. She broke it in two and handed the bigger half to Chloe. She spoke and chewed at the same time.

'You can have my fags,' Emma said. 'I'll nick a packet off my brother. He went to Ibiza last month and he's got a massive carton of duty-free under his bed. He'll never know.'

Chloe brightened.

'And relax about Carl. You don't need to phone him. He'll ring you himself before too long. Just keep your phone on you. Put it on vibrate and keep it in your knickers or something.' Chloe laughed and I could see that it was working – that Emma was doing my job for me and getting Chloe to be reasonable. It wasn't fair.

'He doesn't know your parents know – doesn't even know you've been in hospital. Give him a few days. He'll ring, and then you can update him and he'll get you some money. I'll go and get it off him, or you can send Lola if you want.'

Chloe sighed. 'He better had,' she said irritably, and kicked her foot at the selection box. It toppled and fell onto the floor. 'Pick that up, will you?'

I knew she was talking to me and not Emma so I picked it up and slotted it back onto the table between their feet and tried to think of something to say. Even I could work out that telling her I'd seen Carl the night before would be a bad idea.

'At least you're not pregnant,' I said. 'Carl will be glad about that, won't he?'

Chloe shook her head and pursed her lips at me. 'For fuck's sake,' she said, under her breath, 'can't you keep your mouth shut about anything? Tell you something, and I might as well broadcast it on the news.'

I glanced at Emma, who was frowning.

'Forget it,' Chloe said, 'just sod off home, will you? I never asked you to come round. I'm supposed to be resting. I'll see you when I get back to school.'

I stood up and turned round, making my way slowly through the arch into the living room and towards the front door – walking as slowly as I could to give Chloe a chance to change her mind, to laugh and say it was a joke. I hadn't even had the chance to take my coat off. She could have called me back in then and there and I'd have laughed along with her and Emma and pretended to find it funny. The only noise I could hear as I went out into the street and clicked the front door shut behind me was the noise of their voices, low and murmuring, talking about something I wasn't allowed to hear.

18

Donald and I had been watching videos. Piles of matches and cards from an abandoned game of Crazy Eights littered the coffee table. Barbara was somewhere else – out in her coat and headscarf hacking at the garden, or upstairs beating bed linen into submission. My heart wasn't in the game that night.

Donald and me had a routine, after school. Watch his *Blockbusters* videos in the afternoons, play cards. Drink Lemsips in front of the news and wait for our tea to be ready. I was late because I'd stopped at Chloe's house first, and then had to wash my face in cold water so he wouldn't see that I'd been crying on the way home. Even Crazy Eights, which was a card game I enjoyed and regularly beat Donald at, hadn't held my attention for long.

'Turn it off now, Lola, the news will be on.'

'Dad? Why don't we just carry on with this?'

'Lola, come on.' He poked at the remote control before giving up and tossing it into my lap, 'you know I can't figure these things out.'

I didn't want to watch the news – knowing that it would probably be about Wilson. But Donald wouldn't hear of it. The news was routine for him – when it was finished he knew that it was time for us to decamp into the kitchen for our tea. He liked knowing the names of all the members of the cabinet and tested his memory by making lists of the countries which were at war. He often quizzed me and Barbara on current affairs, tutting when we always got the answers wrong. I knelt in front of the video player and pressed the eject button. The tape slid out into my hands and the news flashed onto the screen.

'Dad?' My voice sounded thin and trembly.

Donald shushed me. 'He's made the reconstruction,' he said, appreciatively. 'He said he was going to.'

'Not the police?'

Donald shook his head. 'Too slow,' he said, 'Terry wanted to take matters into his own hands. Get things sorted. Look.'

Terry introduced the latest, which was, as Donald had anticipated, a reconstruction of Wilson's last movements. The posters had worked and the police had found two girls who'd spoken to Wilson on Boxing Day and they'd got together with a cameraman and a few extras and made a film with them in it.

Melanie and Dawn were the same age as me and Chloe but at a different school. They'd gone to the park in the morning and they'd seen Wilson. Perhaps Terry had found an outlet for his frustration over not getting any of the flasher's victims on his programme. Melanie and Dawn weren't real victims of anything, but they were girls, and fairly photogenic so they'd do until he could get hold of the real thing. He had them in the studio with him, watching themselves star in the short film. They were in their school uniforms: cherry-coloured pullovers, navy blue skirts and solemn, made-up faces. Terry praised them lavishly, Fiona scowled and the two girls squirmed.

It should have been a relief. According to Terry and from then on everyone else, these two girls were the last to see Wilson and not us. They'd been drunk on a bottle of stolen Advocaat they'd smuggled out to drink on one of the wooden benches near the fountain.

But it wasn't a relief because it wasn't true. They'd seen Wilson in the late morning, when they'd been in Avenham Park. We hadn't seen him until the afternoon and across the town in the car park of Cuerden Valley nature reserve.

'I've seen the posters about him,' Donald said, 'they've got them pasted up in the shopping centre.'

'Yes,' I said, 'they're everywhere. The council takes them down at night and his mum and dad put them back up in the morning.'

'That must be a full-time job.'

'They want him to come home.'

I recognised the man who they'd hired to be Wilson as the owner of the video shop near our school. He had the same fine brown hair thinning into wisps at the temples and he was the same height as Wilson. I watched as the man shambled around the park and walked aimlessly around the fountain throwing twigs and dried out conker cases onto the frozen cap on the water.

It wasn't working. It should have worked. The details were right. The North Face jacket was ostentatiously identical to the one Wilson had worn: the camera's eye hovered over the cuffs and collar while Terry provided a voiceover that called our attention to the distinctive white stitching of the design. The video man was doing his best to look like Wilson by letting the skin around his eyes and jowls go slack and pretending to be baffled by a litter bin. He tried to limp, as if this would be shorthand or code for Wilson's disability. He was all wrong. He wasn't Wilson and he wasn't a professional actor, so he was still himself and carrying with him the associations everyone who knew about him would have.

He was a leering, lecherous, nasty little man. He was oily and his whole shop smelled like Dettol and curry and when we walked home from school we'd see him through the window, sitting behind the counter on a ripped and taped-up and ripped again bar-stool, the stuffing coming out behind him and dangling like droppings. He'd perch, and drink hundreds of tins of pop, and spend all day reading the plot summaries on the back of the porn videos and looking up the names of the actresses in a film encyclopaedia.

There were rumours. He had a ball missing from a childhood accident, couldn't get a girlfriend, and lived with a blow-up doll he'd speak to and eat with, as well as everything else. He had snuff films in his back room of cows getting shot in abattoirs and swans being stolen from the canal and tortured. You had to have a fiver and you had to put the fiver on the counter in a certain way, something to do with the Queen's head, and he'd give one of them to you.

It was probably rubbish. All of it. He never did anything to us but we thought, all of us, that he was weird and bad and sinister. The police knew that too. They knew his reputation. Knew that he scared us. I watched him leer as he caught sight of Melanie and Dawn and I realised that while Terry had chosen him because he had a passing physical resemblance to Wilson, the greatest similarity between them was in how they made us feel.

'While the police continue to go through the motions of investigating the missing man's sudden disappearance,' Terry said solemnly, 'they've also been tasked with countering rumours that there's a connection between Daniel Wilson and the several recent incidents of indecent exposure that have taken place in the City's parks and green spaces. But while it is true that the police are looking for a man of medium height and build in connection with the offences and there is, *apparently*, no evidence to connect the missing man to them, the offences seem to have stopped abruptly around the time Wilson was last seen.'

Donald moved the mug around, warming his hands. I looked at him but his expression was unreadable. Barbara came into the room, a corner of a tea-towel tucked into each pocket of her trousers – a make-shift apron.

'Anything new?' she asked.

'Nothing,' Donald said. 'Speculation and misdirection, as always.'

She clipped his shoulder gently, as if to say, 'What are you like?'

But Donald was right. *This*, I thought, was what the world was really like. We weren't supposed to forget. Terry wasn't trying to help Wilson and his parents at all. If he had been, he wouldn't have chosen Video Man, who was bound to make us feel bad and remind us of why we really didn't want Wilson to be found.

'What kind of man approaches young girls in the park anyway, that's what I want to know,' Barbara said. 'I hope they catch him soon. No wonder he's left home and gone into hiding.'

We carried on watching. The camera-work was rough. In more than a few shots, you could see the sound-boom at the top of the frame. They'd not bothered too much with costumes – when Wilson/Video Man walked, his jacket flapped open to reveal, quite clearly, the blue and white short-sleeved tee-shirt everyone who worked at the video shop wore as part of their uniform.

Video Man staggered, half stumbling as if he was drunk, towards the two girls. They pretended not to see him at first. Dawn whispered something in Melanie's ear, and Melanie let her hair fall over her face and laughed. I instantly wondered what it was she'd said – whether they'd been asked to pretend to whisper and giggle for the reconstruction, or if they were really whispering something about Video Man and his balls and his doll or something else, between themselves.

The yellow bottle of Advocaat was on the bench too, but away from them, and although the camera zoomed in on the label and Terry pointed out the windmill and the brand name as if it was an advert and not the news, neither of the girls touched it for the duration of the reconstruction. It was as if it was someone else's bottle, and Melanie and Dawn had just happened to sit down next to it.

'Who is that strange man over there?' Dawn said woodenly, and pointed past the camera.

'I don't know. I have never seen him before,' Melanie replied. 'Maybe we'd better head on home now.' She sounded bored. Dawn was smiling at someone off screen.

Cut then, back to Video Man who was still ambling, still

tossing twigs, and making his way gradually, in an uneven zig-zag, towards the bench the two girls were sitting on. Terry, shrunk to the BSL interpreter's station in the bottom corner of the screen, gesticulated sympathetically and provided a helpful commentary.

'The girls were in high spirits on Boxing Day morning and had left their homes and families for a breath of fresh air.'

I knew what that meant. They were pissed. They'd snuck out to drink more, to smoke, to look for boys.

'They were laughing, and talking about the Christmas gifts they'd each received from their families when an older man neither of them had seen before approached them and tried to tempt them deeper into the park by offering them cigarettes.'

'Listen to that!' Barbara said, 'smoking!' as if girls who smoked deserved everything they got. I thought of the tab-ends in the shed and bit my lip. 'I'm away to dish up now. Don't be too long.' She disappeared into the kitchen.

'What is it?' I whispered to Donald.

He screwed up his face. 'Corn beef hash.'

'Sensibly,' Terry said, 'the girls accepted the gifts so as not to anger their interlocutor, and after a brief conversation, the man left them and walked in the direction of the town centre. Police are still checking CCTV camera footage, but what we do know is that man – Daniel Wilson – never returned home.'

The film ended and the shot returned to the studio, where Melanie and Dawn were sitting between Terry and Fiona. Fiona leaned forward and opened her mouth but Terry leapt in before she could say anything.

'The police refuse to be drawn on the matter and obviously there's a limit to what I'm allowed to say on air until we've dug up more evidence. No such restrictions apply to you, viewers. Call us. Tell us. Do you want this man found?'

Fiona frowned and looked pleadingly at someone off screen but Terry went on: 'These offences are not just the concern of the young girls who are at risk of becoming victims on the cusp of their womanhood,' he swept a lavishly gesturing arm in the direction of Melanie and Dawn, who flinched out of its way. 'Ladies and gentlemen, these offences disturb us all. *I* am offended.' Terry stared hard at us out of the tiny screen and I shivered.

'Of course,' Fiona began, 'there's no actual—'

'Yes, yes,' Terry broke in. 'A police spokesman reiterated that there was no evidence to implicate Wilson in any wrongdoing and that vigilante justice would not be tolerated,' he said.

You could tell he didn't mean it by the way he said it. You always got a good performance from Terry – he made the cold weather sound like a personal affront and something the City should be doing something about when he reported on it. It was his sense of drama. It got people stirred up. It got things done. And when he read out that part about the police saying Wilson had nothing to do with the flashings, his voice was flat and insincere. We knew what he thought, clear as anything. When Donald reached into my lap for my hand, I jumped.

'You're always careful at night, when you're out with that Chloe, aren't you?' he said.

I nodded slowly, hardly hearing what Donald was saying because my eyes were fixed on the screen.

'This afternoon, the missing man's parents made an emotional appeal for any information,' Fiona said.

Now they were showing footage of Wilson's mum and dad. Donald noticed I wasn't paying attention to him and used the remote to turn the sound down, but I watched the pair of them anyway – younger than I'd imagined, ordinary, red-eyed and trembling. They were sitting at a trestle table on a platform and there were photographers there. The woman jumped every time the flash went off and the man – Wilson's dad (I thought about worms, fishing and the ban on smoking) – in a suit and tie, looking hot and uncomfortable, with big rough hands appearing on the table, being drawn away to his lap, and then appearing again. The camera flashes reflected off the lenses of his glasses.

'We're just asking, as parents, for anyone who knows what might have happened to come forward. He can't work out the trains, and he's not that good with buses. If he's gone wandering, someone must have given him a lift. He's chatty,' the man smiled, 'never shuts up.' His voice broke and his wife touched his arm gently. He wiped a finger behind his glasses and drew himself up to his full height. 'He'd stick out in the memory, if you took the time to think about it. He had a bit of money on him. Could have took a taxi. Maybe asked you for directions home.' He shook his head, unable to continue. His wife spoke next, and her voice was clear and hard and cold.

'We don't care what anyone says he's done, or not done,' she said, 'he's our son. He'd never hurt or frighten anyone. Never. We want him to come home.'

She stopped and swallowed. The camera zoomed in on her until her face and hands filled the screen. She shook out a hand-kerchief and dabbed at her dry eyelids.

I wanted to speak then – tell Donald it was all wrong, before I either lost my nerve, or threw up. It was me, I wanted to say. Me. My fault. I did it. I wanted to be honest. I believed what people say: that telling the truth lifts a weight off your mind.

I told him to go and test the ice, and he fell through and drowned.

The words were right there, and Donald was the safest person to tell – the best person to test the theory of getting it off your chest, because he'd forget, and even if he didn't and told someone else, they wouldn't believe him.

But they might. And then it would be me on the television. I stiffened, trying to imagine what that would feel like. How weird would it be to see yourself on the telly? How much trouble would I really be in?

I remembered the conversation I'd had with Carl. The last

time I'd seen Chloe. I was on my own – there was no way they were going to stick up for me, and tell anyone who asked that I only spoke to Wilson, that I didn't mean it.

'I'd make you glow in the dark, if I could,' Donald said thoughtfully, and changed the channel.

'What?'

He squeezed my hand, let go of it and stood up. Stared at me, smiling – although less at me than the wallpaper over my head.

'Or the bushes in the park where you and that Chloe go,' he said.

'We don't go in the bushes, Dad,' I said.

'You've not been out for a while,' he said. 'Is it the weather? Too cold for you?'

I shook my head.

'Shall I get your mother to get you some new gloves?'

'Chloe's not been out.'

'She's recovered though, from her time in hospital?'

'She's out. It was nothing, really.'

'You've been missing her, then?' Donald said. 'In your room after school. Sulking?' he smiled, 'trouble in paradise? Or is it a young man? Something else on your mind?'

I looked at him while I gathered up the cards and slotted them into the packet, making sure all the backs were facing the right way. I was surprised by how much he had noticed.

'Chloe's going to be hanging out with Emma from now on.'

'And there's no room for one more?'

I shook my head. 'It goes like that sometimes, at our school. It doesn't matter.'

'Nothing your old dad can sort out for you?'

'I doubt it,' I said, imagining him turning up at Chloe's house and sitting in the kitchen with Nathan and Amanda, using the reasonable voice Barbara put on when she was speaking to the water board or the doctor's surgery.

'Oh dear,' he said. Without noticing, I'd dropped the cards and they'd scattered over the carpet. My hands were shaking. 'What's up? You hungry?'

My throat closed. I wanted to tell him, but it seemed easy and impossible at the same time, so I hovered and said nothing.

'Things like this blow over,' he said, 'and before you know it, you'll be back out gallivanting with your Chloe. And this Emma too. She can't be that bad, can she, if Chloe likes her so much?'

'No,' I said.

'But when you do go out, stay away from the park. Do your dad a favour, eh? Put his mind at rest and tell him you'll stay away from the park, all dark places, until this,' he gestured at the television, 'is all cleared up.'

'I thought he'd stopped?'

'For the time being. But where there's one, there's another. Creeping about. There's all sorts out there.' Donald touched his mouth, swallowed as if it hurt him. He closed his eyes and put his finger in the air – his signal for me to be quiet. Then he laughed.

'Remember your Uncle Ronald? True love, or whatever stands in for it, knows no bounds.'

'You all right, Dad?'

'Make them glow in the dark first,' he said, and opened his eyes. He was wearing brown trousers and a brown and green shirt with a pattern on it – repeating diamonds between narrow stripes. It was his favourite shirt and it was threadbare to the point of transparency at his elbows.

'Dad?'

'You could do something to their genes,' Donald said. 'It wouldn't hurt them – it would,' he was pacing, '*prevent* such a lot of—' he caught himself and cut it short, as if he was about to say a dirty word. 'Lola,' he said, leaned over, grabbed my shoulders and smiled into my face, 'it would keep you safe.'

I smelled fags then, powerfully, and Barbara was in the room, her hand on Donald's elbow.

'Put her down,' she said briskly. His grip tightened and then relaxed. His smile faded. He rolled his eyes. We'll humour her, he was saying, and didn't need to speak the words out loud.

'Donald? Donald? When did you last eat?' she spoke loudly, as if he had trouble with his hearing, which he never did. 'Come on, both of you. The plates have been on the table for five minutes now.'

She bustled him into the kitchen. I clung onto the edge of the couch as if the floor was moving, and trembled.

19

Chloe was back at school that same week. Paler, a little bluer around the temples, perhaps, but as she assured everyone 'basically all right'.

Except she didn't assure me of anything at all. I arrived at the art room to find Emma sitting in my spot. I should have anticipated it – I should have got myself ready and planned how I wanted to react when I saw the pair of them talking 'confidentially' about Chloe's experiences in hospital; loud enough for everybody to hear.

When she saw me, Chloe blinked, touched Emma's arm very gently with her first finger, and said, 'There she is.'

Emma looked at me slowly. A lazy, only half-interested sneer. She was wearing a gold chain with a heart on it over the front of her school blouse. I recognised it as Chloe's. She looked different too. Where Chloe was pale, the open pores on her nose showing, Emma had colour in her cheeks and her hair was sleeker and glossier than I'd ever seen it before. Her shoulders slumped less and she was smiling more. She was still buck-toothed, but somehow it didn't look quite as bad as it had done a few weeks ago.

'So she is,' she said, and turned her head quickly. 'Anyway.'

I actually went and sat with them. I pretended I didn't know what was going on. Where else would I have sat? I pulled out the stool and felt a strange mixture of things. Cold stones in my stomach and the first real grief I'd ever experienced.

'What's she doing?' Emma asked Chloe. She jerked her head and paused with an open homework diary resting on her palm.

I wanted to tear out the pages and screw them into balls and shove them in her mouth. Her fringe shook every time she exhaled.

'I sit here,' I said, and shrugged. 'I always sit here.'

The rest of the class was at my back, staring. I could hear them, the unknown and largely harmless bragging and racket of the boys and in between their deeper and more rumbling sounds, the high-pitched snarl and snap of the girls, gossiping, testing and comparing.

'Come on,' I said reasonably, and put my bag on the table, 'there's loads of room.'

I was going to ask Chloe how she was feeling. It was easy to get her to talk about herself. I might even have smiled – a sticky and fearful smile, forced and less grown up than I would have wanted. I'd have been Emma's friend, and endured a threesome to avoid being thrown to the rest of the form like bloody chump from the back of a boat.

Chloe stretched her feet out under the table. Her shoes met my shins. It wasn't a kick but more of a push that transferred the mud from the bottom of her shoes onto my socks. She yawned luxuriantly, the back of her hand over her mouth, and then leaned forward and draped herself over the pile of bags and coats on the table. Bizarrely, Emma looked at Chloe through that yawn with a kind of pride on her face. Like Chloe was a new baby or the best sort of clutch bag. There was sheer love in that look, and a kind of smug ownership too, that depended on me being there to see it. I saw myself sitting there, only last week, and understood in a terrible cringing flash of insight what people meant by the lessbefrens thing.

'I don't remember her sitting here before,' Chloe said, and settled over the desk, using Emma's bag as a kind of pillow. I could see the top of her head, her razor-sharp parting and the complication of a French plait so tight it was making her hair come out at the temples.

Emma put down the homework diary and rubbed Chloe's back.

'She's still not well,' she said, with sickly kindness, 'probably shouldn't be here at all, but she was desperate to get out and away from her mum.' She licked her teeth behind her lips and stared glassily into the air between us, determined not to look at me. 'They've decided she's grounded for fucking *months*,' Emma said, as if to no one.

Chloe said something but her voice was muffled by her bag and her head-down position. 'Tell it to fuck off. I don't need the stress.'

'You heard what she said,' Emma said, still rubbing, and made a clicking noise in her throat. It could have been asthma, or purring. 'Why don't you take the hint and go and sit with one of your *other* friends?'

Her smile made her flat face even wider.

Chloe calls you panhead, I wanted to say.

The walls of the art room were covered in drawings mounted on sheets of black construction paper. One wall was devoted entirely to still life: carrots and tomatoes arranged suggestively and sketched by some joker, wobbly bananas done in felt pen, and a painting of a crumpled crisp packet almost hallucinatory in its detail and accuracy. Another wall devoted to blotchy and smudged attempts at pointillism and one more of pictures of knotted rope, balls of wool, hanks of tangled string: all vivid in black and brown oil pastels, thick enough to scrape your initial into with a fingernail.

I got up, dragged my bag roughly out from under Chloe and went to lean against the paintbrush sink at the side of the classroom. Of course there was nowhere else to sit. It didn't feel like anyone else had been paying attention, everyone all caught up in the intricacies of their own dramas, but I scanned the room and saw the gaps close up and the empty stools disappear as if the walls themselves were absorbing them.

I should mention this to Donald, I thought, because he will know something about this: herds, mass minds, schools of tiny fish insignificant and edible as individuals, but fearsome and magnificent as one huge flickering shoal. People do it too, I thought, but I already knew that.

Shanks emerged from his office patting the back of his collar. It looked, I thought with a jolt, and before I could stop myself, as if he'd only just put his shirt on. The thought of him being naked in front of a poster of Marc Bolan, maybe even painting like that, made my feet tingle. I closed my eyes and waited for the sensation to pass. Chloe would have called it a cheap thrill. He clapped his hands, as usual, and sat on a corner of his desk, put one ankle on the opposite knee and reached for his register.

'Glad to see you back in fine fettle, Miss Farley,' he said.

'Thanks, sir,' Chloe said, her cheeks colouring up.

Then he leaned towards her, spoke quietly while the usual classroom noise surged around him, but I heard what he said.

'Come and see me afterwards. A quick word, please. Bring,' he waved the corner of the register in Emma's direction, as if he was wafting away a bad smell, 'Laura if you want.'

He didn't sound pissed off, only stern and calm and deter-mined to be kind. He was going to do his pastoral care voice, I thought, and force her to go and see the nurse.

In the first year or two of high school, the nurse, whose real name was Patsy, was called Nitty Nora the Biddy Explorer, because if you went to get a plaster or a suck on your inhaler, she'd always sneak in a check of your head as well.

In Year Nine the girls would call her Dr Jamrag, because you had to go to her office for supplies if you were caught short. She had a drawer filled to the brim with Dr White's – the sort of hospital-issue sanitary towels that made you waddle and weren't even for sale in pound shops. Someone once asked for a tampon, and got a lecture about toxic shock syndrome, natural flow and the importance of the hymen. Seeing her for the hymen talk was such a terrifying prospect that none of us were ever caught short – there was a trick you could do with toilet paper and a folded-up sandwich bag that would hold you over until home-time, and we taught it to each other in whispers during PE.

If the Year Tens and Elevens spoke about Patsy at all it was with a bit more respect because there was a rumour that you could get little paper bags full of condoms from her, or at least she knew where you could get them for free, no questions asked. It might have been a rumour, but being sent to the nurse, or being seen coming out of her office meant only one thing to the rest of us. And all of us, well, all of the boys, at least, were obsessed with condoms – there were always one or two stuck to the windows, and such a plentiful supply of them spare for water bombs that the rumour about Patsy and her paper bags was probably true.

I imagined Chloe in her office, and under the folding sick bed, a treasure chest of foil packets shining like coins.

'What are you doing perched there?' Shanks said. He looked at me, up on the sink, and shook his head. 'You'll give yourself piles – that porcelain must be freezing.'

I know he didn't mean it. Most adults have completely forgotten the way things are at school. The word 'piles' released such a great gale of laughter that it took Shanks several minutes to get the class under control again.

He was standing in front of the longest wall – the one covered in all the coursework from the Year Elevens who were taking art for GCSE. Usually the ones who had problems reading or writing, or getting themselves dressed properly. They were the best pictures though. Chalk, charcoal, pencil, on blue and white and grey paper. Glasses filled with ice and something carbonated, so well drawn you could almost hear the fizz. Car wing mirrors, windows, the curved reflective bonnet of a car. Lightbulbs, more windows, and the strange lozenge-shaped bulbs of streetlamps. I fell into the pictures, gazing at the glass and water, ice and bubbles, until Shanks banged the spine of the register against the edge of the desk and demanded silence.

'For those of you that have been watching the news,' Shanks said, and held the closed register in front of his crotch like he was taking a penalty, 'the rumours that the school is going to close so you can all stay safe at home and in bed have no doubt got your little minds working.' He put down the register and started to pace. His hair sprung up from his head in thick pale tufts – there was a touch of red in it, as if he'd been a full-on ginger in his younger days. Strawberry blond, although that's not a very manly way of describing it.

'I'm here to tell you that's not even half true – there are no plans for closures, and if there were, I'm sure I'd know about them before Terry Best. While the council has had a chat about 8 p.m. curfews for the under-sixteens, that's not something the school would decide, so there's no point passing around that petition when you're supposed to be listening to me, Rachel Briggs. Thank you. In your bag until home-time.'

The thing is Shanks wasn't even that tall. Chloe said height, the ownership of a car and foreplay were all you needed from a man – expecting anything else was being picky, a perfectionist, and the reason why I shouldn't be expecting to get a Valentine from anyone but Donald this year. Again. She could talk. Carl had *both* ears pierced.

'No closure, no curfew, but I'm asking you – for the sake of yourselves, your parents and my nicotine-addled heart – to be careful with yourselves. I know what you get up to at night. Monsters, the lot of you, sneaking out of the back bedroom window as soon as your parents are asleep. I know what you get up to in the bus shelters, in the back of the train station, on the roof of the Spar, round the docks, underneath the jungle gym in the kiddies' swing park – Danny Towers.'

He stopped for the expected laugh, which came. Danny was shoved and punched by his friends, and smirked proudly.

'I'm a realist,' Shanks said, glanced at me on my porcelain perch and almost winked. 'I'm not asking you to stop. I'm not telling you to stay in at night and I'm not telling you that you need to spend the whole weekend hoovering up for your mother and arranging flowers at St Peter's. I'm not that old that I don't remember what it's like. What I am doing, is asking, imploring, beseeching and warning you that whatever you do, do it in pairs. At least. Promise me, 3Y1, that you'll be sensible until this pest is caught.'

He'd got serious towards the end — his voice slowed and dropped until he had the attention of almost everyone in the room.

'But, sir, he's packed it in,' Danny let his voice slide up at the end as if he was asking a question. We all spoke like that.

'When I say "caught", I mean caught properly — not just taking a rest, not just having a bit of time off over Christmas or while it's a bit nippy out — but locked up somewhere, answering to a cellmate who just happens to be two foot wider than he is, and someone's doting dad. Do you hear me? Now's not the time to start getting careless.'

I saw the back of everyone's heads, nodding at him obediently.

'Chloe,' he said quickly, 'get your head up off the desk and stop whispering. Emma? Turn this way please. Is there something about this you think doesn't apply to you? You think you're immune to what's going on in this city? The last victim was fifteen — you're not far off that now, are you? If he's stopped, brilliant — you won't catch me complaining. But a fortnight without an attack and some rumours about some poor boy who didn't find his way home doesn't mean you're all safe. I don't want to be called into the headmaster's office one morning to be told one of you lot has been caught in the crossfire between Jack the Ripper and a vigilante mob — right? Think about it, and wash that make-up off your face before Mrs Grant sees you and decides to be less tolerant than me.

One more detention this term, Chloe, and it's a meeting with your parents.'

Emma was stiff and pale and horrified – probably because she wasn't used to a telling off. Slowly, very slowly, Chloe lifted her head. Her face was red. She was shaking with laughter.

After the wreck of morning registration, I didn't even attempt the dining hall. There was no chance I would be able to go in there, queue, pay, sit, eat and return my tray alone. My stomach squeaked and popped with hunger.

You're chubby anyway, I thought briskly, and walked in the other direction towards the library and the bank of computers you were allowed to use for homework. I had Donald's paperwork with me. Might as well try to type some of it up.

Despite everything, there was something soothing about the typing. Donald's handwriting was always cramped and erratic – often smudged because he was left-handed. I didn't find it difficult to read because I was used to it – I'd done jobs like this one for him before and it was how I knew how to type. Before Year Nine, when I'd finally been allowed to use the school computers for coursework, I'd used Barbara's old Silver Reed – a portable with a slipping ampersand key and a matching plastic case the colour of a hearing aid – the one that Donald had ruined with a lump of lard. I remember I used to spray the ribbon with water from the plant sprayer and wind it back up again because I didn't know you could buy replacements.

Sometimes what I found out during this typing was interesting, if not exactly useful. The Montgolfier brothers made a balloon, and tested it by offering convicted criminals a pardon if they survived a trip over the Channel. Or Wrigley's chewing gum: the first product in the world to be sold with a barcode.

I sat at the computer furthest away from the door in a corner next to a mural of famous dead writers waving and wearing the school colours. The computer hummed and the monitor crackled with static as it loaded up. I took Donald's exercise books out of my bag, fed my floppy disk into the front of the unit, and started to type.

The 27th of January, at the entrance of the vast Bay of Bengal . . . about seven o'clock in the evening, the *Nautilus* . . . was sailing in a sea of milk . . . Was it the effect of the lunar rays? No; for the moon . . . was still lying hidden under the horizon . . . The whole sky, though lit by the sidereal rays, seemed black by contrast with the whiteness of the waters.

'It is called a milk sea,' I explained . . .

'But, sir . . . can you tell me what causes such an effect? for I suppose the water is not really turned into milk.'

'No, my boy; and the whiteness which surprises you is caused only by the presence of myriads of infusoria, a sort of luminous little worm, gelatinous and without colour, of the thickness of a hair and whose length is not more than seven-thousandths of an inch. These insects adhere to one another sometimes for several leagues.'

'. . . and you need not try to compute the number of these infusoria. You will not be able, for . . . ships have floated on these milk seas for more than forty miles.'

Jules Verne, *Twenty Thousand Leagues Under the Sea*

June 1854. South of Java. Aboard the American clipper *Shooting Star*. Captain Kingman reports:

The whole appearance of the ocean was like a plain covered with snow. There was scarce a cloud in the heavens, yet the sky . . . appeared as black as if a storm was raging. The scene was one of awful grandeur; the sea having turned to phosphorus, and the heavens being hung in blackness, and the stars going out, seemed to indicate that all nature was preparing for that last grand conflagration which we are taught to believe is to annihilate this material world.

The British Meteorological Office has established a Bioluminescence Database, which presently contains 235 reports of milky seas seen since 1915. Surely bioluminescent organisms must be the explanation for them? But most of these organisms simply flash briefly and are incapable of generating the strong, steady glow observed. Marine bacteria alone glow steadily. However, calculations show that unrealistic concentrations of bacteria would be needed to generate the observed light. Herring and Watson admit there is no acceptable explanation of the milky sea and yet urge observers of it to retain the water, spiked with bleach, for further study.

Here, Donald's notes dissolved into fragments. I rearranged, trying to line his words up into coherent sentences. I may have distorted his meaning – I really don't know.

Milky Seas Sightings in British Waters and Their Uses: a request for attention, funding and assistance with further research.

<u>Do not want</u> to hand this project over.

There are commercial as well as social and humanitarian applications to any possible findings that must be explored with all haste.

Letters to BMS and various university marine research departments (unanswered) enclosed for your records and perusal.

N. B. What kind of bleach?

Nearly forty minutes later I set the document to print and packed the folders and papers away in my bag. I went to the printer, which was on the side of the librarian's desk at the front of the room. There was a red biscuit tin in the shape of a telephone box with a slit in the top for your money. Mr Brocklehurst (Broccoli, or Meat and One Veg) never looked up. As long as he heard money going into the tin he was happy enough with you taking your printouts. They were five pence each, but I shoved a handful of pennies through the slit, keeping my eyes on his bowed head. I was paying so much attention to him that I didn't see Chloe and Emma, leaning on each other, grinning like leggy, white-socked vampires, and pulling the sheets out of the printer as they arrived.

'What's this?' Chloe said, the bundle clutched tight between her fingers. She was creasing the pages – holding on tight and expecting me to grab for it.

'Give me it,' I said. Emma leaned over, put her head on Chloe's shoulder and ran her fingers along a line of text.

'*Despite my age and lack of swimming ability it is my fervent hope*,' she read in the seal-like bark that we heard from the remedials who were forced to read out in class.

'What the fuck is that?' she asked.

Broccoli turned his head and smiled.

'You girls wouldn't mind taking that outside, would you?'

'Of course not, Mr Brocklehurst,' Chloe said, and tucked the sheets under her arm. 'Come on,' she said, over her shoulder. Emma sniffed, and followed without looking at me.

I waited until I saw them through the glass doors, huddling over the pages and laughing. I followed too. The corridor outside the library was busy. The second meal sitting was over, and the day was too cold for anyone to want to go outside.

'So,' Chloe said.

'I'm writing a story,' I said. 'It's nothing.'

The trick, I thought, was to keep my hands in my pockets. Sit still, don't lean in, don't grab for it. Stand back, breathe casual. She only wants it because she thinks it's important.

'Really?' Chloe said, got so close it looked like she was sniffing the pages. She turned them like a fan. 'What about?'

'Explorers.'

'Bullshit,' she said. 'This is your dad's, isn't it?'

'What?' Emma said.

Chloe turned away from me. I saw the side of her face – her

mouth opening and closing, a loop of hair curled around her ear. She had a mole on the side of her neck. I stared at it. I wanted to stab it with a pencil.

Emma screwed up her nose. Panhead. Panhead. 'Her dad's writing a story?'

Chloe licked her lips, took a breath, and spoke as loudly as she could without shouting.

'No one's supposed to know, but Lola's grand— I mean, dad – he's gone soft in the head. He's got this junk room where her mum keeps him because he's not safe to wander around the house on his own.'

Emma glanced at me. Are we going too far? she seemed to ask. It wasn't funny anymore and Emma wasn't cruel, not like Chloe. This was worse. This was pity, and the effort of understanding. Ah yes, she was thinking, that's why you're the way you are. That's why you're not one of us – always on the outside, left at home on New Year's Eve, waiting outside the car on Boxing Day. Standing guard. Watching, waiting, following. It's because of your dad. He's soft. I should have known.

I couldn't speak. It wasn't true. Not even half true. There had been accidents with aspirin and disposable razors, but Chloe made it sound like we kept him chained to a bolt in the wall. More than the untruth of it, the betrayal took my breath away. I knew they weren't like ordinary parents, of course I did. Things had been bad enough for me without Donald and the junk room and his writing being made public knowledge. It wasn't a junk room, it was a den, and it had taken me a long time to let Chloe come and see me at my house.

'Give me those back, Chloe,' I said quietly. 'There's no need for it.'

Chloe hooted with laughter.

'Come here, Em, have a look.'

Emma glanced at me again, almost reluctant but not quite,

and leaned against Chloe, reading the papers over her shoulder. She giggled and started to read aloud.

'*The humanitarian applications of this project, assuming we are able to locate and extract the bacteria behind the Heysham milky seas phenomenon* –' She stumbled over that word, but Chloe didn't remark on it even though Emma was in set three for everything and me and Chloe were in set one, '*are vast and wide-ranging. We will,*' she looked at me, frowning, '*be able to fund these aims with proper exploitation of the more commercial applications, but it should be remembered by all readers of this report that . . .*' She trailed off and looked at me.

'What is this? Why's he going on about Christmas trees and rapists? I don't get it.'

'There's nothing to get, you chump,' Chloe said, and elbowed Emma out of the way. 'Her father's a crackpot. And it's catching. She's probably made half of this up herself.'

'Give them to me,' I said quietly. I reached out my hand, and she knocked it away.

'You're a weird, frigid little bitch, aren't you?' she said. Emma was at her side again. 'Sitting in here, typing all this up. You're as bad as he is.'

'He pays me,' I said. 'It's just a job. Bit like you getting on your back for Carl every time you want a new album. You know?'

Chloe lurched forward and I thought she was going to hit me, but at the last moment she bit her bottom lip and turned away.

'You don't know anything about me and Carl.'

'I know *I'm* not the one who's frigid. Last time I saw him, he stuck his tongue down my throat. You not giving it up anymore, Chloe? Or is he just bored with you hanging off his arm all the time? Don't suppose you'd know, would you, now mummy's keeping you locked up at night.'

I expected her to hit me then, I really did. She clenched her fist and the papers crumpled. They'd have to be printed out again, I thought, but that was easy enough. No big deal.

Chloe glanced at Emma.

'He *did not* make a move on you,' Emma said. 'You're a liar. He didn't.'

'Why's it your problem?' I said. 'What's it to you that Chloe can't keep a boyfriend?'

'He didn't,' she said again. 'Admit it.'

Chloe was quiet. I laughed, thinking, like an idiot, that I'd hit a nerve.

'Yes, he did. Don't worry though, I turned him down. Not interested, Chloe. You keep him if you're so keen on him.'

Emma was frozen. Her face looked stiff and horrified.

'Just leave it, Chloe, she's not worth getting a detention over.' She looped her arm through Chloe's and tried to tug her away.

'Go back home to your daddy,' Chloe said. She narrowed her eyes to slits and threw the papers at me. They fluttered between us like birds. The bell rang for the end of lunch and the corridor quickly filled with people charging around getting their bags out of their lockers and hurrying to their next lesson. The typing got crushed under tens of pairs of feet.

Chloe stared at me, daring me to kneel and collect them, but I shrugged and walked away.

'Carl's nothing to do with you,' she spat after me. 'He's *ours*.'

20

In all the photographs printed of her after her death Chloe was smiling, her hair pulled back tight, the collar of her school shirt stiff and blinding white. But sometimes I remember her the way she was that lunchtime – her hair falling out of her plait and hanging down by her ears – her lips pursed, one hand on her hip and a spot forming on her chin. That scowl. A look that could have curdled milk.

Tonight I remember the things that happened during that winter and it is like watching myself in a reconstruction. Some girl who isn't quite real enough to be me stumbles through the corridors in a school that cannot have been so large and sits near a pair of girls that would never have been allowed to be so cruel. Our spats were probably comic and insignificant to Shanks, Brocklehurst and the others. No one noticed anything other than the ordinary ebb and shift of teenage girls' friendships. That's why they had all those inquiries afterwards: someone, they said, should have noticed something.

Sometimes I remember my thoughts so exactly it seems like I knew which moments would be significant, even before the significance of them became clear. Is that possible, do you think? Something happens – the event explodes like a firework and illuminates the memories before it, as well as after? Maybe. At the time I was preoccupied with my guilt and worry for Wilson and with Emma's strange shouldering-in and taking Chloe away from me. I was angry with Chloe, as if what had happened to Wilson was her fault instead of mine. I'd always expected that as best friends we'd share each other's secrets and go halves on all these burdens. And when I needed her most, she was acting like a person I didn't even know.

No, that wasn't right. Nothing about Chloe's behaviour was remarkable. She'd been thrown out of schools before for bullying and truancy. She was only hanging by a thread at our school. But that part of the story has been rewritten now. After she died, 'wild' became 'spirited' and 'bully' became 'stubborn'.

It happens while I am dozing – my eyes gritty and the muscles at the back of my neck slowly stiffening. The quiet hum of Terry's broadcast punctuates the adverts and Emma elbows me awake.

'Breaking news – we're finally able to confirm the identification of the remains found here earlier this evening as Daniel Wilson, who disappeared without trace on Boxing Day, 1997, three weeks before his thirty-fourth birthday.'

Terry pauses a moment but it's not the same – this isn't real solemnity. He's hardly containing himself – almost itching with glee.

Emma nudges me and I look up to see the picture of Wilson on the screen – the one of him in his Christmas hat. He is like Chloe now, and will never get any older than this. I am so absorbed by the picture, so lost in my own memories of the first time that I saw it and the way I carried the poster about in my pocket until it fell into fragments, that I don't notice Emma is clutching the arm of the sofa and shaking her head wordlessly. She's crying. Crying and laughing at the same time.

'What's wrong with you?' I say.

She didn't know Wilson. I am sure she didn't know him.

She tries to speak, but for the time being she can't. She gulps, and smiles, and as she smiles her eyes brim over and tears fall from her eyes onto the front of her jacket.

'Thank God,' she says, 'thank God for that.'

I've never seen Emma cry before. Even at Chloe's funeral she stood next to me with her jaw set and her lips clamped together in a perfectly straight line while the rest of the girls snivelled and wailed like a chorus. I don't understand. I wish she'd shut up so I can watch the rest of this segment – find out what they think they know, and how they know it. Wilson wasn't likely to carry about a nice plastic non-biodegradable driving licence in his back pocket and it's been far too quick for forensics to do anything. How do they know it is him?

'Jesus,' Emma says, and rests her face in her hands, sighing out the air between her fingers.

'What is it?'

'It's all right now,' she says, picks up her glass and takes a long swallow. 'I'm all right.' She takes a tissue – no, not a tissue but a real, environmentally friendly handkerchief – from her pocket, and rubs at her eyes, which are red, and as usual, bare of make-up. The rims look raw. I realise she's been crying for a while – sitting here leaking while I've been asleep. How could I have slept?

'Do you remember him?' she asks.

My mouth is dry. I reach for my wine glass and my hand bumps hers. She's handing me cold coffee, and I sip at it and rub my eyes. I've been dreaming.

'I remember the news about him,' I say carefully, 'that Christmas when he disappeared.'

'Yes, they did a reconstruction, didn't they? Those two girls. Chloe was seething mad because she'd have volunteered to act in it like a shot.' She laughs again, and coughs back her wine.

'What's got you so worked up?' I say, and my voice is irritated – not sympathetic at all.

'I had an idea,' she says slowly, 'as soon as I saw the mayor dig that jacket up, I had this thought. You remember those girls? The ones that got attacked when we were at school?'

'I remember.'

'I thought it was one of those. Someone who didn't just get

a flash or a bit of a feel. Someone who got it worse. Someone who got murdered. I thought they'd be telling us it was a young girl. Someone our age.'

'The age we used to be.'

'Yes.'

'They didn't report anyone missing,' I say, 'no girls disappearing. Someone our age would have been missed.'

Emma shrugs. 'You never know. Not with some families. You were only sixteen when you went. Bet your mum's not got a clue where you are, what you're doing with yourself.'

'Doesn't mean I'm dead,' I say, and I am still irritable. 'Anyway, why should you be so worked up about it? It isn't anything to do with us.'

'I remember it,' she says. 'Hard not to take it personally when every week someone else got grabbed at in the bushes.' She will not look at me, but runs her thumb up and down the stem of her glass as if she's scraping away dirt from the surface. 'I'm not upset, I'm relieved.'

'Yes, so long as it's not some pretty blonde fourteen-year-old, it doesn't matter, does it? That man —' I point at the screen, 'he had parents too.'

'It isn't the same,' Emma says, 'you know it isn't.'

For a while we don't say anything. We watch the screen, but there's nothing new. Emma's breaths are ragged but she's clamer now, and doesn't start crying again.

'What a time,' she says. 'They were on the brink of sticking us all on a curfew. And your dad . . .' She tails away.

Is she remembering that afternoon outside the library when she and Chloe took Donald's application away from me? Maybe she's putting together the events in her head – slotting what she knows and what she's found out tonight into the right order, and realising what Donald was doing while she and Chloe were tormenting me about how soft he was.

'Sorry,' she says, and coughs. I think she's about to touch me, to put a hand on my shoulder, and I wonder what I'd do if she did. But she doesn't. She coughs again.

'Sorry,' she says. She's still giddy with relief and speaks too quickly, her words crashing into each other and slurring slightly. 'It's safer now though, isn't it? Because of Chloe. People haven't ever forgot. They don't let the girls roam about as much as they used to. I think it's a good thing.' Emma smiles. 'Do you remember how much Chloe wanted to be on the telly? She'd have gone mad if she knew her big moment was ruined by a . . .' She's about to say 'Mong' but she bites her lip. I can tell it is the same for her as it is for me. Time, which stuck at the point Chloe died, seems to have come unstuck and started moving again tonight. She's realised we're too old for talk like that anymore – it's ten years later and no longer excusable.

Terry is in front of his van and doing an interview with a hair-dresser that used to own a salon in Longton near where Wilson and his parents lived. She's dressed up as if for a night out, and whenever she speaks to Terry she looks uncertainly towards the camera because she can't forget she is being watched. They must have had her lined up for hours – ready to go on air as soon as the identification was confirmed. There's lipstick on her teeth.

'I'm glad to be here,' she says, and laughs when Terry asks her if she's normally up this late, and if the night isn't a bit too nippy for her. I think about teeth and fingerprints and hair and wonder how they did it. Must have been something in his wallet or in his pocket because forensic tests take longer than a few hours – everyone who's watched *CSI* knows that. I learn some-thing new from this hairdresser though. Wilson had a job. It surprises me.

'He was a lovely man,' she says. 'He'd always be round first thing in the morning with his bucket of water and his sponge. Never asked for any money – in the end we had to insist on giving him free haircuts, whenever he wanted. It wouldn't have been right otherwise, would it?'

'And did you ever notice anything strange? Perhaps the hours he was keeping? Late mornings? Early nights? Ever see him talking to any of your staff or customers? Lots of young ladies coming in and out of your salon, I expect.'

'We ran a successful business,' she beams, 'always very busy.'

Terry bites his lip. You can see he's getting worked up. 'And Wilson, did he attempt to make any friends? Particularly with the *very* young women?'

I know what he's getting at. The ex-hairdresser shakes her head. She's wearing gold chains and they rattle over her chest.

'No, never anything like that. He just cleaned the windows and the pavement sign for us. Never even asked him to, he just liked it. We did look into paying him properly, but we thought it might mess up his benefit, and we'd have had to take the tax and NI off him so it wouldn't have been worth it, really.'

Terry grimaces in frustration and reels off the phone number scrolling along the bottom of the screen. Emma turns the tap on the box and refills her glass. She knocks back half of it straight away. The skin around her fingernails is cracked and brown with flakes of old blood. There's a drop of wine on her thumb and when she notices it she sucks it off, and then starts chewing on her thumbnail. When she runs out of nail, she starts nibbling on the skin, tearing fine shreds of it away. It reminds me of Chloe. I hear her teeth click.

'He's still harping on about that flasher,' Emma says. 'It's been years.'

'He thinks he's finally got his man,' I say. 'Terry always thought Wilson was the pest. He's after an award. Services to young girls everywhere.'

Emma snorts. She's recovered now. Can see the funny side. '*Servicing* young girls everywhere, more like,' she says. She stands up and walks out of the front room. I hear the bathroom door slam as if she is angry with me. As if this is all my fault. The water runs, and I wait, watching Terry who is so excited he's practically hopping. The one that got away. The prolific flasher, whose attacks became more frequent until finally, when it seemed they were about to culminate in a rape or a murder, they stopped – and just as suddenly as Wilson disappeared. He's never been able to prove it although he was never above taking credit for it, but tonight, you can tell, he thinks he will.

When Emma comes out from the bathroom there's a picture of a chunky silver bracelet on the television screen. She looks at it, and does a double-take. I know what she's thinking.

'It's not hers,' I say quickly, 'it's Wilson's. It's something he wore all the time, apparently.'

Her face is red – she's scrubbed with soap and rubbed herself hard with the rough bath towel, and her fringe is pushed back in wet and uneven clumps.

'So they're certain it's him then. No mistakes?'

'They'll have to do the DNA, but it's engraved with his name and phone number. It's a medical thing. He had a heart condition. If he passed out in the street, the ambulance people know to look for it. There's certain drugs you can't give people with bad hearts. Something like that.'

I remember the way my mother used to embroider our telephone number onto the cuff of Donald's shirts. Backstitch in pale yellow embroidery cotton. He'd rub his thumb along it whenever he felt nervous. It was so he could always ring home if he went out and got lost or anxious. So he'd always know there'd be someone he could talk to. I frown and drink more to get the memory to leave me.

Emma rubs her hands over her face, not interested now she knows for sure it can't be one of the girls she worried about, and sits down. I look at her sideways and remember the time I saw her laughing with her friends outside my flat. The heels and earrings. She's not the same person anymore. I ask her about it, but she shrugs.

'I used to go out a lot. Drinking. Boyfriends. So what? I don't like to do it anymore.'

'Why not?' I press her. 'What changed?'

She picks at her hair, running her fingers through the wet ends. She could be almost pretty – if her face wasn't so raw and puffy – her skin, like mine, grey and swollen with too many bottles of wine, too many cheap takeaways and late nights.

'Too much effort,' she says, after a long pause. 'I'm not like that. Not really. I thought I'd feel better, a bit more normal, if I tried to get a boyfriend. Went out a bit.'

'And did you?' I say, curious as a tourist because it is something I have never done. I think I know what she is talking about. The not-feeling-normal. After Chloe died our photographs were on the news so much that our faces weren't our own. People recognised us in the street and wanted to hug us or ask us questions. It was horrible.

She shakes her head. 'I just felt like me – everything was the same, apart from it taking two hours to get dressed and you had to deal with all kinds of wankers in the morning. I felt like a tosser in some of those outfits I used to wear. And I looked like one too. Or a tranny.' She shakes her head decisively. 'I'd rather be on my own.'

She jams her lips together and I know I'll get no more out of her. She'll never tell me how much of the reclusive life she leads now is to do with her panic attacks and her fear of being looked at. I don't know which is more pathetic – me sitting in my house all the time I'm not at work, or her trying her best to live the life Chloe might have had, and finding out, for certain, that she just wasn't up to it.

21

After seeing Chloe and Emma outside the library that lunchtime I avoided the corridors and didn't say a word to anyone else all day. I even skipped afternoon registration because I couldn't stand seeing them as thick as that – egging each other on to wind me up.

It was because of Carl. Because he'd tried it on with me. Chloe might pretend like she didn't care, and Emma might act like it was the most shocking thing that anyone had ever said – but the pair of them were jealous. Jealous. I walked home and started to wish I'd taken him up on his offer – just to show her. I imagined being the one he'd take back to the council house where he lived with his mother. Drinking tea with her, and then after she was safely asleep in her chair in front of the telly, being taken upstairs to inspect the new and finished darkroom. I wasn't attracted to Carl, but even I could see the advantages of having a boyfriend who was older and had his own car. It wasn't all school and walking about parks with him. I couldn't imagine him farting into his hands and pretending to throw it at me, which is something the boys at school did a lot. His job wasn't up to much, but he had projects that made him interesting – like the photography.

Then I remembered the kiss again, the feel of his saliva drying on my mouth as I ran away from the car. How could Chloe stand it? Was there something wrong with me because I didn't like it? When I turned the corner onto my street I was dawdling, thinking about tea, hoping and not hoping that it was chips because of the things Chloe had said about the pimples on my forehead, and my school skirt, which was bunched around my waist and rubbing. I put my hand inside my coat and pulled the elasticated fabric away from my skin. When I was in the toilet that afternoon, I'd seen the red scrunch marks the waistband had left on my belly. They looked like the teeth of a zip, right around my middle. I was thinking about what it would be like if people really had zips around their middles. That was making me think of kangaroos, and wonder about situations where it would be useful to cut yourself in two halves. I frowned at my own stupid thoughts and pulled my fingers away from the damp skin of my waist. I saw the police car in front of my house. I stopped in the middle of the pavement then stepped quickly sideways. The dangling parts of the privet hedge bent against my shoulder and poked the side of my face.

I stared at the police car. It had come and parked right outside my house like Carl had said it would. Two of them in there sitting on my mother's three-piece suite in creaking, not quite comfortable uniforms, and Barbara so flustered she hadn't even had the chance to 'clear Donald away'.

I was in trouble. The biggest trouble I'd ever been in, in my whole life. I wondered how they'd found Wilson. I imagined the noise as they cracked off the ice on the top of the pond, and towed it in jagged heaps onto the bank. There'd be doctors, and examinations. They'd know he'd been smoking because of his lungs or his mouth – some remnant of the nicotine in his blood or on his cold fingers. So they'd have searched and found those fag-ends and my fingerprints and spit will have been all over them, and that means they'd know I was there. They'd come to my house in a car to take me away. I edged closer to the hedge, smelling cat piss and privet and trembling.

As I got near I tried to peer inside the police car without turning my face towards it. Ideally, I needed to look like someone who was examining the numbers on the houses, trying to find a certain address, because I didn't live there at all. I knocked more privet away from my face but my hands were shaking so I stuffed them into my pockets.

My phone was in my pocket. I rubbed my fingers over the buttons and then pulled it out to look at it. I watched the car, which looked empty, and dialled Chloe's number. It rang three or four times then went through to the answer machine.

I knew what that meant. I'd been there, plenty of times, when Chloe's phone had rung and she'd wanted to teach Carl a lesson for not taking her out or taking her home too early or ignoring her or not holding her hand in front of his friends. What she did, when she was in a mood like that, was let it ring three or four times just so he knew that she'd heard it. Then she'd press the red button that meant 'busy' and diverted the call to the answering service. That meant she was with her phone and she just didn't want to talk to him. Carl knew all this, and it pissed him off. It wasn't like when she had her phone in the bottom of her bag in her bedroom: then it would ring and ring and ring until the machine cut in automatically. It was totally different.

Chloe knew that I knew all about this too, because I'd been there when Carl had complained about it and I'd watched Chloe winking and chucking her hair about and telling me that Carl was clingy and needy and paranoid and he should just grow up and stop pestering her all the time. Carl hadn't caught onto this, because most of the time it worked and he was especially nice to her for a few days afterwards. There would be presents. It must have worked, or she wouldn't have done it so much.

I pressed the call button on my phone again, but I didn't hold it to my ear. I pretended I was looking up and down the street, waiting for someone, and listened as the faraway sound of the answer machine cut in after just one ring.

'It's me,' I said, after her stupid message. I coughed into the phone.

'The police are here. At my house right now. It's about Wilson. You need to get hold of Carl and do something. I didn't mean to send him out onto the pond. I wasn't the one chasing him. I've seen it. I've seen his football. Fuck it, Chloe. Ring me back, will you?'

I felt like throwing the phone away, but I didn't. I flipped open the top of my bag and poked it into the bottom in case the police wanted me to empty out my pockets in front of Barbara. I didn't have any fags, but I threw my lighter over the wall of next door's garden. I was going to go in there and tell them about Carl having sex with Chloe under-age. I was going to tell them about Carl chasing Wilson. I was going to say that I wanted to stop it, but I was too scared to, and that I had wanted to ring the number on the posters, but they hadn't let me. I was going to tell them I was frightened, and then show them the place in the bushes where Carl had jumped through to run after Wilson, who I hadn't seen again.

I am sure that is what I would have said.

Inside the house, Barbara was sitting on the couch and she was wearing her slippers. That was a bad sign because it meant the police hadn't rung and made an appointment, but had just turned up. On the hoof. That was one of Donald's sayings. It means the same as 'on spec', which was one of Barbara's sayings. The brown slippers made me scared. 'On spec' meant an emergency. They might have had the flashing lights on.

No one looked up when I went in. There were two police officers. The man was standing by the kitchen door with his hands in front of his privates, like he was standing in a parade. He just stood there, pretending he was looking out of the window but really just looking at the folds in the net curtains. I knew that because I knew no one could see anything through them: they were covered in flowers and leaves and butterflies and were about an inch thick. Barbara was paranoid about her privacy being invaded.

The other one was a woman and she was sitting in the

armchair that no one ever sat in because you couldn't see the telly very well from it. It was much cleaner than the settee. The arms were almost spotless. She was leaning forward and trying to touch Barbara, maybe pat her knee or her hand. She couldn't because the space between the chairs was too wide – on purpose – because there was a stain on the carpet that the single chair was covering. Her hand dangled like a fish in the air, flapping with concern, and I thought about angler fish and Donald and my chest started to hurt.

I'd planned to say something like 'Here I am!', but instead I went in and onto the carpet without taking my shoes off. I knew already that it wouldn't matter. That this was the start of a time when things like shoes would stop mattering altogether. That the idea they had ever mattered was going to become funny. I closed the door behind me quietly and went to sit next to Barbara. Donald wasn't there. Wasn't clattering in the kitchen or shuffling around the landing. Wasn't building something embarrassing in the garden. Wasn't cutting pictures out of the TV guide, or trying to programme the video recorder. The radio in his room was silent.

There must have been a privet leaf on the shoulder of my coat. A waxy, pee-smelling oval shape that dropped from my jacket onto the carpet. I looked at it every now and again while the policewoman told me what she had already told Barbara. Barbara, whose face looked like a tent with the guy-ropes cut, sat very quietly. She pulled at a thread in the hem of her skirt. It snapped off and she started at it then wound it round and round her index finger until the tip of the nail turned black.

One morning after this I woke early. It was still almost dark and there were no sounds outside. The house felt heavy. My hair was wet with sweat and stuck to my neck, and I knew I was supposed to be crying. I got up and looked out of the window. It was still frosty outside. The trees in the garden didn't have buds on them yet, but they had lumps on the stems that were going to turn into buds soon. I wondered if it hurt the trees to have the buds slit the bark open, like it hurts women to get babies out, even though it's natural.

I was supposed to stop eating and brushing my hair and I was not supposed to be wanting to go out to the shed and smoke a cigarette and maybe go into town and see if the new tape I wanted was out in HMV yet. I was not supposed to be glad that I didn't have to go to school. Maybe they'd announced it at school. I wiped condensation off the window with the sleeve of my pyjamas and shuddered. I imagined the silence in the class, and Shanks's serious voice. Now everyone will know that Donald was soft. Chloe didn't call.

I looked at the garden and wondered if it hurt to drown. The day before, I'd gone into the bathroom and run a sink full of water. I had put my head into the water and opened my eyes and looked at the black plug and the chain with the bubbles on it. I had tried to breathe in some of the water. Not so that I died, but because I wanted to know if getting water down the back of your nose and into your lungs was painful. My lungs wouldn't let me do it. I coughed, and my eyes stung and streamed.

Now, I thought. Now while the house is quiet I will get out of my bed and try it again. Just so I know. But before I could move I heard Barbara getting up, heard the shower go, and the plastic rustle of the curtain. I lay down and thought about Donald's hair waving in the water and blue light starting to glow from the ends of his fingers and toes. I thought about his hands resting on the mud.

I could only imagine two kinds of water. Bright blue, clear and tropical water with orange and yellow fish in it. Hawaii water, like the pictures in Donald's books. And the other kind – the water at home kind, which was not as good and must have been disappointing to him if he hadn't expected it. Black water with flashing jellyfish throbbing through it like glow-in-the-dark party condoms. Flasher — which is also the name of Donald's favourite kind of fish, a little thing that pretends to be a leaf by floating sideways, and frightens predators by turning its lights on and off whenever they come near.

Some time later I was standing on a kitchen chair having the hem of an old black skirt taken down. Barbara knelt on the lino and I saw the stripe of grey at her hairline where her roots were coming through. She pinned without touching me and I asked about what it meant when they say someone is going to be buried at sea.

Barbara didn't answer me. It wasn't because her mouth was full of pins; she looked at me and then put the pins in her mouth. It was exactly the same as Chloe pretending she was too busy to answer the phone.

'Other side,' she said, and motioned for me to turn around.

We went to a garden outside a crematorium. The neighbours were there. Uncle Ron came late and missed most of the words. He wore a navy blue pinstriped suit and a shirt that was ironed perfectly. He looked smart and fat. Barbara asked him if he had a woman, and would he like to bring her to the house for the sandwiches afterwards. He hugged her and gave her an envelope. She wouldn't take it off him. At the time I thought it was cards — we'd had lots of cards through the post — but now I think he was trying to give her money towards the funeral. She shook her head and he didn't protest, but put the envelope in the back pocket of his trousers and didn't mention it again.

It was a windy day and when it was time to shake out the container into the little sloping garden, the grey powder flew back at us into our eyes and mouths.

'Jesus,' Uncle Ron said, under his breath, and rubbed his face. My mother blinked and did not flinch. I licked it off my lips and tried to catch some of it to put in my pocket. I didn't like the garden: I wanted to put Donald somewhere better. Somewhere near water.

There was a party afterwards, in the house. People sitting on the arms of the chairs and standing in the kitchen. People behaved like they always do when a person dies – even though it only happens once or twice in your life, you see it so often on the soaps that you're trained in what to expect and what to say and it comes natural. It's easy.

Later, Uncle Ron slipped me a five-pound note and told me I could stay at his new flat if I wanted, in a few months, once he'd got things under control.

'Any time, chickadee!'

This is what happened to Donald. He left the house at three in the morning with the tartan-patterned thermos and my old black PE bag. These are more or less facts, because it is a fact that those things were missing from the house and we never got them back.

He was wearing beige trousers, black wellington boots, a blue and grey cagoule and a brown jumper. He had the finished Secchi disks with him and some bamboo cane from the garden. Barbara's bank statements showed that he stopped for petrol at Lancaster services and paid for it with their Switch card at 4.18 a.m.

The man who served him was twenty-three years old. His girlfriend was pregnant and he'd taken a temporary job doing the night shift at the petrol station to earn extra money. He worked in a betting shop during the day. He was so tired he had to telephone the garage to see if he'd had a shift on the night the police were asking him about. He didn't remember Donald, or any of the other customers. He didn't feel qualified to comment on Donald's state of mind.

We didn't feel qualified to comment either, but it should have been comforting to know that on that night Donald was not memorable. Perhaps Chris (I've given him that name – the police never told us) would have been more likely to remember a man who was muttering to himself, raving or weeping, or who seemed not to know what name to sign on his receipt. There was the implication, we thought, that by doing this investigation there was doubt about Donald's intention. He hadn't driven a car for years, they said, what was special about today?

I wanted to tell them about the *Sea Eye* – the deadline fast approaching, the last days of feverish typing and retyping, scribbling and research until late into the night. There were findings to write up, and evidence to collect: this was not an elaborate suicide note. When I began, Barbara looked at me and shook her head slightly. No, she was saying, we do not talk about those things outside of this family.

The boat had been propped in its metal trailer in Donald's friend's front garden in Morecambe. He crept onto the drive while it was still dark and took it away. Craig and his wife didn't hear his feet on their gravelly drive, nor his engine as he towed it off. They didn't report it stolen until eleven the next morning – long after they'd noticed it missing. They wanted to have a proper breakfast first. It wasn't worth so much to them. Craig said they only kept it because Donald had promised, many times, to take it off their hands. He was planning to 'work on Barbara', although those words don't sound like any I would have heard my father say.

This was a slightly dishonest thing for Donald to do and this part troubled me for a long time. It was an act that didn't seem to belong to him, or what I knew about him. Sneaking out in the quiet grey of dawn to steal a boat that had been promised to him anyway.

'If he'd have asked,' Craig said to us one afternoon, 'I'd have gone out with him. Took him wherever he wanted to go.' He drank coffee in Barbara's kitchen, leaning against the sink.

Things were different afterwards: there was no more anxiety about people turning up unannounced.

'What was he after out there, do you know, love?' Craig asked.

'He just liked getting out and about,' Barbara said, 'and didn't have a realistic understanding of his own capabilities. It was a night and day job, looking after him towards the end.'

'You did what you could.'

Barbara murmured something, topped up his coffee and the man left, blame clinging to him like a thread. He was feeling responsible. Like a murderer, perhaps, even though he'd probably never raised a hand in anger in his life. You could kill someone without even touching them though. I knew that better than anyone.

Maybe Donald forgot the time, and expected his friends to be up and eating breakfast. He might have tried to knock on the door, and getting no answer, decided to take the boat anyway. Or maybe, practising what he wanted to say in the car on the way there, he grew suddenly shy and promised himself he'd make amends later. This trip had been a long time in the planning. There were manuals in his room about outboards and currents, tide-tables and maps of the bay.

They found the holdall on Heysham beach a week or so later. In the bag there were jars and trays and empty ice-cream tubs with their lids tucked inside them. He'd been collecting for a while. There was a net. This was a scientific trip. He was researching. He wanted a specimen. I can only think it was the urgency of the approaching *National Geographic* deadline that prompted him to sneak out that morning – that, and his fear that the flasher would strike once again.

However he did it, he was out there. Say it was five in the morning, nearly six. Cold, and still dark. He parked at the very northern side of the bay – just before a golf course that would have been as deserted as the promenade at that time. He picked a good place. The buildings along the seafront are nursing homes, office space and an old church with plastic sheets bolted over the leaded glass in the windows. The car was parked haphazardly. He hadn't driven in years, and I think he would have been excited.

He was happy on the water even though he'd timed the tides and forgotten about the winter mornings, the lack of sun and would have had to wait. It was a useless time for measuring the phototropic zone and he would have resigned himself to that and smiled at himself with his eyes closed. There are signs all along Marine Road from the Midland Hotel to Bolton-le-Sands and as far up along the coast as I've wandered. A litany of warnings: channels, treacherous tides, mud-flats, hidden rocky outcrops. He would have seen them.

And then? Barbara thinks he overbalanced, or fell asleep in the boat which turned and tipped him out. She thinks he might have beached it somewhere and got out to wade over the flats in search of 'those creatures of his'. That's possible. I heard a whisper – something else they tried to keep from me – that when they brought him to the hospital he was barefoot. Perhaps Barbara was right and Donald was wading.

When Barbara talked and poured coffee and lied to our visitors in the kitchen, I sat in the shed, smoking and watching them through the dirty, paperback-sized window. It wasn't right, what she was saying. I was sure, even though I'd never know. I could see it.

Say the reason he was barefoot was because he took off his shoes and socks to pull the boat through the mud on the shore at Morecambe and into the shallows. Yes, it was cold, but he'd have put up with numb feet before he'd have slathered clean socks and shoes with the grey slime sticking to his soles. Barbara was hot on that sort of thing.

He'd have started the outboard, or perhaps just let himself drift on the water while he waited for it to get light. It was slow – cloudier than he'd expected. He might have cut the engine because he wanted the quiet, or wanted to get rid of the wake in the water that would have disturbed whatever it was he was looking for. He had the black and white disks with him, but knew even before he got out of the car that the water was too churned for that. I don't think he minded so much. I don't think he was interested in the light any longer. Not that kind of light. But he went out anyway – looking for something else, and expecting to be lucky.

Say he let the boat drift and settled back in it, lying back as if the damp bottom was a mattress. Hands behind his head and face to the sky, listening to the noise of the water slapping the sides. Maybe he did fall asleep – the rocking, and being awake so early. Maybe not. There was the thermos, which he didn't leave in the car, and a cold black ring of coffee on the counter top at home. Barbara had wiped it away and blamed me for it before she realised he was gone.

I like the idea of him hunching over the lid of the thermos. Holding the cup between his knees and struggling to keep the flask steady with both hands so that he could pour. Burning-hot black coffee so laden with sugar the liquid could hold no more – there'd be a film of it in the bottom of the plastic cup. The smell of it along with the sea, the rotting weed, the sticking mud. Very alert, after all that coffee. Not likely to make a mistake. And the weather that morning was dry – the wind was light. He would have been able to hear, very clearly, the plop and splash of a tail or a fin breaking the surface of the water and disappearing before he could turn his head.

He looked around – scanned the mechanical rakes and pin-sized figures back on the exposed sands to his left. The horizon was tilting and shifting like a cock-eyed spirit level as the boat rocked and almost too far away to see: the first shift of cocklers, getting ready before it was quite light. He was too far away to hear them shout to each other in their own language. The machines rumbled – they sounded like cars, not fish. Maybe he thought about the sound a seabird might make as it straightened its neck and hit the water, and while he thought he held himself perfectly still, moving only his eyes and waiting for it to reappear. He waited until he realised no bird could dive so deep and stay under so long. He'd have been excited. A mind full of milky blind eyes, softly glowing tentacles and the *Sea Eye*. He tipped away coffee and screwed the cup back onto the top of the thermos when he heard it again – a deliberate splash to his left followed by a nudge and a muffled knocking on the underside of the boat.

Donald would not have been afraid.

He stood up, reached for his net, the sea lurched and he went in.

The facts are the facts, and there are few of them. However it happened, the earth sucked the tide and him back in that afternoon and a tug fished him out of the mouth of Heysham Port.

It's a frightening, ugly place to hang around. The sky, which even out of the City is still and flat and grey, is cut into by the massive metal shadows of the tankers and the jetties and the black and white lego-block building – all you can see of the power station. There are tubes and towers and filters that you don't see and they are using gallons of sea-water to cool the waste, and sucking the water out of Morecambe Bay and filtering the sand and the fish and the weed out of it, and then forcing it through the turbine condensers and spitting it out again, into the bay, warm as a bath. You don't hear a thing – the station works in its own bubble of silence, tucked between a golf course and a caravan park and a nature reserve and the people who work there won't live there and the horns of the freight carriers boom across the water and can be heard over to the north if the air is still enough. You don't see any of this happening – this frantic sucking and cooling and making. It's quiet, where Donald was washed up, although the fishermen complain that fish caught in the out-flows from the power station are half-cooked because of the raised water temperature. I don't think that can be true. It was a toss-up, you see, whether it was drowning or hypothermia that got Donald in the end. The water's so shallow in the bay, you can walk across it, some days.

And I was at school, standing outside the library with Chloe and Emma and fighting over his paperwork. Barbara had already noticed the car was gone and called the police. I think she knew what had happened before the police came because Craig had already rung and told us about the boat. He'd had his breakfast – eggs and HP Sauce – and he wanted to double-check with Donald before reporting the theft. Donald had a bad chest and so had never learned how to swim.

All through that January, I was helping Donald with his application – rereading his drafts and advising him about grammar. They already had us practising our personal statements for our Record of Achievement with the careers advisor – one session a month each, to discuss our GCSE options and think about future careers. It was easy enough to translate the kind of tone and language I learned there into the reams of hand-written pages Donald referred to as his 'accompanying documents'. I worked at night, in my room, until the thing was ready to be typed up. I think some of it got into my head. I had nightmares about being trapped in a deep-sea submersible, and drowning.

Donald, who often wandered about on the landing at odd hours, heard me when I woke and sat on my bed once or twice to tell me about the snow that falls under the sea. He made it sound beautiful. I imagined standing on the sea bed watching it flutter; coloured flakes drifting downwards for miles and resting on the top of my head. Stroking the sides of the fish and collecting on the black backs of huge, slow-moving whales.

Some things I can't think about too much. Like the voices I'd heard on the landing one night – a deep, rumbling sobbing noise coming from Donald, and my mother's voice travelling quite clearly from Donald's room into my own.

It must have woken me. That, or another nightmare. I remember hugging my knees in the dark, smelling the washing powder on the duvet.

'Drink your Lemsip,' she was saying, in a low, expressionless voice. 'Sit in your chair and have this blanket. Here.'

Barbara thought Lemsip cured everything from anxiety to measles, and she often used to tuck a sachet into my school bag when I wasn't looking, just in case.

'Did I make a mistake?' I heard drawers being opened – paper being shuffled. Not a burglary. Donald was looking for something.

'It'll come out all right,' Barbara soothed. 'Back in your chair. Here, I've got this Lemsip for you. Take it now, the mug's burning my hand.'

'I didn't make it up, did I, Barbara?'

I felt bad for listening, but my door was ajar. If I got up to close it she'd have heard me and at that moment I would rather have thrown a brick through a stained glass window than draw attention to my presence in the house.

'Sleep now,' she said. 'You didn't dream it. It's the best application they're going to get.'

There were low, protesting sounds from Donald – but half-hearted. The crisis had passed. Different sounds now – the cupboard on the landing where we kept the towels and sheets being opened, and something being dragged out. I held my breath and tried not to move.

'Sleep now,' she said. 'Sit in your chair and sleep for a while. I'll stay in here with you tonight. Sleep in with you. Look, I've got the camp-bed. Drink your Lemsip. Close your eyes.'

She was more his mother than mine. Always, always and especially when I needed her the most. I haven't thought about this for a long time. Tenderness so raw it hurts to bring it back, I think – and something passing between my parents – Donald understanding, only for a moment, that there was no such thing as the *Sea Eye*, that he'd mistaken his wishes for facts, and coming undone about it. I heard Barbara tucking it all back in, so privately that words wouldn't touch it.

22

I heard Barbara coming unsteadily down the stairs, turned off the television, and waited. For a moment there was no sound but her slippers dragging on the stair treads and the fizz of the static escaping from the curved blank screen in the dark room. A shaft of light from the kitchen fell over the carpet and stopped at my feet. I could smell the booze on her before she got near me.

'Mum?'

She threw the pages at me from the doorway. They fluttered. Twice that week someone had thrown a bunch of paper at me. You flinch, even though you know it can't hurt you, and it's humiliating. I sat still and the sound of the pages fluttering and settling quickly died away. It reminded me of two things. One, the time Donald and I had been playing Crazy Eights in front of the news, and he'd tried to speak to me about Chloe, and I'd dropped the cards. Two, the final stage in *The Crystal Maze*, where the contestants have to dive about catching gold and silver pieces of paper as they blow about in the air under a giant plastic dome. They do it for prizes.

'I told you not to encourage him,' she said. Her voice was hoarse and each word melted into the next, like a bad VHS or a dream: she was drunk.

'I didn't,' I said.

She knelt on the carpet and started gathering the papers – the typed sheets and the pages torn from scrapbooks. She was clumsy, knocked the occasional table with her elbow and swore as the remote controls rained down on her.

'He didn't type all this up himself. You did it all. You took it away from him, typed it up, brought it back – told him he was in with a chance, how clever he was, how impressed those bloody biologists were going to be with him.' She stumbled and lisped over 'biologists' and I didn't laugh.

One of the papers had landed face-up near my foot. She scrabbled for it. A perfect pencil and ink drawing of a bathyscaphe in cross-section. Copied from a Dorling Kindersley book I'd found in a charity shop and brought back for him.

'I didn't do—'

'I don't want to hear it, Laura. What did he promise you? Did he give you money? Tell you he'd put your name in the front of his first article? Mention you to the *New Scientist*?'

She looked up at me. She wasn't crying. Without mascara, her eyes looked bald and strange.

'Half of this I've never even seen before –'

'Don't talk to me. Don't say anything to me.' She was kneeling on the carpet, her nightdress bunched against the back of her knees. 'I know you. Mooning about in the bathroom. Staring into mirrors. You thought if he won, you'd get your face on the front of a magazine, didn't you?'

The light from the kitchen fell on her calves and I could see the blue and purple lumps of veins there and the discoloured skin she hid with American Tan popsocks and massaged with sunflower oil in the bath. She was lining up the remote controls on Donald's side table, putting them in order and fitting them into the shapes they'd left in the dust.

'I'll help you,' I said, and stood up.

'Just get out of my sight.'

I went up to Donald's room slowly because I didn't want to be on my own. Didn't want to go to sleep. We'd both been having dreams, but Barbara was allowed to hose them down with a bottle of Gordon's, and I wasn't.

The stairwell was dark. The door to his den didn't creak ominously. There was no special atmosphere. No comforting sense of presence, or sudden rush of happy memories. It was an empty, half-cleared junk room that belonged to a dead person. The table was empty, the debris swept away into three cardboard boxes on the floor in front of it. The drawers were all open, and the contents stirred and disturbed. She'd taken away his blanket and started to pull down the pictures from the wall. The room stank of fags and her perfume. There was a stack of books and papers on the floor in front of the chair. She'd been sitting in it and reading them. I sat too, and picked up the top scrapbook from the pile.

A lot of it was pasted-in printouts of papers I had typed up for him. Drafts of his application for the *Sea Eye* programme. Experiments he could do if only he had the money for the equipment. Long, digressive arguments for funding, for assistance, for advice. Theories about lights under the sea that were somehow connected to the nuclear power plant at Heysham Port.

I turned the pages, stiff and sweet-smelling with flour and water paste, and carried on reading. I started to understand.

He'd had an idea. According to one of the journals it had come to him while walking on Morecambe beach: either he'd seen something out there in the shallow grey water that had sparked the train of thought, or the boredom of pacing across the featureless, muddy sands had encouraged him to daydream. It was all there, scratched out in an erratic handwriting that was almost too familiar to read. Bioluminescence, and the commercial applications of engineering it into living things that didn't have it naturally. Like privet bushes, or yoghurt, or teenage girls. So that's where he went on those long afternoons when Barbara couldn't find him. We'd never have believed he could have managed the trains.

His dreams of being called an inventor and winning his place on the *Sea Eye* must have seemed so close to being fulfilled they were almost inevitable. Donald didn't know, while he was making this list and scrawling draft after draft of his submission to the *National Geographic*, that the reward was already behind him – somewhere in the grey sucking mud of Morecambe Bay. That was the place the ideas had started coming, the place where he'd first imagined allotments filled with rows of lettuce glowing faintly blue whenever they needed water.

He'd been researching the idea from several different angles at once: there were notes about fireflies; lists of glowing fungus; paragraphs on the luminous solution of frightened squid; and a pencil diagram of an angler fish's lure. How to show them that he was serious – that he meant business? Business meant business and that meant money – he knew that much about the world and so the commercial applications were not the cake, but the icing on it – meant to sweeten the pill of what he really wanted to do, although when these ideas finally came to him, they'd come in a rush.

He wrote about flashing pet mice for fairground prizes. Electricity-free glowing Christmas trees to save the planet, yoghurt that glowed in the fridge – either as a warning that it had spoiled, or to replace the traditional fridge light and so save energy. Saplings planted along the side of motorways that would also become street lights when the night fell and their cold, ghostly light became visible. Specially adapted clothing for pot-holers, search and rescue teams, and miners. Finally, he came to it – tried to smuggle his real idea in amongst the others.

The painless tagging of men who wait in dark places and are apt to rape.

This last was underlined, and cushioned between rustling newspaper clippings from the *Evening Post* counting and detailing the twelve occasions when the flasher had made himself known in the City that autumn and winter. In this part of his scrapbook the writing is erratic and tilted. He never asked me, but I would have had a hard time typing it up for him. In places his biro had run out of ink and he'd carried on anyway – not looking at the page, or not caring – just scratching the words into the paper with the dry metal nib of the pen.

He thought he could protect women by making their predators glow in the dark. Barbara would never have let him join the vigilante group even if the other men would have welcomed him, which they wouldn't. He was impotent, but in his own way, he was thinking of me.

I let the scrapbook fall onto the floor.

Barbara was right. He'd been doing all this for me.

Because of me.

You can kill a person without touching them.

I sat there for a long time. Thinking about the way I had behaved – about how obsessed I had been with Chloe and then with Wilson – never realising the more serious things that were happening both at home and out in the world, the things that had been keeping Donald awake at night, and had finally propelled him out onto the water in a boat he didn't know how to operate.

There wasn't a way to fix this, I realised. No going back, nothing as easy as returning a bottle of perfume and writing a contrite letter to the man in charge. I should have acted earlier. Should have sorted the problem out for myself instead of waiting in the house for someone – Chloe – to step in and do it for me. I was nearly fifteen, and it was time enough for me to be looking after myself. My mind travelled to that frozen pond and the football trapped in its surface like a flag – pointing out Wilson to anyone who might walk past and remember the CCTV image of him carrying it across the garage forecourt and put two and two together.

I could, if I had the guts, go there right now and get rid of it. It wouldn't be perfect, but it would be something.

Even then, with the decision made, I didn't act right away – but sat in Donald's chair for longer, thinking over my plan and wondering how it had got to this. Eventually, I reached into the open drawer next to me, and rooted around at the back between the old gloves and my worn-out baby clothes. All his precious things.

My limbs felt heavy – as if I was swimming through sand. Everything was slow and damp and cold. The air had thickened. The back of the drawer felt as if it was miles away, the wood dry and splintery under my scrabbling fingertips. Barbara hadn't found the margarine tub yet. I pulled it out, opened it and pocketed all the money that was in there. Didn't count it, but there must have been close to four hundred pounds. Enough to get away quickly if I couldn't manage to get rid of the football.

I heard Barbara moving around downstairs, and an hour later, come past Donald's den and go into her bedroom. I waited until the light under her door went out, holding the money in my hand and staring at the torn pictures on Donald's walls and the cardboard boxes full of rubbish that Barbara had been sorting through. When I was sure she was asleep, I went downstairs, drank what was left in the bottle she'd abandoned on the coffee table, and grabbed my coat from the peg in the kitchen.

I half turned towards the river and up the hill to go to Chloe's house, but then I remembered it couldn't be her anymore – that we weren't friends in the way that we used to be. I was half drunk and knew only vaguely where Emma lived. In a house whose back garden backed steeply down onto the canal, and I only knew that because of the time she'd told me and Chloe about her brothers going out on a boat to fish out a large handbag they were sure was full of money, but actually contained a dead bloody cat and seven hairless slimy kittens.

Boats. I had to walk fast, in any direction – just to tear my mind away from boats. I started running then, sloppily – banging into parked cars and hedges, until I came to the taxi rank. I jumped into a black cab and asked the driver to take me to Cuerden Valley Park.

'What do you want to go there for at this time of night? And on your own?'

That's the thing about being young. People always think they can ask about things that are none of their business.

'I'm meeting someone there,' I said. 'My older brother's picking me up. It's all right.'

'You got money?'

I pulled the roll of notes I'd taken from Donald's margarine tub and showed them to him. 'I can pay,' I said.

'Where did you get all that from?' he said. I didn't exhale, didn't want him to smell the booze on me in case he got worried about me throwing up and made me get back out in the cold.

'My dad gave it me,' I said, and jutted my chin at him. Go on then, bloody ask me. Ask me, and I'll tell you.

The driver shrugged, started the engine and turned up the radio. Terry again – talking about a tree branch that had blown onto a primary school roof and destroyed the nesting site of a family of rare birds.

'They're going to put a curfew on for you young girls,' he said, 'keep you in at night.'

'Really,' I said.

'Yes. In with your mums and dads – tucked up early. None of this White Lightning and Blue Bols on a park bench. No boyfriends,' he laughed. 'If you ask me, they should do it for the lads too. Everyone under eighteen can stay in after 8 p.m. whether they catch this nonce, or not.'

I couldn't see out of the windows because the driver had left the interior light on, all the better to stare at me in his rear-view mirror. I felt drunk then, and tried to sit up straight and not breathe out of my mouth.

Nonce. Not of normal criminal experience. Out of the ordinary. He was special, see, this flasher of ours. Like Terry's bird family – a rare breed.

'What time is it, please?'

'Getting up to midnight. Funny time to be meeting your brother, that's all I'm saying. You know?'

I ignored him, and drummed my fingers on my knees. Worried about my brother waiting for me in the cold. Imagined him – pacing, hands in his pockets, a parka hood zipped almost over his face.

The heat and the soft vanilla smell of the shampoo the cleaners must have used the last time someone threw up in the back made my eyelids droop. The low chatter of the radio murmured while the taxi chugged through almost empty streets and along familiar roads where we only stopped for the lights. I was almost asleep when the car drew up. I'd calmed down. Maybe sobered up a bit too.

'I don't see anyone,' he said. 'Shall I wait? Have to keep the meter running though. Still, not like you don't have the cash.' He nodded towards the bundle I was letting get hot and damp between my fists in my lap.

'I'm all right.'

'Still, you want to put that away. Stick it in your back pocket, and zip your coat up. There's all sorts out there.'

'He's stopped now.'

'What?'

'That nonce, the pest. He's packed it in.'

'Nothing like it. He's back in action. Two in the past week. The swimming baths this time, and another one at the back of the playing fields.' He named my own school, and I shuddered. 'It's getting worse. Younger. And the last one, outside the school – he tried to pull her into a car. Wearing a mask, apparently. Where have you been? It's all over the news.'

I marvelled about how cut off from everything Barbara and I had become in our grief. She'd lost interest in Terry and Donald hadn't been there to insist on the news. It had been easy enough to slip into our own twilight realm of late-night films and long lie-ins. Barbara watched Donald's videos until she fell asleep.

The real world had retreated to the other side of the always-drawn curtains.

'That's thirteen now, isn't it?'

'Fourteen. That we know about. I reckon some of them'll be too scared to tell their parents. Don't want anyone to know. Ashamed, too pissed to remember, or shouldn't have been out in the first place. I'm reckoning it's closer to twenty.'

I thought about this for a moment. Wondered about what it meant. If it was Wilson who was doing it, then he was still alive, still out there somewhere. And if it was someone else – most likely Video Man, or someone like him, then why had he stopped for a while? No one believed the joke about the cold weather, not really. Twenty of us.

'All right then, I'll be careful.'

'There's police patrolling everywhere. Make sure you don't breathe out as you walk past them, not unless you want a free ride home.'

He laughed.

'Whatever.'

'Your brother not waiting?' He tapped the meter.

'Forget it,' I said. 'I know where he'll be.' I poked the money through the hole in the plastic divider that separated him from me. He looked at it, at the meter and then claimed not to have change for a twenty.

'Keep it. Keep it.'

I slammed the door.

The cold hit me like a hammer. The wind made it even worse. It was aggressive – that cold – hard not to take personally. I shook and held my teeth together as I ran because I knew if I let them chatter I wouldn't be able to stop. Dark. The trees just black shapes against a black sky. No stars. Half way across the car park I turned, but the taxi had already gone. Nothing. It was so silent. Nothing to distract me, so in my mind I went through the argument I'd had with Barbara again – thought about Donald

– paced and cried, thought about Chloe, and Wilson – and then got myself together and headed into the woods.

I didn't see Carl's car until I'd passed it. It was at the very edge of the car park, tucked under overhanging trees – two wheels up on the verge. In the darkest corner, where the lights from the main road couldn't reach. At least getting angry helped me to stay warm. I spun on my heels, marched over and banged at the windows with my fists. Imagined them in there, pawing at each other underneath Carl's filthy work coat.

Dogging.

The car was still. I leaned forward and cupped my hands around my eyes. Empty. And nothing in the back except for a roll of plastic bin-liners and Chloe's school bag. The footwells clear of rubbish. I thought about picking up a rock and trying to break into the car. I picked one up from the verge – felt its small heft against my palm – the biggest I could find and just the size of an egg. I could smash the window. No keys, so no way to drive it away, even if I could, but the noise would be satisfying and I saw myself sitting in there, huddled under the tartan blanket until they came back.

'Hello, Chloe, hello, Carl,' I'd say. Just the right amount of emphasis. They'd look furtive and a bit ashamed of themselves. I'd have the upper hand. Still, no way of telling how long it would be before they came back.

And back from where? What were they doing?

I let the stone fall and headed along a groove in the soil – more of a track than a path – that led between the trees. I had cried so much over the past few days that the cold along the rims of my swollen eyelids was almost soothing. My fingers were numb. I went quietly, following the track as it curved around tree roots and trying not to step on too many twigs. I could see almost nothing.

It would have been easy enough to turn around and flag down another taxi, but as soon as I left the car park I felt my choices dwindling. All I could do was follow Wilson's path into the dark down towards the water. Deeper into the woods and at an angle, circling the pond, where Wilson had decided to try out ice skating because of how much fun I'd told him it was going to be.

I nearly walked right into them. Would have done, except Chloe retched suddenly and Carl hissed at her to shut up. Tiny noises, but I recognised them, and stopped. Heavy breathing, and little retching sounds again. I thought he was making her give him a blow-job. On a night like this? I squinted through the dark and the trees and didn't see anything except the pale moving shape of her coat with the fluffy collar. I kept still as anything, stayed leaning against a tree, trying to hide myself, and listened.

'Move it,' Carl said, not whispering, but very quiet. His voice sounded odd, and I realised it was his ordinary voice I was hearing – not the one that he used to talk to Chloe and me with, which was slowed down, drawly, pretend-deep and ridiculous.

'I can't, it's heavy. My hands hurt.'

'Shut up your moaning, you silly little bitch. Get on with it.'

They were both out of breath.

'I can't go any faster than what I'm doing,' Chloe whispered – and even when she was talking so quietly, I could tell she'd been crying and would be tearing up again soon.

I listened, out of puff but rationing my breath so they wouldn't hear me panting. There was a crushed Coke can next to my foot – the hole at the top stuffed with leaves and the red and silver pattern on the side almost faded away. I stared at it while I heard them whispering to each other. Time went along. Every minute or so, Chloe would cry out – a little, half-strangled noise of disgust and fear.

It wasn't a blow-job. They could have stayed in the car for that. Couldn't imagine them fucking outside and not bringing the blanket. And anyway, why would you? I didn't know that much about it, but I knew it was freezing. No, not a blow-job then, and the shapes through the trees were bending and moving but apart and not together. I heard the scrape of metal against rock. I knew then. It wasn't a shock. Twice, he stopped and moved over to her to hit her on the back as she vomited.

'For God's sake, Chloe.'

I felt suddenly calm. Calmer than I'd felt in three weeks. And very far away. The ideas that had been upsetting me so much – about Donald, or Wilson, about Chloe and Emma and the way things were at school, my anger at Barbara – all melted away and I had only one, flint-hard thought left.

I'd have lied for her. I knew it – I'd have come with Carl and done this job for her, and I'd have kept it to myself forever. No trouble. Taking my turn feeling the smooth wood of the spade handle slide across my palms. Working with Carl in silence – no flinching, no whinging, no throwing up behind a tree. Working – proper work, in the dead silence of the woods, nothing but our breath to keep time. I'm stronger than I look.

How long would it take? How long had they been there? I thought about the icy ground and the rock-hard soil, the noise of the spade sounding like it was hitting concrete. Chloe was no help – I could hear her whimpering. She wasn't cut out for this kind of work. Wasn't calm enough. I could have done it. I would have done it for her.

Think of it – me, pale and bruised with dirty hair, working with Carl, sweating through the cold. And then back to her house.

Dropped off at the end of her street, and coming up to her bedroom through the back door. She'd be waiting – looking between her bedroom curtains, the night-light glowing softly. Her pink flannel pyjamas and rabbit-ear slippers. Smelling like Body Shop White Musk and the vanilla Shake n' Vac her mum put on the carpet. When I came in, she'd take off my shoes and socks and the rest of my clothes, and sit me in the bath with the Christmas bath pearls, and wash my hair, and take the soil out from under my fingernails and rub hand-cream into the sore places on my palms. Her hands on my skin. I'd wear one of her nightdresses and she'd let me sleep in her bed. No one would ever know – not our parents, not Emma – not anyone.

I would have done all that.

I took a deep breath and backed through the twigs and branches as quietly as I could until I got far enough to think they couldn't hear me and set off running. Tripped, once or twice. Rotting logs – an old bike frame half buried in leaves and dead brambles. Ran over a mattress and didn't realise what it was until the ground went spongy and the wetness bubbled up from the ticking and soaked through the canvas sides of my trainers.

I got onto the main road – the warm glow of the orange streetlamps, the red and yellow illuminated signs at the petrol station. The thrum of the irregular night-time traffic. I stuck my hand out to get a lift – my thumb out, the way they do in films. I think it only really works in America.

I would have lied for her, and she never even asked me to.

Poor Wilson. He wasn't ever going home.

I tried to imagine what had happened. Had Carl pushed him over and made him hit his head on a rock or fallen tree? Had he, frustrated at being outrun by a Mong, thrown something at him and hurt him that way? Perhaps Wilson had tripped in the leaves and Carl had caught up with him and let himself get carried away with kicking and punching. Maybe Carl hadn't hurt him that much. He could have just stamped on his leg and made it impossible for Wilson to get out of the woods. It was so cold at night.

I'd never know what had really happened. But Carl knew. And while he might have lied to Chloe, might have wanted her to believe it was more of an accident than it was, she knew that one way or another Carl was responsible and not me. The both of them had betrayed me. I hadn't done anything to hurt Wilson, hadn't even teased him when it would have been easy to. And because it made things more comfortable for Carl, they'd both let me think that it was my fault.

That night I walked along the grass verge by the main road, I waited for ages on a roundabout for someone to stop and give me a lift. No one did and it was nearly five in the morning before I used my key in the back door and crept through the kitchen into the house. Barbara had got up in the night and was sleeping on the settee, an empty glass in her hand. Her mouth was open as if she was shouting at me even in her dreams. I could have got on the phone without waking her, and reported Carl right away. You can do it anonymously but how could I have put the police on to Carl without admitting that I was there too? And Chloe?

I didn't have any doubt in my mind that if Carl ended up in a police station, he'd be quick to tell them I'd been there and blame it all on me. Chloe would do whatever he told her to, she was so under his thumb. It was hopeless, unless I could somehow get her to talk to me, get her on my side and then make plans for both of us to approach the police together. With Carl locked up, things would get back to normal. And then we'd have our own secret.

I smiled. It could work. We could cry. We could say he forced us to keep quiet, to dig a hole, to say nothing about him. Chloe could convince anyone of anything. I could tell the truth and still get myself into trouble. She could lie and we'd both get away with murder. I should have been worried, should have cried about Wilson, maybe, but that night I slept soundly because I'd already decided what I was going to do.

Now I leave Emma on the couch and walk over to the window. Look out briefly at a whole street full of lighted windows. It's past three in the morning and we are all awake and watching these news broadcasts. Is it just this city? Glued to the glass box, and believing exactly what Terry is telling us.

Emma moves slightly in her seat and the sofa creaks. I turn to look at her and realise she is watching me. She's still wearing her green jacket with the badges – every time she makes herself a roll-up she puts the lighter and the tobacco pouch back in her inside pocket as if she doesn't trust me not to steal from her, or wants to be ready to leave at a moment's notice.

We've never, ever been friends, Emma and me. We were both drawn towards Chloe's light, and exploded outwards along the same trajectory when she burned out. Ten years I've been keeping an eye on Emma, trying to figure out which of Chloe's secrets she's carrying and which I've been left to nurture on my own. And it's taken me this long to realise she's been keeping an eye on me too. Watching me for something. What can she have done? What does she think I could possibly have on her?

Today and every day for the past decade our whole city has sat over its collective picture album and made up its memories of Chloe. Who am I, I am coming to realise, to presume that I've not been doing exactly the same thing – or that my version of Chloe is any more accurate than theirs?

23

I didn't have to wait long. She came to me after school with the dirt still under her fingernails and a red crack at the corner of her mouth, as if her smile was slowly widening.

I opened the front door without thinking about my rank breath or the state of my hair, stood on the step, and waited for her to say something. She'd caught me still in my nightgown and relishing the tail end of my first proper hangover. She stared at me as long as she could manage, and then picked at something on the cuff of her jacket. There was old eye-liner caked in the corner of her eyes like black snot.

'Is your mum here? Am I not allowed to come in now?'

'She's in,' I said. 'She's watching the telly.'

'Well, my dad said he'd pick me up in two hours, so . . . ?'

I turned around and went back into the house, leaving the door open behind me. It was petty, that, but at least she let me enjoy it and didn't say anything as she fumbled the door closed and wiped her feet on the mat. I let her follow me up the stairs to my bedroom. I didn't care if she looked through the hallway at Barbara sitting with her glass in front of the telly in the living room.

'Shanks said about what happened with your dad,' she said, not looking at me. The words ran into each other because she was speaking too fast: trying to get it over with. 'Sorry to hear about it.'

I was almost untouchable now – what would she dare to say to me today? Newly protected and a celebrity at school. I didn't say anything and she opened her mouth again and carried on, ploughing through the silence with her babble.

'Some of the girls talked about clubbing together to get you a card,' Chloe said, 'or making something. Maybe some flowers. We thought you might have had enough of flowers.' She pulled her bag onto her knee and unzipped the top. 'I got this for you. Sorry it's been opened. I got it from home.'

She handed me a bottle wrapped in a carrier bag and I took it without looking at it and put it on my desk.

'Thanks,' I said. 'You got any fags?'

She nodded.

'Give them here then.'

I found my lighter and lit up, right in my room without opening the window, without even closing the door. I stood in front of her and blew the smoke upwards. She stared at me. I said nothing, but leaned over, opened the bottle and swigged from the neck. Vodka. I didn't like it. It smelled like nail varnish remover but I drank it anyway.

'Your mum's going to go wild,' Chloe said, admiringly.

'No, she isn't,' I said, and it was the truth. 'I do what I like now.'

Chloe looked around the room, staring at posters on the walls she'd seen lots of times before, and found something interesting in the folds of a blue and white towel hanging over the radiator. Was she wondering what else was different? I handed her the bottle and she took a sip.

'Who was going to get me a card? Emma? I don't think so.'

Chloe was looking at me funny. It was as if I'd been disfigured, had had something amputated. A deformity she was sorry about, but didn't want to acknowledge. So her pity floated freely around her words, alighting on one or other of them and then taking off – clogging the air and attached to nothing she could mention. She handed the bottle back.

'I brought you this as well,' she said, and pulled out a piece of paper, crumpled from her coat pocket. I thought it was another poster of Wilson and I wouldn't take it so she laid it on the bed between us.

'Science projects. Due in by half term. I'm going to do the calorific value of different kinds of nuts,' Chloe said. 'Emma's going to do that thing with the toilet paper and the felt-tip pens.'

'Right,' I said. I looked out of the window, still blowing smoke.

I admit, it was thrilling to be so uninterested in her and have her still here, chattering and trying to hit on a topic of conversation that might please me. So thrilling that it was hard to keep up the slow movements, the sighs, the slackness I could feel in my face.

'Mrs Fenwick says not to worry. Says I can give it to you, but you don't have to come up with anything yet. She was all right, actually. She said she'll see you when you're next in. No rush.'

'What made you think about the nuts?'

Chloe looked confused, then laughed, then put her hands over her mouth in a dramatic way – as if there were a corpse or a sick person in the next room likely to be disturbed by her noise.

'My dad told me,' she said. 'You set fire to them and work out how much they can heat up a pan of water. Do some sums about the weight.' She flicked her hair. 'He's going to write it all out for me.'

That is how Chloe always came first or second in the class at everything. What her dad didn't know, her mum had covered. I should probably have raided Donald's journals and scrapbooks and done something about fish.

'What are you going to do?' she asked.

Chloe had never spent so much time talking about her school work in all the time that I had known her. 'I bet Mrs F. will have a list, if you can't think—'

'Ice,' I said quickly, and turned on the bed and forced myself into her gaze.

I'll swear down now that I don't know where ice came from. It wasn't planned. It wasn't something I had any particular interest in before then. It must have been the weather, and my near-constant thoughts about the frozen top of the duck pond in the nature reserve. Ice. As soon as I had said the word I imagined fragile sheets blooming over the windows, the ferny spines of snowflakes and skins of frost.

'For global warming?' she said.

I wanted to laugh. 'Ice. It's been on my mind a lot lately.'

She coughed, licked the crack at the corner of her mouth, and stared at the towel on the radiator again. She lit a cigarette uncertainly, glancing towards the door. I counted to twenty.

'What have you come here for, anyway?' I said.

Chloe forced her lips together, and glared at me.

'My mum told me to,' she said. 'She didn't know we'd broke friends.'

Broke friends, as if it was a glass vase on a wobbling coffee table, or a marriage.

'Have you seen Carl?'

Chloe ducked her head. I could see red blotches start to appear on the side of her neck. She played with her cigarette, tapping her ash into the empty metal lid from the vodka bottle.

'You know they've banned me.'

'You've never done as you're told before. They can't stop you having a boyfriend, loads of girls do.'

'He's too old, according to them.'

'Why did you tell them how old he was?'

'They were grilling me in the hospital. Wanted to know where he lived, what school he went to, what his dad did for a living. Mum was going to invite him round for tea to get a good look at him. Dad was after burying him under the patio.'

I thought about that for a while. Relished it.

'I should have kept my mouth shut,' I said, testing. No point holding back now.

'Maybe,' Chloe said. The red on her neck had spread to her face. 'Don't upset yourself. With things the way they are –' she didn't want to say 'because your dad killed himself because he was mental,' but I could tell that was what she meant, 'with things the way they are, it's not that big a deal, is it?'

'I thought you'd go mad,' I said, 'not being able to see him. Have you spoken to him?'

Chloe shook her head, lifted her hand to her mouth to start gnawing on the skin there, and then moved it away sharply – as if it smelled, or she'd only just remembered the crescent moons of filth under her fingernails.

'No,' Chloe said lightly.

'I gave you money for your phone,' I pressed. 'What did you do with it?'

'He's not answering, all right?' Chloe snapped. 'I'm not hanging around with him anymore. Haven't seen him in a fortnight, and don't want to see him. Leave it, eh?'

She was her old self again, lying through her teeth and hissing at me, and in that second I felt a bit scared of her and wanted to do something to make her calm and pleased with me and that meant everything was normal again. I almost felt relieved.

'Sorry. Sorry,' she said, and pushed the bottle at me. 'Have a drink. It'll make you feel better.'

'Will it?'

She nodded, and swigged deeply. 'There's a tablet Carl gets for me and Emma sometimes. I don't know what it's called. It makes you feel like your body's gone to sleep. All your arms and legs get warm and limp. Your mind just floats away somewhere else. It's lovely. I'll ask Emma, see if she's got any left to give to you. You'll like it.' She patted the piece of paper sitting on the bed between us. 'And I'll ask Schizo-Fenwick if we can work together on a project. Do the nuts with me. She'll let you. You probably won't have to do any tests for the rest of the term.'

This was Chloe going into unfamiliar territory and turning the conversation away from herself. I ignored her.

'Carl's a letch,' I said, remembering the spit, and the car, and having to run home on my own through the park. 'He *did* try it on with me, when you were in the hospital. I wasn't lying.'

I expected her to hit me, or shriek, or take fistfuls of my hair and shake me about like a damp shirt. She bowed her head.

'Yes,' she said, 'I bet he did.'

This puzzled me. I paused, wondering what to ask her next.

'He's like that,' she said carefully. She looked like she was about to say something else, but she bit her bottom lip to stop the words coming out.

'Like what?'

'Men are . . . different,' she said, at last. 'Especially older men.' She moved her eyes away from me and started, I could tell, to quote Carl. 'It's the age difference. Maturity in a woman means understanding that a man – fully grown, not like the boys at school – needs more than one woman can give.' I marvelled. Did she really swallow that? Or was that how it worked in real life? How would I know? I thought about Nathan two-timing Amanda and the way she hated it and put up with it all the same. Maybe.

'Anyway, you didn't do anything so it doesn't matter,' she said. 'Let's not talk about it anymore. It's nothing, is it?'

This conversation was not working out the way I'd planned it. Yes, she was uncomfortable, and she seemed to be coming away from Carl at last – but no nearer to confiding in me. No nearer to coming back to the way things were before Emma and then Carl turned up in our lives and spoiled everything.

'Don't say anything more to Emma about it, will you?'

'Why?'

She wouldn't look at me again. I could have slapped her, but my head was swimming with the vodka.

'Carl's all right,' she said, after a long pause. 'He might just be a bit busy at work.' Her hair fell over her eyes and she didn't push it back. 'He's probably just upset that me and him are public now. He was always really worried about me getting into trouble with my parents. Protective.'

I snorted and it made an ugly sound.

'Don't be like that,' she said. 'I've come round, haven't I? Trying to make it up to you?'

'Only because your *daddy* brought you.'

Chloe flinched at that, and while I could see how addictive bullying might be, and why she had such a lot of fun doing it, I didn't want to go on. I stubbed out my cigarette on the side of my desk and poked it into the vodka lid. I motioned for her to give me another fag.

'I might come to your house at the weekend,' I said. 'I need to copy some of your maths off you.'

'I'll leave my book,' she said eagerly.

'No. I don't feel like it now. I might come on Saturday. And I'll decide by then what I want to do about this science thing. Whether I'll come in with you on it or not.'

Chloe nodded. 'All right then,' she said, looking grateful.

I wanted to keep things like they were and hold her on probation until Saturday, but my advantage was wearing off. She leaned back on the bed and unzipped her coat, using the thin edge of the zip to probe underneath her thumbnail.

'What's your mum like?' she said, less carefully now.

'Didn't you see her?'

Chloe opened her eyes wide and shook her head. She was lying.

'Never mind,' I said.

Donald had never been a large part of what we talked about and so long as we didn't mention it he was less embarrassing now that he was dead than he had been when he was alive and shuffling along the upstairs landing in one slipper, or sucking on his inhaler while we were trying to eat our tea, or opening my bedroom door without knocking so that he could interrupt us and ask for scissors or glue or help with his typewriter.

When that happened Chloe would laugh at him openly and I was supposed to join in. Now I kept remembering Chloe's stifled giggles and shaking shoulders, and Donald asking me privately if she was 'quite all right'. I did join in, at the time, and he always hesitated and said 'Sorry, girls,' even if he wasn't asking us for anything, but just telling us to come down for our tea. I think he was sorry, generally, that he was alive and forced to bother other people with the fact of it.

'That boy,' I said, 'on Boxing Day.'

'You are obsessed with that Mong.' She didn't exactly shout, but it was loud, and it came out in a rush.

'Is that what Emma told you to say?' I said.

Chloe stared at me. 'What are you talking about Emma for?'

'Why?'

'What?'

'Why didn't you tell her we were the last people to see Wilson? If you and her are so tight all of a sudden?'

'Oh, she's –' Chloe waved her hand. 'She's too keen. She's a trier – you know? She really cares what I think of her. It's a bit pathetic really.'

I nodded. I was fairly sure that Chloe would have described me like that to Emma too. She was a two-faced little cow when she wanted to be.

'It's just I keep thinking about that football I saw frozen into the ice. Keep imagining him chasing it through the woods and ending up under the water. Do you reckon he could swim?'

'Don't think about it,' Chloe said. 'You're just making stuff up in your head. You've no idea what happened to him. No one does. He probably just ran away.'

'You reckon?'

'How many times have we got to talk about this? It's boring. And you wonder why I'd rather hang out with Emma?'

'It's on my mind, all the time.' I put my head on her shoulder. 'I can't sleep. I'm blaming myself, a bit. I just need to know what happened. To know it wasn't my fault.'

'It wasn't your fault,' Chloe said mechanically. With my head on her shoulder, I could smell her sweat.

'I don't know that for sure. Barbara thinks that what happened with, well, you know. That was down to me. How do I know she's not right about that too?'

I tried to cry, but I was empty.

'What's the matter?' Chloe asked. She shuffled right up close to me until her knee was pressed against my leg.

'Just sad,' I said. 'My head's a mess.'

I did cry then, and it wasn't all pretend, and she knew just what to do with me.

'Poor baby,' she said and squeezed my arm. Tears leaked out until they stopped. She kept squeezing. She probably thought I was going to start wailing or thrashing about. I imagined us in a painting, our heads close together, four white kneecaps and shiny polished shoes touching.

'I've been horrible to you, haven't I, and now this has happened. Your . . . *misfortune*.'

I nearly laughed, and the moment was gone. It wasn't unusual for Chloe to talk as though she was starring in a period drama. She read *Jane Eyre* and for weeks afterwards, instead of asking me if I wanted to come out, she'd enquire if I fancied 'taking a turn around the park'.

I looked at our knees and felt all jangly and hysterical and didn't say anything. We listened to Barbara's feet on the stairs and the sound of the toilet flushing. Silence while the cistern refilled.

'Shall I put your hair up?' she said. I think she was noticing how slowly the time was passing, unpunctuated by Donald's interruptions.

'No. I'm going to go to bed now.'

'Now? But it's—'

'I'm tired.' I flopped backwards onto the duvet and turned my face away from her.

'Shall I go then? I'll ring my dad and get him to come.'

Her voice was tiny. I'd never heard her talking to me like that before, only to Carl. A kind of begging voice.

I shrugged and lay still until I heard the front door open and close behind her.

24

Emma always carried her PE kit in a torn Morrisons bag with her name written on the plastic in black marker. The rest of us had special PE bags with the school badge on, or holdalls from a sports shop. Emma carried her carrier bag around without shame, as if she hadn't noticed she was the only one who did it like that. She had it with her – that and a black violin case – when she came to see me later that week.

'Sorry,' she said. I'd thought it was Barbara and was shoving Donald's journal down the side of my bed in case the sight of his handwriting upset her.

'I thought you heard me call up the stairs. Your mum told me just to come up.'

'It's fine. Is Chloe with you?' I looked over her shoulder but she was closing my bedroom door behind her. She shook her head.

'Just me.'

She leaned the violin case against the wall and put the bag and her school rucksack down carefully before sitting down on my desk chair. All done very deliberately and slowly as if she was putting off the moment when she'd have to speak to me. I sat up properly and swung my legs out of the bed; I didn't want to feel like a patient in a hospital.

'We haven't had a chance to talk,' she said. She tucked her hands into the pleats of her school skirt – she was trembling.

'About what? I'm all right,' I said. 'I'm coming back to school tomorrow.'

She leaned over and smiled at me and there were black clogged pores on her chin and nose. 'They'd let you stay off for longer, if you wanted.'

'I know. I'm bored though. I've got to go back sometime. There's this science project.'

She smiled, as if she knew I was lying. I didn't ask her about chromatography, or if she'd decided to abandon that and go in with Chloe on the nuts. I didn't tell her about ice, and she didn't ask me about Donald's funeral or how I was feeling. There was nothing to say, and the silence was awkward. I didn't rush in to speak – she had come to see me so she could sit there and come up with something to say. And if she didn't, feeling bad about it was her own problem. Maybe she'd just pick up her case and go home again.

'Chloe will be glad to have you back, I reckon,' she said. 'She's not been well lately, did you know?'

I thought of that crack at the side of her mouth.

'Yes,' I said, 'it's her and Carl. It's stressing her out that she's been banned from seeing him. She probably thinks he's going to get someone else to take her place.'

Emma looked at her hands and said nothing for a long time. I got the feeling she was on the brink of confiding something in me. But we'd never been on our own together before. We weren't friends – we were Chloe's friends. I hadn't known she played the violin, I didn't know the names of her brothers, what the inside of her house was like, whether she liked using body spray or just plain soap. And I've no doubt that I was as peripheral to her as she was to me – it was only Chloe we had in common, Chloe who brought us together and in many ways, kept us apart.

'I felt bad after hearing about your dad. The things that me and Chloe said to you. It wasn't on.'

That was not what she had come to say. I shrugged.

'It doesn't matter. Chloe can be like that sometimes, I've known her longer than you. Long enough to know when she means something, and when she's just blowing off steam.'

Emma just fiddled with the pleats in her skirt. Her socks hadn't been washed right – Barbara was very careful about washing only white things together, same as Amanda. Whoever did the washing at Emma's house didn't take the same kind of care, and her socks were the colour of old porridge. Most of the time she was careless about her hair. She never tried to sneak a bit of make-up on for school. She chewed the cuff of her school shirt when she was thinking. I could list the things I knew about her on one hand.

'I've been friends with Chloe for ages,' I said. 'She tells me everything. She's already been round to see me. We've talked it through.'

'I just wondered if you wanted me to start meeting you on your way to school?' she said quickly. 'We can walk in together. I don't mind setting off a bit earlier and coming to your house first. I get up early for gymnastics practice anyway.'

'You want to walk to school with me?' I said.

She twitched, as uncomfortable with this as I was.

'If tomorrow's your first day back, I'll come in with you.'

I stared at her. She stared back. Brown eyes, expressionless and unreadable. She was checking up on me. She wanted to keep tabs on me? Chloe had told her to walk me in – make sure that I didn't get upset and start opening my trap about Wilson, or Carl, or her, or any of the other things she didn't know I knew? None of that made sense.

'You heard, didn't you?' Emma said, by way of explanation. 'I suppose you've had other things to think about the last couple of weeks.'

'I knew there'd been another two.'

'Both from our school – the baths and the playing fields. They're getting extra teachers to stand along the route when we do cross-country now.'

'Barbara's always watching videos,' I said. 'We never have the news on.'

I don't know if Emma understood or not, but she nodded. 'He's started again,' she said. 'It's so close to us now.' Her voice was strange. 'You need to be careful. Very careful.'

The baths were attached to the school – they were our baths really, and our sports hall and tennis courts – but they were also open to the public and there was some sort of complicated timetable that dictated when the pool was available and when we got our lessons. It was so complicated and the barrier between the leisure centre and the school nothing more than a set of unmarked double doors so that half the time you'd be doing your swimming lessons with the spectators' gallery full of people wrapped in towels, waiting impatiently for us to finish so they could get back in. I always found the idea of having a gallery up above the pool weird anyway – who'd want to spectate at a school swimming lesson?

'I've lived this long,' I said, and laughed.

'Terry doesn't think it's the same person,' Emma said. 'He reckons the first ones were that Mong, and this is someone else. A copy-cat.'

I laughed. 'Not that Mong,' I said, and looked out of the window down into the garden which was bare and white-blue with frost. 'Why does Terry think that?'

'The girl by the playing fields – she was a Year Seven. He didn't just get his cock out or have a feel of her,' Emma said, 'he tried to drag her off along that little path. She says there was a car parked at the end of it. He was going to try and take her away, she reckons.'

I shrugged.

'And the other girl,' she said quickly, 'the one in the swimming baths . . .' She paused and followed my gaze out of the window. 'She's still not talking. Not to the police, not to her parents, not to anyone. It's a lot worse. An *escalation of activity*. Doesn't matter who's doing it. Doesn't matter how long it takes for them to catch him. We've just got to stick together. Make sure nothing happens to us. He's not finished yet. They're the girls that got away.'

'So Terry says.'

She sighed, suddenly annoyed with me. 'I'm only trying to tell you for your own good,' she said. 'Even Shanks says it's all gathering around our school – they think the pest is someone very local, he's said we've all to get a partner to walk there and back with – and I didn't know if you'd heard or not. Thought you might want to come with me.'

'You think he's going to jump out of the bushes at me at half eight on a Friday morning?' I said, and remembered the things we said about the man in the Halloween mask. How harmless he was – how it was funny and pathetic and almost sweet in a way.

'I can get us a packet of fags on the way. I know you're probably feeling bad right now – what with, everything – but it might be all right. The two of us, walking in together.'

'Maybe,' I said. Donald's money was rolled up in the toe of a sock, and shoved into a wellington boot at the back of my wardrobe. I wasn't short of fags, not if I didn't want to be.

'It's getting worse,' Emma said again. She was pleading with me.

'Did Shanks really say we had to come in pairs? Is it just our year, or the whole school, or what? Chloe never said anything. She lives nearer to me than you do.'

Emma lifted her hand and let it fall back onto her lap weakly, as if she was planning an argument and had decided to give up before starting.

'I'm just saying, that's all. You don't have to.' She looked away from me, pulled a piece of paper across my desk towards her and wrote something on it.

'That's my phone number,' she said. 'If you want someone to walk with, ring me up when you wake up and I'll come over.'

'I probably won't,' I said. 'Don't wait in or anything.'

Emma should have stood up then. Should have gathered her things and got ready to leave. She didn't, but looked at me again as if she wanted her eyes to ask me something. Begging, almost.

'Chloe will get Carl to take her,' I said. 'Why don't you get him to pick you up as well?'

Emma shook her head slowly.

'I'd better go,' she said.

I heard her walking slowly down the stairs, the bump of her case as it knocked against the banister. Barbara did not get up, and Emma must have let herself out, closing our front door gently behind her.

I walked to school the next morning and the roads were as busy as usual and I felt safe and nothing happened. I was invincible because I was walking around inside my own bright, brittle halo of ice and because I knew the police weren't going to come and get me, my thoughts were so far away from men in Halloween masks it was as if the pest didn't exist.

Chloe got Nathan to drive her – I imagined her sat in the back with her head against the window, her kohled eyes taking it all in as they negotiated the rush hour traffic in silence. Nathan was the kind of dad who talked about himself at parents' evenings, telling Shanks he saw himself as 'firm, but fair'. He'd have tried to talk to Chloe, get her to stop sulking and communicate with him. Share her problems. Her worries about boys, and pregnancy, and her GCSE options. And Chloe would have stared at the window, looking into the eyes of her own reflection and ignored him. I don't know how Emma arrived, but she arrived late, her coat buttoned up wrong and sweat along her hairline. She had to squeeze in at the back because I was in my normal place, next to Chloe.

It was only later that I realised Emma wasn't offering to do me a favour, wasn't trying to check up on me, wasn't on an errand from Chloe. She was scared, and she was desperate for someone to walk with her. I should have seen it. Her house was half a mile away from mine, and in the wrong direction. She didn't have a Carl, and her dad didn't have a car. She must have felt like a sitting duck.

Although Barbara didn't make me go and I had to iron my uniform myself, I almost enjoyed the next few days at school. Home was strange, quieter than usual and in theory, pleasanter, because Barbara had given up getting me to do anything. I ate junk food in front of her, wore my hair loose for school, and let the jam and butter sit out of the fridge all day. I left the bathroom light on all night, just to test it, and she never said a word. I don't think she even noticed. I carried on smoking in my room, stole her gin and left the bottle on my windowsill. This sudden freedom should have made things better but there was something else different about the house too, which I didn't like. A breath-held feeling, a strung-out anticipation for Donald shuffling out of his room after a long sleep, or turning up late for tea. His magazines kept arriving and we pretended that we didn't notice – left them lying in their plastic envelopes in the hallway until Barbara slipped on one. Then she threw the lot away.

I *wanted* to go to school, probably for the first time ever. There was none of that silence at school. No expecting someone to be there who wasn't. And after the pats and the whispers and the first two days I was allowed to slot, more or less, into where I had been before except I wasn't expected to go to assembly, or eat in the main dining room if I didn't feel like it. I let Chloe sit in the empty form room with me while the others listened to the morning announcements and we waited for it to be over and school to start properly. I hated assembly, and didn't mind missing it. Boring announcements about school sports fixtures and warnings that if we weren't sensible the City really would put a curfew in place, whether we liked it or not. We had our whole-school assemblies in the sports hall – and we had to take our shoes off. I never remembered the special instructions because I always had to concentrate on sitting so that my feet weren't lying flat on the floor. If that happened, when I stood up to file out with the rest of the row, I would leave behind a smudged wet imprint of feet on a floor the colour of blue toothpaste.

A death in the family gives you a few benefits. The people left behind become special in a way that they definitely weren't before. And by her proximity to me, constantly clinging at my arm and frowning people's attention and questions away from me (*Would you like that? Do you think that's what she wants to be reminded of?*), Chloe got her own benefits too. She was grounded, probably forever, but Amanda would make an exception for me because I was her best friend and I needed her. And of course Chloe and I were alone together a lot. She hadn't confided in me yet, but I was working on her and I felt we were moving in that direction. She was so solicitous she even came to my house again that week with her Polaroid camera and some of her special clothes.

'Let me do your make-up,' she said, and let a smile tug at the corners of her mouth. She'd brought her make-up bag with her. She was getting thinner. 'I'll do you a make-over and we can take some pictures. It'll cheer you up.'

'I'm not sure,' I said, making a show of being reluctant.

'Come on,' she was cheerful and brisk, 'put some music on. Have a drink. It'll be fun.'

She showed me a how-to guide for smoky eyes in *Just Seventeen* that she wanted to try. 'I'll do it on you, and you can do it to me,' she said. 'It'll be like old times. Remember, we used to do this loads during the summer holidays?'

I let her put mascara on me even though she always ended up poking me in the eye with the wand.

'Ta da!' She winked at me, and spoke with her stupid American accent, 'You look like a million dollars, baby!'

'I feel stupid,' I said, looking at myself in the little hand-mirror.

'That's crap. You look like a model,' she said.

She gave me her basque to try on and made me lie on my stomach with my knees bent and my feet in the air. I felt her fingers on my skin as she adjusted the straps and hooks on the basque so that it fit me, and slid my glasses off my face. She folded them up and left them on my desk where I couldn't reach them.

'Put your tongue behind your teeth and think about something sexy,' she said. She painted my mouth thick with lipstick that smelled like frying pans.

'Chloe,' I moaned, 'I'm cold. I feel stupid.'

She laughed. 'No pain, no gain.'

Chloe snapped handfuls of pictures, and I posed in the itchy red and black basque that Carl had bought her. My flesh came up in goosepimples and I tried to think about something sexy while the world, watery and formless without my glasses, shrank to the sound of her breath as she stuck her tongue out of the corner of her mouth and tried to work out the settings on the camera.

The photographs were okay. Chloe handed me my glasses so I could see them. She blew on them, and lined them up across my desk. I saw myself, looking pale and uncertain, posing with a cigarette, my lips pursed like Jessica Rabbit. I was better at taking them than she was, and most of them were washed-out and crooked-looking. Chloe seemed disappointed.

'Carl's got a proper camera,' she said, and mimed twisting a lens, with one eye closed. 'He develops them himself.'

'Yes,' I said, 'I know.'

It wasn't going to be long before she'd speak to me about what she and Carl had been doing in the woods that night. A person couldn't walk around with that on their conscience forever. She'd need someone to talk to, and that person would be me, and then things would go back to the way they had been in the summer. I got as close as I could to her, prodded her gently when the conversation led in that direction, and waited.

'You look terrific,' she said, and hugged me.

Chloe let me keep most of the pictures.

It was our last week at school together.

25

Barbara still padded about the house in her night-clothes. She kept odd hours, and often woke me up knocking ice cubes out of the plastic tray with a rolling pin. She dusted in the middle of the night and once I found her at three in the morning folding and refolding stacks of Donald's shirts on the living room floor. She never put them away or got rid of them. Her behaviour was getting to be really creepy – no wonder Chloe wanted me to come to her house. And she'd decided it would do me good not to be in my bedroom. She said 'a change of scene'. It sounded like a phrase she'd culled from Amanda, except the two of them were still at war.

I walked. The winter had not broken yet and the sky was white and the windows of the cars I passed were covered in frost. Someone had kicked a half-empty can of Fanta over in a bus stop and the orange trickle had solidified into a spike across the pavement. I stopped and stared at it a while, even though I wasn't really interested. A poster pasted onto the bus shelter caught my eye. Not the one with Wilson's face on it – a different, newer one, with a huge clip-art picture of an eye on it. The details underneath were for the next Community Action Group patrol. Men only, meeting at the train station at 9 p.m. to do a slow loop of the town centre. The eye was anatomically correct – the optical nerve still attached. It looked gruesome. '*Watch Out!*'

I didn't want to go. I didn't want to sit on the peach settee and talk to Chloe's mother: she always wanted me to call her 'Amanda' and chat about period pains and boys and pimples, none of which I had much experience of, any interest in, or any inclination to discuss with her. But even less did I want to stay at home and watch Barbara fluttering the shirts through the air for one last refolding. The arms dangled and made me think of Guy Fawkes dummies.

I was an hour or two later than I said I would be. Amanda opened the door and hugged all the air out of me in an ouff (*Sweetheart! Brave girl!*) and then made me go around the back and take my shoes off in the kitchen (*Just had the carpets done, my angel*). When I got into the kitchen I saw all the nuts and tweezers laid out on the kitchen worktop waiting for me and Chloe to begin. The objects shone, like they were specifically trying to make me feel guilty.

Chloe was in the kitchen too. She talked to me ostentatiously, a long gabbled sentence about the weather, and snow, and needing to wash her hair, and how she thought I'd forgotten. Amanda stood to one side of her, watching, and moving her hands about in her cardigan pockets. When Amanda had taken the television out of her room, Chloe had upped the ante and stopped talking to her altogether. Chloe had told me that she was even refusing to eat in front of her parents so that they'd think they'd made her into an anorexic, feel guilty and relent.

It was working. She looked terrible. Her hair was so dull it looked sticky, and there was sleep in her eyes, yellow crusts along her eyelashes that reminded me of a sick dog Donald had found once, and insisted on keeping in the shed until it was better and could be 'released into the wild' to go back to foraging in bins. She was skinny too – as skinny as she'd ever wanted to be – which made her look sickly and pale and more ill than she'd looked when she'd been in hospital. She didn't look pretty anymore, but I still didn't want to cross the kitchen and stand next to her. Didn't want my thigh next to hers for a comparison.

'I haven't slept more than four hours a night in three weeks,' she'd said, not quite proudly.

She was making herself ill. She told me all this herself and so I thought most of these symptoms were just ploys, and ways of levering her parents into relenting. I didn't think there was anything really wrong. Knowing what kinds of things she had on her mind, I should have.

'They're buying me things to get me to eat,' she'd said gleefully, and shown me a new personal stereo.

'Wow,' I'd responded dutifully, 'can I have your old one?'

'I'll leave you two girls to it, shall I?' Amanda said, but didn't move. She was like Emma, waiting to be asked to join in.

'Lola,' Chloe said, and turned her whole body towards me and away from her mother, 'I'm going to take a quick shower. My hair is disgusting. Can you entertain yourself for fifteen minutes?'

'Sure,' I said, the beginning of a sentence Chloe never heard the end of, because she'd already swished out of the room, slamming the door behind her.

Amanda shook her head at the space in the air Chloe had left. She'd left the smell of her White Musk Christmas perfume hanging around behind her.

'Oh dear,' she said weakly, and pushed the button on the kettle. I listened to the fizz of the element heating up.

'I'm glad you and Chloe have started seeing a bit more of each other again,' Amanda said, 'but you mustn't let it get to be a hassle for your mother.'

'Barbara doesn't mind,' I said.

Chloe's footsteps banged over our heads. The shower started. She was always washing off her make-up and putting it back on again.

'Yes, but all the sleepovers you've been having. You must let us return the favour. We've bought a camp-bed, so you can come whenever you like.'

I registered *all the sleepovers* without letting it show on my face, and then *Carl*. And still keeping my mouth as still as I could manage, I wondered angrily if the camp-bed was a present to me to make up for Donald getting drowned. Chloe isn't allowed to have her boyfriend anymore and she gets a personal stereo. Sony, and not the Alba shit that I've got. Donald drowns himself and I get a zed-bed.

I felt the words bubbling in my throat and wanted to say them so I started chewing at my thumbnail to stop myself from talking.

Amanda wasn't filling up the gap in the conversation, just looking at me sympathetically.

'It isn't any trouble for Barbara,' I said again. The anger evaporated quickly. I was sad. Despite everything, Chloe still wouldn't tell me the truth. She'd probably already confided in Emma.

Amanda poured the boiling water into a pink mug I knew was Chloe's, then led me into the living room and made me sit in the recliner chair, tilted backwards so my feet were up. She perched on the edge of the settee across from me, and smiled, and stared, and nodded encouragingly whenever I put the mug to my mouth. I had to drink hot chocolate with marshmallows in it until Chloe had finished soaping her hair and scraping at her face.

'We've made some ice for you,' she said, and I looked at the brown drink inside the mug. Ice?

'Chloe said you might want to do ice. She and Emma put the trays outside last night.'

She pointed through the arch and I looked along her arm and into the conservatory, through the pointy leaves of some dangling white and green plants and out into the garden. They had filled old seed trays and roasting tins with water and left them to freeze outside overnight. The ice had swelled and the plastic trays were bowed out at the edges.

I'd forgotten that I'd said that, about the ice, but Chloe had remembered and put the water out for me. That was a kind thing to do. I felt bad again, for being late and then silent.

'I think,' I said, struggling to push the recliner down to a proper sitting chair so I could get out of it, 'I'll go up to Chloe's room now. She's got some tapes of mine and I want to take them home with me.'

Amanda looked at me for a long time. She still had her new Christmas earrings on, and blue mascara. I started to feel nervous. She looked like Chloe and her eyes were the same too: glinting at me as if she could guess what I was going to do next.

'She's not eating, you know,' she said abruptly. 'Not here, anyway.'

I didn't know what to say.

'I know you're in the middle . . .' She bit her lip '. . . of your own troubles.'

'It's all right,' I said.

'It's this project. Calories. You know we've stopped her seeing that boy.'

'Yes.'

'It's hard to tell. Revenge, or to get attention. Or something real. Does she worry?'

'What about?'

'Her size. Weight. Does she think she needs to diet?'

I shrugged. Chloe was always more interested in my diet than her own. Some things make your skin worse, she'd tell me, and watch approvingly while I scraped them off my plate and into the bin. Chloe ate whatever she liked. She had that kind of metabolism, she said. I wasn't to feel bad about it. It was luck, genes, and nothing to do with either of us as real people, which to her, was the important thing.

'I don't think so.'

Amanda stood up and started to rearrange the school pictures of Chloe on the mantelpiece. Four different kinds of school uniform and every picture in an expensive silver frame. You could run them together like a flickerbook and see her growing up before your eyes.

'We've never had a teenage girl before, her father and me. People expect you to know how to be a parent by the time your child gets to be this age. But we don't know. She's up in her room with Emma for hours – in and out of the greenhouse – phone calls at odd hours. I've caught her sneaking out at night a few times. What about the times I haven't caught her? She won't let us meet this boy. I daren't think what they get up to together. I had to throw out a pair of her jeans they were so filthy.'

She stopped fiddling with the pictures and turned to face me. 'Is there something I should know? It seems such an extreme reaction. It's hard to know what's normal.'

'We've never spoken about it. Sorry.'

Amanda smiled, and shook her head.

'I shouldn't be pestering you. Nathan told me to leave you alone. Don't worry about it. You just have a nice afternoon,' she waved her hands at me and her voice cracked, 'go on and get your tapes.'

Chloe's room was full of eyes. We spent whole weekends sitting on her bedroom floor cutting pictures out of *Smash Hits* and pasting them to her walls. The shower was still going in the bathroom. I stepped onto the pink carpet and held my breath, listening for the shower water.

Chloe had a special drawer. It was just the bottom drawer of her night-table. She told me that in Year Seven when she'd started wearing bras she'd kept them in there instead of her usual sock drawer. In Year Eight she'd used it to keep her fags in. Now it was full of clear zip-locked bags that were stuffed with condoms. She'd been to a Talkwize clinic in town where they handed them out, for free, no questions asked. Patsy – Dr Jamrag – had told her where to go and what to say. Chloe liked shiny new things. Liked having a special drawer, and accessories, and secrets. She must have got over the embarrassment and been ten times. I'd been with her once, and was embarrassed enough that I had to wait outside (*You can't come in, do you want them to think we're lezzers?*), counting the lumps of chewing gum on the pavement and watching the morning queue outside the pub across the road.

I slid the drawer back and saw the bags. More occasions of sex than any one person would ever have in their life, probably. And underneath them, hardly hidden, the black block of a mobile phone. I picked it up, listened for the continued fizz of the shower water hitting enamel next door, and turned it on. There were holes in the plastic at the ear-piece. I covered them with my thumbs and felt the thing buzz against my hand. Remembered the day the police came to my house and the message that I left on her answering service.

It would have been better if they really had come to talk to me about Wilson.

I touched the buttons, lifted it to my ear, listened. There I was. Pissed off and panicking and as good as admitting to something that she knew full well I hadn't done. And she'd kept this message anyway. Nice insurance for her.

I turned the phone back off again, put it in the drawer, closed it. Opened the drawer, took it out, stuffed it into the back pocket of my jeans and pulled my jumper down to cover the lump it made on my backside. The tapes I wanted were on Chloe's desk, stacked up neatly. I picked them up and went downstairs, not bothering to close the door behind me.

I could have just deleted the message and put the phone back into the drawer. Chloe wouldn't have known, and if she did notice and guess that I had done it, she could hardly come to me and complain about it. I thought about those retching noises she made in the woods. But I stole her phone and I did it because I wanted her to know. I wanted her to notice it was missing and figure out for herself how and why I had taken it. I wanted her to feel scared and confused, like she'd been making me feel − and most of all, I wanted something solid in my pocket – something to hold and take home and look at when I was on my own and doubting that any of this could really be happening.

The ice was stuck hard into the roasting tins and seed trays. Amanda had made Chloe dry her hair before we were allowed to go out, and then given me a tub of salt. I stared at it in my hand and wanted to laugh. The laughter felt like dry, hot stones at the back of my mouth where my tongue started. I tried to let it out, but it turned into a cough.

'You didn't think this through, did you?' she said, poking at the trays with her shoe.

I picked one of the seed trays up and flexed it as if it was an ice cube tray. Blocks of ice, curved at the top like corks where the water had overflowed the individual compartments for the soil, fell onto the lawn and bounced. None of them broke, and I crouched and touched them.

'You have to write about your method,' Chloe said. 'You can't fuck up on this. It isn't possible. So long as you write about what you did, what you used, and what you thought was going to happen, you'll get the marks, even if you end up blowing something up.'

I had stacked the big ice cubes into a tower while she was talking to me. Then I started to pour salt on the top one. The salt wore a dint into it. The dint filled with water, then overflowed. The overflowing water solidified again on its way down. It made the tower less wobbly than it had been before.

'That's all right,' I said, poking at it with my finger.

'You have to write about how you're going to apply it. You can't just mess about.' Chloe's teeth were chattering. I thought about ways to apply it, this stupid tower of ice – this useless thing that I'd made and now had to explain and assign a value to. It made me think about Donald. I wanted to kick the ice tower over, to shatter the cubes into fragments. He did it all for me, and that wasn't fair. I didn't ask him to. It's too much to put on another person's shoulders – to expect me to be happy all the time just to keep Donald on an even keel. I leaned back and kicked the tower. It hurt my foot, right through the toe of my trainer. The blocks broke apart, flew through the air and plopped onto the grass.

'What did you do that for?' Chloe's shoulders were shaking, even though she was more bundled up than I was. It was because she was so thin. 'Don't dick about,' she said irritably. 'I spent ages doing this.'

The ice was harder to get out of the roasting tins because they wouldn't bend like the plastic seed trays had. I put them upside down on the grass and stood on them with one foot. There was a sound, something between a snap and a squeak. When I pulled the metal tray away it was dented and the ice was in pieces.

'I wonder if you can cut yourself on it,' I said, looking at the hard edges and not wanting to touch. It looked like glass, bubbled and broken, but it wasn't glass.

'I'm fucking freezing,' Chloe said, and we went in to burn her Brazil nuts.

What should I say now? I didn't talk to her enough? I talked to her too much? I couldn't get her to listen to me and understand that things would be much better for us both if we'd have confided in each other?

I was fourteen. She was my best friend.

And now it is Emma who I am sitting up late at night with, in something that is nowhere near a companionable silence. I want to ask her if Chloe talked to her about the things that were on her mind – the things she did not tell her mother and would not tell me. I want to ask Emma if Chloe let her listen to the message on her phone – if they laughed over it, or discussed a plan of action. I want to tell Emma that I still talk to Chloe. That I toast her in the early hours. That now I have to try all the things she should have done first, and I have to do it on my own.

I have a pink and white mug I bought for her three years ago and sometimes I bring it out of the cupboard and hold it between my hands like the stem of a posy.

'Here,' I say, offer it out to the dark and try to believe in ghosts. Nothing ever happens. Chloe isn't here and Chloe has never left the City.

Later, we were standing behind the greenhouse, hiding between the wall and the panes of cloudy glass. Smoking.

'I know you're still seeing Carl – don't pretend like you aren't.'

Chloe turned her back to me quickly and shook her head so hard that her ponytail hit the sides of her neck.

'I'm not,' she said, in a strange, muffled voice. Usually, when she was lying, she liked you to know that she was lying. Not that there was a big secret to keep, but that something was going on and you just weren't quite important enough to know about it. Or she'd withhold, to extend the pleasure of the questioning for as long as possible.

'I don't want anything to do with him,' she said, and she sounded like she had something in her mouth.

My hands had gone past cold from playing with the ice, and past sore, and into numb. The skin on my fingers felt like rubber – like it was nothing to do with me at all. As I was wondering what it would be like to have a whole body like that – even tongue and eyes, the warmth in my blood started to prickle back into them and they began to hurt. That seemed more impor- tant – that pain in my fingers – than the conversation I was trying to have with Chloe.

'I know you have,' I said. 'You're talking shite.'

'What?' Chloe blew her smoke at the iced panes of glass,

melting a little circle. She watched the steam and smoke bounce off the surface and didn't look at me. Her eyes were sly, slitty. I could see her eyelashes brushing her cheeks – clumped together with cheap mascara.

'What do you know?' she said, but when she turned and looked at me, her face was red.

'You've been staying out all night with him,' I said.

'No, I haven't,' she said. It wasn't lazy – usually she didn't care if I believed her or not, and usually I didn't bother so much. But this time she was shaking her head, and insisting.

'I think you have. Out in his car at night. In the woods.'

I exhaled a cloud of my own smoke. Didn't try for a ring.

'No.'

'Your mum thinks you've been sleeping at mine,' I said, 'keeping me company. Comforting me.'

I could smell her. After her shower she'd put fresh perfume and make-up on, but got back into her old clothes. She smelled yeasty and musty – dirty knickers and airing cupboards and bathmats, with a choking cover-up of White Musk. It was so weird. Chloe was obsessive about outfits, and hygiene.

'All right,' Chloe said, and dug the cigarette into the gravel with her toe, burying it. 'I've been staying out. So what?'

I pulled the Polos out of my pocket. Only two left, both of them broken.

'Have one of these,' I said. 'You can talk to me about anything.'

She shook her head. 'They'll make me sick,' she said. 'I don't care if she smells the smoke on me.'

'I'm your best friend, aren't I?' I said, still holding out the mints.

She smiled and took one just to please me, put it in her mouth and I could see the scale on her teeth and she sucked it hard, so her cheeks puckered and her eyes popped, like she was trying to make me laugh.

'Best friends,' she said, 'but there's nothing to tell.'

'Where have you been going at night?'

'Carl's, of course,' she said lightly.

'You can't have been,' I said. 'His mother. He'd never take you back to his house.'

'His mother's sick,' Chloe said. 'She doesn't know what's going on. Carl hammered a sheet of wood over the window in the box room and she never even noticed.'

'The darkroom?'

Chloe smiled. 'Nearly finished. I've been helping him.'

'In the middle of the night?'

She shrugged, and smiled at me. 'You're going to get to see it soon. Come on,' she said, 'it's too cold. Let's go in.'

Chloe and I crossed the garden without speaking, sucking on the mints and marching past the ice – the cracked edges and triangular shapes melting into lumps where I'd put the salt on them. We went into the kitchen. She stood at the counter and started sweeping nuts and pieces of burned paper into the bin.

I tried again.

'I want to go back to that pond,' I said. 'Carl's going to have to take us in the car. I want to go and look again.'

'Why?' Chloe said, and shook her head. 'It's nothing to do with me. I didn't do anything wrong. You've already been out there once.'

Her voice was high and cracked. She carried on shaking her head, in a slow thoughtful arc, even after she'd finished speaking.

'I want you to come with me. You're supposed to be my best friend.'

'No point,' she said, more quietly.

'I want you to come. I think he's under the ice. I can't sleep for thinking about it.'

'Why?' she said again. 'Why are you so obsessed with that idea?' She turned her back on me to wring out a cloth aggressively under the tap. 'You're messed up in the head, you are.'

'It's like Carl said. It was me, wasn't it? I told him people went skating on the ice,' I said. 'I told him it was a laugh. I said we did it all the time.'

'We've never been skating on that ice,' Chloe said. Her lips were flaking and cracked, and she licked them nervously. Where was her gloss?

'I know,' I said irritably. It was hard, trying to argue with her in a low voice, while Amanda was ironing in front of the television just through the archway. 'I was just . . .' What was I supposed to tell her? Making things up to impress a Mong? '. . . making conversation.'

'So?' Chloe shrugged.

'So what if he did? What if he went through?'

'It'd be his own stupid fault,' Chloe said, decisively. 'Just because you mentioned it doesn't mean you forced him to do it.'

'You've changed your tune.'

She was certain. I stared at her. Her eyelid twitched slightly and she took her hair from behind her ear and started to twirl it around her fingers. It found its way into her mouth, and she sucked it into a spike. She was so certain it made me doubt myself.

'We're not going to see anything you haven't already seen,' Chloe said. 'You should just forget about it.'

'I want to go and see.'

'He's not there.' Her hands twitched towards a tea-towel on the draining board. 'Can't you just trust me?' Chloe stared at me. I just shook my head and pulled the tea-towel away from her.

'You should just trust *me*,' I said.

'You'll just have to wait until the spring, won't you? See what pops up when it thaws out.'

'I want you and Carl to come, just to double-check. We'll be there and back in an hour if he drives us.'

'He's not going to want to do that,' Chloe said evenly. 'He's busy trying to get this darkroom finished.' She pulled the tea-towel gently through my fingers, spat out her hair and bent her head to scrub at the worktop.

'It's Valentine's Day soon. Tell him he has to take you out, has to drive you wherever you want before you'll shag him. Tell him you deserve a treat, and that's the only thing you want. You can talk to him,' I said.

I spoke more loudly than I needed to, and Amanda popped her head through the arch and smiled at us. She saw Chloe wiping the counter.

'Good girls,' she said, 'but don't waste your Saturday after-noon cleaning up in here, will you?'

Chloe ignored her and she looked hurt and went back into the living room. I wanted to tell Amanda how it worked. To ignore back. To pretend Chloe didn't exist. She'd grow up and pack it in soon enough if we all did that. If we all did it, if everyone in the world pretended like Chloe did not exist, she'd probably die.

Amanda was watching *Countdown* and every now and again she would laugh at the programme, and the steam would come hissing out of the iron.

'I wish you'd shut up about it,' Chloe said, 'you don't know what you're playing at.'

'You'll ask him though, won't you?' I said, and she ducked her head, and then nodded slowly.

'I'll ask him. I'll get him to take us. But don't talk to anyone else about it. There's nothing in it. We're only going to make you feel better.'

'Tell him you're humouring me, because I'm bereaved,' I said, and Chloe looked at me, almost shocked, but saw me smiling and laughed.

'Right,' she said, 'I'll do that. You look like shit. I *am* humouring you because you're bereaved.'

'I want to go home now. So you'll ask your dad to give me a lift back?'

Chloe dropped the tea-towel into the sink and wiped her hands on the front of her jeans.

'I'll come in the car with you,' she said, and her eyelid started to twitch again.

26

It is still dark and the cameras remain with Terry. He's standing away from the bank of the pond where the forensic tent is a pale oblong behind the shadows of the trees.

The crowd is growing as quickly and silently as dividing bacteria. They push against the yellow tape the police have strung between the trees. They are stamping their feet and puffing hot air into cupped hands. They move together, one man's mouth at another's ear. I stare until my eyes feel gritty. These are the hard-core fans: thirty or forty people in anoraks with their hoods up, or duffel coats, or sports jackets with bright, reflective panels. These are the people who follow Terry when he is off-duty, who think they are his friends, who appear like ghosts over and over again in the background of his on-location shots. Some of these people will be his ex-vigilantes from the late nineties and their faces are all the same: solemn, with wide, hungry eyes that track Terry as he moves up and down the tape cordon that separates him from them. He shakes hands over it like the Queen and he nods when they speak, but we at home can't hear anything because they're doing the voiceover bit again.

'It was supposed to be a private ceremony. Close family only, plus media partners and business sponsors. *We* weren't even invited.'

Emma's outraged voice in the dim quiet of my sitting room shocks me. I look at her, but she's frowning at the television.

'I think it's gone past that now,' I say.

My glass is empty and I wedge it between my thighs, testing the pressure – not sure if I want it to shatter or not.

'Something's happened,' she says. 'Look, they're moving.'

The wood was such a dark, quiet place the last time I was there. No one but me, Carl and Chloe wandering along the path and laughing at how often we tripped. Now it's an outdoor studio, and the black bowl of the sky is stained with the spotlights from the camera crew.

A mortuary van rolls along the footpath, its wide tyres crushing the shrubs and scattering the undergrowth in a soft hail of snapped twigs and torn leaves. The engine thrums gently and there's a shuffling, a ripple across the crowd of people waiting as they sigh and reorder themselves. Terry is out of shot, and the van can't get near enough to the tent where the exhumed body is because of the trees. So it stops and two men in navy boiler suits jump out.

The pair move slowly round to the back of the van, open the double doors and bring out a plastic stretcher without a blanket. There's a gasp, as if no one knew that they'd come to collect the body. There's some pointing and head-shaking and the police officers move the tape and divide the onlookers to let them through. They don't unfold the stretcher, but carry it under their arms like a ladder and move along the path cleared through the crowd and marked out by the yellow tape. Heads bowed, and towards the white tent. No rush.

'It's weird, isn't it? It doesn't feel real.'

'What do you mean?'

'Who's to say that they aren't actors? Don't you think it's all just too perfect? It looks like an episode of *Silent Witness*.'

'What would you expect it to look like?' she says vaguely, and refuses to bring her eyes away from the screen. She chews on the cuff off her coat absently. It's an old habit, that.

'Do you remember when we did our interviews?' I say. 'They filmed us, didn't they?'

Emma screws up her nose. 'Not for the telly though.'

'No, but it's creepy to think of it, isn't it? What we said still being on record somewhere. Some tape in an archive. Don't you ever wonder what they're going to do with it?'

She finally looks at me. 'I never think about it.'

'I do,' I say, and swallow. 'I wonder, sometimes, if they were asking you and me the same things, and comparing our stories.'

Emma coughs decisively and pulls her tobacco out of her pocket. The movement is enough to declare the topic of conversation closed.

'I think it's disgusting,' she says, hunched over the packet, 'all those people. This is Chloe's night. We're her friends, not them.'

'It's not that,' I say, half-amused when it strikes me that she could just as easily be talking about party crashers at a birthday or wedding reception, 'it's Terry. There's always a crowd like this when he does on-location stuff. He's not been able to do his own shopping for years.'

'They should be sent home,' Emma says. 'It's disrespectful.'

The men carrying the stretcher disappear between the trees. The police return to move the tape back and the crowd gathers to fill the space. The shot cuts to a view from above – they've got the helicopter out. There's a wide red van in the car park – as big as a tour bus, and the paintwork is so clean and glossy it is almost glowing. This van is painted with the logo of Terry's programme on the side of it and it has a set of aerials and dishes sticking out of the top. It looks like it's had acupuncture. They've set up a mobile studio, and Terry is settling in for the night.

There he is. In front of the van, in his furry hat, with bags under his eyes. He's been there hours. Got to do something to break up the monotony.

'We're busy taking calls,' Terry says. 'We want to know what you think. The number is on the bottom of your screen right now. Dial that number and tell me what's on your mind. We know you're keen to share, and we've already got our first caller. Paul?'

'Terry, I just wanted to say that I went out with the dog

tonight, just to give him a walk, and that big poster of you on Blackpool Road – you know the one on the billboard with your thumbs sticking up?'

'I do, Paul, yes.'

'Well, someone's gone and torn it down. Or it wasn't stuck up properly in the first place. There's bits of it all over the road.'

'A spot of anti-Terry vandalism, or should we say, community-based direct action?' Terry says, and smiles, right through the television screen. There's a beat or two of silence, and then the smile turns into a slow laugh that doesn't get to his eyes.

'Well, whatever you want to call it, I think it's a disgrace, and come the bit of rain we're forecast tomorrow morning, could turn out to be a health hazard. What if some young couple skids off the road on some mashed-up paper? Do you think it's going to be any comfort to their kids that the accident happened because of a picture of your face?'

'Quite so, and I couldn't have put it better myself,' Terry says. 'And anything else, Paul, on this evening's main topic? What's your opinion about the events of the past ten hours? What are your *feelings*?' Terry touches his ear and leans into the screen. 'I'm listening.'

'Well, it's just like this, isn't it, Terry? How long's it been there? They're never going to find out who did it, until they find out when it was done, if you catch my drift. That's what they've got to set about first, isn't it?'

'You're speaking about the unfortunate – the body?'

'Sure,' Paul says, and his voice is warm again – amused and friendly. 'My kids play in that park. I take the dog out there. What I want to know is, how long has it been there, and how long till they get it shifted?'

'Forensics are working on that right now, Paul,' Terry says. There's a twitch in his left nostril. 'In fact, they are *shifting it*, as we speak, and I'll personally pass on your thanks for their sterling efforts tonight. The forensics team is very possibly the least visible and most under-appreciated echelon of our police service, and I know for a fact they'd be grateful you're thinking of them at this time.'

He sighs, too visibly, and reads out the number at the bottom of the screen again. 'Remember,' he says, 'while we want to hear from you all, we're particularly interested in those of you who knew the deceased personally. Those of you with a story to tell about what he might have been doing with himself in these woods when he died.'

Paul is still speaking.

Suddenly, the camera snaps back to the studio. Fiona is there – working a double shift but looking as fresh as she did when she stepped out of Make-up yesterday afternoon. Not a hair out of place and her eyes are as bright as ever. She smiles and it is perfect and blinding.

'Later,' she says warmly, 'we'll be interviewing the men who run the forensics department at the hospital. Real-life *CSI*, and bringing you the facts in small words that you'll understand.' She squints slightly, her hand moves to her ear. I bet Terry or one of his lackeys is shouting at her. 'But for the time being,' she says, 'back to Terry, who's still on location at Cuerden. Terry?'

Terry's red in the face and his mouth is twisted – he's apoplectic, in fact, at the interruption. For a moment the screen is split like a Lynda La Plante adaptation and we at home can see the two of them – him outside in the mud and the cold, and her curled up on the couch in the studio wearing a suit that is perfectly coordinated with it. He does not acknowledge her on the other half of the television but makes a snapping gesture with the flat of his hand – she disappears, and he carries on as if she never existed.

'Remember, Paul, Rome wasn't built in a day and perfection takes patience!' He jerks his jaw to someone off screen. 'Next caller, please! We've got Peggy, here, from New Hall Lane. Peggy – what do you want to say?'

There's a pause – too much dead air for a live broadcast, and they are seconds away from moving on to the next call when there's a crackle on the line and Peggy starts to speak. I can't hear what she's saying because she's sobbing, and the catarrh is rattling in her throat and her own telephone, as well as the equipment in the portable news studio, is amplifying the bubbling, popping sound she is making between every word.

'Peggy,' Terry says gently, 'take your time. I'm listening. We're all listening. This is a hard night for us all. Did you – do you believe you know the deceased?'

He's hoping for an exclusive and not a lonely crackpot who's had too many Babychams and managed to dial the studio's number. He's hoping she's going to make some kind of confession, live on air – you can almost see the awards and the plaudits glittering in think-bubbles over his head.

'When you're ready, my love.'

He may be rehearsing the possibilities but he knows his game – he doesn't smile, doesn't rush her; he looks solemnly at us all through the clank of the digging machinery and the increasing tempo of her sobbing.

'It's just so . . . ugh ugh ugh, so *tragic*,' Peggy splutters. 'She was so young! Does anyone know, has anyone thought to ask, if they're still going to be able to build the little memorial for her? I thought it was such a lovely idea.'

There's a pause while she blows her nose, deafeningly, into the telephone. Terry does not visibly flinch.

'A Wendy house for her friends to play in.'

I glance at Emma and she's wet-eyed: sorrow is still as contagious as plague, and this woman is forgetting that while Chloe is still fourteen, the rest of us are knocking on twenty-five and long past playing in dens in the woods.

'Thank God it wasn't one of us,' Emma says, and I ignore her.

'Ah,' Terry says, and bows his head for a moment, 'a timely

reminder to those of us who are caught up in the drama of the night.' He looks piercingly at the camera. 'This is no soap opera, friends – this is a real-life memorial to a teenage girl.' They cut to a montage of shots taken around the City in the days leading up to Chloe's funeral. The cards and stuffed bears. The drifts of browning flowers. Terry does not stop talking. He writes his own autocue, apparently.

'A teenage girl who loved so deeply, and so completely, that she felt no other option but to end her life alongside her forbidden lover. Ten years has passed – which is why we're here tonight. Let's take a moment of silence to reflect on that and – as Peggy has reminded us – return our focus to Chloe, departed, not forgotten, and loved in death as much as she ever loved in life.'

The minute's silence, the second of the evening, is the opportunity to show the jingle from the chocolate sponsor and cut to the adverts. Emma stands up and goes into the bathroom. She's hunched, and the back of her shirt is darkened with sweat between the shoulder blades. I think, just for a second, about following her in there.

That is what is supposed to happen, isn't it? Girls go to the toilets in pairs. She's supposed to cry and I am supposed to hold her and say some comforting things, pass her loo paper and help her fix her mascara. Reassure her, before we emerge into the glare of the screen in the sitting room, that she looks fine, that it isn't a problem, that no one thinks she's stupid. I mute the television and listen to the water running for a few seconds, then go into the kitchenette to make coffee.

This evening is turning into another Chloe-thon. Terry asked Peggy about the body in the present tense – *'Do you believe you know the deceased?'* – and I think about it, think about how Wilson is still here, not dead at all, not to his parents, not to anyone who misses him and is still waiting for him to come home. Not to Terry, who always refused to believe, despite the last two attacks, that it was not Wilson who was stalking us. I wonder, not for the first time, if Wilson's parents were watching when the mayor started to dig. If they were feeling the sickly churning of anticipation that I've been feeling in my stomach all night.

The present tense is full of possibilities: a future is bolted on to it like time is a row of railway carriages flicking through a train station, one after the other after the other. Now the body has been identified that possibility has been cut off and worse than that, Wilson's mum and dad, wherever they are, are going to know that it never really existed and didn't all the years they were hoping for it.

The coffee smells ashy and foul – there's a ring of multi-coloured bubbles around the rim of the mug that I sweep away with the teaspoon.

'Here,' I say, still standing when Emma comes in.

'I'm not drunk,' she says, takes the coffee and sniffs it without drinking.

'I never said you were. It's four in the morning. I'm knackered, even if you aren't.'

'Yes,' she says, and her eyes are moving around the wall behind me, looking, I think, for a clock. When she finds nothing more than a cracked tile and a cleaning supplies calendar I got free from work and is still showing the page for January (*Supa-Sponge – cuts grease in half!*) she brings her eyes back to my face. 'It is late,' she agrees, and sips quickly. 'Do you want me to go?'

I take my own coffee and we cross back into the sitting room – although it isn't a separate room, it's just the place in this bigger room where you get to walk on worn carpet instead of curling linoleum.

'I'm going to stay up,' I say. 'They've either got to find something out, or put something else on. There was supposed to be a film on tonight.'

She shakes her head. 'You and your films,' she says. The tone of her voice is almost affectionate and her expression reminds me of something.

'You came to my house once,' I say, 'just after Donald—' I still can't talk about it and Emma knows and she nods respect- fully and lets me off the hook. 'You wanted to walk in to school together because everyone had to go in pairs.'

'Yes,' she says, 'Shanks's orders. Danny Towers' older sister brought him in and no one let him forget it for months.'

'You were scared too,' I say, teasing her, 'scared shitless the man in the mask was going to leap out from somewhere and show you his cock.'

I expect her to laugh but she turns on me so suddenly some of her coffee slops over the side of her mug and spatters on the knee of her jeans. It must be scalding her but she doesn't move, doesn't stand up and pluck the fabric away from herself.

'I wasn't scared; I was trying to look after you. I was trying to protect you.'

'You'd have battered him with that violin case?' I joke. 'Or did you have a gun inside it? Emma Capone!' I laugh, but she doesn't join in and the longer the silence between us goes on for the more embarrassed I am at the joke.

'Emma?'

'Leave it,' she says, venomously. She's ashamed of being caught out. At being soft and worrying about me when she pretends to be so hard that she doesn't need friends.

'All right,' I say. 'Fine.'

There's a long pause where we drink our coffee and do not speak. Emma motions for the remote control and turns the volume on the television back up.

'Are you going to be all right for work in the morning?' she says.

I shrug. 'We won't be the only ones staying up. It'll be quiet tomorrow, everyone sleeping in – or taking the day off so they can stay plugged in and see what happens.'

'It's kind of disgusting, isn't it?' she says, 'making a whole programme out of it?'

'Yes. Yes,' I say.

'And those nutters ringing in. Upsetting everyone.'

'Funny they never got Nathan and Amanda on the air,' I say.

'Not really. I bet Terry made that a condition of them covering the memorial and helping to fund the summerhouse. Get a microphone near Amanda and she starts screeching about how old Carl was,' Emma says.

'When Terry does a phone-in in the studio, there's a mute button under that plastic bowl of fruit,' I tell her.

'What?'

'You know – when the callers start swearing or asking him out. There's that button built in to the coffee table and they've put that fruit bowl on top of it so it doesn't show. Watch his hand next time.'

Emma smiles. 'That doesn't make turning the whole night into a circus any better.'

I pause, not sure if I should say the next thing or not because I'm still not sure enough of her to be able to predict how she'll react.

'It's only what they did with Chloe. They wanted to put her *funeral* on the telly.'

'No,' Emma says, and settles herself back on the couch, 'it was different with Chloe. People knew who she was. They wanted to talk about her. Figure out what went wrong and make sure it could never happen again. This –' she points the rim of her mug at the screen, 'this is a mystery. People aren't sad: they think it's exciting. It's stirring everyone up.'

'You're probably right,' I say, and she interrupts me.

'But they'll have those forensic people working overtime. We'll know how he died, what time of day, who did it – everything. Then all this will fade away. In three days' time, they'll get back on with the memorial and everyone will forget about this,' she sniffs, as if she is daring me to disagree with her. 'It's only a matter of time.'

Now it is my turn to stand quickly and head into the bathroom. The bitter coffee on a stomach already tipping and churning with cheap wine is suddenly too much, and I sit on the edge of the bath with my head between my knees. I think of clear cool water, fountains and lagoons and undersea springs. Hydrothermal vents and the frozen, secret sea inside Triton. The tiles in the bathroom are spotted with soap, and I stare at them and try to hear the sea moving, all kinds of other, restful, calming things, and clamp my teeth together so hard I can hear my jaw creaking.

A matter of time.

I lean over to the toilet, flip the lid and vomit quietly and efficiently until I am empty and sober. When I come back, Emma has fallen asleep.

27

Nothing new happens. Terry abandons the phone-in and the programme repeats itself. Replays of the original reconstruction footage, as if the tape is on a loop. It feels like it did at the time: all the repeated warnings about curfews and walking in pairs. The school uniforms look false and dated and I realise even the most exciting things become boring if they are repeated often enough.

I wonder if Melanie and Dawn are watching themselves – cringing at the way the white dimpled fat of their thighs strains against a tight band of school skirt as they sit on that bench. They must have been freezing. I wonder how many times they had to film it – how many takes until it was exactly what the police were after? They make token mentions of Chloe now and again but her parents have long gone home and that decorated spade has been bagged up and taken away. When Emma wakes, she stares at the screen as if it's all new to her.

'Do you remember all those interviews we had?' she says, and I do. I sit on my couch with her and I remember the upstairs classroom. The waiting, the way we looked at the flowers at the front of the school and talked about the different kinds – the ones we liked the best, even – as if we were at a garden centre. I remember that spider plant, and Emma's too-tight school socks.

The police interviews went on for three weeks, and during that time we were allowed into staff sitting rooms and drank tea from teachers' mugs and saw secret places inside the school – smoky lounges behind doors I thought were only cupboards or boiler rooms, rows of pegs with coats and umbrellas, and the sight – tender and thrilling – of Shanks's lunchtime sandwiches wrapped in tinfoil with folded hospital corners, dangling from a peg in a tattered carrier bag.

'They were interviewing loads of people,' I say, which was only half true.

One morning with Shanks and the whole form until they established who were her real friends. Then the focus on me and Emma – as if we were criminals. I remember the look on Emma's face when they asked us to hand in any photographs we had of Chloe. We looked at each other, hostile and questioning, and I knew something was up and she knew something was up and the policewoman interviewing us pushed the tape recorder towards us very gently with her finger, and asked us about Carl.

No one wanted it to be suicide. No one wanted the City to be the sort of place where fourteen-year-old girls who came from good, semi-detached homes south of the river actually drowned themselves. They wanted to get someone for it. Terry wanted them to get someone for it – he'd have probably tried to pin Chloe's death on Wilson if he could have bent time and made the dates fit.

'I only met him a few times,' I said. 'Chloe only went out with him since the autumn.'

'Since Halloween,' Emma chipped in. I nodded. It sounded about right.

'Do you know what she thought of him, what their relationship was like?'

Emma didn't say anything. We were in the staff room, and I followed her gaze up to the high rectangular windows – slices of grey sky and rivulets of rain.

'She loved him,' I said, 'better than anyone else. Better than family and friends. She told me once he was her soul mate. He bought her a charm bracelet.'

There was a short silence, then, far away, the muffled echo

of the bell and the thuds and shouts as the morning classes were released into the corridors. The policewoman – I think her name was Alison – turned away and leaned over the back of her chair. We waited. We were getting used to waiting. She rustled gently inside a cardboard box and a moment later she turned back to us and put a bag on the table. A zip-lock plastic bag with a row of numbers and letters written on it with red marker pen. The last three numbers were smudged – someone had handled the bag before the writing dried. Beside me, Emma laughed – a sudden, choking sound.

'Yes, that's the bracelet,' she said. 'He bought her that.'

Alison stared at her for a second, then swished the bag over towards me. I nodded without looking.

'So he loved her. He bought her presents. She was happy?' I was sitting so close to Emma I could hear the clicking noise in the back of her throat. She said nothing.

'Yes,' I nodded again, 'very happy. She had Carl, she had her friends.'

'They were romantic with each other,' Emma added. 'She liked holding hands.'

'And how was she when her mother stopped her from seeing Carl? What was she like then?'

'Angry,' Emma said. 'Chloe wanted to do what she liked.'

I glanced at Emma. It wasn't as if we were lying.

'She made herself ill she was so worked up about it,' I added. 'Her mum told me she wasn't eating. Asked me to keep an eye on her.'

'She'd been looking forward to Valentine's Day,' Emma said.

Yes, we knew what we were doing. Saying something until it became true and the whole City believed it. Even better, we convinced ourselves. I have not been troubled by sleepless nights these past ten years. My reasons are clear enough. I don't know about Emma's.

'Thanks, girls,' Alison said, 'that's enough for now. We'll let you get back to your classes.' She opened the door and the next time they interviewed us, we were in separate rooms.

'It can't have been legal,' Emma says, 'all that questioning. Were your parents there?'

I shook my head. 'Barbara didn't even know what day it was.'

'They never asked my dad either,' she says. 'There was a letter went back, saying that the police were coming to the school to collect background information. Stuff about her timetable, who her friends were, what kind of person she was. Nothing about interviews. And they taped us,' Emma says. 'Not on, really. They wouldn't be allowed to do that now.'

'It was out of order,' I say, and in this way we comfort each other until the adverts finish and Terry comes back. He never got us on air. His researchers and a troop of other journalists tailed us for two years – until I ran away – but he never got us. I imagine him lying awake at night, burning with the indignation of it. Would we have talked to Fiona?

It is getting light outside but still the coverage of what has happened this evening does not stop. For a dizzy, queasy minute I imagine this footage spinning on a loop for years and years and years. Chloe and Carl, our city's Romeo and Juliet. They will carry on with the memorials and the flowers and the special music until Terry thinks we've all learned the lesson and made sure nothing so senseless and tragic could ever happen here again.

He's still outside the van, gesturing at a digital list that appears on the screen next to him. It must be a knack – being able to point at nothing and talk and talk so that even if the digital people messed up, we'd still be able to picture the glowing words and graphs in our mind's eye – as if they were really there.

'A recap of the facts on the case,' Terry says. 'On Boxing Day 1997, Daniel Wilson left his home for a walk. The house was

299

full of relatives and he told his mother and father he wanted some fresh air. He left his house, and we know he made the long walk across the City to Avenham Park, where he approached two girls and asked for a cigarette. These two girls escaped him, and later took part in an award-winning reconstruction first broadcast on this programme in early 1998.

'The next footage we have of Wilson is on the forecourt of a Texaco petrol station five miles away – it's possible that he walked, but more likely that someone gave him a lift. That person has never been identified, despite appeals from both the police and Wilson's parents.

'At the time of his disappearance, the City was plagued with attacks and indecent exposures on young girls. I was not able to bring you the facts about the perpetrator at the time, but it is true that these attacks stopped at the same time as Daniel Wilson disappeared – which has led some sources to believe the anonymous attacker and this missing man are one and the same.'

'There were two after that,' I say in frustration. 'Why does he always miss out those two?'

Emma looks at me strangely, as if to ask me why I care so much.

'You can't just make things up. You can't just twist things any way you like and put it on the telly so everyone will think it's true,' I say. 'That girl in the swimming baths. She was from our school. That happened afterwards.'

'A copy-cat flasher,' Emma says with sarcasm, 'except he wasn't just flashing.'

'It doesn't make sense,' I say. 'They were constantly telling us he was going to get worse. And when it did get worse, when he tried to drag a girl into a car, Terry said it wasn't him after all, but a copy-cat and we should discount it.'

Emma laughs. 'Well if Terry says it, it must be true.'

Terry carries on, never letting the facts get in the way of how perfect and neat the story could be if he could prove it.

'Was Wilson a victim of vigilante justice? Are you a father, brother or uncle of one of the young victims at the time? What do you think has gone on here?'

'He's the one who got away,' I say, and Emma nods. 'Even at the time I never thought it was him. I had this idea that because he was like he was, he wouldn't be capable.' I laugh. 'I was fourteen, what did I know?'

'You think Terry's right? The last two were someone else?'

I have thought about this a lot. 'I reckon it was that Video Man,' I say. 'He couldn't wait to get in on that reconstruction, could he? Probably gave him all kinds of cheap thrills. Chloe told me Shanks drove a bunch of the Year Seven girls home one night, stopped off at the video shop for some pop and Video Man saw him, and reported *him* to the school. Who'd do that? Shanks got in bother for it because he'd left himself wide open to people saying *he* was the perv.' I pause and think for a while longer. 'On the other hand,' I chopped my palm through the air, 'it did stop. Just like that. The girl in the swimming baths was the last. Maybe Terry was right. Because it *was* Wilson who was doing it and then someone decided they liked the idea and wanted to give it a try themselves.'

He was obsessed with jailbait. I nearly say it, but I don't. The video shop is closed now – has been for years. When people want to watch films they just type in their credit card number on their remote control and download whatever they want to watch then and there. The Video Man is obsolete. He is probably cleaning a shopping centre or something now, the same as me.

'You don't really think that,' Emma says, and she's right, I don't – but I carry on anyway. Doing violence to the way things really are in order to make the story work can be addictive. I can see why Terry does it. I won't get an award but it does make you feel safe.

'It could make sense,' I say. 'He wouldn't have thought he was doing anything wrong. Probably just his way of meeting girls. Chatting them up. They don't think the same way as we do.'

'No,' Emma says.

'Oh, I think so. In his mind, he was probably thirteen or fourteen himself. He wouldn't have felt an age difference between him and the girls he was after, would he?'

Emma looks at me blankly.

'Don't be stupid,' she says, and her voice is thick with contempt. 'It was Carl.'

28

She throws it out so casually I'm sure I've misunderstood, even though I know I haven't. The tracks I think along in my mind creak and shift. It takes a while, and it hurts. My hands feel cold.

'The man in the mask,' I say, 'behind the bandstand.'

Emma nods. 'Yes,' she says.

'The toilets in the swimming baths?'

'Yes.'

'Chloe's Carl?'

'That's how he met her,' Emma says. 'She was the only one who wasn't scared. She told you the truth about that. She thought it was hilarious. Thought he'd picked her out special and surprising her like that was meant to be romantic. She thought it was, at first.'

'How do you know?' I say, and before I can think, 'What makes you so sure?'

I am panicking and I don't want to stop talking but she stares at me until I realise.

'I knew him before Chloe did,' she says slowly, and her eyes are angry and I realise she is looking at me, not in pity, but in disgust. 'I met him first. I was the first one.'

'Where?'

She smiles weakly but her face is pale and this isn't the sort of smile that means she's happy.

'In the launderette,' she said. 'He helped me with the bags. He offered me a lift back to my house and I said no, and then he was there the week after and he brought me some pop and a magazine and I said yes, all right then. I thought he was being kind to me.'

'And then he was Chloe's boyfriend? She *stole* him from you?' Emma shakes her head.

'You stupid cow,' she says. 'Chloe could have told you he walked on water at the weekends and you'd have believed that as well, wouldn't you? Never feel like using your own eyes? Your own head? It's been fucking long enough.'

She turns away. Doesn't talk. Pulls her knees up to her chest and wraps her arms around them. Her jaw is rattling.

'Don't get on at me about it,' she says, 'don't you dare ask me questions. This isn't a fucking phone-in. Not an *interview*. Soul mates. Where did you come up with that shit? He was bad news.'

She was scared of him. She leans forward and refills her glass. Doesn't drink, doesn't talk, but looks at the hem of the curtains, moving gently in the stream of hot air coming off the radiator. She contemplates them for a long time, as if they can tell her something about what to say next. I want to ask her why she's waited this long to tell me, but I don't dare.

'He never went for you?' she says eventually, without looking at me.

'Never,' I say, and wonder about it. I think about the photographs that Chloe took of me and where they ended up. The wondering feels dry and sour in my mouth, like tiny, powdery apples.

'Don't act jealous,' she says. 'It hurt – it was horrible.'

She pauses for a long minute and says nothing. Then, 'I'm glad he's dead,' she says and examines the knee of her jeans. 'If someone helped get him that way, that person saved me.'

'There was that one time,' I say quickly, 'in his car. He kissed me a bit. I didn't like it. I thought he liked me. That he'd gone off Chloe.'

'When was it?'

304

'I told you. Chloe was in the hospital. That time she fainted.'
Emma nods. 'I found her, outside school. Do you remember?
She was crying.'

'She told me she thought she was pregnant,' I say.
Emma laughs. 'She was lying to you. He wasn't that stupid.'
My eyes are stinging and I feel left alone and tiny – very far
away. Emma laughs again – and I get it. She laughs when she's
angry and the more she laughs the angrier she is. That, I think,
would have been useful to know ten years ago.

'You think Carl would have let that happen? The whole world
would have found out about him if he'd have knocked her up.
It only worked – him seeing her regular, pretending he was her
boyfriend, because she liked having a secret.'

'We knew about it,' I say.

'We were *his girls*,' she says darkly. 'There was no way I could
tell anyone – not unless I wanted my own dirty business spread
all over the school.'

'You had brothers though,' I say, 'they'd have helped you.'
She shakes her head at me. 'You've no idea,' she says, and
bites her bottom lip.

I look at her, think about how she lives – alone, touching no
one but her dogs – and get a glimpse of something massive and
black, something I can't catch hold of.

It is cold, where Emma is.

I realise I do not understand it.

'Carl didn't like you knowing,' Emma says. 'He went mad at
her when he found out. Me as well, as if I had anything to do
with it. Still, she thought you would do whatever she told you
to, so long as she kept you sweet and in her good books. Pregnant?
She just needed an excuse for blanking you all holidays.
Something to distract you a bit from the New Year's party. You
were like a pet dog, following her around with your tongue out
whenever she told you to do something.'

'I was her best friend!'

Emma laughs, and mimics me, '*I was her best friend. I knew everything about her. No one knew Chloe like I did.*'

I am so tempted. *I was with her*, I want to say, *I know.*

'Stop it,' I say. It is all I can manage. 'Stop it right now.'

'Or what?'

'Or I'll throw you out.'

Emma stops, and sips at her drink.

'She was getting heavily into things with Carl. Her parents always thought she was with me, or with you. There were things he was into, stuff you couldn't make up.' She shudders. 'It was all catching up with her.'

'She didn't want me to know?'

'You'd have told someone if you'd have known how bad it was. I couldn't have told anyone. Tell on her, and I'd have been telling on myself.'

'You wouldn't have got into trouble.'

Emma points at the television screen. 'Do you think I'd want every detail of what he was doing to me – *to us* – up on the telly for everyone to know about?' she snorts. 'School was bad enough as it was. I think Chloe was just grateful there was someone to take turns with her.'

'That's ridiculous,' I said. 'She was besotted with him. She'd have gone mad if she'd have known.'

'Who do you think she sent out to meet Carl the night she was in hospital? She phoned me in a panic. Her parents knew. Thanks to you. They were going mad. She'd talked Nathan out of calling the police but she wanted me to go and warn him anyway.'

I wonder why, if it was so horrible, the pair of them kept it all to themselves. Why they protected Carl from being found out. Emma might have been ashamed but Chloe wasn't. Chloe *liked* having a boyfriend.

'So I was supposed to go and meet up with him, in her place. She told me not to tell Carl she was ill. That I'd to go and meet him and come up with some kind of excuse.'

'Was that the first time she sent you out to him?'

Emma shakes her head. 'Not by a long shot,' she said bitterly. 'Chloe knew all about me. She didn't care. I think sometimes she thought it was better me than her. Gave her the night off.'

'No,' I said.

'Of course. How else do you think we'd made friends? Look at her, and look at me. At us. What else would she have wanted us for? She'd have shoved you in his direction sooner or later.'

I remember the last time Chloe brought round her camera. For once I wasn't the photographer and just that one time, she was looking at me. For months and years afterwards I could close my eyes and recreate the cool touch of her fingers on my skin, stretching my eyelids taut so she could apply eye-liner. I had felt so loved.

'Did you meet him that night?'

'I was supposed to. He didn't turn up. I waited near the swings for an hour and a half. Some guy came past and asked me if I wanted to earn some money. They're like vampires. I ran home.'

'It *was* that night then,' I said, remembering my run through the dark, the car parked under the bridge near the park. Condensation from the curved underside dripping onto the roof of the car. Emma had been out too, waiting on the swings and watching the street lights warm up from pink to orange to yellow.

'He was with *me*,' I say. 'I phoned him. Told him that Chloe was ill. Said we needed to talk. He drove me somewhere in his car. That's when he tried it on.'

'Were you *that* worried about her?'

I look away and light a cigarette.

'I knew she wasn't pregnant then. I'd been to the hospital. I was annoyed.'

'You went to him on your own. No one made you.' Emma sounds irritated. 'And he kissed you. You were in his car. Anything else?'

I nod, thinking of his hands. Thinking that kissing was another way of hitting me, of shutting me up.

'Did he get romantic with you?' she asks.

'No, it wasn't like that.' I remember the smell of his saliva on my cheek. I'd got off lightly.

'He sometimes did,' Emma says, 'the presents and that. Now and again, when he'd done his business, he'd cry about it. Expect you to comfort him,' she sneers incredulously. 'And I did! As if I'd done something horrible to him, something he couldn't stand, but had to go along with anyway. As if I was twice the size he was, and the one driving the car. Give me a drink.'

I pour the wine into her coffee mug. She doesn't so much smile as open her mouth slightly and show her teeth. 'And I did like it sometimes. When he was gentler, and did it properly.'

'I don't want to hear about it. If it was that great, Chloe wouldn't have put you in the queue for it, would she?'

Emma's teeth are stained with wine.

'That's why she died. It wasn't for love like they say it was. Carl did something to her, wanted to get rid of her and it went wrong and he ended up drowning himself as well. He forced her into the water because she was going to start talking to her parents any day. He'd have gone to jail. She'd never have killed herself just because her parents made it a bit tricky for her to see him. She'd have seen it as a challenge.'

'She was depressed,' I whisper.

'She was seeing him anyway. It doesn't add up. Carl did something to her and you and me – we helped everyone see it the wrong way. Valentine's Day!' she snorts.

'We only told the truth,' I say, 'about the bracelet, his car. She did like those things.'

Emma gestures at the television. 'This will never be over. After she died I thought it didn't matter anymore, not now that he was dead. We were all safe again and I didn't want to explain what I'd been up to. It was disgusting.'

Because she is thinking about Chloe her eyes are wet and soft. Even after all this, and everything that Chloe knew and did and allowed to happen. Even still.

'What he was doing to her. The state of her. Her hair was falling out – the weight dropping off her. Do you remember her skin?' She doesn't wait for me to answer. 'I remember it. Sulking because her parents wouldn't let her see him! Pretending to be anorexic. On hunger strike or something.'

No, I want to say. *That is rubbish. It was Wilson she was worried about.*

I think about how long it must have taken the two of them to dig a hole deep enough in the woods. Hour after hour out there in the cold, grubbing through the earth and getting it under her fingernails. I could tell Emma, but what would be the point? It wouldn't make her feel any better and there are so many lies around what we thought about Chloe and what she thought about us that, even now, I'm not certain what is the truth. Before I can open my mouth she speaks again and the words come out in a rush – as if she's practised them, or it's a burden she can't wait to be rid of.

'Chloe got off lightly compared to me. He had to work gently with her because she wasn't scared of him. She gave him a blow-job here and there. His hand down her jeans in the back of his car while I went to the off licence for them. A few dodgy pictures, long gone now.'

'Maybe she did like it?'

'No. Think of the state of her,' Emma says again. 'She knew what it was like for me. Knew it was in the post for her, as well.'

Me too?

'And he was doing all those other girls?'

'Yes. It was getting worse. He'd have wound up killing someone. That girl in the swimming baths. She still doesn't talk. At all.'

'Maybe.' It's a croak.

'You never saw him when he was in the thick of it. Spit building up in the corners of his mouth, the sweat dripping off him. Dead eyes, like you weren't another person, like you weren't anything. I'd not even treat a dog like that. I'd not even *be able* to treat a dog like that. It hurt.'

I think about Emma's dogs, and her chapped hands buried in their fur.

'He's gone now,' I say, and it sounds clichéd and useless and I am embarrassed.

'Whatever happened to her and the others, he can't do it anymore.'

'I should have threatened to tell someone. Then it would have been me he'd have taken down to the water,' Emma says quietly. 'Chloe sacrificed herself. All this,' she waves towards the television screen, 'she deserves it. Water fountains, page in the paper, the lot. She did it for us. All us girls.'

I look at the screen, expecting to see the memorial that Emma gestured towards, but instead it's showing the photograph of Wilson in his party hat again with another digital list of the victims of the pest, along with dates and ages. Terry is reading the list and it is frightening.

'Shouldn't someone know about it then? That it wasn't Wilson's fault? That he didn't do anything wrong?'

'What difference would it make?'

'It would to his parents. Everyone's saying he's a paedo. Terry's as good as said that someone murdered him to stop him, and that's fair enough by him and everyone else who believes it.'

'Listen,' Emma says, counting on her fingers, 'look at those dates. Carl was at it from the summer, wasn't he? As soon as he got that new job and bought a car. Loads and loads over the winter. Stopped for a bit, over Christmas and New Year.'

'Yes,' I say. He stopped. Busy figuring out what to do with Wilson, I thought. A little break – didn't want to draw any more attention to himself. Had to keep Chloe in line. He was busy then – and a dead body is enough to put anyone off.

'But then he started again, didn't he? January, February? Two more. Tried to drag a girl into his car in the middle of the day.'

I think about Donald and nod.

'My dad was worried sick about it,' I say. 'Chloe wasn't talking to me then, but even if she had been I wouldn't have been allowed past the front door unless it was to go to school. Barbara even thought about getting me a phone.'

'You're not listening,' Emma says. 'They'll work it out. The timings. They'll figure out that Wilson didn't get very far after Boxing Day and that however he ended up dead, it happened before New Year. And the attacks were going on after that. It'll sort it out. They'll know it wasn't him and they'll have to say it —' she points at the telly, 'Terry will have to say it. He can't not do.'

'He hasn't done so far.'

'He'll have to,' she says. 'He can't carry it on anymore. He's wrong and he knows he is. Why else do you think this has been on all night?' She waves at the television. 'No one really cares that much about Wilson. It's Terry. He's hanging on by a thread.'

I think about it and realise she is right.

'So it's done with now?'

'Yes.'

Emma turns away from me, she doesn't ask why I telephoned Carl that night, what was so important that I told on Chloe and demanded we meet. I think about Wilson again, and feel the old pangs of pity and guilt. And then anger.

She hasn't noticed because she's still looking around the room. 'You should have a better flat than this. A better job. Friends.'

'What do you mean?'

'You live like I do, and you've no excuse. No one ever hurt *you*.'

29

This is what happened to Chloe and Carl. I know, because I was there.

Freezing night, and back once again to Cuerden Valley Park, the cowslip and stoat sign with the lighter-burned plastic, and through the woods along a path that wasn't really a path – along to the water and where it first began. Chloe led the way and we followed her as she zig-zagged down a strange route through thicker trees and undergrowth than the real path. The ground sloped sharply and the leaves had settled in black drifts. It was a detour, of course. I pretended not to notice.

Chloe's teeth chattered and she swung her arms and strode, stamping her feet into the frosted, crunchy grass and the sugar-coated leaves. She had a bottle of fizzy white wine with her and she carried it by jamming a thumb into the neck and swinging it against her thigh as she walked. Now and again she'd stop, unplug the neck and tip her head back to drink. The foil label around the neck was in tatters, scratched off and glittering under her thumbnail.

'Have a bit, it's lush.'

Carl wouldn't touch it even though he'd brought it for her, but when she offered it to me I sipped and thought about my lips touching the place she had been drinking from. It felt a bit special.

She sang too, as we walked. I remember the song – 'Jingle Bells' – over and over again. Carl pushed her in the shoulder and told her to shut up but she laughed and started singing louder, gesturing with her hands and opening her mouth and eyes wide as if she were on a stage. She didn't have a bad voice, really. It carried through the cold and through the trees and didn't make an echo. She was giddy and fragile – the embodiment of the phrase 'highly strung'. And I was numb with the cold and with everything else too.

Maybe I should have been scared of Carl, knowing what I did about what he had done and what he was capable of. But it was still hard to look at him with anything other than contempt. And Chloe wasn't scared of him either. Getting her to fear him wasn't the plan – I needed her to want to save her own skin – I needed to convince her, no matter what it cost, to get him out of her life and things back to normal between us. I couldn't do that cowering at home, so I walked behind them, following the whole way.

'Did you bring anything for me, lover-boy?' she said, her voice too loud because she was half drunk. There was a bruise on her throat.

Carl pointed at her hand. 'I brought you the bottle, didn't I?'

'That's not right,' she said, and looked over her shoulder at him, pouting. 'You've to send flowers, cards, chocolates.' She held up the bottle and I thought she was offering it to me so I reached out to take it, but then she rattled her wrist and I realised she wasn't looking at me at all, but showing Carl her charm bracelet.

'You could get me another heart for this.'

'You've already got three.'

'And one more would make four. One for every month you've known me, right?'

Carl turned his head to one side and looked into the woods. We trudged. It was slow-going. He was tense. Jumpy.

'Whatever,' he said. 'I'll give you some money. Go and get it yourself, next time you're in town.'

'Carl, that's not the same . . .' she started to whine. 'It's

Valentine's Day tomorrow. Some girls get weekends away. They get taken out to nice places for meals. New dresses.'

'Aye, all right then,' he said, not listening to her.

'I bet I won't even see you,' she said, and then, as if she'd decided to be cheerful anyway and not care about it, she made a show of taking another long drink from the bottle, waiting for me to catch up and then handing it back to me.

'Have this,' she said, 'finish it off.' Her eyes were narrow and hazy. I wondered if she'd taken one of Carl's special tablets. The bottle was olive green and freezing. The ragged foil around the top scraped at the soft bit of my hand, under my thumb.

'Come here, Carl,' she said, 'come and show Lola what you've got.'

Carl edged nearer to us and clumsily took the bottle out of my hand. He finished the two inches of liquid in the bottom and threw it high over our heads and into the bushes. The motion of transferring his weight from one foot to another made him stagger and he toppled into Chloe. She pushed her face against his chest and giggled. I listened for a smash but it never came.

'Here,' he said, and crooked his finger at me, 'closer. I int going to bite you.'

I took a step or two forward and watched as he pulled a small handful of dog-eared Polaroids out of his inside pocket. I knew he carried a picture of Chloe around with him because she'd told me. But these weren't Chloe. They were me.

'I hope you don't mind,' he said, almost formally. 'Chloe showed me them.'

My face burned and I cringed away and stared at my feet.

'Don't be like that, Lola,' she said, and put her arm around me. When she kissed my cheek I could smell her unwashed hair and the alcohol on her breath.

'You look very nice,' he said, and burped gently. 'These aren't professional quality, but you've really got something. Have you ever thought about taking it further?'

I looked up. He was rubbing his thumb along the bottom of the Polaroid, touching the place where my bare forearms were in the picture.

'You've got a certain magic,' he said. 'It's a special quality really – you see it now and again in the big budget movies. On the catwalks. An unassuming beauty. Not many girls look like this,' he gestured at the picture and not at me, 'and don't know it.'

Chloe laughed. 'He thinks you could be a model,' she said. 'It was the first thing he said when I showed him.'

I didn't say anything.

'You need a portfolio,' Carl said. 'Something a bit better than this.' He shook the Polaroid as if he was waiting for it to be developed, and then put it back in his pocket. 'You should think about it. I could do it for you, if you wanted.' He shrugged. 'Up to you, of course.'

'The darkroom,' I said.

Carl smiled, almost shyly. His front two teeth overlapped slightly and the crevice between them was stained dark with nicotine.

'It's all ready for you. Whenever you like.'

'I don't know,' I said, and shook my head. 'Shouldn't we just go on down to the pond? That's what we're here for.'

Carl laughed. 'I'll make you a deal,' he said. 'How about we get this done, put your mind at rest, and then I take you back to mine so you can have a look at the room? I've a set of professional lights in there, so I could take your picture and get it developed all in one. My mum's out, your mum's – well, not expecting you back soon. We could have all evening. Chloe would be there to do your make-up and make you feel comfy.'

I looked at her and she was nodding, eagerly. 'We do it all the time, Lola, it's a laugh, and you'll look amazing.'

I bit my lip and wondered if Carl could have been telling the truth. An unassuming beauty? Was it possible? What did she show him for?

'Maybe,' I said. He rolled his eyes and put his hand back into his pocket.

'You don't trust me?' he said. 'Here. You keep them then. It was sneaky of Chloe to take them but she knows the sort of thing I like to see. You keep these and come back to the house later.'

'I'll think about it,' I said. Chloe smiled.

'That's my girl, come on then,' Carl replied, and we started walking.

I don't know what it cost Chloe to convince Carl to take us because I never asked her. Still, by the time we got there, all I remember thinking was that they were happy. They were almost giddy with a kind of frantic, forced excitement that seemed to belong to Christmas. I guessed they'd been drinking all afternoon.

We got to the edge of the pond. Carl and Chloe went first, I followed on slightly behind but near enough to hear them talk.

'I left my gloves in your car,' Chloe said. 'Did you bring them out for me?'

Carl shook his head. 'Must be at the house. You should have rung me.'

Chloe put her head on one side.

'Where is your phone, anyway?' he asked.

'Look, we're here now,' I said, 'and we're not going to be long. I've got some mittens you can borrow. Chloe?'

I called after her, but in the time it took for me to pull my mittens out of my pockets they were already too far ahead, their faces turned towards each other so that for one second they looked like that optical illusion you see in books – two heads close on one minute, and a vase the next. You know the one I mean. I still remember it like that – their noses level, Chloe's eyes pointed up at Carl. He pulled her face towards his and whispered something in her ear. She giggled.

'It's been ages, you sicko,' she said, and swished her head away. They bumped each other's shoulders as they walked on and Carl stuck out his foot and pretended he was going to trip her up.

'Come on, dickhead,' he said softly, and poked her in the side with his elbow. Chloe stopped, put her hands on her hips, and pursed her lips at him. It was as if they could talk like that: they had a secret they were sharing backwards and forwards through a code of breaths and eye movements.

Then we were at the pond. Others had walked around it before us and recently too – the grass between the path and the bank was frosty and pressed with footprints.

Chloe complained again about the cold.

'Here we are, Lolly-Lola,' she said. 'What do you want us to look at?'

I didn't answer. I was struggling behind, they'd already arrived and I was trotting through the leaves then – making the effort to catch them up without trying to look desperate or get sweaty.

'I don't see anything,' Carl said. He was bored, his voice was hoarse.

'Further out,' I said, and lost the rest of what I was going to say in a coughing fit. Carl rolled his eyes.

'She needs a fag. Give her a fag, Carl, don't be tight.'

Carl flicked open the packet, jiggled it so one of the cigarettes jumped out at me.

'You got a lighter?'

He pulled it out of his pocket without looking at it. Tossed it through the air. The metal part caught the light and shimmered slightly. I lit the cigarette with the lighter tucked into my palm, and Carl was walking towards Chloe when I turned to give it back to him so I put it away and didn't see what he'd given to me until I got home and I looked for the Polaroids.

It gets to your throat more, when you smoke in the cold. Carl was coughing too. The white air came out of his mouth and I saw it in spumes either side of his head. I remembered being seven and saw myself blowing clouds of warm white air into the cold, pretending I was smoking with a broken twig.

'Come on then,' he said. 'Can we get on with this?'

'It's right in the middle,' I said. Carl stamped over the grass. 'Over there.'

Donald told me that in wildlife documentaries the sound that penguins and polar bears make stepping into the snow isn't real – they put it in afterwards with a sound man squeezing a rubber glove full of custard powder in time to the steps. You want a noise like that, in here. Not loads of custard powder, because it wasn't deep white snow, but grey slush clogging the grass, with a crust of frost. Carl was at the edge of the water. Chloe followed him and if the ground hadn't been frozen they both would have sunk into it because their feet were in the place where the grass turned into reeds.

'I can see it,' Chloe said, and I imagined her at the front of the class, arm waving – always first with the right answer. She grabbed Carl's arm and turned him towards her.

'All right,' he said. 'I see it. It's a football. What are we supposed to do now?'

This last question was for me, but he didn't bother turning his head to look at me and so I didn't bother answering him. Chloe put her hand in his back pocket and squeezed.

'Doesn't prove anything, just looking,' Chloe said, and I didn't know who she was talking to. Suddenly I wanted to touch her. Nothing weird – just a hand on the padded sleeve of her coat, or my cheek against the fluff at her collar. She was with Carl, and miles away.

'We could go out and look,' I said. It was definitely me that said it. I'd been hoping Chloe would suggest it – she was the one who decided on the plans, on what was the best response to any problem. But I'd already decided, at home while I was brushing my teeth and staring at my fringe in the bathroom mirror, that if she wouldn't, I was going to. And that was fine with me.

The ice was thick – bubbled and uneven in places where it had cracked and refrozen. Didn't look like water. Didn't look like ice. Put me in mind of the scorched plastic on the cowslip and stoat sign. Further out the surface was smoother. No reeds or plants to poke through it, just the six wooden stumps of the old platform. Someone had wanted to test the ice – there were branches and bottles, broken bricks and large stones – skid-marks where they'd been thrown and slid over the hard lid on the water. We stared. I imagined the Year Elevens, out here on weekends tossing stones and bottles, someone getting their nerve up to slide right out. It had been all right. No one had fallen so far. If Wilson had got this far he'd have been fine. I imag-ined him, dashing out onto the water and then stopping, delighted, as it held between his feet and Carl gave up the chase on the bank.

'It's a football,' Carl said again, trying to turn away from the pond, but Chloe was still hanging onto his back pocket and wouldn't let it go. 'We've come, we've seen it, it's a fucking foot-ball,' he laughed, and Chloe pulled at his arm. 'Well done, Laura, you were right. A footie.'

'I bet we could see right through though,' I said, but not to him, 'like a window.'

Chloe looked at me over her shoulder, then let go of Carl's arm and turned completely round. She smiled. I could see the back of his head, and Chloe standing in front of him, slightly to the left and facing me. I never imagined it was me she was smiling at. A private, knowing smile. She blinked a few times, and rubbed her chin against her shoulder.

'Come on,' she said to Carl, almost under her breath. 'What difference does it make?'

'We need to go out on the ice,' I said, 'and look through it.'

Chloe darted a look at me.

'Not all of us,' I said, and she frowned.

'The lighter the better,' I explained.

'See if he's down there? Looking up at us?'

She put her tongue under her bottom lip and crossed her eyes.

'Delp ne! Delp ne!' she said, and made her hands into fists banging at an invisible surface over her face. She'd made herself ugly and mumbly, and it was cruel and accurate and funny. I laughed breathlessly, and the air hurt my throat. Carl threw his cigarette into the grass and didn't bother to stamp it out. I watched it as the thin coil of smoke drifted upwards and died away.

Carl looked at her, pulled the packet out of his pocket.

'Fucking hell, Chloe,' he said, like she'd been saying it about Donald, and right in front of me.

It could have been that Carl would have wanted to light his fag then. Patted his pockets, held out the flat of his palm to me for the lighter that wasn't his. And I'd have pulled it out of my pocket, and he'd have seen my face as I looked at it. That could have been dangerous for me. There was a bit of luck due though. Something made a noise then – maybe a car backfiring far away or someone slamming a door closed – and Chloe jumped, strung tight and startled, and stepped backwards onto the ice.

'Chlo—' Carl threw his arms out towards her – it looked like he had lost his balance instead of her. The cigarette rolled away.

'It's solid, it's fine,' she said. She leaned forward – she was only one arm's length away from Carl – and stamped one foot gently. Her fingers were touching the sleeve of his jacket. I wondered again, with more than a little admiration, what Chloe had promised to Carl to get him to bring us out here.

'I'm going out,' she said, and slid her feet backwards as if she was skating. 'I'm the smallest. If someone's going, it should be me.'

Carl reached out his hand. 'Don't be stupid. Get back over here.'

Chloe laughed and stuck out her tongue and pushed herself backwards.

'Solid as anything!' she said, and tried to balance on one foot.

It isn't 'tried', not really. She didn't fall, and she made it look like it was no trouble at all. She turned and slid gracefully, as easily as if she had been wearing blades instead of trainers.

'I'll go out and see if he's there,' Chloe said, as if she was talking about a friend waiting in the park for us. As if she was talking about someone who could, possibly, be there.

'Go on then,' I said, daring her out. I stared, and I wanted her to catch my eye but she didn't. She was still smirking at Carl. Still moving, one foot to another, she reached up behind her head to pull the scrunchie out of her hair. She shook it all loose and it spread out in the air and then fell back along her shoulders. Like an advert for something. Shampoo. Vitamins. She pouted, thinking she was that sexy, and then she was moving, and Carl was nodding his head as if music was coming out of her pores, smiling back at her, dumb and slack-eyed, and she said, 'It's great!' and moved faster, pushing her feet across the ice and swiping her hands through the air like she was swimming.

Even when she was quite far away from us she kept twisting and swishing her hair about and laughing.

'Stupid cow,' Carl said, but his eyes were stuck to her. I watched Carl, not Chloe. I noticed every time she wobbled, he flinched.

'Get out to the middle,' I said, and Carl took a step closer to the edge and took his hands out of his pockets but he didn't say anything.

He could have stopped it. Either of them could have stopped it in a second. I wanted her to stop it. I wanted her to weigh up her options and realise that confiding in me about Wilson was her only and her best choice. All she needed to do was come clean and give me this secret she'd been keeping. I was her best friend. I was first. She could have trusted me with anything. All I was doing was encouraging her: I was making telling me an easier, more attractive option than not telling me. She knew she didn't need to go out on the ice: there wasn't any pressure. I didn't push her; I didn't lay a hand on her.

Chloe started to pick up speed, sliding on flat feet and making rings around the outside of the pond in a tightening spiral to the centre. The far side was in the shade of overhanging trees. When she passed underneath them all I could see of her was flashes of her white hands and trainers weaving through the air, as if disembodied. If it was me out there, I would have fallen. I would have twisted an ankle, or overbalanced and cracked the back of my head against the glassy surface or bruised my backside on a stick.

'She thinks she's in a film,' I said, even though I knew Carl wasn't listening. He jerked his shoulder and grunted slightly, hardly a response at all, and I was overcome with the urge to turn my back on Chloe. She only did these things when other people were watching. That's what Emma was for. I wanted to tell Carl that if he was that worried about her, the quickest way to get Chloe off the ice would be for us both to turn around and go back and sit in the car.

Not that I was that desperate to go and sit in the car with Carl on my own either. Chloe could get scared first, then she would talk, then she would come in off the ice and be safe again.

She came nearer, out of the shadow and trying to spin around. The soles of her trainers were snagging on some groove or imperfection on the ice that I couldn't see, and she was laughing at nothing, and using her left foot like a sweeper, to brush the ice smooth. I looked at her and saw Barbara, pushing the pile of the carpet backwards and forwards with the toe of her slipper, staring at nothing for hours until it went dark and there was nothing to stare at.

'It's stones,' she called, and waved with both hands over her head as if me and Carl were hundreds of miles away. 'Someone's been chucking stones. There's hundreds of them.'

'Come off now,' Carl said, but there was a smile in his voice still. He didn't sound worried anymore, and took another step forward on to the very edge of the ice. His trainers were unlaced and darker at the toes where the blue canvas had been stained by the wet from the grass. I twiddled with the fastening of the Christmas present school coat and stepped forward too.

It was nothing to do with Carl. Chloe always did things first, I'd accepted that, but she accepted that she was testing the way, and that I would follow along shortly after. Carl didn't have anything to do with it.

'Where are your boots?' I said, gently. 'How come you aren't wearing your boots?'

Carl looked at me. Didn't say anything for a long while.

'I didn't want them anymore,' he said, 'they were dirty.' I stared at him, and he laughed, 'So what?'

'Are you coming?' Chloe called, and we both paused, me and her boyfriend Carl, one foot on the ice each and waiting. Chloe carried on knocking the stones away with the side of her foot. They were the grey, straight-edged chips – big gravel from the path and the car park. Industrial – it comes in sacks and someone had chucked handfuls of it out onto the ice. Probably someone we knew. Someone in our year at school, at least.

I put my hands either side of my mouth and made a trumpet. 'Can you see anything yet?'

Carl looked at me when I shouted, and snorted, 'Is that what we're here for? Still?'

I ignored him, and shouted again. 'It's behind you!'

The *oooo* sound didn't echo – we were too much in the open for that – but it sounded hollow anyway, glancing over the ice and amplifying like we were at a pantomime. Chloe looked up and gave me the finger, for no reason at all, and then started stepping, half walking, half sliding, to the centre of the lake.

'He just ran away,' said Carl.

'Chloe said we could come and check. To put my mind at rest. She's nearly there now.'

'Waste of fucking time,' Carl said, and I thought he was getting to something – but I didn't want it to be him to tell me, didn't want it to be something he'd break to her: *Listen* – cocking his head towards me – *I've had to let her in on it, don't start on though, will you?* No. It was not supposed to be like that.

'Chloe doesn't think it's a waste of time,' I said, and Carl laughed at me again and might have been about to say something else when Chloe interrupted us.

'Oi!' she shouted, sounding indignant. It was because we'd stopped looking at her. 'I'm here!' she said. 'You two better not be talking about me!'

She put her foot on top of the football and Carl stepped forward with his other foot until he was completely on the ice.

So this was the way it was going to be. He was going to follow her out there.

I stepped back onto the bank.

'Come back in now,' he said, trying to sound like someone's dad.

'It's stuck right in,' she said.

'Can you see through?' I imagined that out in the middle, where the water was clearer, it would have frozen into something like thick glass.

Chloe stepped back and put her hands on her hips, drew her leg behind her and kicked the football. The ice broke, making a noise like snapped polystyrene. The football bobbed under the surface and popped back out. It rolled across the ice away from her and the leg she'd kicked with sank into the hole it had left.

I suppose she must have screamed.

Carl ran onto the ice as if he were sprinting across tarmac. I thought he might slip, but he didn't. I put my hands back inside my pockets and felt for my mittens.

He got there quickly. When he reached her, Chloe was sprawled awkwardly across the surface. She'd leaned forward – her right leg buried in the black water up to her thigh and her left bent and flat behind her on the ice. Her arms were stretched out as if she was reaching for the ball which had hit one of the branches and stopped rolling six inches short of her scrabbling fingertips.

Carl grabbed hold of her left ankle. He was crouching behind her and pulling at her. It wasn't doing any good. He was pulling her backwards, bringing the back of her thigh against the fragment of ice behind it. He would have done better to stand up and hold onto her hands, or try to slide her out frontward. I was watching them and wondering again if broken slabs of ice could cut a person. No, I decided at last, because a body's heat would melt the edge and dull it.

Carl was shouting something, and Chloe was screaming and flailing and kicking with her free leg. She wasn't doing herself any good. Panicking so much that Carl had a job keeping hold of her ankle. He stood up, heaved her leg up with him and then leaned back. It must have felt like she was being folded in two. Carl wobbled, as if he was losing his balance. I thought he was going to do it. Then he wobbled again, and I realised it wasn't him that was moving, it was the piece of ice he was standing on.

He dropped her ankle and stepped back but the ice cracked again – a slab as big as a table tilting upwards under his feet and throwing him on top of her. I fluttered my fingers inside my pockets, feeling Carl's lighter and the shiny side of the Polaroids. Something in the bottom snagged against my fingertips and under my nails. Something gritty, small and hard. It could have been bits of burned Donald left over from the sprinkling at the crematorium.

Chloe went right down – I saw the top of her head as she bobbed up again between Carl's arms. Her hair was wet and flat against her scalp. Carl's head was submerged, perhaps knocking the ice, and his flailing elbow hit her chin and forced her head back. She screamed in a breath and it was as if they were fighting. They were both under and it was quiet and I waited until they didn't come back up again. I put on my mittens and waited until the surface of the water was still again before I decided to go home.

Chloe and Carl didn't stay there long. The water might have frozen over their heads like a thin film in the dark to cover them up for a while, but in the morning the sun shone and up they came. Joggers and dog walkers emerged on the paths on cue to discover them, wet heads bobbing in the water like corks. It was Valentine's Day, and the long-awaited thaw had begun, and I bet it was a right production to get them out and into their matching pair of ambulances.

I was sleeping when they were found. I never saw any of it.

I have imagined it. Hair plastered to their skulls. The blueness of their skin and fingernails. I had already imagined it for Wilson: transferring the details of the imagery to them was quick and involuntary.

When Terry reported it on the news that afternoon, I was eating a Marmite sandwich and looking at the first Valentine's Day card I had ever received. Anonymous, handmade, and sent in a jiffy bag along with a mix tape of songs I had never heard of. I was examining the writing, trying to picture what the scrawl on Shanks's whiteboard in the classroom would look like if he was writing properly, in a card like this, with a pen.

I knew the report was going to be about Chloe as soon as I saw Terry's tie. He didn't skip to his chair, or do a run and slide over the shiny floor of the studio, as he sometimes did. But he'd walked soberly to his seat before and the news had been no worse than another fuel shortage, or a local carpeting firm going bust, or one more assault with a broken bottle and a bike chain in a pub car park. As I say, it was the tie. What other than a death – a pair of deaths, although it was Chloe's that was important, because she was the blonde – would have induced Terry to wear a black tie on Valentine's Day when Ladbrokes had him down at five to one for the 'kiss me quick, untie me slowly' design that Woolworths had been carrying with him in mind since Burns Night?

Barbara was in her bedroom. It didn't matter how close to the television I sat: no one was going to stop me. The Marmite sandwich was my first and only meal that day – it was like I didn't have a mother anymore. The Christmas tree was long gone, brown and bare and out in the garden, leaning against the back wall, but the odd needle from it was still caught in the carpet and something pricked the palm of the hand that I leaned on.

They showed her school photograph, with her hair French-plaited and tiny sapphire studs in her ears. Taken at the end of the summer, while she still had a tan and before she started getting thin.

I hardly listened to the bulletin. I could tell from the way his eyes were moving that Terry was reading from the autocue. He said polished, careful things like 'local treasure' and 'tragic winter flower' and 'the heart-shattering sorrow of her parents, who will remember this season of love and romance with heavy hearts for as long as they both shall live'.

They showed pictures of the school, and the car park outside the nature reserve, and the pond. It looked the same. You couldn't see the hole in the ice – just the trees, and lots of cars, and blue and white tape stretched between the bench and the railings.

Eventually, I realised what Terry was saying. Not only the words, but the implication of them. Chloe, apparently, had faded in front of her parents' eyes after they had banned her from seeing Carl. Carl, who was not twenty-three, as we'd thought, but twenty-nine (and mourned by his mother who was in a wheelchair, and talked about how he always took her to the supermarket in his car, no matter what, and because of that, Terry made him out to be a hero), had given away a pair of expensive brown-envelope-coloured boots, and an almost new pair of jeans to a friend. And then he and Chloe had held hands and drank Cava and walked out onto the ice towards hypothermia, serious injury and certain death, because of their great and *inordinate* (which is not a word you hear on the news very much) love for each other.

A Valentine's Day Suicide Pact. And the thing is, I thought, licking Marmite off my thumb and considering a banana for afters, that's exactly the sort of overblown, influenced-by-television, schmaltzy gesture Chloe *would* make. The people who knew her were shocked, and they were sad, but they weren't surprised.

It was a special extended programme: they cut into *Family Fortunes* and Terry Best interviewed various experts – including Patsy the school nurse. She tipsily gave five helpful hints to the parents of teenage girls, which were displayed on the screen behind her in courier font as she spoke. She seemed to think Chloe had died of an eating disorder because she talked a lot about the importance of making sure young girls didn't feel self-conscious about their developing breasts and mistake the natural swellings (she sketched a shape in the air in front of her sweater) for unwanted weight gain. That was never Chloe's problem.

I didn't wonder about anything. I was waiting for something else to happen, something worse, or more important, but every time my mind skated forward to think about what it might be, a light went out and everything went dark and I couldn't think about anything. The sensation was new and peculiar, but it has never quite left me.

I stared and I watched my television and I didn't say anything to anyone.

*

It wasn't long after that the interviews started. The photographs. The way they wanted me and Emma to tell them everything. I knew what they wanted to hear. We helped them make Chloe into who she is today.

When the spring came in proper the headmaster got someone to bulldoze up the cement courtyard at the front of the school and filled it with the yellow Juliet roses. The town has never stunk like it did in the late spring of 1998. Loads of people planted them and although now, ten years later, they are a lot less fashionable, you can still smell them occasionally.

In my dreams now it is always night and their soaked heads break the surface again and again. They want to float and my hands and arms are frozen with trying to push them back under.

30

Emma and I are opening the drawers in the tallboy in my bedroom. She's sitting on the carpet next to me. I can smell her trainers and see the pattern on her socks out of the corner of my eye as I jiggle the sticky bottom drawer open. The grain of the carpet digs into my palms as I lean towards her. I feel young, hunched down on the floor with her like this. We might have been better friends, Emma and me, if it hadn't been for Chloe.

'Let's have it all out then,' she says.

The photographs of Chloe are tucked between folded jeans and sweatshirts and hiding under balls of socks and old scarves I've not worn in years. We lift out the clothes, throw them onto my bed or pile them on the floor, and excavate.

Here's one of Chloe's mittens. Here's a homework diary, filled with her round, squat handwriting. A pink pot of raspberry-ripple-scented lip balm. A dangling cubic zirconia pendant. I wasn't as bad at stealing things as Emma and Chloe thought I was. Emma looks at the objects, gathering them in a pile between her crossed legs as I hand them to her. Eventually, I have to go and find her a shoebox.

'There's so much of it,' she says.

'She used to stay over a lot,' I say. 'She spent half the summer living at my house. The other half, I was with her. I bet there was loads of my stuff round at her place too.'

I think of those lost objects. I try to count them, to list the spare socks and abandoned magazines. The notebooks and pens with moulded plastic tops in the shape of cats. I wonder if Amanda still has her things.

'Come on,' Emma says, and thrusts a pile of folded tee-shirts at me. 'Put these up on your bed for the time being, we can put it all back after.'

Here's an envelope stuffed with newspaper clippings. I hitch my finger under the flap but Emma shakes her head and holds out her hand.

'You've read it all already,' she says.

More. There's the cord from her dressing gown. A stack of old tapes, a pair of headphones. I know I'm going to get to her mobile phone, but even as my hand brushes it and I see the cracked black plastic of the casing, I feel shocked. To Emma, it's just a piece of broken equipment. It's nothing. It's not worth anything, not dangerous, not significant. I give it to her, my voice trapped inside it. It goes into the box.

'There can't be much more,' she says.

I give Emma a photograph of Chloe that I took for Carl and kept for myself. She stares at it without embarrassment.

'His mother must have known,' she says, looking at Chloe leaning over the bed in her underwear.

'His wheelchair-bound mother, who Carl, despite having a full-time job, drove to the supermarket each and every Sunday without fail.' I'm quoting Terry, but Emma doesn't know that and glances at me with a strange expression on her face. She's staring at the Polaroid. Chloe's face is a faded oval – there is no definition to her features except for the bright slash of lipstick around her mouth.

'She must have gone through his stuff. Found pictures like this. Chloe. Some of me. God knows who else.'

'She'd have got rid of them,' I say, and Emma nods.

'That's what you should have done. Chuck it all out. It's disgusting.' She tears the picture in half. 'I don't want anyone ever knowing about this,' she says. 'It's bad enough having to think about it.' She reaches out her hand and strokes the carpet beside her. It's an unconscious movement and I wonder if she's thinking about her dogs, about putting her hands into the coarse fur at the back of their necks.

'I'd never say anything,' I say quickly, 'you can trust me on that. I'm your friend.'

Emma snorts, but doesn't answer and I remove the very last thing, something I found in a black school coat pocket, a coat that pretended to be a Christmas present, a long time ago. I hold it in my hands. It's a tiny thing. Could have been a dangerous thing. A cigarette lighter with a woman in a bikini on it. When it was new, you flicked the lighter to ignite the flame and her bikini disappeared. A bit of a surprise. Something saucy and harmless. Now her skin has a greenish tinge and the gas in the chamber is long gone. I hold it between my palms for a second, feeling the cold of the metal top against the web of skin between my thumb and first finger.

I remember this lighter.

I remember.

Emma takes it off me. 'Was this Chloe's?' she asks, and frowns. She tests the wheel with her thumb a few times. There's a scraping sound, but it doesn't spark. The flint is gone. The feel of it in her hand reminds her, I think, that she wants to smoke, and she's leaning forward, easing the green packet of tobacco out of her back pocket. The lighter is on the floor between us as she fiddles with matches and filters, runs the sliver of transparent paper along her tongue.

'Here,' she says, and hands me a cigarette. I light it from a match and we exhale together. My bedroom is tiny and soon the smoke is making a dusky halo around the bare lightbulb hanging from the ceiling, shrouded with its own ropy cobwebs of dust.

'It doesn't look like Chloe's,' she says. 'Is it going in the box?'

I know what she's thinking. It isn't pink. It isn't fluffy. It doesn't sparkle or smell like strawberries, it doesn't glitter or glow in the dark. So it isn't Chloe's. A long minute passes before I speak.

'It was Carl's,' I say, 'and he got it off Wilson. Or Wilson lost it, and Carl picked it up. I don't know exactly.'

'Carl gave it you?' she says carefully. 'Like a present?' She says present with a tilt to it, and I realise what she's implying, what she's offering up to me. I can talk if I want to. I can be her friend like this.

'No,' I say. 'I found it in the woods.'

I gesture half-heartedly at the television in the next room. We've left it on, and across the hallway and between two half-closed doors, I can still hear Terry's voice. He speaks into the silence, talking about human error and regret and despite everything how he'd like to take the opportunity to recap his personal career highlights. Emma was right. He can't get away without admitting he was wrong.

'Those woods on the telly?'

'Yes.'

Emma looks at the lighter, and looks at me. She's calm. She picks it up, examines it again as she finishes the last of her cigarette.

'She's supposed to get naked, when you flick it,' I say.

Emma nods. 'I've seen them before. Sell them everywhere. Pound shops, newsagents, pubs. Hundreds of them.'

There's no ashtray in here. No conveniently placed empty coffee mug or wine bottle. She flicks the ash into the shoebox and stubs out the cigarette in the lid.

'It's Wilson's,' I say, and Emma looks at me again – the same even, unreadable expression on her face.

'I don't want to know,' she says. 'I haven't asked, have I?' She opens her eyes wide and I can see she's biting her bottom lip.

'No,' I say.

'It goes in the box too then?' she says neutrally.

'Yes, okay. Get rid of it.'

She throws it in, and makes a show of pushing everything

down flat and rearranging the papers and photographs so she can get the lid on tight.

'Is there anything else?' She is brisk and efficient now. She sounds like Barbara. I wonder about what's left in that house – whether Barbara cleaned out my room as quickly as she emptied Donald's. I think of my old things, and wonder who there is in the world to tuck them into drawers and keep them safe for me.

'No, that's it,' I say. 'I've nothing else.'

'Good. Come on then, get up and get your coat on.'

'What are we going to do with it?'

'We're going to chuck it out,' Emma says, as if she expects me to challenge her.

'I know a place,' I say. 'Do you have your car?'

She nods.

Outside, it's getting light but the street is empty. I've been up this early before. The bread van should be arriving around now – the milk float, and the first bit of morning traffic. The early bus. But there's nothing, and instead of a street full of darkened windows we can see the lights still on behind the closed curtains; people sitting up late, sitting up early – as long as it takes. The racks in front of the block of flats are still loaded with people's bikes: no one's leaving the house early for work this morning.

'We're missing Terry's resignation speech,' I say, not really meaning it.

Emma turns the keys in the ignition and smiles.

'So what? We'll get home in a couple of hours and catch his concluding remarks. As soon as he goes, Fiona is going to do an interview with Amanda. Exclusive. *What her mother knew.* I'll lay down fifty quid on it for you.'

We smirk. I think it's the first time I've seen her smile properly, ever. It used to flatten her face out – Chloe called her panhead because of it. Maybe something has changed as she grew up, or maybe I was just too quick to believe Chloe in the first place.

The car is clean and the seats are covered with colourful afghans. It looks worn and loved in here.

'Are you going to be all right to drive?' I say. 'We've been drinking all night. You must be knackered.'

She shakes her head. 'I've driven in worse states than this,' she says, which is not reassuring. 'You'll have to give me directions: I don't know where I'm going. And when you want me to turn, don't say left or right – point with your hand. I can't tell, otherwise.'

I buckle my seatbelt and she thrusts the shoebox onto my lap and puts her foot to the floor. The screech of the car engine is deafening in the empty street, but we're not waking anyone up – and no one opens their front door and shouts.

'You want to get on the M6,' I say. 'We're going up to Morecambe.'

Emma doesn't shudder or tremble. Her phobias do not seem to be bothering her this morning.

The place where we stop isn't miles away from where Donald might have taken his boat into the water. We park on the seafront at the northern edge of Morecambe after a long drive through the town and along a deserted, shuttered-up promenade. There are arcades, and the hoarding outside Frontierland tilts and lifts with a strong wind that whips across the bay and onto the hunched and huddled shopfronts flanking the curve of the land. We park on a double yellow line that Emma assures me doesn't apply outside business hours. The road hugs the coast and the sharp outline of the concrete promenade contrasts with the ragged, muddy edge of the shallow bay. There are boats too – peeling, abandoned-looking things half sunk into the mud or sitting, tilted on the sand, chained to concrete-filled oil cans or bolts in the sea defence wall. And there are birds, big white birds sitting on posts and swooping to peck at fag-ends and abandoned polystyrene chip trays.

It's completely light by the time we get out of the car and start walking, carrying our shoebox like it contains something precious. It feels more normal up here. Makes me think it isn't the whole world that's sitting in listening to Terry broadcast a litany of his regrets: it's just our city. I wonder why that should be so, and I want to ask Emma about it but before I can she is climbing the railings and leaning out over the mud.

I'm scared, and before I think about it I rush up behind her, put my arms around her waist and pull. She's tried this sort of thing before.

'Stop!'

'I'm not after topping myself,' she says, in her ordinary voice. 'I'm just trying to get a better look.'

I leave my arms around her waist for a second, press my face into her back – smell the musty, doggy smell of her waxed jacket. It's a mainly unpleasant smell – but I don't move until she shrugs me off.

'Get away,' she says, without irritation. 'Come up and look here.'

I jump up next to her and we are leaning on the railings, the cold coming off them biting through my jeans and making the top of my thighs ache. The clouds are low and pencil-lead-coloured. Can't see out very far. Everything is brown or grey. I'm thinking a lot about Donald now – course I am.

'Here's where my dad drowned himself,' I say, and edge closer to Emma.

'I remember about that,' she says, and doesn't ask me if I am all right.

'He was a bit –' I pause, and realise no one who cares is listening anymore, 'he was a bit soft.'

'I heard about that as well.'

'From Chloe?'

Emma nods. 'Some things you were better off keeping to yourself.'

'You wouldn't have taken the piss, would you?' I say. Maybe me and Emma can be friends now. We've stayed in contact, all these years. That must be worth something. Don't want to think about all those years wasted – would rather have someone else, another Chloe, to sit in the house with me at night, to keep secrets with, to visit cafes and Debenhams and sit on the climbing frame in the park. She could be my friend.

'I'll come with you after here,' I say. 'I'll come with you to the dogs' home. You've got your shift first thing, yeah? Walk them, wash them and that? I'll come in the car with you.' I show her the toe of my trainers. 'These things are old, doesn't matter if they get in a bit of a state. Then we can have breakfast together afterwards?'

Emma doesn't say anything. She is looking out at the moving brown and grey water in the channel – the way the exposed mud-flats seem to dissolve and resolve themselves into shadow and spits of almost solid land, and then back again into moving sludge and stirred-up water. I wonder how long it's been since she's been out of the City, since she's driven on a motorway, since she's been anywhere unfamiliar without being scared. She's just looking out, very calmly. And this is a creepy, dangerous place. You stare out far enough, and the water lightens. It's never blue, it's just less brown. There's a buoy, and further out, a shrimp boat with its red lights on, tailed by a train of screaming gulls.

'You want to make friends with someone,' she says mildly, 'go and see your mother. She still lives in your old house. Still got that same car on blocks in the back garden. Same net curtains. Same cherry tree. Still puts out that wreath on Christmas Eve, and still chains it to the door handle so no one can nick it.'

'You know more about her than I do,' I say. It sounds sullen.

She shakes her head. 'I never went in. Just went to see a couple of times. Wanted to know if you were still going to see her. Talking to her, maybe.'

'I've never said anything.'

'Well, there's no need now, is there?'

I'm not looking at Emma, I'm looking at the water, and feeling the ground whip away from under my feet until suddenly it feels like I am tipping, falling, and there is nothing and nobody to hold on to. It's been a terrible waste. I could cry, and my awareness of the world shrinks to a narrow, foreshortened view of my hands and feet on those cold railings, the paint scabby and flaking against my palms.

'Lola?' Emma touches my arm. 'Come on, Lola, don't be like that.'

I can't speak. I want to speak. I want to tell her my name is Laura and she is never allowed to call me Lola again. Tell her she's never allowed to speak to me again. I want to put my hand in the flat of her back and push her so she tips over the railings and sinks into the mud and I don't have to see her or think about her anymore.

'It'll be all right,' she says, 'you know it will. Everything'll be fine.'

I don't know how she is able to say that to me. How she has got enough of herself left to share. I have done something very bad. I open my mouth and I still can't speak but there's no need because suddenly, far away on the water where the channels fall away into troughs and get deep and treacherous even for experienced sailors, I see a blue glow over the surface of the bay. It's a light. A cold, artificial-looking light – like a fluorescent tube or the glow of a television and it blinks and swirls and then goes out.

I look at Emma, and she nods at me.

'I've seen it before. Something to do with the algae.'

I'm laughing, and I can't help it. She looks at me and pulls a face. 'What's wrong with you?' and before I can answer she's laughing too.

'It's the algae or the plankton,' she says. 'It's dead common in the Pacific.'

'I know how it works. Just didn't think it was possible round here.'

'No,' she shakes her head, 'it shouldn't be. There's the towers at Heysham. They warm up the water. It's bad really. Not natural, at the very least.'

I'm still laughing, even as I'm staring and squinting and waiting for it to happen again. The water is dark and the sky is getting lighter.

'Better at night, I reckon – but I wouldn't bother. You can watch it on YouTube whenever you want.'

Something about what she's said strikes me as hilarious and we're laughing again – egging each other on, breathless and giddy and near-hysterical. Something close to tears. After too long, we stop.

'I think us two are finished after today, aren't we?'

It's like a slap, even though she's not saying it nastily. I hang onto the railing. My head throbs and burns. I want those lights to come back.

'You weren't planning on spending the rest of your life checking up on me, were you? I'm glad we don't need to do that anymore.' She knocks her chin against my shoulder and I can smell the old wine and tobacco on her breath, and then she's away, lifting up the box over the railings and pulling off the lid.

If I'd have imagined this before now, I'd have pictured her taking the things out one by one and letting them drift into the water. She'd say something meaningful. But she doesn't. She doesn't wait to see if I'm watching or not – doesn't ask me how I feel or what I'm thinking. She drops the lid of the box over the side and before it hits the mud, she turns the box upside down and lets it fall through her fingers. It's only ten feet or so and the tide isn't even properly in. The paper and photographs stick to the mud or blow away. She leans over and we watch the mobile phone sink into the grey sludge and disappear.

'Do you want to wait until the tide comes in and covers it over?' she says.

I shrug.

'Might as well.'

We stare until the sea and sky are light and empty and I don't see the blue lights again but I know they have been there and that someone else has seen them with me and that is the best I'm going to get.

EPILOGUE

Imagine this. It could happen.

I am at home. Not at the flat. Not in my front room, or the kitchen, or the bathroom with the toothpaste-coloured tiles. Not in the service corridors at the shopping centre, feeling tiny in the silence as I put my trolley away and wind up the wire for the portable floor polisher. No, my real home. The one with the crooked back gate and the cherry tree in the garden and the shed with the paperback-sized window.

It is sunny. Say we've had a mild winter but a long one, and this day, first of a new month, feels like the first day of spring too. Barbara and I are sitting out in the garden on the mildew-spotted plastic patio furniture and because the sky is improbably blue and even a few bees are flying about the garden, she's asked me to rig something up with the extension cable and the television on the sill of the open kitchen window. It's a warm day, but a fresh one – even after lugging the telly through the house I'm not sweating as I lean back and tuck the kitchen net behind it so it doesn't get tangled in the aerial.

'It'll probably fall in the sink and electrocute us,' Barbara says, but she is smiling and she comes out from the kitchen with no apron, and her hair down, and she's carrying a bottle of Gordon's and two glasses with ice and wedges of lemon in them on a round plastic tray, and she pours the drinks and we sit on our patio chairs with the sun on the backs of our necks, and watch the television. I put my feet in her lap and feel the slats of the plastic chair sticking into my back, but not uncomfortably.

She's wearing a loose skirt with green leaves and red flowers on it – looks like the sort of thing they put in the window in charity shops, but it falls softly around her calves and the breeze twitches the hem and it suits her.

We're watching Wilson's funeral. It's April and it's taken them this long to release the body.

'His poor mother,' Barbara says, and Fiona, who is still in her camel-coloured two-piece suit, slightly shimmering tights and a new hairdo – blonde waves, to celebrate her new job – narrates the slow procession snaking its way along a path and into the dark open mouth of the church. The coffin is at the front of the queue, and it is white, like the ones they use for babies and young girls. The dad is too old to bear it, and he walks behind with the mother and their heads are bowed, not looking at the press, but they do not cry and they are not ashamed.

'Imagine having a photographer at a funeral and you not even being a member of the royal family,' Barbara says, scandalised and admiring. There's an ashtray on the table, a little blue glass lump with depressions in the side, and I light up, and offer one to Barbara, and for a few seconds we're absorbed in the apparatus of smoking – the flick of the lighter, the draw, the crackle, the delicious feeling of the first pull, grey threads of smoke sucked into the lungs, darkening and filtering into the blood. She sighs and puts her head back, exhales upwards towards the sky, and balances the ashtray on my shins so I can't move my feet now, even if I wanted to.

'A nice day for it though, eh?' As if it wasn't a funeral, but a wedding. 'I wonder if they'll ever catch who did it?' The ice cubes click in her glass as she drinks.

I don't answer her, but look away from the television and around the garden, where I have been working for Barbara all morning. The grass is neat and there is a small heap of clippings and pulled weeds at the side of the shed. Fiona's voice still emanates thinly from the colour portable, quoting from Terry's final broadcast where, before retiring, he admitted that the police were able to prove beyond doubt that Wilson was innocent of anything suspected of him. The noise of her is filling the tiny garden, flying up into the air and travelling outwards, the waves getting wider and further apart until we can't hear them anymore.

ACKNOWLEDGEMENTS

While researching bioluminescence I found many books, articles and websites useful. In particular, 'Milky Seas: A Bioluminescent Puzzle' (*Marine Oberver*, 63.22, 1993) by P.J. Herring and M. Watson, and *The Science Frontiers Sourcebook Project* at http://www.science-frontiers.com/sourcebk.htm, edited by William R. Corliss helped inform my understanding. The research forum at *The Bioluminescence Website*: http://lifesci.ucsb.edu/~biolum/ edited by S.H. Haddock, C.M. McDougal and J. F. Case was also helpful.

Thanks are owed to Emma Lannie, who knew about Wrigley's and barcodes, to Kim McGowan who helped with water-cooled power stations and continuity errors in late drafts and to Angela Fitzpatrick: a librarian extraordinaire. Thanks to all the writers from the Northern Lines Fiction Workshop – Tom Fletcher, Andrew Hurley, Sally Cook, Emma Unsworth and Zoe Lambert – for invaluable feedback, advice and moral support. To my agent Anthony Goff and my editors Carole Welch and Ruth Tross for their patient, professional and meticulous approaches.

The time I needed to develop this novel was supported by the National Lottery through Arts Council England. My employer, Lancashire County Council's Library and Information Service, generously agreed to a career break that gave me the space to write and my colleagues at Lancashire Libraries and HMP Garth were especially understanding. Sarah Hymas, at Lancaster Litfest, acted as a wise and patient mentor during the final stages.

Most of all, thanks to Duncan McGowan, for not reading this one either.